PRAISE FOR

# CHLOE LIESE

"Chloe Liese's writing is soulful, honest, and steamy in that swoon-worthy way that made me fall in love with romance novels in the first place! Her work is breathtaking, and I constantly look forward to more from her!"

—Ali Hazelwood, #1 *New York Times* bestselling author of *Love on the Brain*

"Quirky and delicious romance. I could curl up in Liese's writing for days, I love it so."

—Helen Hoang, *New York Times* bestselling author of *The Heart Principle*

"There's no warmer hug than a Chloe Liese book."

—Rachel Lynn Solomon, *New York Times* bestselling author of *Weather Girl*

"No one pairs sweet and steamy quite like Chloe Liese!"

—Alison Cochrun, author of *The Charm Offensive*

"Chloe Liese consistently writes strong casts brimming with people I want to hang out with in real life, and I'll happily gobble up anything she writes."

—Sarah Hogle, author of *You Deserve Each Other*

"Chloe Liese continues to reign as the master of steamy romance!"

—Sarah Adams, author of *The Cheat Sheet*

# *With You Forever*

## A BERGMAN BROTHERS NOVEL

## CHLOE LIESE

BERKLEY ROMANCE
NEW YORK

BERKLEY ROMANCE
Published by Berkley
An imprint of Penguin Random House LLC
penguinrandomhouse.com

Library of Congress Cataloging-in-Publication Data

Names: Liese, Chloe, author.
Title: With you forever: a Bergman Brothers novel / Chloe Liese.
Description: New York: Berkley Romance, 2024. |
Series: The Bergman Brothers
Identifiers: LCCN 2023042046 (print) | LCCN 2023042047 (ebook) |
ISBN 9780593642412 (trade paperback) | ISBN 9780593642429 (ebook)
Subjects: LCGFT: Romance fiction. | Novels.
Classification: LCC PS3612.I3357 W58 2024 (print) |
LCC PS3612.I3357 (ebook) | DDC 813/.6—dc23/eng/20231005
LC record available at https://lccn.loc.gov/2023042046
LC ebook record available at https://lccn.loc.gov/2023042047

*With You Forever* was originally self-published, in different form, in 2021.

First Berkley Romance Edition: January 2024

Printed in the United States of America
1st Printing

Book design by Kristin del Rosario

*For the hearts that love differently,*
*and the hearts that love them for it.*

Dear Reader,

This story features characters with human realities that I believe deserve to be seen more prominently in romance through positive, authentic representation. As a neurodivergent person living with chronic conditions, I am passionate about writing feel-good romances affirming my belief that every one of us is worthy and capable of happily ever after, if that's what our heart desires.

Specifically, this story portrays a main character who is on the autism spectrum, as well as a main character with a chronic illness, which is an inflammatory bowel disease, ulcerative colitis. No two people's experience of any condition or diagnosis will be the same, but through my own experience and the insight of authenticity readers, I have strived to create characters who honor the nuances of those identities.

If any of these are sensitive topics for you, I hope you feel comforted in knowing that loving, affirming relationships—with oneself and others—are championed in this story.

XO,
Chloe

If I loved you less, I might be able to talk about it more.

—JANE AUSTEN,
*Emma*

# ONE

# *Rooney*

Playlist: "Cowboy Blues," Kesha

My eyes are on the road, but my head is in the clouds. Windows cracked, cool autumn air spilling in as Seattle-Tacoma Airport fades behind me and a cozy cabin staycation lies ahead.

Thoughts drifting, I soak up the view: sapphire sky, emerald evergreens mingling with burnished bronze leaves, an onyx asphalt ribbon paving the way. My rental car blasts Kesha because, hello, I'm a woman on a solo trip, figuring out her shit—of course I'm listening to Kesha. There's just one of her songs that I avoid. Because the last time I heard it, I did A Very Terrible Thing.

I kissed Axel Bergman.

Which isn't the end of the world. I'm over it. It's not like I fixate on it. Or daydream about it. Not about The Charades Kiss or Axel, who I haven't seen since.

Who I'm definitely not thinking about now as I drive through his home state, that song filling the car before I can skip it, while a rainbow whooshes across the sky.

Ohhhh, Rooney. Liar, liar, palazzo pants on fire.

My mind isn't on the road or in the clouds. It's in the past, in the moment after our kiss . . .

*The clue—"kiss"—scrawled on a piece of paper, flutters to the ground. My lips tingle, my cheeks are hot as I stand with my head back, staring up at Axel, who I've just kissed.*

*Maybe "mauled with my mouth" is more accurate.*

*A rainbow gale of confetti whips around the room, spun off the ceiling-fan blades that whir overhead. In a haze of soft, warm lights, the air thumps with that upbeat song's opening bars.*

*But it all fades as I look at him. Six feet, many inches of grumpy gorgeousness. An unreadable, dangerously kissable mystery.*

*Who I just crushed my mouth to for the sake of a charades clue.*

*I bring a shaky hand to my lips. "Axel, I-I-I'm sorry. I didn't mean . . . that is, I shouldn't have . . . I'm just viciously competitive, and I . . ."*

*He stands, silent, staring at my mouth. Then, slowly, he takes a step closer. For once, he doesn't leave like he always seems to when I get close. He doesn't run.*

*He stays.*

*"I think . . ." he says hoarsely, leaning a little closer.*

*I lean a little closer, too. "You think . . . ?"*

*Axel swallows roughly as his fingertips brush mine. It's the faintest touch, but it seismic-booms through me, in tempo with the music, as if it's the soundtrack to this tenuous, almost-something moment.*

*"I think," he whispers, "I have a new appreciation for charades."*

*My mouth falls open in surprise. The silent giant just cracked a joke.*

*He takes a step closer, placing us toe to toe, and his gaze settles on my mouth. He bends his head toward mine. He's close. A little closer.*

*And just as I realize he might be on the verge of kissing me back, sharp warning spasms clutch my stomach, punching the air out of my lungs.*

*In the world's worst timing, I'm the one who pulls away. I'm the one who runs from the room. The moment stolen from me before it was even fully mine.*

That's where it always ends, where the daydream leaves me wondering, *What if?*

What if I hadn't had to run off without a word of explanation?

What if, when I finally came back, Axel was still there, waiting for me?

My daydream what-ifs spin cotton candy–sweet but dissolve just as easily when my phone's ringtone overrides the music. I glance at the screen, my throat tightening as I see my best friend's name: *Willa*.

The only sound in the car is the call's rhythmic ring. It's suddenly quiet—too quiet—and my thoughts have backpedaled to what I came up here to escape.

I wish I could say that kissing Axel Bergman in a moment of overzealousness for charades and then having to bolt for the bathroom in gastrointestinal agony was the low point of my recent existence, but I can't.

Because since that night, my health nosedived to the point that I had to take a leave of absence from law school, and when I came back to the apartment after finalizing said leave of absence, defeated, exhausted, so fucking lost, I couldn't stay one second longer.

So here I am, directionless, doing something I haven't in . . . ever. I'm trying to take care of myself.

Willa is still calling, each ring chipping away at my resolve. I take a deep breath, push the right button on the steering wheel, and accept her call.

Finding my *I'm okay* upbeat voice, I holler, "I'm here!"

"You're here! Just got your text that you landed. Where are you exactly?"

"Whoa now, no need for an interrogation."

"You're lost, aren't you?"

"I'm not *lost*." Squinting, I glance at the GPS on my rental's display screen and the winding trail of my directions. Then I peer up at my surroundings. "I'm . . . heading . . . west."

"Uh-huh. You know you have nothing to prove to me, right? You're a biochem geek who's at Stanford Law. It's okay to have a weakness and admit that you're directionally challenged."

"I admit that I have many weaknesses and that I am direction-ally challenged. I do not, however, admit to being lost."

I swear I can hear her eye roll. "The property's entrance sneaks up on you. I can't tell you how many times I've missed it. It's easy to drive past, so go slow when you come to that hairpin turn."

I grimace as I stare at the directions. I have no idea what she's talking about. "Will do. I can't wait to see it."

"Oh, Roo, you're gonna love it. It's so beautiful. I wish I was there to welcome you and watch you take it in. I would absolutely reenact an epic *Chariots of Fire* run to your car if this professional soccer gig wasn't so damn demanding. Crummy World Cup quali-fiers. Crummy flight. Crummy soccer."

"So crummy," I tell her. "Crummy dream come true, crummy playing for the US women's team. Crummy honor of being a rookie who's on the starting lineup."

"Okay, fine, it's not crummy, and I'm very excited. I just miss you." After a beat of hesitation, she says, "How are you holding up?"

"I'm . . . okay."

I set a hand on my stomach, which has started making warning twinges that I'm all too familiar with, especially since my old meds stopped working a few months ago. Thankfully, my new treatment has finally started giving me relief from my most serious ulcer-ative colitis symptoms, so I'm relatively much better—meaning I'm not incapacitated at home or in the hospital for dehydration and pain—but I have lasting damage to my intestines. Even while I'm in clinical remission, some symptoms are a permanent fixture in my life.

But Willa's not asking about my GI troubles. She's asking

about everything else. Because this is the one thing I keep from her.

She and I have most of the West Coast between us these days, but we talk all the time, and she knows I've taken a leave of absence from Stanford Law. She just doesn't know the medical reason. Because Willa doesn't know I have ulcerative colitis. She knows I have a sensitive stomach and make more bathroom trips than most, but not why, not the worst of it.

When I told her I was taking a leave of absence, I explained that I was stepping back to assess if law school was still the right path for me, which isn't a lie. It's just not the whole truth.

I know. I hate keeping secrets from her, but I've had my reasons, and I believe they're good ones.

We've been best friends since we met, which was as freshman roommates and newbies on the women's soccer team at UCLA. It wasn't long into our friendship that she shared her mom's past battle with breast cancer and her new diagnosis of leukemia. That's when I knew the last thing Willa needed was someone else to worry about. With the right medication and sheer unreliable luck, ulcerative colitis is one of those diseases that can behave itself for years. Mine did through college, with only a few minor episodes that I managed to handle without raising Willa's suspicion. I hate lying, and I never wanted to keep it from her, but I simply felt in my heart that she didn't need one more thing weighing on her. The wisdom of that choice was confirmed when her mother died our junior year.

In the past few years since we've graduated, I haven't known how to tell her. I've been afraid to worry her. I haven't wanted anything to change between us. And the longer my lie of omission continues, the harder it gets to tell the truth.

That's why she doesn't know how sick I've been recently. That's why she thinks I've just been crushed by law school, and once again, it's not a lie—it's just not the whole truth. Law school *has* been stressful. I've loved it some moments, hated it others, and it's unequivocally the hardest thing I've ever done.

And then that stress, hours of studying, late nights, anxiety about doing my best caught up with me, and I just couldn't do it anymore. *Your health or your studies*, my doctor said. *Pick one.*

"Rooney?" Willa says. "I think you cut out for a minute."

"Sorry." I shake myself and snap out of it. "Can you hear me okay?"

"I can now. I didn't catch anything after I asked how you're doing."

"Ah." I clear my throat nervously. "Well, I'm doing . . . okay. Just really ready for this time away. Thank you again for offering the A-frame. You still haven't told me what I can give the Bergmans for rent, though."

"I told you that you're not paying rent. You'll never hear the end of it if you even try. You're practically family to them."

Willa's boyfriend, Ryder, is the middle child of the seven Bergman siblings, a boisterous, close family that's welcomed me into their fold. His mom, Elin, is a Swedish transplant whose hugs and homemaking are the stuff of dreams. His dad, who goes by Dr. B, is one of those people who instantly makes any gathering a party. While Willa and Ryder met when we were at UCLA, and Los Angeles is where the Bergmans now call home, their family's early years were spent here in Washington State, often at their getaway property, the A-frame.

The Bergmans are the chaotic, tight-knit family my only child soul always wanted, and they've done nothing but make me feel welcome. Since Willa is as good as theirs, and I'm hers, now I'm as good as theirs, too. At least, I was, until The Charades Kiss with Axel, the oldest Bergman son.

Not that *they* made it awkward. Apparently only Axel and I were traumatized by my rogue charades move. Nobody seemed re-

motely fazed afterward. Sure, they gasped when the kiss happened—
I mean, it shocked everyone, including me—but by the time I came
back from the bathroom and found Axel pointedly absent, they'd
moved on. Laughing, teasing, setting the table for dinner. Like it
was nothing.

Either they're incredible actors, or they weren't terribly surprised that I'd finally flung myself at Axel after nursing a long-
standing crush I've tried very hard to hide—Axel, who threw me a
rare bone of humor when he made that crack about *a new appreciation for charades*, but who was clearly scared away by my antics. The
whole situation was mortifying.

I felt sick. I was embarrassed. So that night I made my excuses,
and since then, the past six weeks, I've made myself scarce, which
hasn't been hard because I've been sick as a dog.

Do I wish I could figure out how to smooth things over? Yes.
Do I wish I knew how to re-engage without dying of embarrassment? Yes. But I have no idea where to begin, and I can't deal with
that right now. I don't have the spoons to think about the Bergmans, especially Axel. I have the spoons to stay at their empty
A-frame for the next few weeks, hiding from reality while figuring
out how I'm going to eventually face it again.

It's an escape I desperately need. Which is why I really want to
give the Bergmans something for my time here.

"Willa, I don't like the idea of staying at the A-frame for free."

"Too bad," she says. "It's there. Unused. Ryder said it should be
empty until New Year's. That's when Freya and Aiden have their
turn, so stay as long as you like up until then."

"Willa, seriously, I couldn't—"

"Listen, Roo, the place is paid off. It's there simply to be enjoyed. Ryder's parents barely bother coming up, so it's free for the
siblings to use how and when they want. There's no need to pay
when none of us are paying. We just do the minimum upkeep."

"I can do upkeep!"

She sighs. "You're *not* spending your staycation replacing lost shingles and resealing the deck."

"Don't tempt me. I love DIY projects."

"You're supposed to be *relaxing*."

"Fine. I'll settle for scrubbing the bathroom grout with a toothbrush."

Willa snorts a laugh. "God, I miss you. Do you think you'll stick around long enough for us to catch up? I'm back in two and a half weeks. I'd be home sooner, but after we play, I've got to do a bunch of press and sponsorship shit—aka, the stuff that actually pays the bills."

I glance in the rearview mirror at my reflection. I still look like I'm sick. Pale skin, shadowy half-moons under my eyes. Well, at least when we meet up, and I finally find the courage to tell her I'm sick, I'll look the part.

"I should still be here." Technically I don't have to be back until a few days before Christmas, to celebrate with Dad, then meet up with my advisor to discuss how I plan to proceed at school, but I'll probably come home at the end of the month for Thanksgiving. The holiday is always a bit of a bust, since it's just Dad and me, but it feels odd to consider spending it apart from him. Even though, if I weren't home, I bet he'd be happy working in his office or on set without feeling guilty about leaving me alone.

"Yay! I can't wait," Willa says. "But listen, no worries if plans change. If you head home before I'm back, we'll make it to Thanksgiving. We'll eat. Then nap. Then play board games. Then there's the soccer tournament in the backyard. . . ."

A wave of guilt crashes through me. Willa assumes I'm coming to the Bergmans' for Thanksgiving, like I did last year, after Dad's and my brief, early meal. I don't want to tell her how unsure I am that I'll make it. If I'll feel well enough, because I just never know when it's going to be a rough day and home is the only place I can handle being. If I can stand the embarrassment of seeing Axel since Kissgate.

Willa's still talking happily, planning our day. "You better brace yourself. I'm going to tackle-hug you. I'm going to squeeze you so hard, you'll squeak like a puppy chew toy."

That makes me laugh. "You're disturbing."

"But you love me. All right, I have to get going. I just wanted to catch up quickly before I had practice. Love you! Text me when you're safe at the cabin?"

"Love you, too. I will."

"And text Ryder for help when you're ready to admit that you're lost."

"I'm not lost!" I yell right as she hangs up. Then I refocus on the GPS.

Okay. Maybe I'm a *little* lost.

# TWO

# Axel

A drop of water lands on my forehead with a *splat*. Annoyed, I wipe it away, then dry my hand off on my filthy jeans. Generally, I don't mind getting wet. I've lived in Washington most of my life, and I'm used to rain. My problem is this precipitation is happening *inside* the A-frame.

"Well," Bennett says on a sigh. "It's as bad as you said."

"Now you get to tell me how bad, in dollars."

Surveying the worst of the water damage, he says, "Lotsa bad. As a contractor, I'm seeing one of my best-paying jobs in years. As your friend, I'm sick to my stomach."

"Right." I turn toward the ladder on the other side of the open window, where Parker's been doing an exterior inspection and is now climbing down the rungs. Bennett's not going to want to bear the bad news, but Parker will have no problem giving it to me straight. "So in dollars, that is?"

Parker lands on the ground with a thud as their kid, Skyler, splashes past him, thrilled with all the water that's accumulated for puddle jumping. "Enough to make you wish you'd taken out the extra insurance that covers replacing not only the old pipes but also the damage they cause when they burst."

I lean my forearms on the open windowsill and glare down at

him. "You only have the balls to say that to me because I'm up here and you're down there."

"Language," Parker says, right as Skyler jumps into a puddle and yells, "Balls!"

"Sky," he tells her, "don't say that." Then he peers up at me. "I'm just telling you what B's too nice to say when you're in the same room. Whatever happens after this, you gotta have that insurance."

Bennett tugs at the dark bun twisted on top of his head, nudging a chunk of waterlogged drywall that's fallen to the floor. "He has to work on his bedside manner."

"I'm hardly one to criticize."

He wipes away a splat of water that hit him on the head. "Park said it wrong, but he's right. If you go through with these repairs, that's mandatory from now on. Between not being regularly inhabited and its exposure to the elements, it's a high-risk property."

"*When* I go through with the repairs," I tell him. "Which, again, are going to cost how much?"

"On top of what we already had scoped out?"

I nod.

Scuffing his boot on the floor, Bennett tugs at his bun again. "How 'bout I write it down, and you open it once we're gone?" He extracts his ever-present notepad from his back pocket and scribbles something. Ripping out the paper, he folds it in half and slaps it in my palm. "I'm serious about the waiting. At least until Skyler's in the car. We just got her to stop saying 'goddammit' last week."

"I told you I'd watch your child. I made no promises to be a role model."

Bennett sighs. "Dude, she's seven."

"She's a board game despot who whupped my ass at Candy Land. Endure that, and let's see how clean your mouth is."

Bennett arches an eyebrow. "I'll admit she can be brutal when it comes to Candy Land, but no more bad words from Uncle Ax."

"Fine," I mutter. "Go away."

"Going." Bennett pockets his notebook again and sticks the pencil he used back in his bun. "Don't tell Parker I said this, but if it takes you a while to come up with the money, we can afford to start on half the normal retainer that we ask for. Just enough to pay the crew."

That's not a good sign. Not at all.

I stare at the folded piece of paper. "*That* bad?"

"Let's just say, even if you took out a construction loan, banks usually require twenty percent down. So that's going to be . . ." Bennett clears his throat and nods toward the paper. "Well, yeah. You'll know soon enough."

My jaw clenches. "Great."

"You still can't paint?" Bennett asks carefully.

I shake my head. He knows the financial and professional situation I'm in, that this crisis at the A-frame could not have come at a worse time.

Normally, faced with this predicament, I'd paint a few solid pieces, have a quick show and sale, and I'd be fine. Until recently, after having sold my art at a level that I never used to dream I could, I *had* a shit ton of money saved, and it would have been no problem. I put some of it into A-frame repairs that I hired Parker and Bennett's crew for a few months ago, but once I'd addressed the most pressing issues, I paused that work and invested the bulk of it in my brother Ryder's just-underway business, an REI-style shop that also offers outdoor activities he's working to make accessible to anyone who wants to experience nature.

Ryder's undergoing training, getting certified, interviewing people to build an inclusive team, buying expensive equipment, outfitting the facility, all of which requires a large up-front sum. Rather than him dealing with interest rates through a bank loan, I told him to take the money and consider it an investment in his business.

That's why—even though he only lives an hour away, and if there's anyone I'd trust with helping me handle this crisis, it's him—I haven't told my younger brother what's going on. He'd offer the money back, put his dream on hold. And I won't let that happen. Not when he's happier than I've seen him in years. I'm not doing a damn thing to compromise that.

I'm not telling anyone else in my family, either. If they knew what I've done and plan to do for the A-frame, my parents would say it's an unreasonable investment, and my siblings would think they owe me. It's not, and they don't. This is the least I can do.

I know I'm not easy to feel close to. I'm not warm and affectionate like the rest of my family. I don't hug spontaneously or laugh often or thrive in the intimate chaos that defines our large family.

I don't love the way they do.

So I do this. I protect the place we care about, the A-frame that's been the heart of our family since my parents bought it. This is a way that I love them. And nothing's going to stop that.

I just have to get . . . creative. I have to get past this painting crisis because until I can paint, there's no money to fix the A-frame in this small window of time before it's my sister's turn here and everyone in my family knows what's wrong.

Bennett shifts on his feet and clears his throat. "What about the inheritance?"

I give him a sharp look. I've vehemently ignored my inheritance since the moment I was told about Uncle Jakob's will. Because it came with the worst possible condition he could have placed on me. "Did you conveniently forget the condition?"

"So follow the letter of the law, not the spirit of it. You don't have to find true love to get married. Just someone willing to partner with you and treat it like a business venture. You could find someone in a heartbeat, I bet."

Sighing, I massage the bridge of my nose. "Right. Because I have such a wide social circle, and it's made up of single people champing at the bit to marry for money."

"I mean . . . we could figure it out. Park and I would help you."

"B!" Parker yells from outside. "Leave the man to brood in peace!"

"All right," Bennett mutters, heading for the hallway. "Hang in there. Let me know what you decide. And if you change your mind about the inheritance, I mean it—we'll help you find someone."

"I'm not that desperate." I stare down at the paper burning a hole in my hand. "At least, I don't think so. But thanks, Bennett."

Following him down the stairs and outside, I stop on the porch.

Skyler pauses puddle jumping and squints up at me. "You look extra grumpy today, Uncle Ax."

"What can I say, Skyler. It's a good day to be grumpy."

Hands on hips over her superhero-cape rain jacket, she tips her head and examines me. "I think you need a good kiss."

Parker covers his laugh with a cough.

"Really," I say to her. "Wonder who's been telling you that."

"No one!" she says, leaping for a puddle right next to me and dousing my legs.

"Skyler," Bennett chides.

"They're already soaking wet," I tell him.

She lands in another puddle. "I just know that when Daddy's grumpy, BiBi kisses him, and then he's all better. So go find some-one and get a kiss. Then come back for more Candy Land so I can kick your butt."

"This child," Bennett says wearily, taking her by the shoulder. "All Parker."

Parker grins as he backtracks toward the car. "Out of the mouths of babes, Axel!"

I give him the appropriate hand gesture when Skyler turns her back and gets into the car. Then I watch the three of them leave, hands waving out the windows from their extended-cab truck. When it turns onto the main road, I open the paper Bennett handed me.

And it's a very good thing Skyler isn't around to hear what comes out of my mouth.

I am so absolutely fucked.

Pocketing the quote, I lower myself onto the porch. Wind moves through the trees, sending fiery gold and scarlet leaves fluttering to the ground and painting the earth, doing a damn better job at making art than I have in months.

A knot tightens in my chest. I shut my eyes, and there she is, vivid, breathtaking.

Rooney.

This is all her fault—not the house, but those blank and half-finished canvases back in my studio. It's her fault that I've been fighting a losing creative battle for months. And it's that fucking charades kiss that was the death blow.

Now, every time I pick up a brush, it's not abstract lines and bold colors. It's peaches and pinks, ocean blue greens and spun honey gold. I paint something—*someone*—I shouldn't.

That has to end. I need so much money, and fast. I haven't painted anything I can sell in over two months. Everything I *have* painted is already sold. If I can't get past this creative block, I don't know what I'll do.

Well, that's not true. I know what I'll do. I just really don't want to do it.

Pushing off the steps, I turn back inside, shut the door, and lock it behind me. My eyes land on the family photos along the hallway wall. My parents' wedding day. My siblings and I, in all stages of childhood. Formal family portraits and candid photos of skinned-kneed kids—flushed faces; suntanned, freckled skin.

Then there's the photo from years ago. I spot my mother's brother, Uncle Jakob, who came all the way from Östersund, a man whose quiet intensity, whose daily ritual of sitting outside early in the morning, drinking coffee and sketching the view, I recognize in myself. A man who I *thought* would respect a person's choice for a solitary life if they decided that was for the best.

And then he left me a shocking amount of money with the condition that I had to be married.

It felt like being slapped.

He didn't know me well, but he saw me enough times that I'd thought he would intuit marriage wasn't likely for someone like me, someone who can barely talk to unfamiliar people, whose words come out blunt and sharp with the people I *do* know and love, who avoids unfamiliar touch and rarely hugs and disappears when rooms grow loud, no matter how happy the occasion, because it's just too much.

I've tried not to be resentful. But right now I am. That inheritance could really come in handy. And I have to get married in order to access it.

Could I marry someone, even if only for the sole purpose of money? A business arrangement in which I get my inheritance and they barter their cut?

I stare at Uncle Jakob's photo and sigh. "What were you thinking?"

He doesn't answer. Of course he doesn't. He's a fucking photo, and he's been dead for over a year. I'm losing it.

Beneath my feet, I hear an ominous clunk, then a surge of water, meaning something else just went wrong. I'm not even surprised at this point. Sighing, I turn and make my way toward the basement.

# THREE

# Rooney

Playlist: "Alex," Wild Child

I didn't get lost. I took a detour. That's my story, and I'm sticking to it.

After my "detour," I reach the end of the drive and throw the car in park. I almost kiss the ground when I step out and shut the door behind me. My drive took nearly two hours, and my stomach pains are persistent—not bad enough that I was worried about needing a roadside stop but bad enough that I'm thoroughly relieved to be here. Pain is always a warning, and it's vulnerable, not knowing when pain will become urgency.

I take a deep breath, more relaxed now that a bathroom is within reach if I need it. Thankfully, I don't need it right now. For now, I can stand and drink in the view before me.

My gaze settles on the A-frame. Two tall stories. Floor-to-ceiling glass, the exterior rain-darkened to a deep brown black. Towering evergreens and deciduous trees flank the property. The rush of nearby water marries the sound of rain slipping off branches to the earth in a soft *pit-pat*.

It's so peaceful—quiet and hushed. The kind of silent stillness I never thought I'd be drawn to, but here I am, mesmerized. A carpet of crimson and copper rain-slicked leaves spreads across the clearing, a trail leads into the woods, a view of the lake is to the other side, and . . . there's another car here.

That's strange.

I frown at the black Jeep Wrangler that looks like it's as old as me. I don't recognize it. Probably an old standby car that the Bergmans keep here.

After grabbing my suitcase, I make my way up to the porch, each step's gentle creak adding to the chorus of chirping birds and dripping rainwater. I stretch on tiptoe and feel along the doorframe, like Willa instructed, until my fingertips find the cool metal of the front door key.

I let myself in, and the door swings open, revealing an open-concept great room frozen in time. The dated kitchen decor, the long, well-loved dining table and a dozen mismatched chairs, the cozy living room with its oversized furniture all look so loved and worn and lived-in, I can feel the memories in this place. A pang of envy thrums through my chest. What must it be like to belong to something like this, to be surrounded by family and history and memories?

All I want to do is explore every inch of the house, but that giant bottle of water I drank on my drive has hit my bladder. Time to find a bathroom. Dropping my suitcase in the foyer, I head down a hallway that looks promising.

Pictures of the Bergmans flank the wall as I walk. Elin and Dr. B on their wedding day, then a series of steadily growing family portraits. First, baby Freya, her fluffy white-blonde chickadee hair and Elin's pale blue-gray eyes. Next, baby Axel who—oh my *God*—is frowning adorably, dark brown hair sticking straight up in a mohawk, his dad's bright green eyes narrowed in suspicion. I snort softly and stop long enough to look closer, my fingertips tracing that frown.

His frown was so fucking cute. It still is.

Forcing myself not to dwell on that, I resume my family photo tour as I walk down the hall, the pictures growing busier as the family grows, too.

There's Ren, same copper hair as he has now and pale blue-gray Elin Bergman eyes, nestled in Freya's arms as Axel—you guessed it—frowns at the camera. Then Ryder, who's easily recognizable, the only one in the family with the combination of green eyes and blond hair. Not surprisingly, the next photo involves both of the wild "man cubs," as the family calls them, who are only twelve months apart—Viggo and Oliver, like night and day, with matching blue-gray eyes but brown and blond hair, respectively. Then finally, baby Ziggy, with her dad's copper locks and sharp green eyes, surrounded by all her siblings.

My heart twists. I've only known the Bergmans for a few years, since Willa and Ryder got serious, but they feel as close to a real family as I've ever known. And, unless things become miraculously not-awkward between Axel and me, I'm going to have to leave it behind.

I reach the last of the family photos. And I feel unreasonably sad about that.

Just as I turn away from the picture wall, I spot a door across the hallway that looks promisingly like it's hiding a powder room. Since I got sick in high school, I've become an expert at scoping out bathrooms when I arrive anywhere, because you just never know when you'll need to go. I recognize a powder room door when I see it.

Just as I reach for the handle, I hear a sound. A very human sound. Like footsteps.

Someone's here.

Probably the someone who drove that Jeep outside. God, what is wrong with me? Why wasn't I suspicious when I saw the car? Why am I incapable of assuming the worst?

Unless I'm just paranoid and working myself up.

I freeze, hand poised over the doorknob, and listen harder. I try to convince myself that I'm imagining things.

But then I hear it: steady, increasingly louder footsteps coming from behind the door I was about to open. This is right out of a horror movie. Some murdering fucker is coming for me from the basement.

Adrenaline floods my system, panic pricking my skin. I glance around wildly, hoping to find something I can defend myself with. My gaze flicks quickly to the hard-shell suitcase I left in the foyer. A decent weapon. I consider running toward it, hoping I'll be able to sweep it up in time to defend myself, but too late. The door opens. I stand face-to-face with a tall man hidden in shadow, only his boots illuminated by a flashlight.

I scream because holy *shit*, this is terrifying, then push the guy, hoping I can catch him off guard long enough to run away. He yells in shock and drops the flashlight. Then he reels backward, teetering on the edge of the step, arms pinwheeling at his sides.

As his head tips back in the effort to find his balance, his features catch in the flashlight's beams. That's when I recognize who I just shoved to his staircase doom.

Axel Bergman.

---

It happens in slow motion, and my imagination is running wild, picturing Axel flipping down the steps and breaking his neck. I reach for him, grabbing a fistful of his shirt in an effort to slow him down.

Here's the thing. I'm five-eleven and—when not coming off a bad flare-up—pretty fit. Axel, though very lean, is nearly six and a half feet tall, and whatever is on those bones is muscle. Muscle, my friends, is *heavy*. Meaning holding on to Axel does nothing, except send me with him.

I try to stop myself from pitching forward, too, but it's hopeless.

I fall into him, just as he arcs backward like a diver. Axel plants his hands on the slanted ceiling behind him, stopping us from plummeting down the steps.

Our bodies connect with a clattering *oomph*.

Oh God. He's so big. So tall and lean and *big*. I feel his hard thigh muscles. The undeniable . . . bulk at his groin. His sharp hip bones jut into mine, my breasts are smashed against his chest, and my hands rest right over his pecs to steady myself.

Air saws in and out of our lungs, echoing around us.

"I'm so sorry," I say hoarsely. I'm still clinging to him as we hover at an unnervingly steep angle over the stairs. "You startled me, and I just . . . reacted."

He doesn't answer me. On a grunt, he pushes off the ceiling, which thrusts his body into mine. Heat rockets beneath my skin, and the moment my heels touch down on the landing, I step away, embarrassment pinking my cheeks.

Clearing his throat, Axel picks up the dropped flashlight and turns it off. Then he steps forward and calmly shuts the basement door behind him as if we didn't just rub bodies and nearly tumble down the steps.

"What are you doing here?" he finally says. His voice wraps around me, deep and soft as a midnight caress.

I blink dazedly, then snap out of it. "Uh . . . what? I'm . . . I'm here for a staycation. Willa said the A-frame was mine to use when I mentioned I needed somewhere to get away."

His eyes travel me, slide down the hallway, then land on my suitcase in the foyer. A long, heavy sigh leaves him.

"Why are *you* here?" I ask carefully.

Swearing under his breath, he pockets the flashlight and strolls past me. "Outside."

"Outside?" I watch his long strides make quick work of the hallway. I'm so confused.

Axel picks up my suitcase and points with the flashlight toward the front door. "Outside. Please."

Is he seriously kicking me out?

Walking my way, he uses the suitcase to nudge me toward the door. I'm being corralled like sheep. "Please, Rooney."

"Okay, okay. I'm going. Is something wrong?"

"Just about everything," he mutters.

I glance over my shoulder, staring around for signs of home disaster. The place seems well-loved, but it hardly looks like it's falling apart. Then again, looks can be deceiving. If I had a nickel for every time I made the mistake of telling someone I was sick—and they said disbelievingly, *But you look fine!*—I'd be rolling in shiny little Thomas Jeffersons.

"Is that why you're here? In the basement?" I ask. "With a flashlight?"

"Dealing with major plumbing issues. No electricity on for safety, thus the flashlight."

Well, much more logical than him being a murderer. God, I can be such a drama llama.

Opening the front door, Axel follows me outside. As we step onto the porch, then face each other, every thought evaporates. The evening sun bathes him in golden light as he stands tall, his face unreadable but handsome as ever—rich brown hair, sharp cheekbones, eyes dark as the rain-drenched evergreens around us.

He looks different than when I've seen him at his parents' house, or—holy God—that one time when he showed his art in LA and wore the fuck out of a charcoal-gray two-piece suit— bright white button-up, cognac leather belt and dress shoes, no tie . . .

Wow, I sound creepy remembering all of that, but if you saw

Axel Bergman looking like sin in a suit, you'd remember the fine details, too.

Today, though, his normally tidy hair is going every direction, and he has a thick five-o'clock shadow of stubble that makes him look surlier. There's mud and water all over his jeans and boots. He's not wearing a jacket, despite the cold, just a threadbare flannel shirt, its plaid print echoing our surroundings—cloud gray, sky blue, thin stripes that are wet-earth burgundy. His shirt's undone four buttons, revealing a narrow wedge of pale skin, a dusting of dark hair across the shadow of his pecs.

Axel notices me staring, then peers down. Twin splashes of pink bloom on his cheeks as he swiftly refastens two more buttons on his shirt, until it sits open just below the hollow of his throat.

"So . . ." I fold my arms across my chest, as much to hide my body reacting to that peek of Axel's skin as to brace myself against the wind. "What now?"

He runs both hands through his hair and swallows.

I do not watch his Adam's apple bob.

Or think about licking it.

Shit, who am I kidding. If liars' pants really caught on fire, these stretchy palazzos would be a heap of ash.

He finally glances my way, his gaze barely slipping across my face before he turns and stares up at the A-frame. He clears his throat. "I don't know. It's not safe for you to stay here."

I turn and stare at the A-frame, too. So much for a cozy staycation.

Tears well in my eyes. I'm beyond disappointed. And, as if I wasn't already feeling miserable, a fresh wave of pain hits my stomach.

I suck in a breath and bite my cheek to stifle a groan.

But Axel notices. His head snaps my way, and his gaze meets mine so briefly, I almost doubt it happened. Except I feel it. A millisecond of those sharp green eyes locked with mine knocks the air right out of me.

"Are you all right?" he asks.

There's a softness in his voice, a gentleness I don't recognize that inexplicably makes me want to cry. So of course, I force a smile. "Yeah. I could just use the restroom before I get out of your hair."

He frowns, glancing over at the house. "Not here. The water's shut off."

Another spasm racks my stomach, the pain intensifying. I grit my teeth. Sweat breaks out on my skin. I'm too uncomfortable to be embarrassed as I say, "Can you . . . tell me where I *can* find a working bathroom, then? I need it."

There's a long, heavy silence in which I start wiggling my knees and take a slow, deep breath. I can hear Axel's gears turning. He's been raised too well to do something like send me to a gas station and tell me I'm on my own, but what else can he offer? Not that I'm even sure I'd make it to the last gas station I drove by on my way here. Let alone find it.

I look around, desperate for some magical solution to appear. But it doesn't. Trees. Water. More trees.

I'm screwed. I'm going to have to wander into the woods and pull a Laura Ingalls Wilder.

Ax hoists my suitcase tighter in his grip. "This way."

Before I can ask where we're going, he's opened the Jeep's trunk and is setting my suitcase inside. Then he opens the front passenger door. I could stay here and ask where he's taking me that has indoor plumbing, but honestly, what does it matter? I'm not going to look a gift toilet in the bowl.

I hustle down the porch's steps and slide into the passenger seat. After he shuts the door behind me, Axel smoothly rounds the car, starts the engine, then pulls a quick, efficient U-turn before he guns it down the drive.

My hands white-knuckle the worn leather upholstery of my seat. This is partly because I am focusing all my energy on not shitting my pants, and also because Axel has the hot forearm thing going, driving the car—it's a stick shift, so those muscles and tendons flex as he drives, eyes fixed on the road. To add insult to injury, the car's the first place I've ever been able to pin down his scent that's as evasive as he is. He's brushed by me a few times. And then of course there was The Charades Kiss, which was when I got a decent lungful, but so much was happening, my brain didn't have time to sort it out.

Now I'm soaking in his scent, and it's indecently appealing. Not a harsh cologne, like so many guys wear, but something gentle. A whisper of sage and cedar. Woodsy, warm, clean. Like maybe it's just the bar of soap he washes with.

And there my horny mind goes, daydreaming about Axel showering, soap clutched in one of those big hands, slipping down his chest, that lean, flat stomach, lower, right over his—

"Rooney."

"What?" I yelp.

There's an awkward silence before Axel clears his throat, eyes on the road. "You said Willa sent you here?"

I need a word with the universe, whoever's in charge up there, because I truly resent that this man who leaves a room whenever I enter it seems genetically designed to turn me on. Just hearing him speak, quiet and deep, makes me want to shut my eyes and arch into the air like his voice is a taunting fingertip tracing my skin. If I weren't so physically miserable, I'd be despicably turned-on.

"I told Willa I needed to get away. She said the A-frame was empty. Which is . . ." I frown, staring out the window. "Really weird. Why would she send me here if she knew you were here and that all this stuff was going on?"

An uneasy hum rumbles in Axel's throat. I catch his hands

white-knuckling the steering wheel and gear shift, but he doesn't say anything.

Thank God, just a few seconds later, we've pulled into a small clearing surrounding what I can only describe as a modern cottage. Dark wood. Clean lines. It reminds me of a bigger version of those trendy tiny cabins that always advertise on Instagram with photos of couples cuddling in a sea of white sheets and fluffy pillows that definitely don't make me feel hopelessly alone or anything.

Axel throws open the door of his Jeep, his strides long and brisk as he rounds the car and opens my door before I've so much as unbuckled my seat belt. He holds the door open, but backs away as soon as I'm out of it, like he both wants as much space between us as possible and can't help being a gentleman.

"What is this place?" I ask him.

Glancing my way, he pulls my suitcase from the trunk. "Somewhere you can stay tonight."

"Oh, that's not necessary. I just need the restroom, then I'll get back on the road."

He frowns, glancing up at the sky. "It's almost dark. Stay the night. Figure out your plans tomorrow."

I want to argue with him, but I'm not exactly excited to get in the car again and get myself lost driving these winding roads back to the airport, especially if my stomach stays finicky.

Resigned, I start for the house behind Axel, who strolls ahead of me, unlocks the door, and opens it.

Relief and desperation win out. I plaster on my brightest smile, call what I hope is a chipper "Thanks!" over my shoulder, and speed-walk inside.

---

I don't get a detailed view of the cabin on my way in, but after using the bathroom, I'm able to take in the space. It's beautiful. Tidy and minimalist. Clean lines. A familiar, calming scent I could swear reminds me of Axel, but I think his sexy smell might simply be stuck in my nose after the car ride.

A main room divided into living sections, its dominant feature is a wooden platform bed, smooth white sheets and pillows, and a matching nightstand beside it with a lamp, tucked in one corner. On the other side of the bed, to the right of a long, low-profile dresser, there's a door leading to where I'm not sure—maybe a garage? A woodburning fireplace faces the foot of the bed, with floating tiered shelves above anchored to the chimney. Dominating the central space is an oblong reclaimed-wood dining table encircled by mismatched chairs. And past that is a long sofa tucked along the other wall, a narrow side table with another lamp, and more floating shelves above the sofa. An island divides the main living space from the kitchen, which is small and spotless—appliances that catch my reflection and sparkling, uncluttered countertops. The place is a soothing palette of cloud white, dark wood tones, and shades of deep earthy greens and stormy grays. It feels familiar and calming.

I'm tempted to snoop around further, but I've got too many questions, like why Willa sent me to the A-frame when it's in some kind of structural crisis, when Axel of all people was there and clearly didn't know I was coming. I have a funny feeling when I get some answers, I'm not going to like them.

I step outside onto a fragrant carpet of fallen pine needles and search the space for Axel. But I don't see him anywhere. Only a circle of tidy stones clearly dedicated to a campfire. A pile of split wood, with a heavy-looking hatchet wedged into a nearby tree stump. There's the Jeep, too. But no Axel.

Then I see a note trapped beneath the windshield wiper, fluttering in the wind. I snatch it up and read the long, tidy scrawl.

*Sorry about the A-frame. As I said, feel free to stay here tonight.
If not, keys are in the Jeep for you to drive back and grab your
rental.*

$$—A$$

*PS My number in case of emergency is 555-231-4542.*

I reread his note, running my fingers across the letters as fatigue sinks its teeth into me. Between sickness and stress, the long day of flying, then driving, I'm exhausted. Humbling reality hits.

I'm *tired*. Too tired to do anything but accept this.

On the threshold, I listen to the quiet sounds of wildlife around me, the whisper of wind dancing through the trees. I stare down at Axel's note, sliding my thumb across that solitary letter *A*. Then I fold it in half and tuck it into the safe square pocket of my sweater, right over my heart.

# FOUR

## Axel

Playlist: "Social Cues," Cage the Elephant

What the *hell* have I done?

*Stay here tonight.* I just . . . blurted it, which is so unlike me, and then—as if I hadn't been clear enough—I said it again in that goddamn note.

With my phone number.

Fuck me.

It was like I was possessed, driving her to the house, telling her to stay, writing that note, when all I want is for Rooney to be as far away from me as possible. Because for two years I've hidden my attraction to her, and that's been possible through one thing: distance.

So what do I do when she tumbles into my life? I invite her to spend the fucking night.

Brilliant, Axel. Just brilliant.

The best I can do now is make myself scarce, which is exactly what I'm doing. Not that it's helping much. I can still smell her, soft and peaceful as a meadow at twilight, blossoms swaying in the breeze. Most perfumes are so cloyingly strong, they give me a headache. But this was so . . . soothing. I wonder if it's simply the scent of her skin and her hair.

But it's dangerous, wondering that. Because then I picture nuzzling the soft, warm, sweet places of Rooney's body, breathing her in. And that's not going to happen.

Ever.

I pick up my pace, each step placing more distance between us, even though I know it's pointless. I can still smell her soothing scent, still *feel* her soft body leaning into mine as I braced us over the stairs. Her breasts pressed into my chest. Her hands' warmth branding my skin.

"Fuck." I swat a weed with a stick I've had in my hand, then toss the stick.

My strides eat up the ground as I start across the small soccer field behind the A-frame, home to countless family pickup games.

Speaking of my fucking family. I move one thousand miles north of them, and they still manage to meddle in my life. Even though they don't know what's going on with the A-frame, there's no good excuse for Ryder and Willa sending Rooney here. This is *my* stretch of time, and they both knew it. Something's up. I don't know what, but it's got Bergman bullshit written all over it.

Storming across the field, I yank out my phone, pull up my text messages, and open my thread with Ryder, then type, What the hell are you playing at?

Three little dots show up immediately, then his response: I love a good vague text.

Don't act like you don't know Rooney's here at the A-frame, I write. She said Willa told her she could come here. Meaning YOU told her it was free. It's my time at the cabin. What the fuck were you thinking?

His response: I was thinking it's no big deal.

"No big deal!" I yell, stomping up the porch. I open the front door, then slam it shut behind me.

I can't tell him about the state of the A-frame. But I can tell him having Rooney here is the last thing I need. Well, it is. She can't be here.

Why not? he texts.

I rack my brain for what to say. I can't explain how serious things are here, but God, do I wish he understood what a mess this makes. She's already fucked my creativity from a thousand miles away. Now that I've seen her, smelled her, touched her, what's my chance at painting what I need to? I know how my brain works. It will have one thing consuming it when I pick up that brush, and it sure as shit won't be abstract art.

I pace the house, the severity of this situation tightening like a noose around my neck. I have two months to get the biggest repairs on the A-frame handled and paid for. I have Parker and Bennett's crew ready to do the work. I just need *money*. I have to paint brilliantly and sell fast, or suck it up and marry.

*Christ.*

Uncle Jakob's photo. I swear it's looking at me, taunting me from across the hall. "You might as well have told me to climb Everest," I tell the picture. "Shit, I'd probably have a better chance at that!"

His serious expression stares back at me. I drop my forehead to the wall and bang it. I'm losing my mind.

When my phone dings with a message from Ryder, I nearly jump out of my skin.

Willa said Rooney's going through a rough
patch and needed somewhere to stay for a
while, so I told her to have at it. You don't
even stay at the A-frame, Ax. You built your
own damn house on the property. What's the
big deal? Are you going to catch cooties from

sharing an acre of land with her for a
few weeks?

Oh, God. *Weeks?* She can't stay here for weeks. I'll be done for.

I don't stay at the A-frame, I type, but I had projects I was
working on.

Pause the projects, he says. Or work on them & stay out of
her way. Find your big-boy pants & talk to her about it yourself.

I can't talk to Rooney, not at any length, and be coherent. I can
barely look at her and breathe properly. Make Willa invite her to
stay at your place instead, I type.

My phone dings again with his next message. Fuck no. We live
in a shoebox bungalow and Willa's not even around right now.
The A-frame's empty & it's perfectly reasonable to offer it to a
family friend. If you have to be a jerk about it, go hide in your
little troll cottage in the woods & stay there until she leaves.

It dings again. While you're at it, pull that stick out of your ass
about being around her, because she's invited to Thanksgiving,
which means post-turkey-dinner charades.

Shit. The memory of Rooney's kiss comes back in full force—
the sweet softness of her mouth on mine, the flush of her cheeks as
she stared up at me. That *can't* happen again.

My asshole brother has the audacity to text, I'm putting "make
out" in the basket this time.

Fuck. Off, I type.

His response comes instantly. LOL.

I groan and drop my phone into my pocket. This is terrible.
Ryder says Rooney came here because she's going through a rough
patch, and while I don't know what's going on, I know she didn't
seem like herself, either.

And that's what turned me inside out, what made me throw
her suitcase in my trunk and drive her to the house. I wasn't think-

ing. I was reacting. Because after I nudged her out of the A-frame, it felt like my heart was splintering in my chest.

I stared at her profile as she peered up at the house, that honey-blonde hair just past her shoulders, wind-whipped and dancing, like the breeze couldn't help but slip its cool fingers through those spun-gold strands. And I knew something was different. Something was wrong. Her wide blue-green eyes weren't sparkling and there were half-moon bruises beneath them. Her normally glowing skin was pale, no rosy flush in her cheeks. Two deep dimples that flash every time she smiles were nowhere to be seen.

She was hurting. And I didn't want her to hurt anymore. I don't want her to hurt ever.

So now what do I do? I can't kick her out if she needs somewhere to stay. But if I don't send her packing, there's no chance in hell I'm going to paint. Shit, who am I kidding? Even if she were to leave first thing tomorrow, crashing into her today has sent me into a tailspin. I have to face the facts:

I am not in the right frame of mind to paint.

Because I can't paint, I can't sell.

And because I can't sell, I can't make money.

With no money, the A-frame's done for. My parents will find out. They'll absolutely veto the financing necessary to shore up the place, and that will leave one thing and one thing only: selling it. And then this place will be lost to us.

Unless I bite the bullet and take Bennett up on his offer, let him and Parker help me find someone who'll enter into a legal union only for the money and with no other expectations, a marriage that's purely transactional. It's bleak, but it's the only solution.

Before I can talk myself out of it, I pull out my phone and dial Bennett. He picks up on the third ring. "You okay?" he asks.

A fair question. I never call. "When you said you'd help me find someone so I could get the inheritance, did you mean it?"

There's a pause. "Of course, Ax."

I inhale slowly, relief funneling into my lungs. "I'm going to take you up on it."

"I think you're making the right call," he says. "It's a shit ton of money, with the plumbing disaster."

Stepping through the sliding doors onto the back deck, I look over the field toward the cabin where I left Rooney. "Yeah. There's no way I can force painting right now."

"He finally comes to his senses!" Parker calls.

I scowl. "Speakerphone. How lovely."

"Hi, Uncle Ax!" Skyler bellows.

I yank the phone away from my ear. "Hi, Skyler."

"I'm eating your favorite," she says loudly around the sound of chewing. "Carrots with grape jelly."

"Gross."

"Hey! Give Uncle Ax another mark on his chart. He yucked my yum!"

Parker laughs in the background.

"Sky, put BiBi on the phone, please."

"Hey," Bennett says, amid footsteps and the sound of a door being shut. "Sorry about that. We were in the middle of dinner, but I answered because the last time you called me, you were in the hospital, so the precedent was set."

I scrub my face and groan. "I don't know why I called. I could have texted."

After a beat, Bennett says, "Ax, are you okay?"

My eyes fasten on the exact spot in the woods where the cabin sits. My heart pounds. "I will be."

"All right. I'm here for you, remember? All three of us are."

"I know."

"Good," he says. "Well, talk tomorrow."

"Yeah." I hang up, then pocket my phone. After a walk-through to remind myself why I'm going to marry a stranger for money (which works—this place is so deceptively good at hiding its problems, I'm surprised it hasn't caved in on us already), I lock up the A-frame.

Standing on the porch, my back to the clearing, I hold my breath, not knowing when I turn around what car I'm more terrified I'll see: the Jeep or Rooney's rental.

If the rental is gone and my Jeep is in its place, she passed up my offer and left. And then life will be back to normal—well, minus marrying someone for money—and I can focus on the tasks ahead. But if the rental is still here, that means she stayed. And then . . .

Air rushes out of my lungs. Her rental sedan glows in the dying light.

She stayed.

She *stayed*.

My heart pounds against my ribs. My chest tightens. I take a deep breath, concentrating on the logistics. I changed the sheets on my bed this morning, coincidentally, so that's good. I'm fastidiously neat, so the place is spotless. When I let her into the house to use the restroom, I threw a handful of clothes into a duffel bag to tide me over for the night since I wouldn't have access to my stuff.

But I'm pretty sure the fridge is almost empty. I should pick up food.

Once I grab my bicycle from the shed, I double-check that the dual storage bags are secure and take off. I ride hard, trying to outstrip the unsettling hum beneath my skin when I think about Rooney in my house.

In my bed.

In my shower.

I mentally slap myself for going down that dangerous path. Then I ride harder.

Soon, I'm parking the bike outside Shepard's, bracing myself

for the inevitable. Bike bags in hand, I push open the door. The
bell dings, and—

"Heartbreaker!"

I frown at the store's owner, Sarah Shepard. Hip-length silver
hair, wire-rimmed spectacles, and a sly smile, she's known me my
whole life and lives to give me shit.

While Shepard's is the only place within reasonable cycling
distance, I shop at the small café and locally sourced grocery store
even when I have the Jeep. I could drive a little farther to the near-
est chain store and avoid the harassment, but my mother would
disown me. Sarah took Mom under her wing when she and Dad
bought the A-frame, and they're still incredibly close friends. It's
ingrained in me to shop only at Shepard's, even if Sarah drives me
up the wall.

I lift a hand in hello, grab a basket, and head for the fresh food.

Sarah smiles and says nothing else, fussing with the flowers sitting in a vase on the checkout counter. I know better than to think
I'm going to get out of here unscathed, though. Sarah's quiet is like
the calm before the storm.

Focused on buying what will fit in the bike bags, I grab ingredients for a quick campfire dinner. I'm not cooking in that tiny
kitchen with Rooney nearby and my bed twenty feet away. Not a
chance in hell. I'll give her a good outdoorsy Washington welcome
and make a simple meal in a cast-iron skillet.

On my way to check out, I stop at the aisle that I never go
down. I'm not exactly sure what to get, I just know in the handful
of times I've seen Rooney, at some point she was sighing over whatever sweet my mom had made. They're no homemade Swedish
dessert, but I grab the biggest bag of marshmallows, a brick of chocolate, and graham crackers. Seems like a safe choice.

Sarah scans the items and arches her eyebrows. "So," she says.
"Who're you hiding at the little house?"

I blink at her in shock. "What?"

"Dear, this is not my first day as local busybody, and I've known you since you were frowning in diapers. You hate sugary food. The sweetest thing you'll eat is an apple. Whereas this evening, you have, in fact, purchased all the fixings for s'mores. Which means, my sweet, surly thirtysomething, that you have a guest." She bats her eyelashes. "A special someone waiting for you? Warming up that cozy cabin in the woods?"

"A guest," I tell Sarah distractedly, fishing around my jeans for my wallet. "She's Willa's best friend."

"Oh!" Sarah beams. She loves Willa. "Well, in that case, it's on the house. Go. Shoo. Woo her with s'mores."

"I'm not woo—" Clenching my teeth, I exhale heavily and hold out enough cash to cover everything. "I'd like to pay."

Sarah stacks the items neatly inside my bike bags, then shoves them across the counter. "I said it's on the house, heartbreaker. Now get wooing."

# FIVE

# *Rooney*

Playlist: "Make Out," Julia Nunes

Since I walked back into the cabin, flopped onto that big, dreamy bed, and crashed, I've been dreaming about a tall, green-eyed man I couldn't deny is Axel if I tried.

In the dream, I stand with him in the rain. The world is soft and diffuse, only cool water and almost kisses, the wind whispering between us. Axel's green eyes glow as he watches me, and his hands drift over my waist, pinning our hips together. I sigh with each kiss that drifts along my jaw. My fingertips dance across warm skin and lean shoulders, then dive into the silky softness of his hair. It's quiet, and it's dusk. The air crackles around us with an impending storm, and holding my eyes, Axel pulls me closer, his mouth descending toward mine—

A loud, upbeat bark outside the window wrenches me awake.

My eyes snap open. I fumble for my phone on the bed, and a quick glance at its time display tells me I've been napping for over an hour, which makes sense, given the growing darkness. Rolling onto my back, I stare up at the ceiling, flushed and achy, unresolved need heavy between my thighs. My cheeks burn. I honestly can't believe myself. It's been . . . God, over two years, and this absurd crush I've harbored, made up of a handful of fleeting interactions and stilted conversations, is ridiculous.

My head knows this. Everything else in me . . . does not.

Sitting up, I rub my face and flick on the bedside table lamp. I drooled on the bed. There's a pillow crease on my cheek. I'm tempted to slump over and give in to sleep, but I feel gross from traveling and I'm nervous I'm going to fall straight back into that dangerously good dream I was having.

I'm also a little curious about that dog bark, which I don't hear anymore. Is Axel here? *Does* he have a dog? Shit. Picturing the sexy, silent giant cuddling a puppy dog makes me hot and bothered all over again.

A cold shower it is. That'll knock the lust out of my system.

Traipsing to the bathroom, I turn on the water, admiring the sage-green tiles and spotless grout. The showerhead is ridiculously high, so I angle it down and screech the moment the cold water hits my back. Seems I'm too much of a wuss to freeze my ass off. I turn the water hot and scrub my skin pink.

Warm, clean, slightly less turned-on, I wrap a towel around my hair and walk out in my birthday suit, because I would be a nudie if I could. There is seriously no greater joy in life than air hitting the delicate bits after a long day.

My first step out of the bathroom onto the cool wood floor makes me yelp. Okay, maybe I'll wear socks with my birthday suit. Socks on, I dance around to Harry Styles and, on a spin, fall onto the bed, my eyes wandering the room. That's when I catch sight of something just underneath the dresser. Curious, I roll off the bed, pick it up, then stand and examine it.

It takes me a second to process what I'm holding before it clicks. Boxer briefs. I yelp and reflexively launch them into the air, as far away from me as possible.

"What the *fuck*?"

What's a pair of boxer briefs doing here?

After a moment, when my heart's settled down, my rational thought process takes over. This seems to be a guesthouse. Logically, the boxer briefs were most likely left by the last person who stayed here. Yes. That's it. Everyone forgets their underwear sometimes.

I whip around, the towel wobbling off my head as I search for the boxer briefs I just slingshot-ed across the room. That's when I spot them. They landed on top of the tallest of three staggered floating shelves above the fireplace.

My gaze travels the floating shelves, eyeing up the height. I'm going to have to stand on a chair or something. That top shelf is *up* there.

I frown down at myself, naked except for socks. Maybe I should put on some clothes for this.

Clothed, dining chair set at the foot of the fireplace, I stretch on tiptoe for the boxer briefs. They're *just* out of reach.

"Dammit." Blowing out a breath, I try one more time, calling on those obligatory childhood ballet lessons and pushing onto my toes. Just as I triumphantly sink my fingers into the fabric, the chair wobbles under my feet. Scrambling for stability, I grab the middle floating shelf that's within reach and screech as the chair flies out from beneath me.

My grip slips off the shelf, which groans, then tips. I fall in a flurry of books and papers, landing on my back with a thud.

"Ouch."

Sitting up, I take in the wreckage around me. Paperback books lie in a heap, pages fanned out every which way. Beside them, what looks like notebooks and journals, as well as a few folders whose contents have spilled across the floor. My gaze drifts their way, and my law school–attuned brain instantly recognizes pages of legalese.

I squeeze my eyes shut. I have a vivid memory, and the last thing I need is to accidentally read and forever remember something personal of the Bergmans'.

There's pounding on the door, then Axel's voice. "Rooney."

"Come in," I wheeze.

The door wrenches open, and Axel crosses the room, then bends over me. "Are you hurt?"

"Just a bruised ego," I groan. "And ass."

"What happened?"

Slowly, I sit up. "It's the underwear's fault."

Axel's eyes travel the mess, then land on the boxer briefs. His cheeks heat as he snatches them up and pockets them. Then he turns and stacks the paperbacks, gathers the notebooks, folders, and papers, too many of which my disobedient gaze quickly sees bearing the name *Axel Jakob Bergman*. Oh God.

Oh *God*.

Is this his house? The pieces snap into place. How good it smells. How tidy it looks. How *tall* everything is. The boxer briefs. The papers.

Cheese and fucking rice, this is mortifying! What is he doing, giving me his house to stay in without telling me?

I open my mouth, but a dog's loud, relentless bark echoes from outside, cutting me off. Axel stands, strolls toward the door, then opens it.

"Hush!" he yells out the door. "I can't think when you bark like that."

There's a soft canine whine, followed by silence.

I scramble upright, straightening myself out. My phone's still playing music, and I thought it was just my best of Harry Styles mix, but apparently it's my self-pleasure mix, because the next song starts, sexy words wafting through the air.

I lunge for the phone, jab buttons until it stops, then drop it into my pants, forgetting I'm wearing leggings. My phone slips immediately down my hip until it's wedged somewhere very uncomfortable. My cheeks heat. Somehow Axel manages not to look like he just noticed that.

"All right?" he asks.

I blink at him. "I—"

The barking resumes, and this time, it's even more insistent.

"Sorry," he mutters, turning and opening the door again. A lean brindle greyhound dog stands outside. "Lie down," he says gently. The dog scoots closer and nudges him, earning Axel's attention long enough for me to fish my phone out of its undesirable location in my leggings.

After Axel gives him a few head rubs, the dog tucks itself into a small wood structure next to the front door that I somehow failed to notice earlier—what looks like a tiny A-frame doghouse, complete with a plush plaid fleece sleeping bag tucked inside. The dog plops down on top of it and blinks big brown eyes our way.

Axel turns back toward me, seemingly unaffected by the absurd level of cuteness. "Go ahead."

"First things first." I fold my arms across my chest. "You *live* here," I tell him accusingly.

He has the grace to blush. But he doesn't say anything.

"This is your home, not a guesthouse. Why did you tell me I could stay here tonight?"

His blush deepens. "Because the A-frame's not safe, and you needed somewhere to stay."

I open my mouth. Then shut it. "I don't . . . understand. I don't understand what's going on with the A-frame or why Willa said it was okay to come, and why you're giving me your house and—"

My stomach makes an obscenely loud gurgle, silencing me. I set a hand over it. "Sorry about that."

Axel glances between the kitchen and the front door. "Why don't we . . . Let me make some dinner. Then we can talk."

Talk? Axel? He's going to . . . talk to me?

"Okay?" I say slowly.

He nods, then strides past me into his kitchen, opening drawers and cabinets. "Do you like cheese omelets?" he asks.

"I love them."

"With vegetables?"

"Yes."

"Anything you can't eat?" he asks, stacking utensils, oil, salt, and pepper onto a tray.

"I don't eat meat. Or gluten. I'm a joy to cook for."

I get a grunt of acknowledgment, then, "Won't take long."

He's gone in a handful of long strides, the door thudding behind him.

Well. All right, then.

Slipping on my rain jacket, stepping into my boots, I glance out the wide window over his bed, a perfect view of Axel bent over the campfire. His greyhound companion trots unevenly out of the doghouse, then lies on his belly, head swiveling as Axel roams around, preparing dinner.

There's a bike nearby propped on its kickstand with two bags attached to the back. Axel pulls food from them, then sets to work, cracking eggs, opening what looks like a container of pre-chopped vegetables, adding them to the skillet, which glistens with oil.

I watch the greyhound edge closer, blinking up at Axel, who turns and speaks to it. And because I'm curious, I use the crank to open the window just a little.

"No barking at her," Axel tells the dog. "Or begging."

The dog ruffs and whines.

"You heard her stomach growl. She gets food first. You'll just have to wait."

Another whine.

"No, I'm not cooking human food for you."

A small laugh leaves me. This is the most comfortably I've ever heard him talk. He's always so tight-lipped and serious. Watching him carry on this one-sided conversation feels like seeing an entirely different person.

Feeling guilty for having eavesdropped, I crank the window shut, then run both hands through my hair and try to detangle it. It's a half-dry, uncombed mess, and I'm in lounge clothes, but oh well. He's made it clear he's immune to my charms. If I look rough, what difference does it make?

As I step outside and shut the door behind me, Ax straightens, then glances my way. His gaze flicks up my body before he turns back toward the fire. Like each time I've seen him, the brief, unaffected dismissal stings.

At least the dog notices me. I smile as it pushes up onto its haunches and walks slowly toward me. The pup doesn't seem to use its back right leg very well. "Hi, cutie."

Wagging its tail, it smells my hand, followed by a hearty lick. I crouch down and pet it, my hands running along its bristly, short hair. I peer up at Axel, who's frowning at me. He glances away. "How long have you had a dog?"

"He's not my dog."

The dog spins away from me and ambles toward him, as if to prove him wrong. Firelight dances in Axel's green eyes as he leans and indulges the dog with a scratch behind his ears.

"Well, he seems like a sweet animal," I tell him.

"He's a nuisance." Axel pats the dog's side, then gently nudges him away from the food and crouches over the large cast-iron skillet on the campfire that's burning hot and bright. Eyes on his task, he points to a folding chair that sits open with a plaid fuzzy blanket draped across it. "Go ahead and sit. Should be done any minute."

Lowering myself into the chair, I tug the blanket across my lap as he works in silence.

"Can I help?" I ask.

He shakes his head, scooting the eggs around and adding cheese to them. Then he stands quickly and disappears inside the house. He's gone maybe thirty seconds before he's back with an armful of items, including a bowl that he sets right in front of the dog. I don't miss the way he scratches behind the dog's ears again and pats his head gently. I don't miss the way the dog looks at Axel, then dives into his food like this is all part of the day's routine.

*He's not my dog*, my ass.

The snap of the fire is soothing against the quiet dark closing in on us. I watch Axel cook as firelight paints his face in sharp shadows—lips pursed, brow furrowed in concentration.

"I appreciate this," I tell him.

He clears his throat and folds the omelet. "Least I could do, given the shit show with the A-frame."

"I feel bad about that. Seems like my showing up made a stressful situation worse. I just don't get why Willa said to come up here when you're dealing with so many issues on the property."

Axel clears his throat again, sliding the omelet onto a plate. He cuts the omelet in half and sets one piece each onto two plates. My mouth waters. It's simple food, but it smells so good, and when he hands it my way, I can't help but smile.

"Thank you," I tell him. I taste my omelet and almost have a foodgasm. How does a cheese and veggie omelet taste so good? "This is incredible."

"Good." He turns back toward the fire, and his worn jeans pull across a high, hard ass as he picks up his plate. I nearly drop mine.

I have to get myself together.

"So," I squeak. Then I clear my throat. "I feel like you're avoiding this topic."

"What topic?"

"Willa and Ryder sending me here, given what's going on with the A-frame?"

"Ah." Axel sits on a tree stump nearby, scooting his food around. "So . . . they don't exactly know about the A-frame's problems."

"They don't?"

He frowns and seems to hesitate, then he has a bite of omelet and chews. "No one knows what's going on, except for me and my friends who own a construction business, and that's only because they're going to do the work on it."

"Why?"

The dog flops to Axel's feet again, setting his chin across his boot. Axel pats his side and says, "The place needs significant, expensive updates. The siblings handle small tasks and troubleshooting when it's each of our turns here, but the bigger issues have compounded, some of which I already knew about, others which I didn't realize until it was my stint here. I'm the only one who knows about those big updates and their cost."

"Why not tell your family? You don't think they'd want to contribute or have ideas for how to handle it?"

"My siblings would feel obligated to pay or obligated to me if they knew what I've paid, neither of which I want. And my parents will certainly have ideas for work this expensive." He stabs a bite of omelet and brings it to his mouth. "Ideas involving a For Sale sign."

I lower the bite of omelet I had halfway to my mouth. "But they love the A-frame, don't they?"

"Yes, but they're also practical people. They've brought it up occasionally, selling the place, with the precise concerns I share—like any property, eventually just patching things up isn't enough. They've said they don't want the siblings to shoulder a heavy financial burden, and they aren't willing to invest much in it, either, since Dad's planning to retire soon and they can't exactly afford to empty their savings." He pokes at the fire, sending a shower of sparks flying into the air. "So I'm handling it."

My heart spins as it clicks into place—*why* he's doing this, *who* he's doing it for. His family. He's taking on this heavy financial and mental burden of saving the place behind their backs . . . because this is how he loves to love his family, because somewhere under all that surliness is someone with a big soft spot for his people.

I tip my head, examining him in the firelight, seeing him with new eyes. "This is your love language."

He freezes with the poker. "My what?"

"Your love language."

Axel frowns. Another jab of the fire sends sparks into the air. "I don't have a love language."

"Everyone does."

"Not me."

I grin and lean toward him. "You show the people you love what they mean to you through sacrificial, generous action. That's all it means."

Axel doesn't say anything, just cocks a dark eyebrow as he eats his food.

"So, have your friends started working on it?" I ask.

He's quiet for a minute. Then he slowly says, "No."

"Why not?"

"I'm still working on the financing."

"Are you not painting? I'd imagine you'd be able to cover it, with how well your stuff sells."

"Not right now," he says, staring into the fire. "Creative block."

I feel a wave of sympathy for him. "I'm sorry. What are you going to do?"

"I have a plan to handle it. My friends are helping me with that, too."

I want to press him for more information because I'm curious by nature, but Axel doesn't seem to want to share. So I let it go.

"I'm glad you at least have friends in your corner on this."

He nods. "Please keep this between us. You can't tell Willa. She'll tell Ryder, then everything's ruined if he knows."

"I won't." The guilt of another deception weighs on me, but it's not Axel's fault I have a running tally of lies of omissions with my best friend. "I promise."

"Thank you," he says.

As we focus on our food, my thoughts wander and I mull over what he's told me. There's still one part of this scenario that doesn't have an explanation.

"Axel, did you say it was your turn here, at the A-frame? As in, currently?"

He nods, not pausing from eating. "Yes."

Unease dances down my spine. Willa and Ryder don't know what's going on with the place, but they knew Axel was here. So why didn't Willa tell me? What was she doing?

Unease becomes suspicion. I've heard of the Bergman family's capacity for meddling, and I assumed that because I'm not one of them, I was immune. But what if I'm not?

Are they trying to set us up?

Why? Because of The Charades Kiss? That was just an embarrassing accident . . . unless it wasn't. Unless they gave me that *kiss* clue on *purpose*.

Holy shit. I am a plausible victim of Bergman meddling.

Embarrassment heats my skin as I revisit the charades night with fresh eyes. Me, swept up in my competitiveness, my frustration when no one guessed "kiss." They knew what I'd do, that if they didn't guess it, I wouldn't pause and think, *Gee, huh. Wonder why none of my teammates are guessing "kiss" when I'm giving them obvious clues? They aren't trying to get me to kiss someone, are they?*

They knew that, as the time dwindled, I'd grow desperate. They knew I'd grab Axel, the only age-appropriate and unclaimed Bergman son (who I may incidentally have a massive, purely sexual crush on) and kiss the hell out of him.

Damn. Those Bergman girlfriends and sisters played me like a well-tuned instrument.

And now I'm starting to think they had a hand in this A-frame adventure, too.

Why, though? They really think Axel and I have a chance? They're in for a sore disappointment when they realize Axel doesn't see me that way. That there's nothing more than my lust and his indifference between us.

It makes shameful regret burn through me again. I should never have kissed him.

"Axel."

He glances my way. "Yes?"

"Thank you for your hospitality. You didn't have to offer it to me, but you did. Even after I made things so awkward with charades last time. With the kiss."

Axel fumbles with his plate and nearly drops it, catching it right before it hits the ground. The dog looks deeply disappointed. He clears his throat. "It's fine. It was nothing."

*Nothing.* I should be relieved that he's not more upset by a kiss I didn't ask his permission for, but just like his indifference when he looks at me, this stings, too. "Well…good. That's good. We just need your family to get the memo that meddling is an exercise in futility."

"You think they interfered with the game?"

"I think they pretended to slip the clue right into the basket before it was my turn. I bet it was Willa." I gasp as I remember. "It *was.* She handed me the clue."

"I hadn't considered that," he says, "but now what Ryder said is even more incriminating."

"What did he say?"

Pink floods Axel's cheeks again. He glances my way, his gaze landing on my mouth. "That he was tossing 'make out' as a clue in the basket when we're there for Thanksgiving."

The unbidden image of Axel—his hands frantic down my waist, cupping my ass, as his mouth meets mine, as that beard scrapes along my cheek—bursts through my mind. I grip my plate so tight, my hands hurt. "What a . . . ridiculous idea."

Axel nods, swallowing roughly. "Absolutely. Ridiculous."

Heavy, thick silence stretches between us. Then Axel shoots upright, startling the dog. He nearly drops his plate again, but steadies it, then reaches my way. "I'll take yours, if you're done."

I reach for his plate instead. "No. You cooked, I'll do the dishes."

He flicks it out of reach, frowning at me. "That's not necessary."

I stand, which places me very close to him. "I'm. Doing. The. Dishes."

The frown becomes a scowl. I smile. Then I gather everything he used to cook, and stack the dishes on the tray. Tray in hand, I stroll inside.

I've just added soap to the water in the sink when Axel shuts the door behind him and strides into the kitchen after me, plate in hand. "Rooney—"

"Please, Axel. Please just let me wash the dishes." When I turn to face him, we nearly collide, making me intimately aware of the scent of campfire smoke and woodsy soap mingling in his clothes, the rapid rise and fall of his chest.

I reach for his plate, and our fingertips inadvertently brush as I take it from his hands. Axel exhales roughly, and I glance up, then freeze. His green eyes flicker like dying embers, locked on my mouth. Heat flies through me, and my body sways toward him. His head bends, the world melting away as my heart thunders.

It's like The Charades Kiss all over again, those beautiful eyes locked on my mouth, air rushing from his lungs, our mouths close, closer—

The dog's loud bark outside the door shatters the moment, wrenching us apart. Axel's gaze drops to his boots, pink high on his cheeks. I am burning from head to toe with lust, flushed, dazed, heartbeat pounding in my ears.

Holy shit. *Were* we about to kiss? *Is* he attracted to me?

Axel clears his throat and glances up as far as my mouth, then to the ground again. "I should go."

I nod, uncharacteristically speechless for a moment. Finally, I find my words and say, "Thanks for dinner."

"You too." He grimaces. "Uh. I meant—" He sighs. "Never mind. Good night."

"Wait." I'm so worked up from whatever that was just a minute ago, I'm processing on a delay, but I'm finally caught up. "If I'm in your place, where are you staying? Not the A-frame. You said it's not safe."

"I've got a tent."

"A *tent*? Are you serious?"

He scratches the back of his neck and shrugs. "Yes."

"Axel, no. Please at least sleep on the couch. Just one night. Then I'll leave tomorrow. I promise. Bright and early I'll be out of your hair."

"I'm not . . . you're not—" He clenches his jaw. "You don't have to, Rooney. It's not a problem."

"Then if it's not a problem, sleep on the couch."

He scowls as the wind picks up outside, howling around us. "I can't."

"Why not?"

"I . . . snore. Loudly."

"So? I sleep like a rock. Won't wake me."

His mouth presses into a thin line. He shoves his hands into his pocket. "No."

"Axel Bergman, if you don't sleep on the couch, *I'm* sleeping in that tent of yours and you're taking the bed."

"You're not sleeping in a tent," he says. "Especially when a storm is coming." He crosses his arms, shoulders filling the doorway. I think he's trying to intimidate me, but all it does is make him look annoyingly attractive. Grumpiness should not be this hot.

"Then neither are you," I argue. "I'm not kicking you out of your house." I try an old, reliable tactic, widening my eyes as I pout. "Please, Ax. Just sleep on the couch—"

"No," he says firmly, opening the door behind him. "You sleep here. I'll sleep—" He throws a thumb over his shoulder, where wind whips the nearby trees into ominous dark slants. "Out there."

I sigh hopelessly. "You have a disturbingly deep sense of chivalry."

Axel takes another step back, hands braced on the doorframe. "An unfortunate symptom of being a Bergman. Good night, Rooney."

"Good ni—"

The door slams shut.

Groaning, I plop down on the bed as rain starts pelting the windows. This is going to be a very long night.

# SIX

# Axel

Sunlight seeps through the tent, warming my eyelids, but I don't wake up. I don't want to. Not when I'm in this dream. A dream where Rooney is soft and warm beneath me.

A groan rumbles in my throat, dreamworld and reality coalescing as I shift on my stomach and every aching inch of me rubs into the soft give of my sleeping bag. I'm so hard, so close I can barely catch my breath, when in my dream her body arches into mine and—

"Rise and shine!" she says.

I thrash awake, flipping onto my back and gasping for air. Thinking better of that exposing position, I curl onto my side, just as Rooney peers inside the tent, thermos of coffee in hand, flashing a smile brighter than the sun behind her. She's wearing an outrageously fuzzy highlighter-yellow hat that clashes with her hair. Her cheeks are flushed pink from the cold air.

She's so beautiful, it hurts.

"You okay?" she asks. "Sounded like a bad dream."

I groan as I sit up. "Something like that."

"I come bearing coffee." She extends a stainless-steel tumbler that smells like heaven.

"Thank you." I pop off the lid and breathe in the aroma.

Making herself at home, she steps inside, plops down, and leans back on her elbows. My gaze snaps to her chest. She's wearing an ice-blue thermal shirt that hugs her breasts as they tighten in the cold. My dick throbs angrily. First the dream. Now this. I'm in agony.

I shut my eyes tight and take a long gulp of scalding coffee.

"So," she says breezily. "We have company."

I choke on my coffee. "What?"

"Your friends and their daughter?" Smiling, she tips her head and peers at me curiously. "She called you 'Uncle Ax.'"

*Christ*. I clear my throat and take another deep drink of coffee. If Parker and Bennett are here with Skyler, I'm going to need all the caffeine I can get.

"Greetings, earthlings!" An alien mask echoing with Skyler's voice pops inside the tent and startles me so badly, I spill coffee all over my sleeping bag. "You okay, Uncle Ax?"

"What the hell kind of mask is that?"

"Ooh, bad word. I won't tell them you slipped." She rips off the mask, revealing dark springy curls and mischievous brown eyes. "Daddy and BiBi let me watch a documentary on aliens that changed my *life*, and they said if I kept my room clean for a week, I could get an alien mask, so I did, and it's *awesome*, isn't it?" She takes a deep breath after that marathon and smiles. "We made cinnamon rolls. Daddy and BiBi said this was an *e-germ-ency,* so we brought you some."

"Emergency." I snap the lid on my tumbler and set it aside. Clearly, this is not my time to have coffee. "Get out, E.T. I'll put on some clothes and be there in a minute."

Skyler looks at Rooney. "Your name's E.T.? I thought it was Rooney."

Rooney laughs. "It's an old movie about an alien, and another word for alien is 'extraterrestrial,' or E.T. for short. He's calling *you* that."

"The takeaway," I tell them, "is that you both need to leave. Out."

Skyler tumbles out of the tent, followed by Rooney, their voices blending as they walk away. I flop back on the sleeping bag, letting out a long, pained groan. This is a terrible development.

I change quickly into the clothing that I shoved in my duffel bag last night. Jeans, a flannel, socks, and boots. Then I step out of the tent.

And there sit Bennett and Parker, Skyler, and Rooney around a campfire, mugs in hand, talking like old friends.

"There he is!" Park calls. "Speaking of the handsome devil."

I glare at him as I cross the clearing, then drop onto the tree-stump seat, coffee thermos in hand. Skyler smiles up at me, icing on her cheek and the alien mask tipped back on her head. I gesture at it with my thermos. "Aliens, huh?"

"It's Parker's fault," Bennett says, offering me the platter of cinnamon rolls. "She's obsessed. Brought you two without icing."

"Uncle Ax doesn't like sugar," Skyler tells Rooney around a mouthful. "Maybe that's why he's so bad at Candy Land."

Rooney snorts a laugh. "Ouch."

Grumbling, I take an un-iced cinnamon roll and fill my mouth with a bite. If I talk, nothing nice is going to come out. Might as well fill it with breakfast.

"Sure you don't want one?" Parker asks Rooney.

She shakes her head. "No, thanks. I'm not very hungry."

"She's gluten-free," I say around my bite. "She's just too nice and doesn't want you to feel bad that she can't eat it."

Rooney gives me an alarmed, wide-eyed look.

Parker smiles, offering her the plate again. "Luckily, you *can* eat it. I'm sorry, I should have mentioned. Skyler has celiac disease, so our kitchen's dedicated gluten-free, and these are, too."

Rooney blinks from me to Parker. "Oh," she says hesitantly. "Really?"

Sky nods, knobby-kneed kid legs and yellow rain boots swinging off her chair. "Yep. You got celiac, too?"

"No," Rooney says, shaking her head. "I'm gluten-intolerant. My stomach feels best when I don't eat it."

Sky nods. "Cool. Have one! These are good."

"Took us months to perfect the recipe," Parker tells her.

Skyler shudders. "Those early batches sucked."

"Hey." Bennett gives her a look.

"Stunk," Sky amends, licking icing off her fingers.

Smiling, Rooney accepts a cinnamon roll, then takes a bite. Her eyes slip shut. Her head tips back, exposing the long line of her throat. "Oh my God," she says on a sigh. Then she moans. Deep in her throat.

And then real estate in my jeans' groin area is hard to come by.

Strategically shifting, I rest my elbows on my knees and drop my head as I visualize that time Viggo and Oliver put ice on my junk while I was napping and I woke up with my dick on the verge of freezing right off. That works wonders.

"Okay, Uncle Ax?" Skyler asks.

"Yep. Peachy."

Rooney groans again and slides an icing-laden finger deep into her mouth to lick it clean. I shove the rest of the cinnamon roll into my mouth and decide if I choke, it won't be the worst way out of this hellish situation.

"Well," Bennett says, accepting the platter of cinnamon rolls from Parker and snapping a fitted lid over them. "We came to be helpful, but it seems we're no longer needed."

Rooney glances between us. "What do you mean?"

I try to talk, but my mouth is so full of cinnamon roll, the words aren't remotely intelligible.

Parker frowns at her, and I already know what's coming, but—mouth full of cinnamon roll—I'm helpless to stop it. "Getting this guy hitched, of course," he says.

I choke on the cinnamon roll, eyes watering. Skyler smacks my back, which helps nothing. Everyone else ignores me.

Rooney leans forward. "Wait, what?"

"Axel called us in a bit of a panic last night about marrying to get his inheritance," Bennett tells her. "I assumed that you and he had worked something out. But . . . you didn't?"

"Inheritance?" Rooney tips her head. "Panic? What?"

This is the world's largest bite of food ever. I'm trying furiously to chew and swallow, but I keep gagging. Goddamn gluten-free baked goods. This cinnamon roll is twice as dense as a normal one. It's gluey sawdust in my throat.

"You know about the situation at the A-frame?" Parker asks.

Rooney nods.

"We're ready to do the work," he explains, "but Ax needs the money for it. If he marries, he can access the inheritance his uncle gave him. Then he can pay for everything the place needs."

"We figured we'd come by with some consolation cinnamon rolls and brainstorm options," Bennett says, glancing my way. "But then you were here when we showed up, and we just . . . assumed he'd beat us to the punch."

"So, how do you two know each other?" Parker asks.

Finally, I get the cinnamon roll down my gullet. "Guys, ease up."

Parker settles deeper in his folding chair and props his boots on one of the stones around the fire. "We're just making conversation."

I throw him a death glare.

"Go ahead, Rooney," Parker says.

Rooney glances my way, then back down at her cinnamon roll. "I've spent time with Axel's family through Willa. She's my best friend from college."

"We love Willa," Bennett says warmly.

"Makes two of us," Rooney says on a smile. "Obviously, I missed her once she moved and got busy playing here, and she missed me. The Bergmans invited me over to visit whenever Willa and Ryder were in town to make the most of their time in LA, and in the past few years, I've come to love them. I mean, who wouldn't love the Bergman family?"

"And Axel?" Parker prompts.

Rooney bites her lip, a soft blush kissing her cheeks. "We actually met at Willa's first game here. And since then, I've just seen Axel when he comes down every once in a while for one of those visits."

"I'm bored," Skyler says, hopping off her chair as she tugs on her alien mask. She skips over to Rooney and says, "Hey, E.T., want to play?"

Bennett sighs and looks at Parker. "See? See what you did to our child?"

"It's okay," Rooney says. Standing, she pops the last of her cinnamon roll in her mouth and dusts off her hands. "Do you want to go look for Axel's dog, Skyler?"

"He's not my dog," I remind everyone.

"Oh, right," Parker says. "The one you got up-to-date on his vaccinations, who you feed and bathe, who you built a mini A-frame doghouse for because he won't come inside your place, even though it's getting too cold for him to sleep outside, and who spends all day with you. *That* dog that's definitely not yours."

I open my mouth to answer, but first Rooney says, "Yes." She turns toward Parker and Bennett. "That one. If it's okay with you, I mean. I just thought we'd head that way, stay in your sight line but out of . . . earshot?" she says pointedly.

Bennett nods. "That's fine. Stay with Rooney, Skyler, and no going in the water."

Skyler gives him a thumbs-up. "It's too cold anyway. Let's go find this dog. I didn't even know Uncle Ax *had* a dog." She shakes her alien head. "Secret keeper."

"He's not—" My voice dies off because Skyler's already on her way, holding Rooney's hand, skipping across the clearing.

Parker and Bennett watch them walk. Then the moment Sky and Rooney are out of hearing, Parker's and Bennett's heads snap my way.

"What is happening?" Parker says.

"It was a mix-up. Rooney needed a break, and Willa told her the place was hers to stay in."

Bennett leans back in his seat, tugging at his bun. His thought pose. "Could she work, for you to marry for the inheritance? Is she available?"

"How perfect would that be?" Parker says. "Come on, why not? It's fortuitous. Kismet. A sign."

"Absolutely not."

"Why not?" Bennett asks.

"Because I said so."

Parker narrows his eyes at me. "What aren't you telling us?"

"Nothing."

"Experience dictates," Bennett muses, "if you want to gauge Axel's interest in someone, the quieter he is, the more it says."

"There's nothing to say, that's why I'm quiet. She's my brother's girlfriend's best friend. I have no idea if she's available to marry me for strictly financial purposes, and I have no plans on finding out."

I am *not* marrying someone—for money or not—that I'm desperately attracted to, that I've spent years avoiding because there's no chance in hell anything is ever coming of that.

"I'd reconsider if I were you." Parker drops his feet and leans forward, lowering his voice. "She's someone you can trust, right? I can't see Willa bothering with anyone except good people."

I stare down at my hands, picking at a callus. "Yes."

"Great. So there's that going for her. She also said she loves your family, so I'm sure she'd want to do something that helps them."

Bennett chimes in, "I agree with Park. She's perfect. Ask her to marry you."

I tug at my shirt collar, yanking it open another button and taking a deep breath. My throat is too tight. "I can't. I shouldn't. She wouldn't want to."

"Why not?" Parker says, watching Rooney and Skyler greet the dog, who comes loping toward them, a stick in his mouth. "I mean, sure, she may have romantic notions about marriage and not be interested, but you don't know until you try. It's just a business arrangement anyway. You're not wooing her. No pressure to make it anything other than what it is."

"But this is what you were going to help me with," I tell Bennett, hearing how pathetically desperate I sound. "Right?"

Bennett swallows nervously. "Oh. Um. Yes. Of course! We were . . . eventually. We'd find someone."

I sigh.

"I'm sorry, okay?" Bennett says. "Parker was supposed to help me come up with a short list."

"Hey." Parker nudges his chair. "Don't drag me into this."

"The dog is so cute!" Skyler hollers, running toward us as he chases her, tongue lolling out of his mouth.

"How's it going?" Rooney asks, following in their wake.

"Terrible," I tell her as Bennett and Parker say in unison, "Great!"

"Skyler," Park says, shooting out of his seat and dragging Bennett with him. "Why don't you show us what you taught Uncle Ax's dog with that stick?"

Hustling Skyler and the pup toward the other end of the clearing, they're gone in the blink of an eye. Now it's only Rooney and me, alone.

I stand from my seat on the tree stump, feeling uneasy. "Did you hear all of that?"

"Hard not to," she says. "You three have deep voices, and you weren't very quiet." Taking a few slow steps, she turns and leans against a tree, looking out toward the lake. "So you need someone to marry?"

"For purely financial reasons, yes."

She nods, eyes still on the water. "It would take care of the A-frame. Fix whatever you need, take the pressure off of you, so you can pay for it quickly and keep your family in the dark."

"Yes," I say slowly.

"I'll do it," she says simply, pushing off the tree. Then she straightens the big fuzzy yellow hat and turns my way. "If you want me, that is."

I blink at her, stunned. "*Why?*"

"Because I can. Because your family has been so kind to me, and now I can be kind back. Even in this small way."

"It's not *small*. It's getting married."

"'For purely financial reasons,'" she repeats. "It's not a big deal. I'm not a romantic, at least, not when it comes to marriage. I'm single and legally free to be your wife."

*Wife.*

The word hits me like a body blow.

"It should be straightforward," she says. "I'm no expert on family law, but I know enough to understand the basics of wills and conditions. There's very little beyond demanding proof of marriage that's enforceable for an inheritance condition in a court of law. So, like I said, it should be easy to take care of. Civil ceremony. Marriage license. Witnesses. Proof of that provided to the will's executor. I'll take a look at the documentation, if you like, make sure the terms are reasonable. I'm sure there's a subsequent condition, too, like 'after X amount of time.'"

"I . . . yes. There is. One year."

"That's fine. I'll be your legal wife for a year."

I blink at her, stunned. "You're serious."

She shrugs, toeing the ground. "It's not like I have much of anything else going on with my life."

"What about law school?"

"Not that you can't be married and in law school, but I took a leave of absence," she says, still staring at the ground. "I've got time on my hands."

I want to ask why, if it has anything to do with how unlike herself she seems to be, whatever personal stuff that Ryder mentioned in our texts, but it's none of my business, is it? She's not mine to be concerned about. "If you did this, I'd give you some of the money. I'm sure there'll be some left after I pay for the A-frame—"

"No," she says forcefully, shaking her head. "No money. I don't want a cent."

"Then this isn't an option. I couldn't let you do this without getting anything in return."

Did I just say that? Am I really considering this?

*What other choice do you have?* the voice of reason says.

Rooney glances up at the trees, biting her lip. "I don't need your money, and I don't want it, either. I just want to help. I just need . . ."

*Somewhere safe.*

I'm not very good at intuiting how other people feel. I struggle to know what *I'm* feeling often enough. But looking at her, I'm so sure I know exactly what she needs, and I know it's going to be the death of me.

"You can stay here," I offer. "In my house."

*You jackass,* that same voice hisses in my head. *You really did it now.*

Her head whips my way. "What?"

"Stay," I tell her. "That's what you need, right? Somewhere to stay for a while?"

"Yes," she says carefully. She glances my way, staring at me curiously. "Are you sure?"

I nod.

A faint smile warms her face, and God, am I a fool for it. "I promise I won't bother you," she says quickly. "Or kiss you. Sorry. I shouldn't have brought that up. Again. I just handle self-consciousness with self-deprecating humor, and you said me mauling your mouth with mine was nothing, but it doesn't feel like it, and if I'm staying here, I need to feel like it's okay between us."

"Rooney."

Slowly, she peers up at me. But I don't meet her eyes. I stare at her mouth because it's impossible not to. It's so quiet, I can hear the cadence of Bennett and Parker's conversation across the clearing, Skyler's bell-like laugh, the playful growl of the dog as they play tug-of-war with a stick.

"Maybe," I say hoarsely, before clearing my throat, finding my voice. "Maybe we can just agree to . . . leave the kiss in the past and move on. Maybe then it would feel more comfortable."

Lowering my gaze to the ground, I see our boots, nearly toe to toe. That's when I realize how close we're standing. How I can smell her, soft and peaceful, and see the fuzzy yellow ball adorning her hat. And then her hand enters my field of vision, outstretched, waiting.

"Deal," she says quietly.

I take her hand in mine, shocked by the raw pleasure of our fingertips brushing, the warmth that spreads up my arm as our palms connect.

That's when I realize "comfortable," no matter how much we leave in the past, is the last thing this marriage is going to be.

Over three days' time, Rooney and I divide and conquer, tackling what's necessary to get us legally married as soon as possible. Rooney insists on handling the legal side of things since that's her expertise, and I handle everything else. After seventy-two hours of barely seeing each other, exchanging only necessary information and signatures, we have a valid marriage license, rings, wedding attire, an officiant, and witnesses—everything we need to ensure we have proof for the executor of my uncle's will.

The morning of the wedding promises one of those bright, crisp days at the gasping end of autumn that makes me want to spend every moment outside, soaking it up. With the sun beaming down on us and no chilling wind, I'm comfortable in my uniform for art shows: charcoal suit, white shirt, no tie—because *fuck* anything tight around my neck—matching brown belt and chukka boots. I have no idea what Rooney's wearing, only that she assured me she had what she needed.

Not that it's important what she wears.

Seeing as this isn't real.

Well, besides legally.

I just need my nervous system to get the memo.

"Don't pass out on me," Parker says. "Take some breaths."

I roll my neck side to side and take a deep breath, hoping it'll pop the anxious bands wrapped around my chest. "I'm not going to pass out. Where's Lloyd?"

The officiant, Lloyd, is Parker's cousin. I haven't seen him since we were in high school together, but Parker reassured me he's qualified to do this, free of charge.

"He's here." Parker straightens his cuffs and glances over his shoulder toward the woods. "Just had to take a piss. Seriously, relax. You're giving me contact stress. Breathe or some shit."

"I'm breathing," I grumble, scrubbing my face, then raking my hands through my hair.

"You have some pent-up energy, my friend." Bennett nods in the direction of the A-frame. "We'll save you a few soggy walls to rip out tomorrow."

"Too bad you and Rooney don't plan on working out tension the old-fashioned way," Parker says.

I roll my eyes.

"I'm just saying," he continues, "that's how Bennett and I started. No-strings sex. Friends with benefits. Now look at us."

In an ideal world, I would have found strangers for witnesses who wouldn't harass me as I anxiously awaited marrying for money, but they're the only nonfamily people I can mildly tolerate, and beggars can't be choosers. I'm reminded of that last point as I watch our "officiant" jiggling his zipper, clearly returning from a pee in the woods.

"We do have indoor plumbing," I mutter. "It's literally the reason we're doing it here, not the A-frame."

Bennett chuckles. "That's just Lloyd. He's low-maintenance. Woods are as good a place as any for him."

"Remind me not to shake his hand."

Parker snorts. "You didn't run this morning, did you?"

"I did." I roll my neck again side to side, then glance up, watching the sun dart behind a thick cloud. "I just didn't get enough miles in."

I was never going to get enough miles in for a day like this.

Before either of them can bust my ass anymore, the dog bounds up to my house's door, favoring his left leg just a little as always. An old injury healed wrong, according to the vet. That was before she asked if I wanted him to be mine and after I had him screened for a chip that wasn't there.

The dog looks like a greyhound, but he's actually a lurcher, a crossbreed that's much less valuable, which made his lack of a chip also much less surprising. Lurchers are used as hunting dogs and more likely to be discarded by their owners when they get hurt, like this one clearly was when he wandered toward my home last month, whining and shivering but refusing to come inside and warm up.

I said I'd build him a house and keep an eye on him. The vet said I could call it whatever I wanted, as long as I signed papers and paid for his X-rays, because otherwise, if he went to the shelter, it wouldn't be long before he was put down. He seemed like a safe bet, a living creature that would be hard to disappoint or inadvertently neglect when he wouldn't even cross my threshold. When all he wanted was a few pats on the head, two meals a day, and somewhere safe and warm to sleep.

But as he barks happily at my house's opening front door and bounds back and forth with the kind of energy and strength he didn't have when he first started living here, I wonder if maybe we've done more than just coexist. If maybe being with me *has* been good for him. If, for once, showing something a little love in the way that I could hasn't been a complete disaster.

When he pounces on Rooney as she steps outside, a furious ache blooms beneath my sternum. Her hair is braided gold, an intricate knot accented by a sprig of plum-colored heather. Her ivory sweater dress swirls around her like wind-whipped snow, torturously leaving the silhouette of her body to my imagination. And then the dog lands his muddy paws on her pristine clothing.

All of us wince, except Rooney. Rooney laughs, warm and bright, all teeth and dimples and crinkled eyes, a face of pure happiness, right as the sun bursts out from behind the clouds. Soft, glittering, she looks like fresh snowfall kissed by sunlight.

Watching her, that ache in my chest burrows and deepens. I glance away and adjust my shirt cuffs, then my collar, my brain making the connection as I inspect myself—my goddamn bouton-niere matches the heather in Rooney's hair. I scowl at Parker, who snuck it in there half an hour ago, but Parker just smiles at me and wiggles his eyebrows.

Bennett sighs at Rooney and dabs his eyes.

I turn toward Lloyd, the officiant, who's finally decided to join us.

"Aaaaaxellll," Lloyd says slowly on a broad, lazy smile. "Con-grats on the big day." As I feared, he extends his hand.

"Shouldn't shake." I point to my nose and sniffle, probably unconvincingly. "Think I'm coming down with something."

The lazy smile widens. "That's cool, man. That's cool. I appreci-ate the consideration."

There's something about his tone, the languid delivery and slow movements, that's familiar. Curiosity forces me to do what I find intensely uncomfortable for how intimate it feels, and I meet his eyes. That's when I notice they're bloodshot, his pupils blown wide.

Fuck's sake.

The officiant is high as a kite.

# SEVEN

# Rooney

Playlist: "It's Nice to Have a Friend," Taylor Swift

I've had three days to think over this marriage that I agreed to. I think I surprised myself as much as Axel when I volunteered to do it.

At first, I thought perhaps it was as simple as the fact that while I'm a lover and probably always going to be a bit of a romantic, I am deeply disillusioned with marriage, and so marrying someone for such purely practical reasons is nothing to me. But then I got thinking. And I realized it's a little more complex than that.

I offered to marry Axel because right now, I feel helpless, at the whim of my unpredictable body and my furloughed plans. And *doing* something, having a purpose, a way of being helpful has given my life that structure and purpose that I was starving for. Without my days crammed from sunrise to sunset with school, without the grueling pace of the past few years, I've felt so lost.

But not now. Now I have intention again and a plan in place that I admire, even if only for a little while. I'm happily not getting an inheritance out of this, but I am getting something I desperately need: a direction, a purpose . . . and oddly enough, a sense of belonging. It's not just Axel saving the A-frame, loving his family this way—it's *us*. Together. Not as lovers, and probably not even quite as friends, but as partners. This plan takes both of us, fully committed to it. And that sense of connection, however practical and strategic, is something I didn't know how much I wanted until it was right in front of me.

So here I am, looking a little more like my old self, thanks to a flattering, swingy dress and the world's best under-eye concealer. Ready to get married.

*Married.*

At least, once I deal with the dog's enthusiastic, muddy hug.

"Well." Standing behind me on the cabin's threshold with a tiny spring of purple heather in her hands, Skyler sighs. "You got dirt on your dress."

"I did. Nothing a little soapy water and a towel won't fix, I think."

"Here," she says, handing me her heather posy, then skipping into the house. She comes back a moment later with a soft rag, wet with water and a squirt of soap.

"Thank you, Skyler."

"You're welcome." Tipping her head, she watches me as I scrub the dirt out with a fair amount of success. "Are you gonna kiss Uncle Ax?"

I squeak and almost drop the rag. "Uh. Well. I'm not exactly—"

"He could use a kiss is all I'm saying." She holds out her hand for the rag.

Hesitantly, I return it to her. "Why do you say that?"

"'Cause he's *grumpy*. And kisses make the grumps go away."

I bite my lip, trying not to laugh. "I don't think he's that grumpy."

She gives me a disbelieving look. "He's *so* grumpy."

"He's serious. And quite possibly very shy. Not everyone is as social as you and me."

"Why not? I don't get it."

Glancing over my shoulder, I watch Axel adjusting his cuffs, clearing his throat. He looks nervous. "I don't, either. But that doesn't mean we can't try."

"I still think a kiss would do the trick," she says, walking back inside with the rag. "But I'm just a kid. What do I know?"

On a soft whine, the dog nudges my elbow and peers up at me. I pat his head gently, waiting until Skyler joins me again and takes my hand. "Let's do this," she says, tugging me along with her.

We cross the clearing together, and while I try to drink in the beauty of fading autumn—a rain shower of golden leaves swirling to the ground, the sun cutting lacework through the branches— all I see is Axel, daylight sparkling bronze in his rich brown hair, making his deep green eyes glow.

Looking at him, I feel my heart leap, wild and happy, not un-like the pup who jumped into my arms. My heart has no business doing that. So I yank it back to heel with a gentle but firm re-minder: this marriage is a mutually beneficial arrangement, noth-ing more.

Stopping across from Axel, I smile at him and try really hard not to give him a good, long once-over, but he's wearing that suit he wore to his LA art show, so resisting is impossible. He's shaved, his face smooth once again, every angle in sharp relief—long, straight nose, those high cheekbones, lips pursed in a thoughtful frown. His gaze roams my hair, my mouth, then darts to the ground, pink warming his cheeks. He clears his throat and throws a look at the officiant Axel told me is Parker's cousin, Lloyd.

"Lloyd." I turn toward him and offer my hand. "Nice to meet you."

"Likewise," he says, his voice mellow, a dazed smile on his face. In fact, I think he might be high. Like, *really* high. Not that I'm judging. Weed's been one of my go-tos when my stomach is in bad shape, so I don't mind that he's smoked. I'm just curious how we're going to get through wedding vows with a guy who's properly stoned. Should at least add some levity to what suddenly feels like a serious event.

Smiling, Lloyd extends his hand to shake mine, but before he reaches me, Axel's hand shoots out and grabs mine.

I glance over at him, surprised and confused. "Ax," I whisper, "what are you—"

"Let's get started," he tells Lloyd, his voice clipped and low.

In juxtaposition to the sharpness of his words, his hand gently slides down mine and intertwines our fingers. I stare down at our hands, braided together. It feels so unexpectedly good. Like sinking into a just-hot-enough bath, relaxation unspooling my limbs.

"Lloyd," Parker says, "take it away."

Lloyd nods. "All right. Here we go." Sighing, he shuts his eyes and opens his hands, arms wide. "Friends, first, let's take a moment to bask in the magnificent, vibrant energy filling this space. Nature has been good to us."

"Christ," Axel mutters, staring up at the sky.

I bite back a smile as I squeeze his hand. His gaze darts to our tangled fingers, and he looks at them the way I did, like he's not exactly sure how that happened or why it's happening. I wait for him to pull away, to do what has defined the majority of our interactions, which is to retreat when I get close. Instead, after a moment's hesitation, his hand softly squeezes mine back.

Bennett moves around, snapping candid shots. I'm no photographer, but with the autumn leaves around us, the soft, diffuse sunlight, I can't imagine they won't turn out beautifully.

Lloyd's been talking this whole time, waxing poetic about nature and energy and love bringing life full circle, but I haven't absorbed it. All I've heard is the snap of the camera. All I've felt is Axel's hand, strong and calloused and warm, his fingers knotted with mine.

"And so," Lloyd says, "embracing the reminder that nature gives us, let's celebrate this fecund joining—"

Bennett snorts and nearly drops his camera.

"*Fecund?*" Skyler wrinkles her nose. "What's that mean?"

"I'll tell you later," Parker mutters, tucking her against him and earning her scowl.

"Axel," Lloyd says, having missed that little exchange, "do you take Rooney to be your wife, your partner and fellow traveler on the journey of life?"

Axel clears his throat, then says in his deep, soft voice, "I do."

"Rooney," Lloyd says to me, "do you take Axel to be your husband, your partner and fellow traveler on the journey of life?"

I inhale slowly as nerves jostle my body, working to steady my voice. "I do."

We make our promises to love and cherish each other, to forsake all others, in sickness and in health, for richer or poorer. First Axel, then me, each word more daunting to say than the last.

Maybe it's my guilt complex about lying. Maybe it's my love of truth and facts and right vanquishing wrong, but it's unsettling, making vows that I know, in one year, I'll break. By the time I finish, my voice is shaking, as is my body.

And Axel knows. He's felt every tremor, every wave of tension cresting through me. Because not once has he let go of my hand. Until now, when he gently releases his grip and pulls out the rings that we agreed were wise to wear for the sake of the photos that will be sent to the executor of his uncle's will.

Handing his ring to Skyler for when I'll need it, Axel then slides the thin white gold band down my finger in a slow, steady glide. He begins to let go, then stops and leans in, gently adjusting the ring. I can see in that moment the way he must step back from his paintings, frowning as he examines it, then step in to make it just so.

Gently, Skyler nudges me and offers the ring. I take the wide, matte metal band, then I take Axel's hand in mine and feel him tense as I slide the ring down his finger, a strange sense of déjà vu rippling down my spine.

I feel Axel's scrutinizing gaze on me. I hate that I'm like this right now, unable to tuck in all these vulnerable, frayed loose ends beneath the surface of my usual bright smile and upbeat energy. I hate that I look unsteady and that my voice might have sounded unsure when I was really just caught off guard by how intense this felt.

I hope I haven't offended Axel, that I haven't made him feel like I'm having second thoughts or regretting this or him or—

Suddenly, his hands are sliding up my neck, cupping my jaw, and—oh, God—his lips are on mine, warm and soft. My head falls back, and the shaking in my limbs dissolves. Air rushes into my lungs as I breathe in cool air and warm Axel.

He's kissing me. He's *kissing* me.

Hands limp at my sides, I sway toward him as he steps closer and tips my head to deepen our kiss. His mouth nudges mine gently as he breathes and our lips meet, hard and slow, a dizzying, patient rhythm. My eyes flutter shut as his fingertips drift down the nape of my neck in soothing strokes, as his thumbs slide along my jaw.

Our mouths don't open. No tongues or teeth or groaned pleasure. And yet it's a kiss more powerful than any from my past. It's a kiss that echoes through my bones and grounds me to the earth. It's a kiss that calms and soothes and caresses with tenderness.

It's exactly what I needed.

When Axel pulls away, I feel as dazed as Lloyd sounds when he says, "I was gonna say you can kiss your bride, man, but you beat me to the punch."

---

I'm *still* dazed after the ceremony is deemed complete and Lloyd says his goodbyes, strolling off while lighting up a joint I'd give a lot of money for a hit of right about now.

Axel and I stand close, waiting as Bennett adjusts his camera's focus to take photos we'll send as part of our proof of marriage. A perk of the will's executor living in Sweden, it just requires scanning a handful of documents and a brief email from Axel. After this photo session, my part is done.

"I'm hungry," Skyler whines. She flops onto the tree stump, hands over her stomach.

"Just a few more photos," Parker tells her. "Then we'll have brunch."

Hunger pains are hitting me, too, and I grimace just as Bennett's camera clicks. He laughs. "Rooney, the camera loves you, but try to relax."

"Sorry," I say weakly.

"Ax, put your arm around her," Parker calls from behind Bennett.

Axel sighs, then bends his head and drops his voice. "Do you mind?"

His breath whispers over the sensitive skin behind my ear. Goose bumps dance across my skin. "N-no, I don't mind."

Carefully, he slips his arm around me, his hand sitting neatly in the notch of my waist, fingertips brushing my ribs. I swallow and take a deep breath.

"How are you?" he asks, looking at Bennett's camera.

I glance up at him, caught off guard by the care in his question. "I'm okay, I think. You?"

I turn back to face Bennett as the camera clicks, and Axel says, "Same."

As Bennett calls for one more, the dog rushes toward us, colliding with Axel's shins, then sitting right on my toes as he glances up. Tongue wagging, eyes wide with excitement, he falls backward from craning his neck so far and knocks into me, which sends me stumbling backward. I shriek in surprised laughter as I start to fall, but Axel lunges just in time and yanks me back, tumbling into his chest.

I hear the camera click.

And I know of all the photos Bennett took, that's the one I'll want.

# EIGHT

*Axel*

Well. You could say the wedding proceedings got away from me.

I kissed her. I *kissed* her.

I can't think about it, or I'll spiral. I'll do something drastic like rip off my suit jacket, kick out of my boots, and take off into the woods so I can outrun the reality that I kissed my wife when I had no business doing so.

This situation really is surreal.

The moment Bennett tells us our photos are done, I step back and tug at my collar, popping loose another button.

I don't look at Rooney's mouth. Or think about kissing her. I think about brunch and the pancakes I'm going to make.

"You did it!" Parker says, clapping his hands. "And may I say, it felt pretty legit."

"Minus the stoned officiant," I mutter.

Bennett chuckles, packing away his camera. "Lloyd is a trip."

"He's a free spirit," Parker says defensively.

Rooney laughs. "He was great. He made it memorable." Petting the dog as he sits on her feet, she smiles.

For the first time, I notice she has faint freckles just on the bridge of her nose and the barest hint of copper in her hair.

It makes my hands ache to paint just as much as it makes my legs ache to run away from the reality of that kiss, to disappear and escape this . . . *feeling*. This sharp, aching feeling right beneath my breastbone.

I have to fight that impulse to escape and disappear. I'm not going to do that today. Because I told myself I'd do this right.

To thank her. To show Rooney how much I realize she's sacrificed. In her marrying me, I get an inheritance and everything I need to save the A-frame. Whereas Rooney gets somewhere to stay for a month. If I weren't so desperate for her help, I'd have said no simply because of how unequally this serves both of us. But I *am* that desperate, and she, in her determined kindness, is that eager to help.

The least I can do is marry her and not vanish afterward.

"Is it time to eat yet?" Skyler asks, hopping down from the tree stump.

"Yes." Tugging off my coat, I breathe deeply and enjoy the relief from its constricting structure.

Rooney shuts her eyes as she tugs the heather from out of her hair, then the tight coiled braid, sighing with pleasure. I try not to watch her hair fall in a sheet of spun gold tinged with copper, to fantasize about burying my nose in that sunshine silk and breathing her in.

"Can I help?" She glances up and catches me staring at her.

I avert my eyes and scrub the back of my neck, skin prickling with nerves. "No. Just relax."

"What do you think I've been doing for three days?" she says.

"Everything on the legal side of things," I tell her, starting to cuff my sleeves.

"It didn't take much. And I have news for you, Axel. I don't do well with nothing to do. Please let me help?"

I sigh heavily. "All right."

"Great!" Turning to Skyler, she says, "You heard him! Brunch time."

I lead Rooney inside the house and make sure Skyler's been supplied with a granola bar to tide her over. A glance out the window shows her happily playing with the dog in the clearing, where Bennett and Parker debate how to set up for brunch.

Strolling past the dining table, I drape my jacket on one of the chairs and quickly shove my cuffed sleeves past my elbows. Then I rummage through the kitchen, pulling out the brunch items and ingredients I picked up at Shepard's yesterday, including everything I need for omelets and pancakes.

"What can I do?" Rooney asks, tugging her hair into a messy bun on her head.

"You can read this mix's ingredients and make sure it's safe for you." I point to the gluten-free flour blend sitting on the counter.

Rooney reaches over the counter, picking it up. "That was nice of you."

"Making sure you could eat brunch?" I ask, eyes on my task. "I would think that's decency."

"You'd be surprised how inconvenient some people find having to accommodate it." She stares at the mix, reading it. "It's perfect."

"Good."

I try not to think about the fact that we're in this tiny kitchen again, and last time we were, I nearly kissed her. Instead, I focus on the recipe that I've been making since I was a teenager, when the older siblings started having weekend cooking responsibilities. While the butter melts in the microwave, I beat the eggs and some milk, then add flour and sugar.

"Family recipe?" Rooney asks.

I nod.

Her gaze tracks my movement as I add the melted butter and more milk, then the remaining flour and milk. "You're just eyeballing it."

"I grew up making it. It's muscle memory now. Everyone has recipes like that."

She shakes her head. "Not me. I'm a terrible cook."

I glance her way, watching her fingertips dance softly along the counter. "How do you eat, then?"

Rooney laughs. "Thank you for not throwing false praise my way. I cannot tell you how many people have said, 'Oh, I'm sure you're not!' when I really am a terrible cook. Well, except, I can heat up a mean bowl of soup."

I tilt the pan until the butter is spread thin across the surface, then add the first pour of batter. "You weren't taught to cook?" I ask her. "Your parents never showed you?"

She shakes her head. "No."

For being such a talkative person, she says very little about her family. "Who cooked, then?"

"My parents had a chef." Rooney turns and leans her back against the counter, looking through the window over the sink. "Which was a luxury, obviously. It just didn't feel like my friends' family meals when I ate with them. I love that about your family. All the traditions and family recipes your mom talks about. I envy that sense of . . . belonging? Belonging and connection to all these people before me who are part of what made me who I am."

I want to tell her that you can have all the traditions and family recipes you like and still not feel like you belong. But I would never tell her that. I've never told anyone that.

Quiet settles between us as I watch the pancake's edges for signs of bubbling and browning. She leans in and watches me closely as I flip the pancake and turn down the heat. "Do you want me to teach you?" I ask her.

Oh, hello, self-sabotage. I'd say it's been long time no see, but—considering I just kissed the woman I agreed to marry, when she's the same woman I've done everything possible to keep my distance from the past two years—I can't. Or if I did, I'd be lying.

Why? *Why* do I keep doing this?

All I had to do was make it through today. Then I'd have my space from her again. What did I do? Kissed her. And now I've offered a fucking cooking lesson.

"Really?" she says eagerly. It's the biggest smile I've seen on her face since she came here, and despite my panic, satisfaction swells in my chest, warm and proud.

"Really." Stepping back, I vacate the space I held in front of the range. "Go ahead."

She glances between the pan and me. "Now?"

I nod.

Quickly, Rooney moves in, staring down at the pan. "What am I doing?" she whispers, a smile tipping her mouth.

"You're watching the edges get bubbly and brown. Then we'll slide this off the pan, onto a plate, and make another one."

"Okay." She frowns in concentration, bunching her dress's sleeves up to her elbows. "Now?" she asks.

I lean in for a closer look, my chest inadvertently brushing her back. "No."

A beat of silence passes. "Now?" she asks again.

"No. Be patient."

"I can't." She wiggles her shoulders in eagerness. Taps her toes. Glances from the clock to the pan. "Okay, how about now? Come on. They're brown!"

"Now, yes."

Rooney grips the handle and tips the pan until the pancake slides onto the plate. "Wow," she says. "They're like crepes."

"*Pannkakor* are close to crepes, except, as my mom would say, crepes are not nearly as good."

She smiles. "What is *pannkakor*? 'Swedish pancakes'?"

"Yes." I reach for the bowl of batter and set it in her hands, then spread a little more butter around the pan. "Go on, pour a scoopful."

"What's the difference between crepes and *pannkakor*?" she asks, following my direction.

"Besides one being French and the other Swedish—which inherently makes the latter far superior, according to my mother—Swedish pancakes are less flour, more eggs and butter. Done right, they're light as air."

Instinctively, I grip the handle to tilt the pan and spread the batter evenly. That's when I realize Rooney's hand was already there. She's unnaturally still inside the bracket of my arms—one hand on the counter, the other guiding the pan.

"Sorry," I mutter. "Autopilot."

She shakes her head a little. "It's okay. I forgot that part."

"I also forgot to tell you."

A soft laugh fills her throat. "I keep distracting you with questions."

I release her hand gripping the pan's handle, but I can't for the life of me make myself step back. I stare at the curve where her neck meets her shoulder, the soft wisps of blonde hair kissing her skin.

*I* want to kiss that skin. And I'm definitely not supposed to.

My hands turn to fists at my sides. I turn away, fumbling through the fridge. "Know how to make omelets?"

"I'm going to be honest," she says over her shoulder. "There is very little I know how to cook. And what I do turns out atrociously. So, consider this my blanket statement: no."

I shut the door with my hip, then grab a new pan. "How about we change that?"

---

Food was a bad idea.

A very bad idea.

Maybe it's because anytime she's been at my parents', I made sure I sat at the opposite end of the table, as far from her as possible (standard operating procedure around Rooney), but I never knew she enjoyed her meals . . . like this.

Moaning. Sighing. Tongue sliding up the tines of her fork.

I have an erection the size of Seattle. And now I'm panicking.

"I'll do the dishes," she says, reaching for my plate.

"No!" It comes out louder than intended, but I need her to sit and relax and stop being so damn helpful. Problem is, I can't stand right now and take over, because—erection.

"Just . . ." I glance around. "How about tea?"

I don't want tea. I want an ice bath. But for now, it'll give me time to get my body under control.

"Sure," Rooney says, smiling as she stacks dishes. I tug them away from her, earning her playful glare. "I'm assuming it's in the cabinet above the kettle?"

"Yep."

She rounds the table. I dig my fingers into my eyeballs once she passes me so I won't ogle her ass. This is hell. Marrying someone you're in lust with is hell.

"Anyone else want tea?" she asks, leaving our outdoor dining setup behind and opening the door to the house.

"Please," Bennett says. "I'll help." Standing, he stacks the rest of the plates and silverware, then follows her.

"Save me the dishes," Parker calls over his shoulder.

"I was planning on it," Bennett calls.

Rooney laughs, the sound fading as she and Bennett disappear inside the house.

Parker fusses with the flowers he arranged in a vase that I'm pretty sure he nicked from the A-frame, then wipes crumbs off the table. His gaze slides my way. "Doing all right, my friend?"

Taking deep, slow breaths, I've been visualizing sinking my

body, inch by inch, into the lake in the dead of winter. Now that my dick's no longer in danger of busting through my zipper, I drop my hands and glance up at the sky. Dammit. Weather is still perfect for a hike.

"I'm fine," I tell him.

"Still planning on your—"

"Yep."

Parker nods, glancing at Skyler where she sleeps beside him in a folding chair, wrapped in a blanket from my house. "I think it's a nice gesture."

I sit back and tug at my collar, taking a deep breath. "Just for today."

Knowing me well enough to sense when I'm at the end of my rope, Parker leans back in his chair and watches Skyler sleep, letting quiet have its place for a few minutes. The faint sound of Bennett and Rooney making tea inside wafts our way. Skyler twitches in her sleep and smiles.

Finally, he breaks the silence. "Can I say something?"

I groan. "You're going to anyway."

"I think she's a little . . . unmoored right now."

I frown at him. "How could you possibly infer that from the amount of time you've spent with her?"

"Because I recognize it. I've been there. I sense it. And listen, maybe I'm way off. But I just want to say, stick to your plan if you want, keep it platonic and businesslike, but . . . at least try to be a friend to her while she's here."

"That's the last thing I'm going to be to her."

"You're so stubborn," he says, gaze drifting toward Rooney and Bennett as they come back from the house, bearing trays of teacups and fixings, a steaming kettle, and a plate of gluten-free cookies.

"Trust me," I tell him. "It's for the best."

"Bullshit," he says through his smile as the two of them join us at the table.

I'm still scowling at him when Rooney calls my name.

"Black tea?" she asks. "And no sugar, right?"

I nod.

She pours it smoothly as Bennett readies the next cup, taking Parker's order. It's a strange feeling, sitting next to her, over tea with my friends. As strange as it was to sit at the table and feel like maybe she didn't mind that I was so quiet while we ate. Which is probably all wrong. She's gracious to a fault. I'm sure she's only tolerating my reticence.

Her fingers brush mine as she slides the cup my way, jolting me out of my thoughts.

"Thank you," I tell her.

She smiles, then turns back toward Bennett and Parker, setting cookies on plates for them. Their conversation fills in where I fall short. I sip my tea and watch them talk so easily, like they've known each other for years.

Not until they stand, Parker and Bennett acting like they're actually going to go into my house and wash up after me, do I find my voice. "Go the hell home," I tell them, pointing at their truck. "You've done enough."

Parker rolls his eyes. "Fine." He picks up a sleeping Skyler, who could barely sleep last night, she was so excited about the wedding.

Bennett hugs Rooney goodbye and winks at me. "I'll edit those photos once we're home, then send them your way."

I nod. "Thanks, B."

"Thank you for *everything*," Rooney says, accepting Parker's one-armed hug goodbye, too, her gaze lingering on Skyler asleep in his arms. I watch her expression tighten for a moment, then smooth.

And then we stand side by side, watching my friends go.

"Well," she says on a sigh as their truck disappears down the path.

I set my hands in my pockets because they're shaking. "Well."

She peers up at me. "Everything okay?"

"Mm-hmm." I clear my throat, staring at the ground and toeing the dirt with my boot. "I thought maybe . . ." I clear my throat again when my voice breaks like I'm some squeaking adolescent. "Maybe we could go for a hike later."

A beat of silence. "A hike?"

"Nothing too technical. Just . . . relaxing, with a nice view at the end."

She tucks a loose strand of hair behind her ear. "I'd like that."

"Great." Relief washes through me. "I'll clean up in the kitchen, let you have a quiet afternoon, then maybe we can head out around dinnertime. That is, if you feel up for it."

"I'm up for it, yes. Thank you . . . thank you for checking."

I nod. "Well. I'll just—" I point to the house. "The dishes. I'll just do them."

"I'll help."

"Rooney—"

"You promised," she says, strolling ahead of me. "You promised you'd let me help today."

Defeated, I open the door and hold it for her. Except the dog bounds up to us and goes in first. I stare at him.

He came inside. He's *never* wanted to.

He whines and glances at Rooney, big brown eyes pinned on her.

Rooney crosses the threshold, then crouches in front of him, running her hands down his body in slow, steady strokes.

"You're such a sweetheart," she croons to him, affectionately massaging around his ears. The dog shuts his eyes and sways dreamily.

Lucky bastard.

"Is he allowed in?" she asks as he starts wandering around.

"It's fine." I watch him sniffing everything, his ears perking up. He glances from the bed to me.

"Don't push it," I tell him.

He runs toward me and licks my hand. I still can't process that he's comfortable in the house. But then I watch him trot behind Rooney into the kitchen, eyes pinned on her again, and it clicks. He's a sucker for her. Of course he is.

While Rooney pets the dog, I run water and soap in the sink. A few minutes into scrubbing, I sense her straighten and step up to my right. She starts rinsing the plates, then drying them. The dog snores on the rug behind us.

Then he rips a fart, making Rooney snort in laughter.

"Second-guessing wanting him to stay?" I ask, glancing over my shoulder at him. He kicks in his sleep and farts again.

"Not a bit," she says, gently taking the plate from my hand. Her fingers brush mine and heat climbs up my arm, flooding my body. "Not his fault he's got gas. I think Skyler fed him half of her eggs."

Quiet settles between us, and while I wish I knew how to fill it for Rooney's sake, I never will be a small-talker. I blank on what to say and have no energy for it. And yet, as I steal occasional glances as we tear through the dishes, Rooney seems content—a small smile on her face as she works.

Only when the water is swirling down the drain and she's set the damp drying towel over her shoulder does she break the silence. "Ax," she says quietly. Picking up her half-drunk tea, she cups it and says, "Today . . . when you held my hand, when you kissed me—"

"I'm sorry," I blurt. Humiliation sweeps through me, turning my cheeks hot. "I didn't . . . that is, I wasn't . . ."

Words evaporate on my tongue.

I knew I got it wrong. Well, I stand by grabbing her hand, because like hell was she touching Lloyd's germ-infested fingers after his unsanitary piss in the woods. But kissing her . . . that was a risk. I find people difficult to read, but Rooney's whole body was a portrait of nervousness. Shaking limbs, pale skin, her lip wedged harshly between her teeth until I was worried it would draw blood, and I couldn't let that happen, so I kissed her. I kissed her because I hoped that, like holding hands, it would help.

And I hoped that we'd never talk about it ever again, that if she hated it, she'd be her usual gracious self and not tell me.

But here she is, about to lower the boom.

Rooney tips her head, examining me. I turn so she can't see my face, picking up my leftover tea, which is cold and brackish. I drink it anyway.

Leaning against the counter, she cradles her mug in her hands, dunking the tea bag in and out. "I was going to say thank you for that. I know it wasn't in the job description today, but it helped."

I freeze, stunned. "It . . . helped?"

"Why do you sound so surprised? Isn't that why you did it?"

"Yes," I admit slowly. "I'm just . . . surprised it worked."

"It worked, all right," she says into her mug.

Satisfaction ebbs through me, rare and peaceful. "Well . . . good."

"It was pretty forward of you, though."

My head whips her way. She's smiling. She's *teasing* me.

"I suppose . . ." I sip my tea, then shrug. "I owed you for an unsolicited kiss, though, didn't I?"

Her gasp echoes in the kitchen. In one smooth move, she pulls the damp dish towel off her shoulder and whips it my way, hitting me in the stomach. "So much for you being a gentleman."

"I never said I was a gentleman."

She rolls her eyes. "What do you call a man who always opens my car door and insists on sleeping in a *tent* while I take over his house?"

"A man who's been raised by Elin and Alexander Bergman."

Rooney laughs. "Fine. Okay. You're no gentleman, Axel Bergman. You're a coldhearted rogue."

The deep, foreign feeling of laughter catches in my chest and rumbles. Perking up at the noise we're making, the dog wakes up from his nap. Then he rolls onto his back, tongue hanging out. Rooney extends one long leg and softly rubs his belly with her socked foot.

"You actually do owe me an apology," she says.

I pause with my mug halfway to my mouth, not sure if she's still teasing or not. "What for?"

She steals a sip of her tea and smiles to herself. "For making it such a *good* kiss."

"I'm very sorry."

"You should be," she says primly. "Next time—if a kiss is necessary for whatever reason—please make sure it's absolutely terrible."

I glance over at her and spy a faint, secret smile playing on her lips. Hips against the counter, a sink between us, I raise my mug in a salute. "I'll do my best."

# NINE

# Rooney

Playlist: "You and I," Wilco

Hands in my pockets, knees wiggling with nerves, I wait outside Axel's house, gazing up at the sky as a bird circles overhead in great, steady swoops.

A twig snaps, and I spin toward the sound.

Axel stands in the clearing, looking so perfectly in his element, it leaves me a little breathless. Tall, straight-backed, with wind-swept hair, rich as poured chocolate. He's back in worn jeans and dirty boots, a soft, faded plaid flannel undone a few buttons. The perpetual surly expression is more severe, with that five-o'clock shadow making an appearance and—

Oh *fuck*.

"You wear glasses?" I ask hoarsely.

His hands go to the frames, like he's not even sure they're there. "Uh. Yes."

"I've never seen you wear them before."

"Contacts were bugging me," he says.

Thin frames, their pattern is a swirl of coffee and cream that brings out the rich chocolate color of his hair and lashes, the tiny flecks of caramel in his green eyes. He looks absolutely decadent.

Barely swallowing an embarrassing moan of want, I tug my hat tighter on my head, when what I really want to do is drag it over my face and hide the blush heating my cheeks. My entirely platonic (meaning totally off-limits) husband went from dangerously hot to bespectacled sex on legs.

Cruel, cruel universe.

Shutting my eyes, I take a deep, centering breath, and when I open them, feeling slightly less frazzled, I see Axel's staring at my hand. I follow his gaze. And then I blush again.

I'm still wearing my ring. My gaze snaps to his hand, and my stomach does a weird flip-flop.

*He's* still wearing his ring.

And the hand that wears it is splayed wide, like a fist he just unclenched and flexed. He glances down and fists his hand tight, eyes on his ring. "I, uh—" He clears his throat. "I just realized now that I'm still wearing mine, too. It's oddly . . . comfortable."

I laugh quietly, peering down at the smooth white gold band. "Same. I mean . . . we could just wear them, to be safe—authentic, that is. Especially with the crew coming—not that I'm implying all construction workers are lecherous creeps, most of them aren't, but there's always a few bad apples, and I wouldn't mind sporting the universal signal for 'taken' so I don't have to worry about getting hit on. Not that I'm saying I get hit on all the time or that I'll get hit on by them—" I gasp for air after that verbal monstrosity, forcing myself to stop.

What a disaster. I haven't nervous-rambled like this in years.

Axel rubs his knuckles against his mouth, and watching him do it, his wedding ring flashing as his left hand drags across his lips, does weird things to the pit of my stomach. Good-weird things.

"I'm on board with that," he finally says.

"Great!" I tell him. "Good. Okay."

"Ready?"

"Yep. Totally. Born ready."

He turns and starts walking, adjusting the big bag on his back.

"What's with the gear?" I ask, stretching my stride to catch up to him.

"It's a surprise," he says.

I adjust the much smaller bag on my back and peer up at him, curious. "A surprise?"

He nods.

Axel has a surprise for me. He planned a hike for us. *Why?*

"Axel?"

Slowing to a stop, he glances my way but keeps his eyes down. "Yes?"

"Why are we doing this?"

Silence hangs in the air but for the sound of wind on the nearby water. Axel scrubs the back of his neck, then adjusts his glasses. "It's not every day you get married. Even if it's for . . . nontraditional reasons."

Just like when he held my hand, when he kissed me, when he asked how I was during photos, it's unexpectedly sweet. A soft laugh jumps out of me. "Fair enough."

Satisfied, Axel turns and starts walking again.

"I feel bad that I don't have a surprise for you," I tell him. "If I'd known we were celebrating our nontraditional marriage, I would have pulled something together."

Axel points ahead to where a small tree trunk bisects the path. I hop over it. "You've done more than enough. Thanks to you, saving the house is possible. That's all I need. Tell me if I go too fast," he adds.

I frown up at him. "Don't worry about me. I'm a little run-down lately, but I'm not fragile."

"I—" He hesitates, lifting a branch that I nearly just walked into. "I'm just trying to be considerate. I tend to lose track of when I'm moving too quickly for other people, which isn't hard, given how long my stride is."

"Oh. Right." I clear my throat nervously. "So . . . where are we going?"

He throws a glance my way, the glasses making his side-eye doubly hot. Rude, glasses. Very rude.

"You're at Stanford Law," he says evenly, "and you don't know the meaning of the word 'surprise'? Admissions standards are slipping."

"Oh, ha ha! Very funny."

His mouth twitches like he was about to smile, but his expression's serious before I'm even sure it happened.

"I didn't know our *destination* was a surprise, too, smart-ass."

"It is," he says. "Watch."

I hop over a small ditch just in time not to twist an ankle. "I thought you said this wasn't very technical."

He shrugs. "I guess it is if you're a novice."

"Axel Bergman. If I didn't know better, I'd think you were *trying* to get under my skin."

Another mouth twitch. I will get a smile out of him!

"I was answering your question," he says. Then, after a beat: "And maybe teasing you a little."

"Very husbandly."

He shakes his head. "Not the way I grew up. My dad knows what's good for him."

"I've absolutely seen your dad tease your mom."

Ax points toward a smaller path off the main trail and leads the way. "True. But he knows what teasing she likes and how far he can go, and he never goes beyond it."

I smile. "Your parents are so cute. You can tell they're still very much in love."

"It's oppressive," he says. "I have walked in on them making out way too many times."

"Well, I mean five more of you had to come about somehow—"

"That's enough out of you," he says, cupping his hands over his ears and wrinkling his nose.

I cackle. "I get it. But I also think it's pretty sweet. My parents weren't—" I bite off the rest of my sentence and glance around, scrambling for a shift in gears. "So, we're ascending. Sunset view?"

Axel peers my way, his gaze dancing up my face, then to the sky. "Why'd you change the subject?"

"The polite thing to do would be to roll with said change in subject."

"Not really my thing," he says. "Politeness. I'm shit at it. Like when I asked you to tell me if I was going too fast and somehow I'd implied you were fragile."

I bite my lip. "Oof. That was my bad. I'm sorry."

"Make it up to me. Tell me what you were going to say." He reaches off the path quickly, snaps a long stick across his thigh, then hands half of it to me. "Should be a good height."

"I . . . what?"

He stands the stick beside me and wraps my hand around it. "The stick. Go on."

"What, with the stick or the topic?"

"Both," he says, using the other half of the stick for himself and gently nudging me forward.

As we move forward on the path, I try the walking stick, enjoying how it sinks into the ground and gives me leverage. "My parents just weren't like that."

"Like what?" he says.

I stare at the ground, focusing on my footsteps. "In love. At least, not for long."

I hear him falter behind me, and I glance over my shoulder. He frowns down at the ground. We walk in silence for a while, Axel pointing us in a new direction, the trail winding higher and higher.

"I don't know what to say," he admits.

"Sometimes there's nothing to be said. It's okay."

He peers my way, our eyes meeting too briefly, before he glances ahead. "You can talk more about it," he says. "If you want. I'll listen."

A lump forms in my throat, and I keep my eyes ahead. "Not much to say. They divorced when I went to college. Apparently they thought it was important to stay together for me through high school, thinking I couldn't tell how miserable they were before that. Now my mom spends most of the year in Italy because she loves the weather and Paolo, her second husband. My dad spends most of his time working because that's what he loves. My parents love me, too, of course, and I love them, and they're both happier now that they're divorced, but we're just not close, as a family—whoa!"

Axel's hand shoots out, grabbing me by the upper arm, like he knew I'd trip on the rock ahead of me before I did. My body lurches and then immediately straightens in the steadiness of his grip.

"Okay?" he says.

I nod, drowning in embarrassment that I both tripped and just told him all that.

Why am I spilling my guts like this? Maybe it's the closeness that's come from our unlikely partnership, all this work we've shared to make the wedding happen. Maybe it's the simple intensity of having him so close, having more of his attention and conversation than I ever have before. Maybe it's those damn glasses.

"What is it?" he says, noticing me staring at him.

I look away, scarlet-cheeked. "With the glasses, you've got a bookish woodsman vibe. It's messing with me."

"'A bookish woodsman'?" He wrinkles his nose. Holy shit, he's cute when he wrinkles his nose. "What?"

I try to shove him away, but he neatly sidesteps me, sending me tumbling. Once again, his hand shoots out, catching my elbow and spinning me back onto the path. "More like a bookish *warrior*," he says, before releasing me.

"You do have impressive reflexes. With your height and those reflexes on a soccer field, you had to play goalie. Am I right?"

"I always preferred defense, but yes, my grand soccer history is starting as a right back and ending up dragged into goal."

"You still play?"

"Not now that the A-frame is falling down around me, but otherwise, yes. Just a rec league. You?"

"Too busy. I hope to once school's done."

Pointing ahead, he says, "Almost there."

I follow his direction, where the trees thin and evening sun drips golden tangerine across the ground. The view stops me in my tracks. "This is . . . wow."

Axel stands beside me, drinking it in, eyes on the horizon. "It's my favorite place."

I look up at him as he looks down at me. And I remember that kiss from the ceremony a little too well. The scientist in me wants to test kissing Axel again and again and again. To see if it was an outlier or if his every kiss really will make me weak-kneed.

But even if it does, so what? What am I going to do, make a habit of kissing the man I married until I go home?

Even I'm not that good at compartmentalizing. The kiss during the ceremony was one thing—a touchingly thoughtful, sweet gesture on his part that I never expected. Especially when, up until very recently, I'd have sworn he didn't even find me attractive. You have to be at least a little attracted to someone to kiss them like that, don't you?

It doesn't matter. It can't. That kiss is just going to have to be enough.

"Rooney?"

"Huh?"

His mouth lifts the faintest bit at the corner as he looks away, eyes on the lowering sun. "Hungry?" he asks.

I stare at him, tousled dark hair and lashes, the long line of his nose, the shadowy stubble that I can't stop imagining scraping against my thighs. "Starving."

———

"Well, Ax, if you decide to move on from painting, I think your calling is vegetarian, gluten-free charcuterie boards." Rubbing my full stomach in soothing circles, I stare at the sunset, a lush sky of plum, peach, and rose-petal pink.

"I just might have to," he mutters.

Adjusting my bag, which I'm using as a pillow, I glance over at him. Hands behind his head, eyes on the horizon, he looks so deeply serious. "What happened?" I ask. "With painting?"

He doesn't answer me immediately. I watch his gears turn, the way his jaw works before he says, "I can't paint what I used to."

"Is that bad?" I ask. "As in, isn't it natural for an artist's aesthetic to evolve?"

He clears his throat, still watching the sunset. "Yes. However, what I *can* paint right now isn't for an audience."

"What do you mean?"

He sighs. "And I thought Skyler had a lot of questions."

I push up on my elbow and toss a leaf at him, but he doesn't so much as blink my way. "I'm a curious soul," I tell him.

"Well, you're just going to have to stay curious about that topic, then."

"Fine." I flop onto my back again and stare at the horizon. "You're welcome, by the way."

Axel gives me sexy side-eye through the glasses. "For what?"

"I ate too much. I took one for the team and made that sacrifice so you wouldn't have to haul all that picnic food back down the hill. Now it's in my belly instead of on your back."

Axel's mouth twitches in another thwarted smile. His gaze settles on my mouth. "I'm glad you liked it."

Heat spills through me, warm and rich as the fading sunlight bathing everything the eye can see. "So much."

He swallows roughly, his eyes darkening. But then he glances back to the horizon again.

"Why is this your favorite spot?" I ask.

"Best view of sunrise and sunset. My favorite times of day."

"I bet you love to paint them."

The wind picks up, ruffling his hair. "No."

"'No'? What do you mean 'no'?"

"I've never painted a sunrise or a sunset."

"Why?" I ask, peering out at the sunset, too.

After a long beat of silence, he says, "Promise you won't laugh?"

I turn slightly, facing him. "Of course."

"I've never painted a sunrise or a sunset because . . . I'm not sure I can do them justice. Both times of day, the light changes so quickly, it's absurdly difficult. I have this fear that I won't be able to get it right, and it'll ruin it for me, this thing I love that's so beautiful it makes something in me"—he sets a hand over his heart and rubs—"ache."

I stare at him, stunned and unexpectedly moved.

I asked Axel about painting, and I got an answer about *him*. About how deeply he feels, how hard he is on himself.

"I think I understand," I say quietly.

Axel glances my way, our eyes meeting. "You do?"

"The deeper you love, the deeper the risk of disappointment, and hurt, and loss. The more you care, the more pain you might face. And yet, I hope you won't always let that stop you," I tell him.

"Fear of failure, fear of not living up to these standards you hold yourself to, which sound pretty damn high. Because . . . well, have you ever considered that the depth of feeling for the subject is the reason you're the very best person to paint it?"

His gaze slips away again, back on the sun, just a sliver of bronze remaining. It's quiet for so long, I start to worry I've offended him, gone too far, talked too long. I breathe in and hold it, dread building inside me.

"No," he says finally. "I hadn't considered that."

His answer is brief, but I sense that he's simply lost in his thoughts, considering what I've said.

I exhale, relieved. "I think if anyone could do it, Axel, paint something so complexly beautiful, it would be you."

"And if I do it terribly?" he asks.

"Art is subjective. You're the judge of it, right? Of course you have your standards, but maybe you'll come to realize they need to be adjusted or they were unreasonable to begin with. Maybe you'll muscle through a few rough attempts before you make something you're proud of, and it will be everything you wanted." I reach carefully toward him, extracting the leaf I tossed into his hair. "Maybe even more."

And then I realize how close I am, how somewhere along the way, I ended up almost leaning over him.

"Do you . . ." Axel swallows roughly. His eyes darken, fixed on my mouth.

"Do I . . . ?"

He sits upright suddenly. "Do you mind if we head back? It's getting dark, and I don't want you to twist something on the way down."

My mouth drops open in offense. "'Twist something on the way down'? Listen, Bear Grylls, not all of us have the terrain memorized." I try for a shove, but once again, he deftly spins and springs upright, letting me tumble onto the grass. "You're supposed to be chivalrous and catch me," I remind him, starfished on the ground.

He shakes his head. "You'll never learn your lesson."

"And what's that?"

"That I'm not the kind of person you count on to catch you."

My stomach drops. "That's not a very kind thing to say about yourself."

"Kind or not, it's true." He packs up the last of our picnic items, then swings his bag onto his back. "Come on. Up you get."

Standing and shrugging on my own backpack, I do what I always do. Put a smile on and try to keep things breezy. "This was nice, Axel, thank you."

He nods.

"Actually." I stop on the path. "There is one more thing."

I've given in the past few days to his insistence that I stay at the cabin while he continues to rough it in his tent. But this can't go on for the remainder of my stay.

"I'm not okay with you sleeping in a tent anymore while I stay at your place. I'm not—"

"Rooney, I *like* sleeping outside. It's comfortable and peaceful. I'm not a martyr," he says quietly. "Trust me."

Fine, he's not a martyr, he's just damn stubborn.

"I'm willing to negotiate," I tell him. "I'll allow you to sleep in the tent—"

"You'll *allow* me?"

"That's what I said. I'll allow you to rough it for sleep, *if* you and I eat dinner together inside, then you get yourself comfortable for the night. A hot meal and a shower in the house for you, not whatever you've been doing thus far."

He massages the bridge of his nose, beneath his glasses. "I have a wash-up space in my studio."

"Yeah, and I imagine it's meant for rinsing off paint and cleaning brushes, not showering a grown, taller-than-average man. A proper meal and a proper indoor shower. These terms are non-negotiable."

He sighs wearily. "I had to marry a lawyer."

"Almost lawyer," I remind him. "I'm just naturally good at arguing. A Sullivan family trait."

Our shadows grow longer as we walk in silence for a moment. "Fine," he grumbles.

"Excellent. Starting tonight. We already had dinner, so when we get back, you shower first."

"No. Guests go first."

"If not," I say casually, adjusting my bag as we gain momentum and descend the trail, "I can always head to a hotel so you'll have your bed. It's late, but worst comes to worst, I can pull an all-nighter in the lounge area until a room's open tomorrow—"

"Absolutely not." He glares down at me. "You're . . ."

"Incorrigible?" I offer, smiling sweetly.

He mutters something under his breath, then marches ahead on the trail. The rest of our walk passes in silence, but I don't mind. While my husband's off-limits to my hands, tell that to my eyeballs. They are shamelessly ogling the back half of him.

When we hit the bottom of the trail at the clearing around his house, Axel comes to an abrupt halt, causing me to trip and barely sidestep him.

Curious as to what stopped him, I try to follow his line of sight. I can't see anything in the almost darkness except the faint outline of his tent, and farther off, the little house. "What is it?" I ask.

On a grim sigh, he says, "Skunk."

# TEN

# *Rooney*

Playlist: "The Circle Married the Line," Feist

Axel walks into the clearing, toward his tent. "Stay back," he tells me.

I ignore that mandate and follow him from a distance as he searches the space. When the wind shifts, I catch a whiff of something that's not particularly strong but is definitely unpleasant. It's bad enough to pinch my nose.

"You're sure it's a skunk?" I ask, my voice nasal.

"No," Axel says, approaching his tent. "I think a little flower fairy danced through here and sprinkled her petal perfume."

"Note to self. Axel is a grumpy asshole after a long day."

Disgust paints Axel's face as he walks the perimeter of his tent. "Note to self," he says. "Axel is *always* a grumpy asshole."

"That's not true," I counter, still nasal-voiced, following him. "You were very ungrumpy with Skyler when she complimented your pancakes and blackberry sauce over brunch, and you were pleasant company over our picni—" My word dies off with a dry heave. "Jesus Christ," I gasp, turning and running toward the house, away from where the smell is at its worst.

Standing outside the door, I squint into the darkness, waiting for Axel to resurface from wherever he's wandered. Finally he materializes from the shadows, looking bleak.

I drop my fingers from my nose and take an experimental sniff. The smell here isn't too bad. "What is it?" I ask.

"It's in my tent."

My eyes widen. "*In* your tent?"

There's a rustling sound that startles Axel. Betraying his freak-ish reflexes again, he's got the door unlocked behind me, dragging me inside before I can even yelp in surprise.

The door slams shut as he slumps against it. "Those fuckers are terrifying," he says.

"Are skunks . . . violent?"

He gives me a sharp glance, then pushes off the door. Sliding his bag off his back, he drops it on the dining table with a *thunk*, then strolls into the kitchen. "Their scent is a violence to my nose."

I turn, watching Axel open a cabinet above the refrigerator and pull out a bottle. "What is that?"

"It's coping." He yanks the cork from the bottle with his teeth, spits it out, then pours a hefty serving into a small Mason jar. "Want some?" he asks.

I shake my head, biting back a smile.

He catches my expression and freezes, tumbler halfway to his mouth. "Skunks are no laughing matter, Rooney."

"I've just never seen you this worked up."

"That ass-reeking rodent," he says, gesturing with his glass, "is crawling around my valuables, and knowing my luck, the god-damn dog's going to come by, piss it off, and make it spray all over my shit, and then everything will need to be replaced."

Guilt smacks me. "Oh. I didn't think of that. I'm sorry."

Axel mumbles darkly into his glass before he drains . . . all of it. Wow. Okay. And then he pours himself another one.

"Will Harry be all right?" I ask.

He frowns. "Who the hell is Harry?"

"The dog," I tell him as I shrug off my backpack and plop onto the bed.

"That dog does not have a name."

"He does as of yesterday," I tell him, nudging off my boots and sighing as I flop back onto the mattress. "Harry and I decided over a veggie hot dog campfire lunch—he loves those veggie dogs, by the way—that he needs a name and someone to love him. For the next couple of weeks, I'm his gal."

"Absolutely not," he says.

"Why not?"

"When you're gone, he'll have expectations of me."

"Would that be the worst thing?" I ask.

"Yes." Setting down the Mason jar, he turns and leans his hips against the counter, showing me the breadth of his back, the narrow taper of his waist. He runs both hands through his hair and tugs. "Go ahead and shower," he says.

"Okay, bossy."

"Bossy and grumpy. Not just at night. Not just after a long day. All the time. No false advertising here."

Sighing, I push off the bed. "Fine. I'll shower. But then you're next."

"All my clean clothes are in the tent now," he says. "There's no point."

I step into the kitchen and lean against the counter beside him, close but not touching. "I've got a pair of pajama shorts those long legs of yours would look great in."

Axel's head snaps my way. His mouth twitches. "This isn't funny."

"I know." I peer up at him and smile. "But just because it's not funny doesn't mean you can't laugh. Sometimes laughter is all you have."

He peers down at his glass. "If anything, I'm stealing that robe of yours hanging in the bathroom."

I picture my red silk robe, which I keep in the bathroom in case Axel happened to be inside the house and my nudism wouldn't be appreciated. A surprised laugh jumps out of me. "See?" I tell him. "That wasn't so hard, was it?"

---

Axel capitulates to a shower after remembering he had a pair of paint-splattered jeans and a faded, slightly less paint-splattered T-shirt in his studio. His hair's wet, and his clothes cling to his long, lean body, making me picture what he looks like when he's painting, brow furrowed, lost in his creativity.

I feel a stab of disappointment, knowing this tiny glimpse of him in his natural habitat is all that I'll get. Glum about that, I snuggle lower in the bed, cozy in pajama pants and my UCLA hoodie. Axel sits on the edge of the mattress and peers out the window, eyes glued on the skunk that wanders around his tent. It's been hours, and the animal refuses to leave.

"Why don't you just sleep on the couch and give up the skunk vigil?"

Axel doesn't blink, gaze locked outside. "Then the skunk wins," he says. "Stop tempting me with promises of sleep, Margaret."

I wallop him with a pillow, making him grunt.

"Shh," he says seriously. "The skunk."

"My first name is something you take to your grave, Axel Bergman. I rue the day I had to share a marriage license with you."

"I don't know why you're so upset about it. Margaret's a pretty name."

His humor is so dry, I can't tell if he's teasing me, so I wallop him again, just to be safe.

"Hey." He takes the pillow and wallops me back. "Stop it. I was being genuine."

I set the pillow behind my head. "It doesn't suit me. They chose it because it was my dad's mother's name and it's close to my mom's name—Margo. But it's just not me."

Axel's mouth lifts faintly in the corner, his focus otherwise unin-terrupted. "It's a nice name. It's just not a good fit. You're a Rooney."

My stomach swoops. I like this side of Axel so much, the one that teases a little and talks more, the one that sits on the bed and waits out a skunk. The one who kisses me and takes me on a sunset hike. And I know he'll be gone in the morning. I know walls will go up and things will have their proper place, and I realize I'm go-ing to miss this sliver of time when he treated me like I wasn't just another peripheral person in his life.

After a stretch of silence that I use to not so covertly ogle Axel in those glasses again, he says, "Why Harry?"

"The dog is named in honor of my other husband, the one and only Harry Styles, of course. Because like the icon, that pup makes me smile and moves to his own rhythm."

A muscle in Axel's jaw twitches as he takes another sip of whis-key. "That guy's overrated."

"You watch your mouth. Harry Styles is a gift to humanity."

Axel shrugs. Silence falls between us.

Feeling sleep start to tug at me, I pop my daily immuno-suppressant pills that make my infusion meds most effective and chase them with a long chug of water. The pills make me nause-ated, so I take them right before bed in the hopes of passing out before the queasiness hits. I burrow deeper under the blankets and reach for the electric heating pad I packed and always sleep with.

Eyes still outside, he says, "Stomach hurting?"

I pause, hand hovering over the heating pad I've lodged be-neath my hoodie. "Oh, uh . . ." I clear my throat. "Can you keep a secret?"

"I think I've proven I can."

"So . . . I have an IBD. Ulcerative colitis."

He glances my way, his eyes not quite meeting mine in the darkness. "I don't know what that is."

"An inflammatory bowel disease. Sexy term, I know. It's an auto-immune disease that targets my large intestine."

Axel's quiet. I try to swallow the nervousness tightening my throat. "Sorry if that's uncomfortable," I mutter. "I know stomach troubles and bathroom stuff aren't polite conversation—"

"I'm not uncomfortable," he says. "I'm just—" Turning on the bed, he actually abandons his skunk vigil to face me. "That sounds serious."

"Well, it can be. Mine's pretty well managed. Well, it was, after I was first sick and diagnosed in high school. But it got out of control recently again, which is one of the reasons why I'm here, living in your house instead of wrapping up law school."

Axel stares down at my hands held protectively over my stomach, and then he sets his hand over one of them, dragging it his way. Studying my palm, he slides a finger along my lifeline. "I'm sorry."

"It's okay," I tell him quietly, watching in bewilderment as he touches me this way. Gently. Tenderly. "It was the right call."

"You don't have to say it's okay," he says. "It hurts, doesn't it?"

*In so many ways*, I almost admit.

I stare at him, moonlight tracing his face, his eyes on my hand, which he's . . . massaging. He's massaging my hand. Maybe he had more whiskey while I was in the shower.

"It's not too bad," I tell him.

Air huffs from his nose. "Coming from you, that means it's excruciating."

"Sometimes," I admit. "But not now. It's more just . . . how it affects everything. That's part of what's fucking with me. I'm on a new medication that works, but what if—no, *when*—it stops working and I have to hope another med will be as effective? It's a chronic condition—it's not going anywhere, and I'll always have it. How will that affect my ability to do a job down the road? To engage clients, work on a case, if I'm sick to my stomach, always having to rush off to the bathroom or in bed with pain?"

Axel goes still. The massage stops.

"Shit," I mutter, trying to pull my hand away. "Sorry. My mouth gets going sometimes and—"

"Rooney." His grip on my hand tightens.

I stop resisting and peer up at him. "Yes?"

Slowly he sets my hand back before reaching for the other and massaging that one. "Please don't put words in my mouth. I—" Swallowing slowly, he slides his thumb down my palm, making me arch reflexively in pleasure. "Sometimes I just need time to say what I want. It's harder when people jump in."

"Sorry," I whisper. "I get nervous when I talk about it."

He nods. "I understand. But you don't need to, with me."

Tears prick my eyes. It's just a little kindness, but it's toward such a tender part of my life, it feels like the hardest hug and the biggest smile and the sweetest kiss. It feels good to be accepted, to be not only told but shown that I'm safe to be not just smiley Rooney or happy Rooney but all-of-me Rooney. Even the one who's really fucking sick sometimes.

I smile, hoping to blink away the threatening tears, but one slips down my cheek. Axel goes still as he notices it. Then, carefully, he reaches up and thumbs the tear away. His hand cradles my jaw, fingertips whispering over my skin. My eyes drift half-shut in pleasure that's soft and gentle as starlight.

I want so badly to lean deeper into the comfort of his tenderness. I want there to be more to it than there is. But I have to remember what we are, what today's been—married but not in love, a comforting kiss, a picnic hike of appreciation. Gestures of gratitude for helping Axel, nothing more. But even so, I want to show him *my* gratitude. For making me feel safe. Accepted. Seen.

My hand slides across the comforter to his leg, over his hard thigh stretching his jeans. I hold my hand there, tipping my head, leaning into his palm as it cradles my face. Eyes on my mouth, Axel bends closer, fingers slipping through my hair. I lean closer, too, our mouths a whisper away. But I stop myself, not wanting to repeat history.

"May I kiss you?" I ask.

His eyes darken, fixed on my mouth. "I was going to ask the same thing."

Gently, I slide his glasses off his nose and close them before carefully setting them on the nightstand next to me. "We have a small problem."

"What's that?" he says roughly.

"You promised, if another kiss was necessary, you were going to make it terrible."

Air leaves him unsteadily as he leans closer. "I'm not going to keep that promise."

My hand settles on his chest, and his hand wraps around it, holding it hard against him. "I was hoping you'd say that."

And that's when he tugs me close and his mouth finds mine, warm and tender and so perfect, air catches in my throat. It's the kind of kiss I never really thought I'd experience. The kind that builds, warm and deep inside me, then spills and fills every corner of my body. The kind that makes the need for air an annoyance, and only two hands to feel a maddening frustration.

I dissolve into the bed as Axel's body stretches out beside mine, long and strong, his arms wrapping around me as he pulls me close.

"Terrible?" he asks, breathing harshly.

I sink my fingers into his shirt and tug him closer. "Awful. You should try again."

I feel him hesitate for just a moment. "You'd tell me if it's actually terrible?" he says quietly.

Meeting his eyes, I sweep away the hair falling onto his forehead. "I would, and it's not. I promise."

His mouth brushes mine again, harder this time, more insistent, deep, long kisses as his hand wraps around my waist. "We shouldn't do this," he says.

"Probably not," I agree, sliding my hand over his ribs, feeling the solidity of his body, warm and strong beside me. "But it is our wedding day. I say we give ourselves a pass."

He groans when I bite his bottom lip. "Just tonight."

"Just tonight," I whisper as he yanks me closer and lines up our bodies.

Bending his head, he meets my mouth again, nestling his pelvis against mine. I feel the hard ridge of his length inside his jeans and gasp. My mouth falls open, and I taste him—mint toothpaste and cool water, but mostly something that's just Axel. Mind-bending hunger burns through me.

Oh, this is dangerous. Because now I want more. I want tongue and teeth. I want his hands clutching my waist, rocking me against him. I want him filling my hands, filling me, his weight pressing me into the mattress, the headboard knocking against the wall in rhythm with our bodies.

As if he's read the dangerous turn of my thoughts, Axel gives me one more long, soft kiss to my lips, then pulls away.

"Why'd you stop?" I whisper, far too horny to care about my pride.

He sits up and slips his glasses back on. Gently, he smooths my hair off my face, tangled from his fingers. But he doesn't answer me. He only traces his fingertip across my forehead, down my temple, over the bridge of my nose to my other temple, before his touch slips along my jaw, then my mouth. Then he does it again, a lulling circuit that makes my eyes drift shut. That makes me sink back into the pillow and smile dreamily.

And when I open my eyes, the world is sunny and bright, the bed empty.

Except for a small piece of paper resting on the pillow beside me. Pushing up onto an elbow, I drag the paper closer. A drawing. A dog that looks just like Harry the greyhound, with a speech bubble. *The skunk's gone. I know we planned on cuddles, but if you know what's good for you, keep your distance, seeing as I'm the one who scared him off.*

As a signature, there's a tiny drawn paw print, then a messily written, *Harry*.

I smile at that paper, taking it with me as I ease out of bed. And then I tuck it safely in my suitcase, hoping that it won't be the last one.

# ELEVEN

## Axel

Playlist: "Sunflower, Vol. 6," Harry Styles

After so much shit timing propelling me into the most surreal season of my adult life, I've been waiting for something to go wrong the past two weeks. But I've been working with Bennett, Parker, and the crew, who've been busting their asses on the A-frame, and our progress is better than expected.

In short, things have gone shockingly well.

At least, if I don't think too hard about how scarce I've made myself with Rooney. Like my marriage, keeping my promise has been, as Bennett said, the letter of the law, not the spirit. For the past fourteen days, I've slept in my tent—the skunk, thank fuck, did not spray in it, just decimated my granola bar stash—but I've kept my promise and showered before bed in the house's bathroom each night. Have I done it after I saw her light go out so the chance of talking was virtually erased? Yes. Yes, I have.

As for dinner, I've technically shared meals with her, too. When Bennett and Parker gave me the schedule and I saw it ran until 8:00 p.m., I suggested providing the crew a simple catered dinner through Sarah's café at Shepard's, since, with the inheritance, I could actually afford it. If I created a group meal, I wouldn't have to sit across the table from Rooney in the quiet of my house, enduring her soft, meadow-blossom scent, watching her sigh and smile as she ate her meal.

So every night the past two weeks, I've built my plate and wandered off for some desperately needed peace and quiet after working with the nonstop noise of tools and equipment and barked communication. Then I've sat for a few minutes at the table to get credit for being present.

Rooney's always there, at the other end of the table. She sits next to Skyler, sharing the gluten-free food and a private animated conversation that I've tried not to be too curious about.

If Rooney minds how I've bent the rules, she hasn't said. Which is fine. No—good. I wouldn't *want* her to mind, to care that instead of dinner, just the two of us in the cabin, it's a bunch of rowdy people gathered around the table.

"Ah," Park says when I come back from my walk, smiling up at me as he serves himself more chicken. "Good of you to join us."

"Saved you a seat," Bennett says, adding salad to his plate.

Blinking away from watching Rooney, I drop into an empty chair at the table.

"And how are we this evening, Mr. Bergman?" Parker asks.

"Fine," I mumble, pilfering a roll from a basket as it's passed.

"Fine?" Bennett drops the salad bowl with a *clunk*. "We're killing it on the house. You know that, right? Everything critical and time sensitive has been replaced, repaired, or is underway and stabilized. We've had perfect weather, no material holdups. We're days ahead of schedule—"

"Ay!" Parker points a forkful of chicken at him. "Don't jinx it."

"*Tournesol!*" one of the guys calls. "Pass the water, please?"

Rooney breaks from her conversation with Skyler, then smiles at the guy as she hands him the water pitcher. I watch him smile back at her and something snaps, dead center in my chest.

"What did he call her?"

Bennett glances between me and the guy down at Rooney's end of the table. I put in a new floor with him, but even now, I can't remember his name. I remember his faint French accent, but I'm shit with names.

"Who, Vic?" Bennett says. "He calls her *tournesol*. Means 'sunflower.'"

My hand wraps around my knife so tight, my knuckles throb.

Parker clears his throat, then leans toward Bennett. "In case you're wondering, Axel is fine. He's not sexually frustrated, and he's definitely not jealous. He's just been married to, avoiding, and celibate with a woman he clearly wants. Two weeks down. How many more to go?"

"Two," I mutter. "She's going home for Thanksgiving. That endearment. Does everyone call her that?"

"On the crew, yeah." Bennett shrugs. "Vic started it, and it caught on. She stops up every day and hangs with Skyler between when I pick her up from school and when we have dinner, so the guys have gotten to know her."

"What?"

"Yep," he says airily. "You're just always conveniently not around at that time."

Rooney laughs at something Vic says, all bright teeth and sparkling eyes, and dammit, he even gets her dimples—*both* dimples.

"Say"—Parker reaches behind his chair to the kitchen island and plucks up two gluten-free cupcakes Sarah sent, then turns and sets them in front of me—"why don't you go offer Sky and Rooney some dessert?"

Fueled by that twisty, sore ache beneath my ribs, I snatch up the cupcakes and walk the length of the table to where Rooney and Skyler sit, heads together, bent over a piece of paper.

"Does that make sense?" Rooney asks.

Skyler glances up at me, then back down to the paper, which has what looks like a chemical reaction written down. "Not really," she says.

Rooney's shoulders drop. "Shoot. I'm trying to think of another way to explain it."

"Explain what?" I ask.

Rooney glances up, her smile smaller than I'd like as our eyes meet. She glances back down at the paper. "Skyler said they made a volcano at school with baking soda and vinegar today, and she wanted to know how it happened. I just showed her the chemical equation for the reaction between sodium bicarbonate and vinegar, a diluted solution containing acetic acid. They're actually two distinct reactions, did you know that?"

She points to the formula and continues. "The first is the acid-base reaction, when vinegar and baking soda mix together. Hydrogen ions in the vinegar react with the sodium and bicarbonate ions in the baking soda, and that reaction results in two new chemicals: carbonic acid and sodium acetate. And then the *second* reaction is a decomposition reaction, actually, which is a little different. Carbonic acid that's a result of the first reaction breaks down into water and carbon dioxide gas—thus the bubbles."

We stare at her. Skyler shakes her head. "What did you just say?"

Rooney sticks out her lip in an adorable pout. "I'm sorry, Skyler, I don't know how else to explain it. This is why teachers are superstars. They don't just learn their subject, they learn how to teach it to you."

I crouch down, draw the paper closer, then pick up their pen. Quickly I sketch and label the molecules with the periodic symbols that Rooney used—probably not placing them entirely accurately, but arranged together based on her equation. Then I slide the paper toward Rooney. "Why don't you draw arrows for what goes where in the reaction. Use black pen for the first reaction, then"—I pull out another pen from my back pocket—"blue for the second."

Sky bounces in her seat, staring at the drawing. "Yes! Do it!"

Rooney looks at me curiously. When she takes the pen from my hand, her fingers brush mine. She bites her lip and narrows her eyes at me.

"What?" I ask.

"You've got a lot of nerve, strolling down here with gluten-free dessert and the perfect solution to my problem."

She's teasing me. I think I like it when she teases me, even if I usually don't catch it at first. It's worth watching her playfully glare at me, then figuring it out. "My apologies."

"Forgiven," she says, spinning on her chair and diagramming the reaction. "There, Sky. Does the diagram help? What do we think?"

Skyler bites into her cupcake and smiles. "I get it! That's so cool. You two should make a science book. You write the words, Rooney. Uncle Ax can draw the pictures."

As that thought flashes through my mind, an odd, unsettling warmth spills through my limbs.

Rooney smiles as she plucks her cupcake from where I set it on the table. "Maybe in a couple days, we'll make Uncle Ax draw some biology material. What do you say, Ax? Single-cell organisms?"

"Why not tomorrow?" Skyler pouts.

"I have to go get some medicine tomorrow," Rooney says, before biting into her cupcake.

My gaze snaps to her. "You okay?"

She nods and smiles again. "Yep. This is a medication I need once every six weeks, and I'm due. I called my doctor's office, and the admins there are a dream. They worked out somewhere here that I can get it, and I'm scheduled tomorrow." Directing herself to Skyler, she says, "The medicine just makes me really sleepy afterward, so I'll probably crash and sleep through dinner. It's what I've done in the past. But we'll pick up where we left off soon, okay?"

Skyler seems to think it over, having another bite of cupcake. "I guess so."

"So you're going to pick up your medicine, then come back?" I ask her, still crouched between them.

Rooney chews her mouthful, shaking her head. "No, I take the medication there, then I'll come home—I mean, back here."

"I'll drive you, then."

"What?" Rooney blinks at me. "Why would you do that?"

"You said it makes you tired. That you crash afterward. I'd prefer that to happen on my bed instead of the highway."

"Axel," she says, rolling her eyes. "I was being figurative about crashing. I can make it back."

"We're fairly remote here. Wherever you're headed has to be a bit of a drive."

She shrugs. "Half an hour."

*Half an hour.* Like it's nothing that she'd be driving lethargic behind the wheel. "I'll take you. Tell me when."

"But it's going to take hours. It'll blow your entire afternoon and take you away from the house. You don't have to—"

"Rooney. Let me drive you."

Sighing, she glances down at Skyler. "Is Uncle Ax this bossy with you, too?"

"Yep," Skyler says, chomping on her cupcake. "He makes me go to bed on time when he babysits."

Rooney laughs and tells me, "Fine. I appreciate it. I do tend to get tired pretty soon afterward, so maybe it's for the best."

"Good." I stand, my hand still lingering on her chair. The one with my wedding ring.

Purely to keep everyone away from her. Not because she's mine or anything. Not because I'm feeling toxically territorial—well, not *too* toxically territorial—but because she's here to rest and relax and be on her own, not to be teased and flirted with by a bunch of good-looking, fit guys her age working on the house, calling her *sunflower*.

"Uncle Ax!" Skyler yells, dragging me from my thoughts.

"Yes, Sky."

"I asked Daddy and BiBi for a dog like yours, and they said no, but they said I can get a fish."

Crouching back down so we're eye level, I ask, "What are you going to name it?"

"Rachel Carson," Skyler says.

"Why Rachel Carson?"

Rooney smiles as she watches Skyler slide off her chair and jump an imaginary hopscotch across the foyer. "Rooney told me about her the other day," Skyler explains, "and then I got some books at the library and she's so cool. She made people care about spraying poison that was supposed to kill pests but actually made people and animals and plants sick. Did you know that's the kind of lawyer Rooney wants to be?" She spins and says dramatically, "A toxic chemical *explosion* lawyer."

"Exposure?" I ask.

Rooney shrugs and smiles wider. "I think she liked the superhero vibe 'explosion' gave me."

In her own world, Skyler plops back onto her chair and polishes off the last bite of her cupcake. "She wants to help people who get sick from chemicals and tell that to judges and make companies take better care of the earth when they use chemicals. And since she studied chemicals, she can do a good job. I want to do that, too. I want to study science and tell judges about science and help people and make the world poison-free."

She has icing on her nose, and I wipe it off. "You can do anything you want, Sky."

"I know," she says happily.

When I glance at Rooney, our eyes meet. Her expression is unreadable to me, but I know I don't recognize it—brow furrowed, eyes soft, her mouth tipped in a faint smile. Blushing, she turns back and fiddles with the pen she was using, then the cupcake wrapper.

Standing again, I ask her, "When do you want to leave for your appointment tomorrow?"

"It's at noon," she says. "I'd like to leave at eleven fifteen, just to be safe."

I nod, then reluctantly release my grip on her chair, taking a step back.

"Axel?" she says quietly.

"Yes?"

She peels the last of her cupcake from its paper and sucks a dollop of icing off her finger. "Thanks for the dessert delivery."

I tell myself I'm not going to stare at that full mouth wrapped around her finger. I'm not going to watch her finger leave her lips with a sensual *pop*.

Except I stand there and torture myself until every last crumb is gone.

Two weeks down. Two more to go.

———

"This is it," she says, pointing toward the entrance. "But seriously, you don't have to come in. If you want to just circle back for me, I'll be ready by two."

"Do you not want me to come?"

She exhales slowly, biting her lip. "I mean . . . I wouldn't mind."

"Then I'll come. Lead the way."

I follow her in, identifying the least occupied part of the room and leaning against the wall. Rooney fills out paperwork, then finds me, joining me to my right. "You can sit," I tell her. "I just prefer to stand."

She wiggles her knees and shakes her head. "I'm good. It helps with nerves, to stand."

"Are you nervous?"

She nods. "Needles aren't my favorite."

*Needles?*

A cold sweat breaks out on my skin. "What kind of medicine is this?"

Rooney's oblivious to my panic, lost in her own unease. "An infusion. That's why I'm here for two hours."

Oh *fuck*. Two hours of sitting there, watching Rooney have a needle in her arm. I have to get out of here.

I could make up a call, pretend like there's been some emergency at the A-frame. Rooney would smile and be gracious as I excused myself. She'd tell me she's fine.

But as I watch her, staring at the television talk show yet not watching it, her hands tight, nervous fists behind her back, I know I'm not going to leave. Eyes on the television, too, I reach until my knuckles brush hers.

Rooney's breath hitches. She blinks, then swallows quickly, gaze pinned to the screen. And then slowly her fist unfurls, her fingertips brush mine, our hands link tight.

"Deep breaths," I tell her as we stare at the TV.

She nods.

I lean a little closer, my nose brushing her hair. "Actually take a deep breath."

She laughs nervously, then takes a slow, deep breath, then another. I take them with her, telling myself this isn't too bad, that I'll manage it all right. Sure, I don't like needles going into *me*—and by don't like, I mean am deathly afraid of—but in someone else, it'll be fine, I bet. Totally fine.

When her name is called, Rooney squeezes my hand, then releases it, but she glances over her shoulder as she starts walking, as

if to make sure I'm following her. I nod encouragingly, then hold
the door for the nurse and her as we make our way out of the waiting room.

I catch my first glimpse of an IV pole and feel my knees change
states from solid to liquid. Breathing deeply, I clench my jaw until
my teeth ache, and form fists with my hands, making sobering,
painful crescents dig into my palms. I focus on that sensation as
the nurse directs us to an alcove with a reclining chair that Rooney
slides onto gingerly. There's another chair beside it, along the wall
but close enough that I can hold her hand, if she needs that.

Shit, maybe *I'll* need that.

While Rooney answers the nurse's questions, signs papers, and
makes small talk, I sit still, eyes shut, visualizing happy things. A
quiet walk in the woods, the soothing peace of standing behind a
waterfall, the last painting I did that I loved.

Until Rooney's hand is clutching mine, and my eyes snap open.

"Okay?" the nurse says, rubbing her thumb along Rooney's
vein.

The world swims a little.

"Yep," Rooney says cheerfully, sounding convincingly fine, except that she's almost breaking my hand, she's squeezing it so hard.

"Nice deep breath," the nurse says.

I take one at the same time Rooney does, looking anywhere
except the needle approaching her arm. I'm fine. This is fine. I'm
going to be fine. Until Rooney startles at the pain and whimpers.

That's when the world goes black.

# TWELVE

# Rooney

Playlist: "Fever Dream," mxmtoon

"One minute you're holding my hand," I tell Axel, his reclined chair parked right next to mine, "taking a deep breath with me. The next, you're slumped over the chair."

The nurse chuckles to herself and checks the machine distributing my medicine. "Poor guy. Wait until you have babies. He's going to need his own hospital bed."

Axel's still ashen as I hold his hand. He gets one look at my arm and shuts his eyes again. "Is it over?" he asks hoarsely.

"What, honey?" the nurse asks. "The infusion? Oh, no, it's just getting started. We'll cover it with a towel so you can't see it. That should help."

Exhaling slowly through his nose, Axel squeezes my hand. "Sorry."

Something dangerously close to affection swells inside me. "Why are you sorry?"

"Because I *fainted*," he says tightly.

"You were trying to be there for me." I stare at him, his lips pursed in a frown, the prominence of his Adam's apple as he swallows. "It means a lot that, even though needles freak you out, you stayed."

"Hm." He squeezes my hand, head dropping back again.

"Try not to mention the word," the nurse whispers, winking at me.

"Sorry, Ax." I rub my thumb over his hand in, hopefully, soothing circles. "I'm the worst."

"No you're not," he says. "That honor is reserved for skunks."

"Here's some juice for you." The nurse sets an apple juice box on the arm of his chair.

Axel thanks her, but he doesn't open his eyes or move to take it. His skin is still white as paper.

I pick up the juice box, puncture it with the straw, and bring it to his lips. "Open up."

He parts his mouth and accepts the straw, drinking slowly.

"Want me to tell you a science joke?" I ask.

Turning my way, he opens his eyes and looks straight at me for the briefest moment before those emerald showstoppers disappear behind his lids. "Sure."

"Too bad. The good ones argon. Get it? Argon?" I snort a laugh and sigh.

Axel shakes his head slowly. "That's not a joke. That's a pun worthy of my nerdy eighth-grade science teacher."

"Hey, you." I tap his mouth with the straw again, until he parts his lips and drinks more. "I'll have you know I was going to *be* a nerdy eighth-grade science teacher."

He frowns. "What changed?"

I stare down at the juice box, spinning the straw. "It's a long story."

"I've got time."

Sighing, I give him a look, but his eyes are shut, and if he senses me staring at him, he doesn't let on. "It was a lot of things. Partly my personality—I'm very competitive with myself and achievement oriented. Partly my family life."

"Your family life?"

"My parents' marriage was rocky. Lots of tension and hissed arguments in the kitchen when they thought I was studying or watching TV or up in bed. One night, I came down to refill my water glass, and right when I was about to enter the kitchen—"

My throat catches as I remember it, such a visceral memory. I'm thirteen again, braces hurting my mouth, my hair up in a haphazard ponytail, all scrawny long limbs that I haven't quite grown into. And I see it just how I did over a decade ago—my mom right in my dad's face, the pain in her expression.

As I pull myself out of that memory and swallow the lump of tears in my throat, I'm more grateful than ever for Axel's quiet way, the patience in his silence. He doesn't push me or pressure me. He just slowly takes the juice box from me and links our hands together.

"My parents fought," I tell him. "And I overheard things I wasn't supposed to. I was an unplanned pregnancy from a fling they had while working on a movie together."

Axel is quiet, but he's listening. I feel his attention, his presence, as he watches me, his thumb gently circling my palm.

Pasting on my *I'm fine* smile, I explain, "After I heard that I was a mistake, I wanted to prove myself worth the trouble. I thought, maybe if I did everything right, if I got the best grades and the highest scores, they wouldn't see me that way, and they'd be happier. They'd realize they'd made the right choice in having me and getting married, then they'd fall back in love, and we'd finally be a close, happy family."

I shrug, blinking up at the ceiling so the tears that are blurring my vision won't spill. "So I threw myself into that. And by the time I realized that wasn't going to happen, I'd graduated valedictorian, had an academic-athlete scholarship to undergrad. And as my family felt like it was falling apart, I built myself up in my achievements. Majored in biochemistry, minored in public policy, got into Stanford for law school. *Thought* I'd figured out a career that would be meaningful and not too hard on my body. And all that busting my ass got me a mom who lives in Italy, a dad who's married to his work, and chemo drugs to deal with the price my body's paid for all the stress.

"I know they did their best, and I know, in their way, they love me. But sometimes people love you their best, and it's still not enough."

Silence rings in the air. My cheeks heat as I process everything I said, how long I talked. So much that I've bottled up for years just came pouring out.

Axel's still quiet, frowning in thought. He squeezes my hand. And then, slowly, he tugs me close until my head lands against his shoulder.

"You're the furthest thing from a mistake," he says. "You know that, right?"

I nod as I breathe him in, the clean, comforting scent of cedarwood and sage that warms his skin. "Yes, I know."

"Good." Axel shuts his eyes again and rests our interlaced hands across his stomach. I feel the hard muscles beneath his shirt, his steady breathing. For a while, we simply sit in silence, until the nurse comes and checks on my infusion.

When she walks away, this time leaving behind a bag of gluten-free pretzels on our neighboring armrests, Axel reaches into his back pocket and pulls out a small book with a woman and man on the cover in Regency-era clothing, locked in a clinching embrace.

"Reading historical romance?" I ask him.

Axel pops open the bag of pretzels and brings one to my mouth. "It's my brother's fault. Viggo's filled my library with surly dukes and feisty bluestockings."

I smile as he sets a pretzel on my tongue. "You were going to read that while you waited for me?"

He nods. "This one's pretty good."

I nestle back against his shoulder and chew my pretzel. "You could read me some. If you feel like it."

"So long as you promise never to tell Viggo that I'm actually enjoying them."

"I promise. But why?"

"Because if he finds out, he'll be insufferably smug." Clearing his throat, Axel opens the book, not where it's dog-eared halfway through, but at the beginning, before he pauses and feeds me another pretzel. "Now, prepare yourself. I have a stunning English accent."

———

I've started to wonder if Axel isn't so much surly as he is slow to warm up. And I've wondered if once he warms up to you, it freaks him out a little.

Because the transformation from the silent giant of my casual acquaintance to the considerate, caring guy I married and bonded with over a stoned officiant and a breathtaking sunset and a fear of needles, back to the quiet serious man driving me home, are night and day . . . and night. It's like as soon as he started to open up to me, he snapped shut.

He's been unreachable the past two weeks. I expected it. I needed the distance, too. I had no business indulging my lusty thoughts about him and coming damn close to acting on them. And so I shouldn't be so stung that he's withdrawing again.

But I'm such a sucker for the Axel that held my hand and plied me with gluten-free pretzels. Who read historical romance with a range of voices that made me laugh so hard, we got a look from the nurses' station that made us apologize in unison and gave me that us-against-the-world feeling, like on our wedding day.

It makes me wonder what it might take simply to be his friend. *Just* a friend, of course.

But it's a delicate dance with someone who's clearly got his reservations about closeness, who says things like *I'm not the kind of person you count on to catch you*, who won't name a dog that he clearly loves and is clearly his, who doesn't want the dog to *"have expectations"* of him. And so I tell myself not to be disappointed as he drives us back and the silence grows and the frown returns.

Axel's eyes stay pinned on the road, his hands shifting gears fluidly. I slump sleepily against the window, watching raindrops slither down the glass, and try not to feel glum.

When we're back at the little house, he opens my car door, shuts it, unlocks the front door of the house, opens that, too. I plop onto the bed and drop my bag to the floor. Now I'm too wiped to even be glum.

"You don't look good." Axel stands over me, arms folded across his chest. Frowning.

I smile up at him, knowing he doesn't mean it in a rude way. He's just blunt, and somehow it's endearing that he's unguarded enough to simply speak his mind. "I know. I'll be better after I sleep."

"You're okay, though?"

Ah, there's that sweetness, served with a side of scowl.

"Yeah." I slump sideways, curling up onto the bed.

The frown deepens. "Well. I should go."

"Yep. Thanks again."

He nods. Opens his mouth. Shuts it. Then walks outside.

Then the door swings open again, and only his head pops back inside. "Call if you need anything."

I smile sleepily. "I will, Axel."

On another one of his nods, he shuts the door, quieter this time, the sounds of his footsteps fading. I know by now not to listen for the Jeep's engine. Instead, I listen for Harry's friendly bark, the snap of a twig being broken, before Axel sends it on a whistling lob through the air for the dog to chase. He'll walk to the A-frame, the dog lumbering alongside him. He walks whenever he can.

I know things like this about him now. And it's oddly comforting. It's also really not strategic-marriage, platonic-relationship territory, either. Which is concerning. I'm just too tired to worry about that or analyze it right now.

So I shut my eyes, letting fatigue drag me toward sleep. Just as I'm starting to drift off, my phone rings. Groggily, I tilt the screen up until I can read it.

*Willa.*

I swipe it open to answer. "Hey, you."

"Hey! Guess what? I'm back early!"

My eyes widen in panic, adrenaline making me suddenly wide-awake. The plan was to get as much heavy-duty work as possible done on the A-frame while Willa was gone and we could count on her and Ryder staying away. But now that she's back early, what am I going to do? Tell her I'm here and risk a visit, or lie to her again?

I can't. I can't keep one more thing between us. Not when I'm already mentally writing my confession of all that I *have* kept from her.

"Rooney?"

"Sorry, that's great! How'd everything go?"

"So good," she says. "I played well, press and sponsorship stuff wasn't too painful, and one gig got postponed, so here I am! Are you still at the A-frame? Can I come see you?"

I'm sweating like a pig in a barbecue joint. What do I say?

"Uh, I am, yes. But . . ."

*Think, Rooney! Think!*

"But?" Willa asks.

"But . . ." The lightbulb dings over my head. "Axel said he needs to . . . do a few things on the place. I should get out of his hair." And isn't that the truth? "Why don't I come to you?"

"Are you sure?" Willa asks. "I'd love to have you, but I don't want to make you drive down to Tacoma."

"You mean you don't *trust* me to drive down to Tacoma."

She laughs uneasily. "I mean, sorta."

"I'll be fine," I tell her. "That's what Google Maps is for."

"You sure?"

"Absolutely."

I can hear the smile in her voice as she says, "Then let's do it!"

# THIRTEEN

*Axel*

Playlist: "Ready to Let Go," Cage the Elephant

Rooney is off to Willa's for a long weekend visit, and it's not the relief I thought it would be. I loaded her suitcase into Bennett's Subaru, which he insisted she take because Rooney returned her rental car last week, and she can't drive my Jeep's stick shift to save her life. Then I watched her program Willa's address into her GPS and made her promise to call—hands-free—if she got lost.

And ever since I saw her disappear from view, I've had this ache in my chest that feels like indigestion of the heart.

I don't like it one bit.

Normally, I'd paint, work out whatever's cooking inside me as I dragged color across canvas in the silence of my studio. Unfortunately, there's only one thing I'd paint if I tried, and it's the last thing I should be painting. So I plan to putz around at the A-frame this weekend and distract myself with tasks I can do alone, while the crew's not working.

Which means I have two whole days of quiet to look forward to, starting this evening. No more late nights as of today, now that the time-sensitive work has been handled, so the crew stopped at five, and everyone's gone, which is a deep relief.

Except it means catered dinners are over, and *that* means when Rooney is back, I'm going to have to suck it up and share meals with her. Tempting as it is, there's no point in getting worked up right now about how I'll survive her moans and sighs, her fork tines and finger licking. I'll cross that boner-inducing bridge when I come to it.

No, right now, I'm going to savor that I am, for the first time in two and a half long weeks, going to be alone. Once Parker gets the hell out of here. Bennett left a few hours ago to get Skyler from school, but Park's been walking around, checking progress, making notes.

"Ax!" he calls.

"Out here."

He steps onto the porch, where I've been standing, enjoying the sunset, and shuts the door behind us. "Well?" I ask him.

"I'm not going to say too much because I'm superstitious." He knocks on the house. "But we're kicking ass. Your goal was to be done mid-December, and we're looking real good for that. I *could* say we might be done a week early if this keeps up, but I won't tempt the construction gods."

"This means a lot, Park. All you've done in such a short time."

Bennett rolls down the drive in the truck, Skyler's singing voice echoing from the open windows of the extended cab. He flashes his lights and honks, just to fuck with us.

Parker waves at them. "Hey, you hired the best. I'm just doing my job." We take the steps down from the porch together, and he walks toward the truck. "How long is she gone?"

"Who?"

"Okay, sweet cheeks, don't play dumb. You know who I'm talking about."

I swallow what feels like a hot coal lodged in my throat. It burns all the way down. "Four days."

Parker grins. "Plenty of time."

"What's that mean?" I call.

He doesn't answer. I can't say I like the taste of my own medicine.

After Parker hops into the truck, followed by a brisk trio of honks, they roll down the drive. Standing on the porch, I shut my eyes and savor it—the deepening darkness beyond my closed eyelids, the absolute solitude and silence.

Finally.

Until the faint rumble of a new engine cuts through the air. I keep my eyes shut. Tell myself it's a car that got turned around and took a wrong turn. Any minute now I'll hear tires crunching as they make a sharp U-turn, the sound will fade away, and all will be well.

Except the engine sound grows louder. Then the *pop* and *thunk* of a car door opening and closing echoes in the clearing. My eyes open, then widen in disbelief.

"Oliver?"

My youngest brother hikes a duffel bag higher on his shoulder and walks my way as his Uber makes a three-point turn, then starts down the drive. Oliver's light blond hair is half out of a small ponytail at the nape of his neck, and his blue-gray eyes, just like Mom's, are red-rimmed. He looks like hell, which is . . . unusual for him. He's the golden boy, the last son, brilliant at soccer, brilliant in school. Life goes Oliver's way, and he looks it.

He also looks like he's grown three inches since I last saw him. What do they feed these kids at UCLA? Human growth hormones?

"What the hell are you doing here?" I ask.

Oliver tries to smile up at me, but it's more of a grimace. He blinks away the wetness shining in his eyes and sniffles. "I . . . needed somewhere to go."

"Somewhere to go."

"I needed to not be at school for a couple days."

"What happened?" I ask.

"Uh." He swallows thickly. "I really don't want to talk about it. I just want to be miserable."

"Which brings you here?"

Wiping his nose on his sleeve, he shrugs. "Yeah. You're the one person in the family I feel like I can be miserable around."

"Thanks?"

Sighing, he tugs his hair loose, then pulls it back again. "I just meant that you let people be how they need to be. Everyone else in the family would try to fix it, and it's not something you can fix."

I stare at him, this boy-turning-man, and feel the deep tug of protectiveness. Something that makes me take a steadying breath and open my arms. "Come here."

With two steps forward, Oliver dumps himself against my chest, a single sob hiccuping out as I hold him hard against me. If I control a hug, it's not too uncomfortable. It's when people's hands wander my body that makes my skin crawl. But Ollie's too bereft to hug me back. He just hangs, loose in my arms, silently crying.

Suddenly, I'm very aware of what's barely hiding beneath my shirt—the chain I put on that holds Rooney's ring. That's when I remember I'm still wearing mine, too. Carefully, I slip it off while holding him and hide it inside my fist. I'll add it to the chain when Oliver's not paying attention.

Sighing, Oliver pulls away and wipes his eyes. "Thanks," he whispers.

Shoving my hands in my pockets, including the one with the ring, I take a step back and nod.

"What's going on here?" he asks, pointing to the equipment left around the property, the signs of work.

Panic rolls through me, then quickly ebbs. He doesn't know a hacksaw from a hatchet. He'll have no idea what all is being done or what it might cost.

I shrug. "Just a few repairs while it's my time here to do them."

He blushes and scrubs the back of his neck. "Yeah, sorry to crash it."

"It's all right. You can stay. I just have everything turned around in the A-frame, so it'll have to be the cabin."

He groans. "We have to walk, don't we?"

"No, I thought we'd fly by broomstick."

"Ha ha," he mutters, switching the shoulder his bag is on. "It's so Dad. Walking everywhere when you have a functioning vehicle."

"Well, then take these thirty seconds to rest your weary legs before the brutal trek. I have to close up."

After shutting off the lights and ensuring nothing's amiss, I lock up the A-frame. Oliver eases off the steps on a groan, falling in line with me and grumbling under his breath.

"Grumble all you want, but walking is good for you," I remind him. "It's mentally clarifying. And it saves fuel."

Another groan. "My legs hurt from practice this morning."

"You did say you wanted somewhere to be miserable."

He *hmph*s. "At least you'll feed me. You will feed me dinner, won't you? I'm starving."

"Yes, Ollie. I'll make you dinner," I tell him as the dog that I've begrudgingly begun to acknowledge as Harry runs toward us, barking happily.

So much for peace and quiet.

And yet it seems I'm grateful for these happy sounds echoing through the trees as we walk. With Rooney gone, everything already feels emptier, subdued . . . *too* quiet.

I stop myself from heading further down that mental path. It's a dead end, and there's no point in going there. She's only gone for a few days now, but soon enough she'll be gone for good. She'll leave, and life will go on without her.

It has to.

———

I make a simple dinner, and Oliver eats enough to feed three adults. He yawns almost constantly, but he helps me clean up, then passes out on my bed in a long-limbed diagonal of messy-haired, snoring twenty-year-old.

And once again I have nowhere to sleep. Oliver's taken my bed. I broke down the tent this morning when Parker gave me the all clear to safely stay in the first-floor main bedroom in the A-frame, but I can't stay there tonight without raising Oliver's suspicion.

I haven't minded camping out the past few weeks, but the first-floor bedroom of the A-frame seemed like a smart upgrade now that it's inhabitable and nighttime temperatures are dropping. The place is still in pretty rough shape; it'll only be an air mattress on the floor, but at least there's a bathroom and working plumbing. Sneaking into my house late in the night to shower and get ready for sleep, trying not to notice Rooney out cold in my bed, her blonde hair splayed like a splash of sunlight on the cloud-white pillows, did funny things to my insides. Made me want to smooth the hair stuck to her cheek, tuck the blanket up to her chin.

Shit I have no business wanting to do.

Oliver snores and mumbles something under his breath. Resigned to sleeping on the sofa, which is at least long enough for me, I brush my teeth, then crash, my dreams full of Rooney. Rooney walking the path with Harry the dog. Rooney laughing, eyes crinkled shut, bright, wide smile. Rooney tucked in my bed. Naked. Panting my name—

"Wake up, sleepyhead!"

I jackknife upright and nearly smack heads with Viggo. "What the *fuck*." I shove him away. "First him. Now you? What do I look like, a goddamn Airbnb?"

Viggo plops onto the far end of the sofa, nudging my legs out of the way until his ass is squarely on one of the cushions. "A deeply repressed part of you clearly wants visitors. Why else keep a spare key above the doorway?" He tips his head and inspects me, smiling brightly. "You're so cute in the morning."

I might murder him. "You are satanically alert."

He laughs and pats my leg. I kick him in the back, making him slump sideways. "I'd say I missed you," he groans, "but I can't breathe. I think you broke my kidney."

"You only need one of them," I grumble, burrowing beneath the plaid blanket I slept under. I want to be sleeping like Oliver, who snores, in the exact position he was when he passed out last night. "Viggo, what are you doing here?"

Slowly easing upright again, Viggo props his feet on the sofa, right in front of my face. I knock them off. "Ollie didn't answer his phone," he explains. "And he always answers his phone. I couldn't track it for a while—duh, because he was flying, little did I know—which freaked me out, but once it came back on the radar, I put two and two together and realized I needed to come for moral support, stat."

I frown at him. "You track Oliver's phone?"

"Only in emergencies. He does it to me, too. It's consensual."

"You two are strange," I mutter.

Viggo smooths back his brown hair, the exact same shade as mine, and sighs heavily. "I might also be avoiding Mom."

"Why?"

He grimaces and shuts his eyes, hiding the pale blue-gray irises Mom gave him. "I dropped the ball on a massive baking order for one of her countless charitable fundraising doohickeys. She was . . . not pleased."

This is not unusual. Viggo's the definition of scattered. Dozens of interests, a hundred talents, none of which he can seem to settle on. Whereas I have one—painting. His charisma saves his ass on the regular, but Mom's one of the few people who won't be charmed by it.

Viggo glances my way. "Go ahead. Lecture me."

"I'd rather you make me coffee. You woke me up. It's the least you can do."

"I don't drink coffee, so I can't say I'm sure of what I'm doing, but—"

"Never mind." I throw back the blanket and sit up. "Don't touch my kitchen."

Swan diving onto the vacated couch, Viggo takes my place. He spreads the blanket across his legs, then sets his arms behind his head. "I'll take mint tea."

I give him a death glare.

He grins. "So, did O tell you what happened?"

I shake my head as I fill the kettle with water, then begrudgingly set a sachet of peppermint tea in a mug. "Said he didn't want to talk about it. We ate dinner, cleaned up, then he passed out."

Viggo looks at me like I have four heads. "And you just . . . left it at that."

"Yeah." I add pre-ground coffee into the French press carafe, breathing in the aroma. I prefer the taste of fresh-ground beans, but I cannot stand the noise a grinder makes, so Sarah at Shepard's does it for me every week when I grocery shop.

"Axel," Viggo says wearily. "When Oliver says he doesn't want to talk about it, that means he really wants to talk about it."

"That makes no fucking sense."

"This is why I came. I knew you'd need help. Looks like you could use some help at the A-frame, too. What all are you doing?"

I freeze midair with the boiling kettle. *Shit.*

Shit, shit, shit.

Viggo's not quite as oblivious as Oliver about this stuff. I have to tread carefully. "I have Parker and Bennett cranking out a few projects with me. Nothing major."

It's dangerously quiet as I pour water over the grounds and into Viggo's mug. I learned pretty much as soon as he could crawl that when Viggo was quiet, something terrible was happening or was about to happen, so I brace myself for whatever's next.

"I see." He sits up and eases to his side, reaching for his back pocket. I swear, if he foists one more romance novel on me, I'll—

A pair of peach-pink panties unfurls from his hand. "By the way, I found these on the floor in the bathroom."

Slowly, I set down the kettle. Leave the kitchen. Take them from his grip. And pocket the panties. Then I walk back into the kitchen and resume making coffee, willing my face not to heat. I have Rooney's panties burning a hole in my sweatpants, my fingertips scorched by the soft fabric.

Outside, I am cool and calm. Inside, I'm a boiling-hot mess.

"Now," Viggo says, stretching out on the sofa again, a devious grin lighting up his face. "Why would a boxer-brief-wearing person like yourself have a pair of fancy underpants in your humble abode, Mr. Declared Bachelor?"

"Bachelor. Not monk." The best lies contain the most truth possible.

His grin widens. "Well, tell me about them."

"No."

"Why not?"

"Because it's nothing."

His smile tightens. "Is it *actually* nothing? Or are you trying to convince yourself it's nothing? Not being sarcastic. I'm honestly asking."

I don't answer him, because if I did, I'd have to admit something I don't want to, that with Rooney it doesn't feel like nothing. It feels like *something*—something I can't make sense of.

"Listen." Viggo sighs. "It's okay if it is nothing. I know I go a little hard on the romance lectures, but it's not everybody's thing, and I respect that."

I point to the floating shelf Rooney busted that I've since fixed, the tidy stack of mass-market romances lined up along it in alphabetical order. "Really?"

Crossing the space to the counter dividing the main room and the kitchen, he sweeps up his tea. "My aim was to *expose* you to romance, not to bash you over the head with it. And I'm sorry if I've been heavy-handed. Like I said, I know not everybody wants romance, and that's valid, I just don't want you denying yourself *if* that desire is there."

Oliver's snore pops in the air, the punctuation mark on Viggo's statement.

Viggo asks me what I "desire," if I want romance with someone, like it should be this easily answered question, but for me it's not. I don't *know*.

"Oh." Viggo cups his tea and leans in. "Maybe you're not sure?"

Creepy mind reader with his goddamn feeling words and romance novels. I press down the carafe lid and imagine it's something delicate of his anatomy being crushed as I go.

"You're envisioning pulverizing my nuts, aren't you?" he asks.

I arch an eyebrow but say nothing. That's answer enough.

Shuddering, Viggo hightails it with his tea to the dining table, placing much-needed space between us. He sips from the mug and winces. "Fuck. Burned my tongue. Just a reminder before you daydream anymore about my torture, I only want you to be happy."

"Mm-hmm." I pour myself a cup of coffee, then sit at the opposite end of the table. Taking a sip, I shut my eyes and imagine that I'm alone, that I slept peacefully in my bed and woke up to restful quiet, instead of this hellscape of the man cubs infiltrating my house.

But I can't even find contentment in that daydream. Because that sharp, bitter ache throbs beneath my sternum again.

Fuck. I think I . . . miss Rooney?

How? How is that possible when I've barely seen her the past two weeks? How can I miss someone I've bent over backward to keep my distance from? Who I've avoided doing anything with that would make me feel closer to her, hungrier for her.

"So." Viggo sips his tea again, then sets down his mug. "We hit a wall with the romance talk. Let's backtrack. Tell me about Peach Panties, or whoever it is who's got you looking miserable."

"I'm always miserable," I snap.

Viggo raises his eyebrows, drums his fingers along the table. "Ooookay."

I hide behind my coffee mug and let silence hang between us. Viggo hates silence.

Sighing, he pushes off the table and strolls toward the floating shelf that holds the romance novels he's foisted on me. Slipping one off the shelf, he flips through the pages, then snaps it shut.

"Why do you read these?" he asks.

"Because you sneak one into my suitcase every time I come home for a visit?"

He gives me a nonplussed look. "Axel. Be serious."

"I'm always serious. It's what you all give me shit for."

"Not that kind of serious. Not grumpy serious, genuine serious. And yes, I snuck them into your suitcase, but I haven't made you read them. You could have used them for kindling, but you've read at least some of them, judging by those cracked spines. Why?"

Staring down at my coffee, I tip my cup side to side, watching the dark liquid slide and kiss the ceramic surface. "Because I'm curious, I guess. I'm not . . . against romance. I just don't know that I'm cut out for it, either."

Viggo's uncharacteristically quiet for a moment. He eases onto a seat closer to me and softly fans through the book's pages, over and over. "And after having read a few of these?" he asks. "What do you think?"

"I'm not sure. I don't talk and act like the people in your books."

Viggo sets down the book. "No one does. That's the point. Certain parts of historical romance are highly unrelatable—the marriage mart, the clothing, the elaborate etiquette, the formal language—and yet that's what makes the stories poignant. Reading about people who look and live and speak so differently from us, yet struggle like we do with their inner demons and outside forces, fight for love in their friendships and families and the people they've fallen for, reminds us that not only romantic love, but familial and platonic and sacrificial love is universal, and romance is timeless, that there's a love story for anyone out there who wants one."

How do I explain how unsure I am that romantic love like that is something within my grasp, when I feel like, even with my family, that bridge to closeness is so difficult to cross? That all my life, people have been difficult to understand, to be intimate with, to be around for long before I need room to breathe and quiet to think and space to move so I can function?

How do I explain that even with the people I do love, when my tongue gets tied and I don't want the noise of a rowdy group or anyone's body near mine, that it's so damn complicated to find ways to show them I love them that they'll recognize? That closeness is so much fucking *work* when I seem to have a lot more boundaries and sensitivities than most, when it feels like what I need makes others feel held at arm's length?

I don't doubt that I'm capable of love—I've just learned that I don't communicate it in a language that most recognize. And if I can't find that common language, that understanding with the people who have no choice *but* to love me, who've known me longest and know me best, what kind of chance do I have of building romantic love with anyone else?

I know I'm not broken or defunct. But I know I'm different. And finding how to make my difference fit in this world has been hard, sometimes painful. I've found a place and a way of being that makes my difference safe, that lets me paint and find peace in nature, that gives me the quiet I need and the beauty that fuels my creativity. It's just a deeply solitary existence.

And yes, sometimes I've felt a tug of loneliness, a sense that my life is rich but could be richer if someone else was there, sharing it with me, but this world I've made, one where I don't constantly feel the edges of my limits, isn't for most, is it? And I can't change it very much. Whoever wants me will have to want this. Because this is the life that's healthy for me, that subdues my anxiety and leaves me with enough reserves to love my small circle of family and friends as well as I can.

Could someone want that with me? And if they did, could I take that risk and share it with them? Let them in and let them rearrange it a little? Could I love them the way they need, too?

"Ax," Viggo nudges.

I glance up at him. "Sorry. Just . . . thinking."

He sets the book on the table, peering at me curiously. "I'm going to say something, then I'm going to drop it, promise. In my humble opinion, romance novels aren't just epically sexy, heartfelt escapes—they're little homecomings to *ourselves*."

"I don't understand."

Viggo shifts closer, elbows on the table. "Remember, when Freya and Aiden were in trouble this summer, I gave Aiden a romance novel?"

I nod.

"I didn't do that because I thought he needed a book to teach him how to better love his wife. I gave him a romance novel because they're a safe place to step deeper into our emotions, the happy ones and the hard ones. To recognize and process complex, sometimes difficult feelings within ourselves that the world, in all its gendered, toxic bullshit, tells men we have no obligation to face and feel, when we really do. As *humans*, we owe it to ourselves to know our hearts."

What I'd give to know my own heart, to make sense of this *feeling* aching and tugging inside me whenever Rooney's around, and now that she's gone. But it doesn't seem like romance novels work for me the way they work for Viggo or Aiden or others.

Viggo's quiet for a moment, then careful as he says, "Just because you experience your emotions differently from other people, Axel, doesn't mean that experience isn't valid, or that someone can't love you for it. With the right person, love is possible for any of us who want it."

Then he slides the book he had in his hand my way. "This one isn't dog-eared."

"Yes, forgive me. I haven't suffered through *all* of them yet. I've been a tad busy."

He taps the book. "That's the one to read."

"Why?"

"Because I think this one has a character you'll identify with."

"Unlikely." I rarely identify with anyone.

"He has highly specialized interests, is blunt to a fault, and may actually be more emotionally constipated than you."

"Give me that." I look at the back of the book, scanning it.

"Give it a chance," Viggo says. "Reading a book is just like opening your heart to someone. You won't know if you'll connect until you try."

After having read the back cover, I set down the book, unsettled. I'm not so sure I like the idea of reading about someone I identify with after all.

"*Now* do you want to tell me about Peach Panties?" he asks. "Because I see your gears turning. You're thinking about them." He taps the book. "Thinking about this."

"No."

He groans loudly, making Oliver snort-snuffle in his sleep and then flop onto his back. "Come on, man. Denial is not a way to live."

"Would you kindly use your mouth for that peppermint tea I made you, and stop talking already?"

"You're thinking about this, about *someone*, and I will have that information out of you, Axel Jakob, if it's the last thing I—"

"Is there breakfast?" Ollie asks out of fucking nowhere.

Viggo and I both jump a foot in our chairs.

"Jesus Christmas Christ," Viggo snaps, hand on his heart. "What is wrong with you? Are you a vampire from another life?"

Oliver stands at the foot of the bed, scratching his stomach. "Geez. All I did was get out of bed," he mumbles. Then he blinks, rubbing his eyes. "What's V doing here?"

"I followed your trail," Viggo tells him. "You didn't answer my calls. What's going on?"

Ollie's expression shutters. "I don't want to talk about it."

"Okay." Viggo lifts his hands in surrender. "We don't have to talk about it. *Yet*. But we're going to talk about it. About how you're AWOL from school and the team right now, which is so un-you, it's scary."

"I'm not talking about it," Oliver says, eyeing the kitchen hopefully. "But you will make me feel better if some *pannkakor* appear after my shower."

"You and your hollow leg," I mutter, standing and taking my

coffee mug with me. "Go shower. You smell like airplane air and cafeteria food."

Viggo snorts. "This is who you run to? The comforting arms and words of Axel?"

"Misery loves company," I tell him.

Oliver smiles my way as he watches me pull out ingredients for pancakes. I'm trying desperately not to remember the day I taught Rooney how to make them. "He hugged me last night," Oliver gloats.

Viggo gasps and throws me a wounded glance.

"It was extenuating circumstances," I state for the record, scooping out flour.

"What do I have to do to earn a hug?" Viggo demands.

"If you ever fly a thousand miles and arrive on my doorstep in tears, I'll hug you, Viggo."

"*Psh*. Easy. I already flew a thousand miles up here. Now I just need some tears, which is—" He blinks, sniffles a little, and don't you know, his eyes are glistening. "Look. I'm in tears. Practically a puddle."

I throw a stick of butter at his head. "Get off your ass and help me with these pancakes."

# FOURTEEN

# *Rooney*

Playlist: "Cover Me in Sunshine,"
P!nk and Willow Sage Hart

Sunrise tips over the horizon and spills a dozen blazing shades of orange and yellow. Peering up at the trees, I watch the cool blue sky glow brighter against a lacework of half-bare branches, and what leaves remain are sunlit and dancing in the wind like tiny tongues of fire. I'm trying very hard not to miss Axel and remember him gazing at the sunset on our wedding-day hike. I'm trying not to think too deeply about the fact that he shared his favorite place with me.

And then my phone buzzes on the coffee table. I pick it up and swipe it open. A smile lifts my cheeks as I read Axel's message.

Thank you for telling me you got there safely.
Sorry I'm just responding. Oliver showed up
last night out of nowhere (very on-brand for
him) & by the time I fed him, which took
hours (also very on-brand for him), & got a
chance to look at my phone, it was so late, I
didn't want to risk waking you up.

"Shit," I mutter.

What's he doing there? I type. Did he notice the construction?

He's thankfully completely ignorant of home reno work, Ax

writes, or what it entails, so I'm in the clear. As for why he's here, I'm not sure. Whatever it is, I think he just needed a break from it.

I smile at my screen as a new message from him comes in: By the way, Harry says hi.

There's a photo of the dog, brown eyes wide, snout angling toward the camera lens. But what makes my heart twirl in my chest is that it's a selfie, Axel's lean, muscly forearm wrapped around him. It's only from his mouth down that I can see, but I drink in every detail. The shadow of the beard he keeps neglecting to shave because he literally seems to work sunrise to sunset until he collapses in that tent. The long stretch of his throat and the shadowy hollow at the bottom that I definitely have not fantasized about tracing with my tongue.

I hover over the photo and hit save.

Tell Harry hi, I type, and that I miss him.

Three dots dance right away, and my heart spins like a top.

Harry said he misses you, too.

"Cute dog."

I yelp and drop my phone like it's a hot potato. Willa gives me a curious look as she sets my tea on the coffee table, then joins me on the porch swing that Ryder built.

"Thanks," I say in my best chipper voice.

"You okay?" she asks.

I nod. "Yep. Totally. Absolutely."

Willa searches my eyes for a minute before seeming to decide I'm just being my marginally weird self. Sighing, she sets her head on my shoulder as we gaze out at the sunrise from her screened-in porch. "I'm so happy you're here," she says.

"Me too," I tell her. "I'm glad I found the place. Eventually."

She snorts, then sips her coffee. "You poor woman. I told you I was happy to come to you, but you are so stubborn."

"Takes one to know one."

We clink mugs, and I sip my tea, missing coffee but knowing that when my stomach's throwing a fit, coffee is the last thing I need. That bottle of wine we drank and the unexpectedly spicy fusion food we ate last night, on top of my anxiety about coming clean with Willa about my sickness, has my stomach spasming uncomfortably.

"Rooney?" Willa says, setting her hand on my knee. "Where'd you go?"

I meet her eyes, wide set and brown, sparkling with tiny flecks of gold and amber. Her wild waves are in a messy bun on her head, and when she smiles at me, I feel a flood of tenderness for my best friend, the closest thing to a sister that I'll ever have. I'm so scared that she's going to be hurt by this confession, but waiting is only going to make it worse. It's time to suck it up and be honest.

"I have something to tell you."

Willa tips her head. She squeezes my knee, then releases it, cupping her coffee mug in both hands. "I'm listening."

"First of all, I want you to know how sorry I am for keeping this from you. I didn't want to, but I didn't know how to be the friend I wanted to be and tell you the truth."

Her brow furrows in confusion. "Rooney, what are you talking about?"

I swallow the lump in my throat and force the words out. "You know how we are. We have this *Gilmore Girls*, Lorelai-and-Rory love. Me, juggling too much, with complicated, albeit well-meaning, bougie parents. You, kicking ass at your dream and forging your own path. We lean on each other hard and eat shitty food together and talk too much and hug like we're kids instead of full-grown women, with reckless, bone-squishing abandon."

Willa nods. "I know. And I love you for it."

I nod, too, and blink away tears. "And I . . . wanted to protect you. I didn't want to worry you when your mom was so sick, when you were carrying so much already. You didn't need someone else you loved weighing on your mind, not when this wasn't going anywhere for me. Because what I'm dealing with is here to stay. It's chronic."

"Rooney." She grips my hand and squeezes gently. "What is it?"

I explain the disease, how I got diagnosed at the beginning of high school, and by the time we were in college, I was in clinical remission. I tell her how the meds were doing their thing, and my worst symptoms weren't present, so I took a chance.

"I reasoned it would either stay that way," I explain, "and I would stick to what I told you, which was that I had a sensitive stomach, or I'd get sicker, and I'd tell you because I'd have to at that point. I had a few minor episodes, but I passed those off as going home and spending a few days with my parents. I'm really sorry I kept it from you, but I hope you understand that I was only trying not to add another burden to your life unless absolutely necessary."

Willa opens her mouth, but I barrel on.

"Plus, it's really not a big deal. I mean, lots of people—over one hundred thirty million, actually—live with chronic illness in the United States alone. Did you know that? I mean, more than *fifty percent* of Americans are chronically ill. It's not ideal, but I'm honestly fine. I'm okay—"

"Rooney." Willa cuts me off and squeezes my hand. "Take a deep breath."

I do.

"I want to hug you really hard," she says, blinking away tears. "But I feel like I shouldn't be squeezing the crap out of you if you're not feeling so good."

"Probably not. Unless you want to risk squeezing the actual crap out of me."

There's a long pause. Then the first burst of Willa's laughter, bright and loud. "Oh my God. I'm the worst."

"Laugh it up, asshole! Actually, my *asshole* is the asshole."

"Rooney!" she shrieks, laughing harder. We're both laughing now, and the sound is threaded with tears, too—the cry-laugh we've shared plenty of times since we met freshman year. And that's the best kind of friendship, isn't it? Friendship that lets laughter and tears hold hands, where grief and gratitude can be friends, not enemies.

The sun climbs higher past the horizon, and a new stretch of light reaches us. As our laughter fades, Willa's expression turns serious. She sets her hands on either side of my face and says, "I wish you hadn't kept this from me. But I love you so hard, and I know all you wanted was to protect me when—" She swallows and blinks away tears. "When my life was falling apart."

I nod. "I didn't want you to worry. Then. Now. Ever. Please don't, Willa. I'm really okay—"

"You don't *have* to be," she says firmly. "You don't have to be 'okay' for us to be okay, Rooney. You are allowed to have a tough time and be in pain, just like you made space for me to do so for fucking years."

I wipe my eyes as tears spill over. "I just never want you to worry."

"I will," she says gently, holding my gaze. "And that's okay, too. You're not responsible for my feelings. I get to worry about you because I love you. And I will say that these past few years of therapy have helped me with more than grief and the shit from childhood. They've helped me cope with all kinds of challenges that come when trying to have healthy relationships. Managing my concern for my best friend just got added to that list, and that's a *good* thing."

I hang my head and take a deep breath. "You're making me feel like *I* need therapy."

"Oh, you do," Willa says as she sits back. "Everyone does. Therapy should be as commonplace as annual physicals and regular dental cleanings. How have you *not* been in therapy? You're the one who convinced me to go."

"Ugh." I prop my mug on my stomach, enjoying the comfort of heat seeping through my shirt. "I keep telling myself that I will. But then I've been so busy with law school, and before that it was soccer and undergrad. I've always had an excuse to avoid it. Because if I go, then I have to talk about Margo. And Jack. And my dysfunctional childhood. And I really don't want to. I know it needs to happen, though."

Willa sips her coffee and nods. "Parents are complicated. Trust me, I know it's not fun talking through this shit. I've had to work through the stuff my mom said and modeled that was unhealthy, and it's hard to dig into, especially when she's not here to hash it out with me, but it's worth it. It's made me a better person."

Glancing over at Willa, I tell her, "I'm proud of you."

"I'm proud of myself, too," she says.

"And I'm sorry for making our girl time a bit of a downer."

"You didn't, Roo." She smiles gently. "I want to be here for you. The way you were there for me all through college. I mean, God, remember after Mom died? You literally had to walk me to the shower because I got so depressed, I wasn't even bathing myself."

"But that's diff—"

"It's *not* different. It's being human. This is existence. This is friendship. We love each other. We take turns holding each other up."

I stare down at my tea and sigh heavily. "You're right." Glancing up at her, I meet her eyes and pout-frown. "I'm sorry I kept it from you. Forgive me?"

She uses her pointer and thumb to turn my frown upside down and smiles back at me. "Forgiven. I'm touched by why you kept it from me, but I wish I'd known. Because then I could have been a better friend to *you*."

I give her a hug. "You're an incredible friend."

She hugs me back, then pulls away. "Well, I'd say most of the time I'm not too shabby, but . . . I do owe you an apology for one of my less-than-stellar moments."

"What do you mean?"

She clears her throat and smiles tightly. "I talked about it with my therapist, and while I'm pretty sure it made her laugh—she hid it behind a cough—she did tell me I can't puppeteer people's lives with meddling. Even if it's, like, a Bergman rite of initiation. So . . . I'm sorry about the charades game back in September. The girls—ladies, that is—well, we sort of . . . planted that 'kiss' clue when it was your turn."

"I've figured that out. What I haven't figured out is *why*. You thought after I attacked Axel's mouth, we'd just ride off into the sunset together?"

"I'm sorry," she says a little desperately. "It's just, you two have been dancing around each other for *years*. We thought maybe just the littlest nudge was all you needed. . . ." Her voice dies off as she looks at me. "I'm not going to make excuses. I'm just going to say sorry. I'm sorry for trying to push you two together because I selfishly want you to be a part of our family for the rest of our lives. More than anything, of course, what I really want is your happiness, and if that's not going to come from this sexual-tension thing you and Axel have that I swear turns the room ten degrees hotter every time you're both in it, then I will respect that."

I arch an eyebrow. "And the A-frame? You sent me up there so I could crash into him—literally, I'll add—and have an adorable meet-cute take two, but I'm here to tell you, it just made it even more awkward, which I was very sure was impossible."

"That!" Willa sits up and sets down her coffee. "That I can defend myself on. Ry said Axel's told him repeatedly he just stays in his cabin and paints, that he doesn't even mess with the A-frame at all. So, yes, I knew it was his stint there, but I was pretty sure you two wouldn't cross paths."

My eyebrow arches higher. Willa bats her eyelashes. "I mean—" She laughs nervously. "Maybe I thought you might bump into each other on a sun-dappled walk in the woods, but—"

I palm her forehead, sending her tumbling back. "You read too many romance novels."

"It's Viggo's fault!" she says, scrambling upright. "He's got me hooked. *Hot* historical romance, Rooney, I swear to God, you'll never look back. Ryder's not complaining, if you know what I'm saying."

Our laughter fills the air, then fades, and Willa takes my hand again, holding tight.

"Forgive me, too?" she asks.

I nod. "Forgiven."

Willa offers me her pinkie. "Let's promise. No more interfering. No more secrets."

I hook pinkies with her and cross my toes.

This sucks. I don't want to lie to her anymore, but I can't tell her about marrying Axel. Even though I want to pour it all out, to tell her about the tiny moments between us that have made me see the tenderness beneath his gruff exterior, that make me wonder what it would be like to see even more of him.

As much as I want to, this isn't my secret to tell.

"Promise," I tell her. Pinkies unfurled, we hug gentler but still just right. And then we sit back and face a sunrise, the world's daily reminder of a fresh start.

***

"Are you happy up here?" I ask.

Willa snaps a bite off her Twizzler and whirls the remaining licorice stick in a circle, smiling into the middle distance. "So happy. I love the weather, the hiking. I love being somewhere that makes Ryder happy, too. I wish I didn't travel so much, but I'd do that no matter where we lived. I just miss him awfully when I'm gone, but . . . it makes reuniting extra sweet."

"I'm glad, Willa." I pop a gummy worm in my mouth and chew before diving my hand into the bag again.

"Subject change," she announces around her bite of licorice. Glancing over at me from our spots on the porch swing we've barely left all day, she says, "*Have* you and Axel hung out? I'm not pressuring, just curious, because when we planned this, you said he told you he has projects to handle at the A-frame, meaning you *have* talked at least a little, not that it needs to mean anything more than—"

"Simmer down, sailor." I pat her hand. "We've hung out a smidge."

This isn't a lie. While basically cohabitating for over two weeks, we've spent very little time together. I mean, sure, the time we *have* spent together has been . . . intense, but I can't exactly explain the nature of that, now can I?

Willa's frowning at me when I meet her eyes. "That's all I get?"

"Yep."

"Do we need to be drunk to talk about this? Because if so, we gotta start now so I don't go to bed wasted and wake up hungover tomorrow."

"No more alcohol," I groan. "We did enough damage with that

wine last night. And drunk or not, I've got nothing more to say about Axel."

"Fine," she says sadly. "I guess it's for the best. I have a bitch of a schedule for conditioning and practice tomorrow."

I smile. "I can't wait to watch."

"Watch me die a thousand deaths, you mean. She makes me run so fucking much." Willa's words are misery, but her face is pure happiness. Professional athletes are weird, wonderful creatures. "We can get wrecked tomorrow night if necessary, because then I'm off."

"I think last night was enough wreckage for me."

"Seriously? We're getting tame in our old age. Our wildest activities last night were taking photos with weird Snapchat filters, and you dancing around in your underwear to Harry Styles."

I give her my *How rude!* face. "First of all, *you* were dancing, too, on this coffee table, I'll add. And *I* was wearing my sleepy T-shirt that goes to my knees. There's none of my drunk nudist dancing with the lumberjack in the house."

"Speaking of that, the lumberjack"—this is Willa's nickname for bearded, outdoorsy Ryder—"offered to make himself scarce whenever we needed while you're here, so you may get plastered and do whatever your nudist heart desires so long as I'm too drunk to remember your nakedness. He said he could head up to the A-frame and see how Axel's doing—"

Panic hits me as I process what she's said. I bring the swinging sofa to a screeching halt, which sends Willa bouncing back, then falling off the thing.

I burst out in laughter as she hits the ground. "Shit, Willa. Are you okay?"

Down on the floor, she's wheezing, she's laughing so hard.

"Here." I offer her my hand. "Come on. Get up—*ack!*"

Willa yanks me to the ground. I flip over top of her, landing on my back beside her with a *thud* as laughter leaves us in cackles.

After a minute, Willa gropes around, finds her lost Twizzler, then goes to take another bite.

"Gross!" I yell, yanking it from her hand before she can chomp down. I toss it on the coffee table, then fish around the bag for a new one.

"That was a perfectly good Twizzler!"

I smack her on the shoulder with the fresh licorice. "You didn't study microbiology. Trust me when I say what's on your feet is on the ground and what's on the ground is on the Twizzler, and what's on the Twizzler is not what you want in your mouth."

She narrows her eyes at me and bites off the end of the Twizzler with a brutal *snap*. "Why'd you crash the sofa? I mentioned Ryder visiting Axel, and you short-circuited."

I yank a Twizzler from the bag—contains wheat, so none for me—and make myself a red licorice handlebar mustache. "You *mustache* so many questions."

She bends her Twizzler in the middle and gives herself the world's biggest licorice unibrow. "I'm being serious."

"Willa," I groan. Peeling the Twizzler from my face and avoiding her eyes, I twist it into an infinity symbol. I can't tell her everything about us, which sucks—because, ya know, newfound promise of transparency—but I can tell her something, I guess.

"Axel has been . . . kind while I've been there. Not around a lot, but when he is, he's kind. We've spent some time together and talked a little—"

*Got married. Made pancakes. Kept a skunk vigil. Made out. Held hands. You know, as one does with the man for whom you hold an insatiable, lusty torch.*

Yeah, can't tell her that.

"You have?" she asks quietly. And I hear it in her voice. Hope. Thinly veiled hope.

I sigh and turn my head, meeting her eyes. "We're just *barely* friends, Willa. And while he's been a gracious host, I think he could use some solitude now that I'm gone. Tell the lumberjack to stay, please?"

Flipping her Twizzler so that it rests across her mouth, Willa gives me a wide licorice smile. "You got it, Roo."

# FIFTEEN

# *Axel*

Playlist: "That's What's Up,"
Edward Sharpe & the Magnetic Zeros

"You missed one." I point to a single maple leaf that's dropped to the grass. Viggo looks like he's contemplating murder. Which is how I want him: pissed enough to leave. He and Oliver have been here for a day and a half now, Oliver demanding anything to keep his mind off whatever or whoever has made him miserable at school, Viggo trying to show Ollie solidarity while avoiding Mom's calls.

I keep throwing increasingly torturous tasks their way, because I can't figure out what else might scare them off. Tomorrow the crew is back to work, and I only have a day and a half until Rooney's back. There's no way I'm risking the man cubs overlapping time with any of them.

Oliver wordlessly rakes that lone leaf into his pile. I'm starting to worry a bit. He's not precisely a smiley sunshine like my brother Ren, but Oliver has this . . . unbridled confidence in life. Always motivated, always moving toward his next goal, he lives with a confident, carefree optimism that life will go his way. This despondent, defeated guy raking leaves, forcing a smile at Viggo's antics that are absolutely failing to make him laugh, is nothing like the Ollie I know.

Viggo frowns at Oliver—I think sharing my concern. "Ollie. Let's steal Ax's Jeep and go to Shepard's, buy a cake. Leave the evil mastermind before he thinks of any other hellish landscaping projects for us."

Oliver shakes his head. "No, thanks, V."

"What? No *cake*? Oliver—"

"Just—" Oliver drops the rake and digs his palms against his eyes. "Just let me be sad, Viggo."

"You've been sad. Now it's time for anger. We're going to process this shit and move forward." Viggo dusts off his hands, strolls toward Oliver, and yanks him by the shirt.

"I don't want to move forward," Oliver groans. "I want to wallow. I want to drown in the misery that there's no escaping him when he's in half of my classes and on the *fucking* team!"

Well. Now we're getting somewhere. Oliver has refused to discuss what's upsetting him. Until now.

"That's it," Viggo says, dragging him toward the nearby tree. "Now climb up there, give a good scream, and jump. Get it out of your system."

Oliver yanks himself out of Viggo's grip, folds his arms across his chest, and scowls. He looks eight all over again. "No."

"Fine." Viggo shrugs, climbing ahead of him. "I'll go first."

Oliver's eye twitches. His hands drop to his hips and turn white at the knuckles. He's so like Ryder right now, with that short blond ponytail, the newfound gravity in his expression. "Goddammit," he mutters, climbing the tree and quickly outpacing Viggo. "*I'm* going first."

Viggo grins before quickly hiding it behind a competitive, *don't fuck with me* growl. "No way, Oliver. I'm going fir—"

Oliver shoves past him, walks to the end of the branch like it's a tightrope, and on a high-pitched shriek, does a cannonball into the massive pile of leaves beneath him.

Viggo whoops, then follows, landing in a noticeably less cushy part of the pile with a *thud* that makes me wince.

"Oh God," Viggo groans from inside the leaves. "I'm getting too old for this."

Harry, who's been especially up my ass since Rooney left, whines, head tipped as he stares at Viggo and Oliver.

"Don't worry," I tell him, scratching behind his ears. "They're clowns, but highly resilient clowns. They'll be fine."

He whines again.

"I mean, Viggo might have broken something, but that's not my problem. He's got to learn his lesson someday."

"I'm okay!" Viggo calls, crawling upright. "Just maybe a minor hairline sprain of my spine."

"You dipshit." Oliver sits up and pulls leaves out of his hair. "You can't sustain a hairline sprain."

Oliver not only somehow manages to play Division I soccer for UCLA, but is also on a premed track and seriously considering medical school, meaning he survives on despicably little sleep and functions like a walking, talking, soccer-ball-juggling *Gray's Anatomy*. The book, not the medical drama that my dad, a physician, and my sister Freya, a physical therapist, have made many a night out of hate-watching, booing as they lobbed popcorn at the screen for its countless medical inaccuracies.

"Whatever. The point is, I'm hurt," Viggo says pathetically.

Oliver just shakes his head and starts to climb out of the leaves, but before he can escape, Viggo launches himself at Ollie's ankles and knocks him back down. Oliver sits up from the massive pile, glowering at Viggo, fresh leaves caught in his hair.

"You know you want to pummel me," Viggo says. "C'mon, get it out of your system. I can take it."

Oliver's glower deepens. "I don't want to fight."

"Well, you can't make love," Viggo says. "Seeing as some jackass clearly did a number on you—"

"Argh!" Oliver launches himself at Viggo, and they roll through the leaf pile so violently, a Charles Schulz *Peanuts* cloud of chaos hovers in the air above them.

Harry the dog whines again. "Really, Harry, they're fine," I reassure him. "They've been doing this since Oliver could crawl."

The dog peers up at me, setting a paw on my hip. I wrap my hand around it, shake it, then set it down and pet his head. When I glance up, Oliver's got Viggo in a headlock, the beginning of a smile brightening his face.

I roll my shoulders, a restless tightness tugging them, constricting my ribs. The dog beside me. My brothers in the yard. I should feel content. And yet . . . I'm not.

And I can't stop thinking about Rooney.

I thought maybe it was just the first day, the fact that change unsettles me and Rooney leaving after two weeks of always being in the periphery of my awareness, if not front and center, was definitely *change*.

But two days have passed, and I'm not better. In fact, I think I'm worse.

Unable to stop myself, I pull out my phone, snap a photo of the man cubs in mayhem mode, then text it to Rooney.

Three dots pop up almost immediately, and my heart starts to pound like a bass drum in my chest.

Wait, Viggo's there now?? she asks. What are they doing?

Torturing me, I type back. But I gave them an acre of leaves to rake with tools from 1998 that have half their tines missing, so things are shaping up nicely.

LOL, she responds. What I'd give to see that.

I text her a few more live-action shots, some from earlier while they were raking, some that I snap now as they tumble through the leaves.

Wow, her message reads. That is incredible. And they actually did it all. Just shows how much they love you and that house. You're giving them a lot in making the place its best self again.

I stare down at her words, a deep, quiet warmth filling my chest. All possible because you went along with this marriage, I type.

You made it very easy to propose, she answers.

I swallow roughly. That ache in my chest comes thundering back.

Harry's whine is a welcome distraction. I turn and snap a photo of him, then send it to her. Harry says he still misses you.

I still miss him, she answers. I've seen everyone but you, so far. I'm worried you sustained a construction injury & you're hiding it from me.

I roll my shoulders, self-conscious. I didn't sustain an injury.

I'm a scientist & three-quarters lawyer. I need
proof.

"Dammit," I mumble, raking a hand through my hair. But as much as I'm self-conscious, I'm also a tiny bit pleased she's demanding a selfie.

Sighing, I flip the phone's camera, eyes narrowed a little against the sun.

"Taking some headshots for Peach Panties?" Viggo yells.

I flash him the middle finger, snap the shot, then send it before I can analyze it or tell myself it even matters how I look.

See? I type. Uninjured.

The photo and text show "Read." But there's no response for what feels like a decade. Then Rooney finally writes back two words: Those glasses.

I frown as I type, What about them? You don't like them?

LIKE THEM, she texts. They are sex in spectacle form.

Seeing those words, I nearly drop the phone.

I'm sorry, she says before I can respond. I had to be honest. Objectively, purely objectively, those glasses do great things for you, Ax. Once you're out of your brutally transactional first marriage, we're sending you into the dating world, glasses on. You'll have to peel people off of you.

I shudder. The idea of that is repulsive, of course, but it's the fact that she's so ready to match me up with someone else that rankles.

No, thank you, I type.

The dots appear. Disappear. Appear. Then: Party pooper. Will the man cubs be there or gone when I get back? Do I need a story to explain myself?

I glance up at Oliver, who's finally laughing, and Viggo, who's shrieking so high, it makes Harry's ears pin back as Oliver hits his tickle spot.

They'll be gone by then. I'll make sure of it.

---

"You broke me," Viggo says, easing out of the car in front of the drop-off zone for Alaska Air.

"That kind of work is character building," I tell him as I pull his suitcase out of the Jeep. "Now I can be a reference when you decide to give landscaping a try."

He glares at me darkly. "Never will I ever."

Amused, I set his suitcase at his feet. "Thank you for your help, V."

"Yeah, yeah," he says.

He's reaching for his suitcase when I yank him into my arms and give him a hard squeeze. After a moment's delay, he slowly wraps his arms around me and holds them still. As hugs go, it's pretty good.

"Thanks . . . for what you said yesterday," I tell him. "It meant a lot." Pulling away, I yank the handle up from his suitcase. "Now get out of here. Wear your seat belt on the plane. And text when you're back."

Viggo grins. "You're such a dad. When are you giving me nieces and nephews—"

"Go. Away. Now." I shove him gently, right into Oliver's arms. They hug, exchanging words as they do, then step apart.

Viggo yanks his suitcase up off the curb and says to me, "Take care of him. Make sure he eats."

"Jesus, guys," Oliver groans.

I open the car door and nod. "I've got it in hand."

On a final wave, Viggo jogs into the airport, disappearing from sight. Oliver and I slip into the car, silence thick in the air as I pull into the slow-moving drop-off traffic.

"It's so quiet without him," he says, head resting on the window glass.

I shift gears and accelerate. "Considering he never shuts up."

Oliver huffs a laugh. "He's a pain in the ass, but he's our pain in the ass."

"That he is."

Oliver frowns when I take a turn in the opposite direction of the A-frame. While I managed to scare Viggo into an evening flight with the threat of more landscaping projects tomorrow, Oliver scheduled his flight for early tomorrow morning because he wanted to stay away as long as possible before he's due back for an exam. "Where are we going?" he asks.

"Where do you think?"

His eyes light up as I take the next turn. "Oh my God, seriously?"

"I told Viggo I'd take care of you."

It's not a long drive from the airport to Pier 57. We find parking, then walk down and order dinner. The younger siblings have fewer memories of living in the area, but certain ritual treats are cemented in their brains. Anything we wanted to eat and a ride on the wheel is one of them.

Oliver peers up at the city's iconic Ferris wheel lit up and glowing against the evening sky. Crab-and-shrimp roll in hand, he smiles like a kid at Christmas. "Thanks for this, Ax."

Mouth full of fried fish, I nod. "'Course."

"You didn't have to do it, driving V and me around Seattle, taking me to my favorite place, when you've got stuff to do. I really appreciate it."

I glance his way. "I know I'm not always very available, and I moved back here as soon as I could, but I do want to see you, Oliver. I just . . . don't always have it in me. I'm glad I did this time."

Oliver pauses midchew, then slowly resumes and swallows. "Axel, you know I understand. Viggo and I give you hell about moving back to Washington, but we're happy you're here. Because it's where *you're* happy. We were just telling you in our ass-backwards way that we miss you."

A weird lump settles in my throat as I peer down at my food. "I miss you, too."

"In that case, I should come up here more often." Ollie smiles, then bites into his roll. "Maybe I'll move in with you."

"Not a chance in hell. I'm the recluse in the woods, and it's going to stay that way."

He tips his head, examining me. "I'm not judging, asking you this, but do you want to be on your own, *forever*?"

I set down my food and glance out at the water because it's easier to say shit like this with the wind in my face and a break from eye contact. "I'm not sure. Whether or not it's what I want, there are parts of relationships I'm not great at, and being with me means signing up for a simple, private existence. I'll never be someone who has a ton of friends or a large social circle. When I'm selling art, doing shows, I don't even have energy for my best friends. It's . . ." I shrug. "It's not what most people want."

"Someone will," Oliver says, smiling into the wind as it whips his hair across his face. "I know it."

First Viggo's romance pep talk. Now Oliver and his unwavering confidence. It makes me feel . . . strange. In a good way. In an unnerving way. I point up at the wheel. "Don't you have a giant bucket to ride?"

"Hell yeah! Come ride it with me."

"No, thank you," I tell him. "The only heights I like are the ones I climb."

"Also, don't think I didn't notice you changed the subject," he says, before he tears off another bite.

"I redirected us. We're not here to talk about me. We're here so you can eat your feelings and talk about your stuff."

Oliver groans around his mouthful. "I don't want to talk about my stuff. I want to get away from it."

"Well, Viggo's gone, so no one's going to force you to do otherwise. But . . ." I clear my throat and shrug. "If that changes, you know, when you're back in LA, I'm here. Just texts? I can text all day. But phone calls"—I grimace—"only in emergencies."

Popping the last of his roll into his mouth, Oliver grins. "Texts it is."

# SIXTEEN

# Rooney

Playlist: "Waiting for You," The Aces

After leaving Willa's with a tentative promise to "do my best" to attend Thanksgiving, I hop into Bennett's Subaru and get on the road. It's a little easier this time, retracing my steps, but it's still nerve-racking.

And then it goes from nerve-racking to nuclear disaster when my stomach decides it's one of those times when I have thirty seconds to find a bathroom.

On the highway.

Have you truly experienced nature until you've shit your brains out in a field? I think not. I'm telling myself there are silver linings to my roadside mishap. It has a) given me outdoorsy cred that I was sorely lacking and b) brought me the tiny kitten that's currently meowing from the passenger seat floor of Bennett's car.

Having dealt with my traumatic pit stop (this is not an uncommon reality for people with stomach issues like mine, meaning I always have the essentials to handle it, waiting in my bag), I was walking back to the car and nearly tripped over a tiny gray fluff-ball, meowing all by herself in the tall grass. I scooped her up, and we wandered around for a while, her meowing, me setting her down periodically to let her sniff in the hopes that she'd lead me to her siblings and mother. But there wasn't a single sign that they were anywhere nearby. I almost left her. I didn't want to take her from her family, but what was I supposed to do?

It was leave her for imminent death by one of the many birds of prey that swooped overhead as we carried out our search, or bring her home—that is, back to the cabin.

It's with an odd sense of homecoming that I park outside the A-frame, staring up at it and knowing nothing is like it was when I first got here. My heart does a little leap as I remember walking up the steps, letting myself in, tumbling into Axel, and having the world's most awkward post-kiss reunion.

Just a few weeks have passed, and so much is different. Not the least of which is the tiny, fuzzy kitten blinking up at me.

"Meow," she says as I open up the passenger door and tuck her in my arms. Rather than stash her in Axel's home without his permission, I figure we'll try to find him first and make introductions, wow him with our foresight in stopping at the mom-and-pop store on our way back and buying compostable cat litter and organic wet kitten food. And if *that* doesn't impress him, I just have to hope two pairs of big, sad blue eyes will be enough to convince him to keep her.

We walk around the A-frame, searching for Axel. Oddly, it's only just dinnertime, and the crew isn't here. I expected to walk into another big dinner, but no one's around.

"Meow," she says again. It's the tiniest meow I've ever heard.

I kiss her head. "I love you, too. I'm not sure what you're named, but I'll think of something good."

She's pale gray with big blue eyes, so adorably small and fluffy, it shouldn't be possible.

Walking around the house, we get to the addition on the back end of the A-frame, which Axel explained was the selling point for his parents and their growing family when they bought the place.

Calling Axel's name, I try the first bedroom door. The door swings open and makes me stop in my tracks. The view is breathtaking. Sunlight bouncing off the lake, dwindling autumn foliage dappled with evergreens. Light streams in through the windows and turns the floors butterscotch. Not for the first time in these past few weeks, I think I could get used to living somewhere this beautiful all the time.

"Meow," says the cat again.

I snap out of my daydreaming and hug her gently. "You're right. Time to take you to the little house and set up your litter. If anyone can empathize with the stress of being in a no-potty zone, it's me."

"Meow," she agrees. Then she starts fidgeting, clawing at my arms. She seems suddenly deeply distressed.

"Meow!" she says. *Loudly.*

The sound strikes my heart like an arrow. "What's the matter, sweetie?"

"MEOW!" she says again. I'm not really sure how it's anatomically possible for a sound that large to come from such a small kitten. She also sounds like she's being skinned alive.

I rush down the stairs with her safe in my arms. She lets out another ear-splitting, "MEOWWWWW!"

"Oh, sweet pea! What's wrong?" My baby talk is absurd, but my heart's wrecked, and the kitten sounds wrecked, too. "It's okay. I've got you."

"Meow?" she says, tiny paw on my arm.

My insides are putty. If this is what pets do, what's going to happen if I ever have babies? Will I dissolve into a puddle of feelings? How will I survive this?

"Oof."

I've walked right into a very solid wall. A warm, good-smelling wall. My eyes process what they're seeing—a deep blue plaid flannel, threaded with green, rolled up at his forearms. A few buttons undone, a delicious wedge of man chest and—

My smile is ridiculously wide, but I'm helpless to stop it. "Hi."

Axel frowns down at the tiny, sweet creature nestled in my arms. Who I think might be peeing on me. I dash past him across the porch, rush down the steps, and set the cat in a little patch of grass. She instantly squats and poops.

"Well," I tell her. "Like mother, like daughter."

Axel's footsteps cross the porch. He leans on the railing. "What is that?"

"A kitten."

Our eyes meet, and it's like lightning, jolting my body.

"I can see that," he says dryly, staring back down at the kitten, who's scuffing her tiny paws and dancing away from a deuce that, like her meow, I'm shocked could come from such a little body. As Axel shoves his hands in his pockets, I notice a blue-green streak of paint on the side of his wrist. It feels oddly intimate. "You know what I meant," he says.

Sitting on the top porch step, I tell him, "I found her on the side of the road. I couldn't leave her there."

Small, gray, and absurdly fluffy, she waddles like an oversized ball of dust up the steps and pounces on Axel's boot. Then she glances up at him and lets out the tiniest meow in the history of meows.

She and I both know what she's capable of, but she's pulling out all the cute stops.

"She likes you," I tell him as she attacks his shoelaces with gusto, yanking so hard, she falls backward with a little *thump*.

Axel crosses his arms and stares down at her, one eyebrow arching. "She likes shoelaces."

"Ah, but they're *your* shoelaces."

Meowing, she climbs onto his boot again and stretches upward, setting her miniature paws on his shin.

"See?" I smile as I scratch her tiny cheek. She leans into it but stays firmly planted on Axel's boot. "It's more than just your shoelaces. It's you."

He frowns down at her. "I sincerely doubt that."

She meows again.

"I think she feels at home here." I gesture toward the stunning view in front of us—a smoked-glass gray sky pierced by countless evergreens. "It's beautiful, isn't it?" I singsong to her as she climbs onto my lap and starts purring. "And you're the same color as those gorgeous clouds. You belong here, don't you?"

After a long stretch of silence, Axel says, "Maybe she does."

When I glance up, he's not looking at the kitten. He's looking at me.

There's a thunder boom in my heart. I think I'm imagining things. He was talking about the tiny cat, not me. His gaze dipped to my mouth and stayed there because he's watching for what I say next, not thinking about kissing me senseless.

Except Axel's lowering onto the porch right next to me, long legs stretched down the steps, elbows on his knees. He leans in slightly and our arms brush as he reaches, scratching behind the kitten's ears. Her purr doubles. Another way she and I are similar: the slightest touch from Axel Bergman and we're purring our hearts out.

I breathe in, and dopamine floods my brain with pleasure. He smells like fresh air and that cedar-sage soap and the heat of his body. I want my hands gliding up his skin, sinking into his hair. I want his weight over me, *in* me—

"Where were you?" he asks. His eyes are on my hair, something so close to a smile tipping his mouth.

I lift my hand reflexively, but Axel beats me to it, extracting a small white wildflower from the crown of my head.

Oh, dear. A flower from the field of digestive disaster.

I can't tell him I had a stomach emergency while on my drive home. Well, I can—I just won't. It's too embarrassing. It's one thing to generally explain that you have an IBD, but no one likes the specifics, given everything in the few square feet of the human body between our navel and thighs is taboo. I know—rationally, I know—there's no shame in my disease, but it's hard. It's hard to find the courage to tell him the reality, when I want Axel, when I want to feel attractive to him.

"Rooney?" He spins the flower softly back and forth, pinched between his thumb and forefinger.

"I was in . . . a field. Of . . . wildflowers."

The mouth tip comes even closer to a smile. "I figured that. What field?"

I stare down at the cat, petting her and hoping my hair falling over my face hides this blush of embarrassment. "A gal needs her secrets."

He's quiet. I feel his eyes on me. So I keep my eyes on the cat, praying he drops it.

Mercifully, he does.

"How—" He clears his throat, then starts scratching under the kitten's chin. She stretches her tiny face toward him, eyes shut, blissed out. "How was your visit with Willa?"

"Really good. I've missed her. Visiting reminded me how much." The kitten flops onto her back in my lap, arms up, a pose of sleepy surrender. "She keeps telling me they need lawyers in Washington, too."

Axel tenses beside me, then leans a little closer as he pets the kitten's tiny white chest and tummy. "Would you . . . ever want to live up here?" he asks.

"Before this trip, I probably would have said no," I admit. "I'm a SoCal girl. I love my sunshine and hot summers and days reading on the beach, but . . ." I glance up, my gaze poring over his handsome face. "Now that I've seen what this place has to offer, it's tempting."

He swallows roughly, dragging his knuckles across his lips. The movement makes me ache right between my thighs.

And then suddenly that hand is cradling my jaw, his thumb stroking my throat. His mouth brushes mine, a kiss as soft as the wind that whispers around us. A daydream come to life.

Axel pulls away, looking stunned. "I shouldn't have . . . I'm sorry."

"Why not?" I ask him. I hold his eyes, and it's a rare gift to truly see them—vivid green, slivers of amber, summertime leaves dappled with sunlight.

I'm not sure why I asked the question. I just know I need the answer. Why the kisses, the kindness, the care?

*Why?*

His grip intensifies, still gentle, yet desperate. He sighs, the sound of weariness meeting comfort, the bittersweet relief of falling into bed after a long day. "Because I . . . I think I missed you. Because I hate kissing, but I love it when it's you, and that means something. I don't know what, and I wish I knew more, but I do know this," he says roughly, and then he *nuzzles* me. I don't know how else to describe it, this tender nudge of his temple against my cheek, the whisper of his mouth over the shell of my ear. "I want to kiss you so badly, it's obliterated every other thought in my brain. There's nothing but wanting it. Wanting *you*."

I told myself I'd accept only the most direct, unconvoluted language to satisfy my curiosity, my love of systematic order and clearly defined terms. But he gave me poetry. The man of few words, who's so gone for the way the sun paints the world at day's beginning and end, he's terrified he'll fail to do it justice. The man who reduces himself to grunts and distance but draws dog doodles and holds hands. Of course he gave me a complex, heart-wrenching answer.

An answer that's making me face something I haven't wanted to before: how scared I am of that kind of complexity, and why I love the logic I learned in preparation for law school, the objectivity of the scientific method. Relationships are so . . . illogical, and their subjectivity is where I've been hurt. Those gray, messy spaces have taught me you can be loved and yet left, wanted yet regretted. So I've avoided them. Because I haven't wanted to get hurt again.

What does it mean that, right now, the fear of pain dims as I contemplate the pleasure I could feel with Axel? As I look at him, I feel a thousand new nerve endings beneath my skin, like everything of me was made to touch and know everything of him. I *want* him.

He's so patient as I deliberate, and yet he never stops touching me—his thumb sliding along my throat, his fingertips sweeping over my jaw. That sharp green gaze settles on my mouth, like my answer is already known, like *yes* is in the air between us.

"I want you, too," I tell him.

The softest groan leaves him as his mouth brushes mine again. Featherlight, reverent. Then deeper and desperate. His hands are in my hair, his tongue tracing my lips, begging me to open up, and I do. And then I moan, a sound for the ache that's in my throat and my breasts and low in my belly, sweet and sharp between my thighs. I fall toward him, anchoring myself on muscles that jump beneath my palms. My touch slides up his thighs and sinks into the butter-soft fabric of his jeans.

Our kisses find a slow, deep rhythm. We share air and breath, and then we're kissing harder, all while a tiny, helpless kitten nestles in my lap, a shower of sun-gold autumn leaves raining down on us. It makes me smile the kind of smile I haven't in years, one that starts at the heart of me and lights up my insides, a dying flame that's found its fuel.

My grip tightens on his thighs as his tongue serenades mine, as Axel's hands leave my hair, drift down my neck, and whisper over my collarbones to my shoulders. He holds me tight and kisses me once more, hard, urgent, before he pulls himself away, breathing ragged and fast.

He looks at me the way I imagine I looked the first time I peeked into a microscope—shocked, riveted, desperate for more—knowing that something I thought was clear and obvious was actually wildly, stunningly complex. That there were endless things to learn and countless possibilities, if only I looked closely enough.

Slowly, he bends his head, his mouth settling at the tender space where my neck and shoulder meet. He presses the faintest kiss there, branding my skin.

"Axel?" I whisper.

He nuzzles my neck, plants another faint kiss along my jaw. "Hm?"

"I think I missed you, too."

## SEVENTEEN

## *Axel*

Playlist: "We're Going Home," Vance Joy

I blame the meddling man cubs for this. I blame Oliver for making me feel just a sliver of hope, and Viggo for that book he recommended that I *might* have read half of last night as I lay in my bed, on top of sheets and pillows that, despite enduring a few days of my brothers, still smelled like twilight in a meadow. Like Rooney.

I sound like a fucking creep about the sheets, but let the record show, I didn't do it on purpose—I just crashed on the bed after I cleaned up from dinner and started reading. Before I knew it, I'd fallen asleep, and then I was dreaming about what you'd expect after reading half of a hot romance novel while bathed in the scent of the woman you're always hard for, always thinking about, always wanting.

Wanting so badly, you kiss her without asking the moment you see her, then you tell her things you didn't even know you had in you to say.

The sheer, free-falling terror of that. It felt like Rooney caught me only a moment before I hit the hard surface of a brutal rejection. And then I felt weightless, because she said, *I want you, too.*

"Axel?"

"Hm?" I blink, drawn from my thoughts, and peer down at the kitten. Carefully, I scratch her chin. She's out, arms up, sleeping.

That dust ball is too cute. I'm just waiting for it to show its devil side. Something that adorable is too good to be true.

"Can we keep her?" Rooney asks.

*We*. The sound of that word makes a shiver bolt down my spine. But then reality rushes in, reminding me of what's coming. How soon *we* won't exist anymore.

"I'm not sure that's a good idea," I tell her, dropping my hand. "Considering we're only a *we* until you leave in a few weeks."

Rooney pouts. "You might love her by then. She could be best friends with Harry by then—"

"She could have a home by then," I interject, "with Parker and Bennett, because Skyler's been begging for a cat."

She lights up. "Really?"

I sigh heavily. "We'll need to take her to the vet first. Get her used to a litter box."

"I can do that," Rooney says. "I'll be responsible for her. Will you ask Parker and Bennett about adopting her once I'm—" She pauses and frowns, petting the cat. "Once I'm gone?"

*Gone.*

I used to count down the days until she'd be gone, because all I wanted was to survive them. Keep my head down, keep my mouth shut, keep my distance. But now, here I am, surrendering. I want to kiss her when I want—when *she* wants—and touch her and know her just a little, for a little while.

And then let her go.

Because someone so sunshine bright and outgoing will never want forever with a quiet, private grump like me, but maybe she could want me for a while. Long enough to enjoy what I can give her, to give her whatever she needs in her brief escape from the outside world.

And then she'll go back to reality before I can fall short. Before I'm too quiet and not expressive enough. Before I get so absorbed in painting that I make her feel ignored, so reclusive that I frustrate her when she wants to socialize. Before either of us has to experience the painful truth: that I'm not someone she'll want forever.

I watch Rooney as she murmurs to the cat in baby talk, as she grins and the corners of her eyes crinkle happily.

"I'll ask them," I tell her. "About taking the cat."

Rooney peers up and gives me a smile as breathtaking as a sunrise. "Thank you, Axel." Glancing back down at the sleeping creature in her lap, she runs a fingertip down the soft, fuzzy gray fur on the kitten's head. "I can't think of a single name that suits her. What should we call her?"

*We.* That word again. I savor it shamelessly.

"Skugga," I tell her.

She glances my way. "Skugga? Is that Swedish?"

I nod. "It means 'shadow.'" Slipping my finger beneath the kitten's paw, I feel the tiny, velvet pink pads. "I have a feeling she'll be following you everywhere. She'll be your shadow."

"Skugga." Rooney smiles. "I like that."

"Skyler will probably change it. But for now, Skugga suits her."

She laughs. "If Skyler knows you thought of it, she'll love it. She's wild about you. She told me you're her favorite uncle."

Surprise, chased by affection, blooms in my chest. "Parker has more siblings than me. I doubt she really means it."

"It's what she said," Rooney whispers before pressing a kiss to the kitten's head. "You haven't heard her talk about you every night at dinner. Seeing as you're hardly *around* for dinner."

I deserve that barb for my suppertime evasion. Then again, I thought she was insisting I eat with her at the cabin rather than eat by myself out of polite kindness. What if she actually wanted to spend time with me?

No. No, that's not it. Or if it was, maybe it was the fact that

Rooney's a fire hazard in the kitchen, and I'm not, and she knew I could make us a decent meal. Or maybe, like me, this electric *thing* between us is something she's tortured by, and dinner would be a prelude to getting it out of our system.

That thought is one I've been stuck on obsessively since she left. What if, just once, we did it, went all the way, didn't stop at kisses and touching but peeled off our clothes and fucked this right out of each other so we could have some peace already?

Before I can take that thought any further, Rooney's stomach growls loudly. "Hungry?" I ask.

A blush heats her cheeks. "A little."

"C'mon," I tell her. "Let's fix that."

———

Rooney requested something "gentle," which, as she explained through a fresh blush on her cheeks, rules out highly fibrous things like lentils and beans, the ingredients I'd generally use to supplement animal protein, which she also doesn't eat.

I walk through Shepard's, adding food to the cart that already contains cat toys, cat treats, and everything I need for potato leek soup. I add a pound of local bacon, a bunch of spinach, and a dozen eggs for a hot spinach salad that I can make for both of us, hold the bacon for Rooney. I've logged more miles than usual the past few mornings, trying to outrun the gnawing ache of missing her, and I'm starving. Potato leek soup isn't going to cut it.

I try to walk past the sweets, but I can't. I know how much Rooney likes them. I turn down the aisle, picking up more gluten-free flour, cocoa, and a bag of white sugar. I'll make brownies.

Sarah's watching me behind her wire-rimmed glasses, pretending she's reading the Beverly Jenkins novel in her hand. It's the same one Viggo was reading while he was here.

"Viggo pay you a visit?" I ask. Must have been one of his and Oliver's late-night snack runs while they were here.

She lowers the book and gives me a coy smile as I set my items on the counter. "Of course he did. Brought me a new romance novel, as always. Now what about you, heartbreaker?" she says, taking in my items and starting to ring them up. "Another week you're buying gluten-free flour. And—*hm*—ingredients for dessert."

I grit my teeth.

"Why don't you grab a bottle of that local dry Riesling? It's with the chilled wines," she says. "That'll go great with the potato leek soup. Oh, and the red blend for chocolate dessert."

"Wine's not necessary."

Is it? I'm just cooking dinner.

"Suit yourself," she says, ringing up the items. "I'm only pointing out that a nice wine pairing can make it feel special."

"Fine!"

The suffering I endure.

I stroll toward the wine section, grab the recommended bottles, then set them on the counter with a hard *thunk*. "Happy now?"

Her mouth lifts in a smile. "It's not me you want to make happy. It's *her*."

I freeze, hand on my wallet. "Excuse me?"

Sarah frowns up at me, wrapping the bottles of wine in recycled paper before she sets them in my reusable canvas grocery bags. "You don't remember?"

"Remember what?"

"You were distracted that night, when you came in all out of sorts, but I figured you'd remember. You said a woman was visiting. Willa's best friend?"

My stomach drops. Sarah and my mom are close friends. They

talk on the phone every day. How did I do that? Slip up so terribly? What was I thinking? "Sarah, have you said anything to my mom?"

She gives me a look of deep offense. "What do you take me for? A gossip?"

"Yes."

"Fair," she concedes, bagging the last of my items and accepting my card. "But even *I* can be discreet. Especially when I know how private you are. I haven't said a word."

Relief buoys me. "Thank you. But listen, even if you did ever slip up—which, kindly don't—it's not like that, okay? She's just . . . she's not . . ."

"Mm-hmm." Sarah rips the receipt off the printer and sets it down for me to sign. "Just someone you've been hosting for weeks, bending over backward to cook and bake for, who's staying *in your home* unless my little birdies that keep me apprised of all things around here were lying about how big of a crew Parker and Bennett have at the A-frame."

My eyes widen. "What the hell kind of spy network are you running around here?"

She grins. "Resident busybody isn't a title you claim without seriously living up to it. Now—" She yanks a box of condoms off the wall behind her, where she keeps stuff that kids steal too often, and throws them in my canvas bag. Then she freezes, fishes them out, and switches them for a new box stamped with a bold, oversized letter *L*. "If you're anything like your mother says your father is—"

"Jesus," I groan, burying my face in my hands. "Stop. I don't need those, Sarah. I told you, it's not like that between us."

As much as I'd like it to be, just once. Just one time to get over this and be able to move on with my life.

Sarah doesn't remove the condoms. She gives me a long, hard look that makes me glance away. "That's what Meg said about us, too."

The photo of her late wife sits on the counter by the cash register. Meg's red hair, threaded with white, is spun into a bun, her smile as bright as the striking constellation of freckles on her skin. Sarah grips the frame and slides her thumb softly along Meg's cheek. "If there's something there between you, don't waste a fucking minute, you hear me?"

Gently, I drag my bags onto my shoulders. "I hear you, Sarah. Good night."

---

"You're back!" Rooney bounds my way and takes half of the grocery bags from my arms. "Thank goodness. We only had two accidents, and I already cleaned them up. I don't think she likes the bathroom. Don't—" The door swings shut. "Let the door slam."

"MEOW!" says the cat. How does something so small make so much noise?

"She *was* asleep," Rooney mutters, traipsing toward the bathroom door. "Okay, so, given that the litter box in the bathroom isn't going so well, where else should we try to put her?"

"The closet."

Rooney nearly drops her armful. "The *closet*? We can't stick her in the *closet*!"

"It's a big closet."

"Axel Bergman, the cat is not going in a closet. She needs sunlight to sunbathe. Cuddly corners to burrow in. Plenty of space to play."

There's a scary liquid sound on the other side of the bathroom. If that cat shit on my tiles—

"And maybe somewhere with a scrubbable, nonporous floor, too," Rooney adds sheepishly.

That leaves only one space. Another sigh leaves me. "Give me five minutes."

I unlock the studio door and let myself in, shutting it behind me. It's quiet and peaceful in here, the floor-to-ceiling windows on the west- and east-facing sides letting in mauve dusk light through the blinds I have only partially closed. I packed up things pretty thoroughly when I accepted that painting wasn't happening, but this morning, finally with a little time alone, I found myself in here, working on a canvas I had no business working on.

I pack that away, and the rest of those half-finished, highly incriminating canvases lying around. I turn them to lean against the wall and throw a drop cloth over them.

Then I make sure my concept sketchbooks are shut and stashed in the organized, thin shelves I have for them. I check that my oil paints and turpentine are all tightly sealed and set up high, brushes out of reach, too. It's like babyproofing, based on what I remember when Parker and Bennett had Skyler.

"Okay," I call, opening the door. "You can bring her in."

A minute later, Rooney enters, kitten in arms. She's wearing a hoodie that swallows her up, the deep green color making the green in her eyes pop. And then I realize why that hoodie looks familiar.

"Nice sweatshirt," I tell her.

She shuffles in, then crouches down, letting the kitten spring from her arms to the ground. "I needed something to protect me from her needle claws. You should see how ripped up my arms are." Standing, she dusts off her hands and folds her arms across her chest. "I found this in the *closet*. The one you wanted to stick the cat in."

"Then you saw—as you pilfered *my* hoodie—how big it is. How comfortable she would have been."

"It has no sunlight!" she says.

"It's cozy," I counter.

"It's behind us now. This is your room, Skugga," she tells the kitten, bending and scratching her cheek. Skugga purrs, then pounces on my boots, attacking the shoelaces.

"Stop," I tell her, taking her by the scruff and gently plucking her off my boot.

"You'll hurt her!" Rooney says.

"This is literally how mother cats carry their kittens." Setting Skugga on a pile of clean drop cloths, I brush the fur off my hands. "Go," I tell the kitten. "Attack those."

Surprisingly, she does, pouncing on a shadowy fold in the fabric. Satisfied that the kitten's amusing herself, we set up her litter box in one corner of the studio, her water and food dish on the other end, close to the door.

"Bye, sweet pea!" Rooney calls as I nudge her toward the door. I'm starving, and I need a distraction. Rooney in my clothes is making more of those uncomfortable achy sensations throb in my chest. And elsewhere.

Skugga is too busy with the drop cloths to notice us shutting the door.

"Think she's okay?" Rooney asks.

I nudge her again. "She's fine. She'll meow if she's not."

"I feel like I'm abandoning her."

"You're not. You're giving her a cozy space to eat, shit, sleep, and play."

"I already feel bereft. My arms are empty of needle-claw kitten cuteness. I can't stop worrying about her."

Something damn close to a smile tugs at my mouth. "Let's distract you, then."

"How?" Rooney moans, flopping onto my bed.

Her moan. My mattress. I need a distraction, too.

Thank God for pushy, nosy Sarah Shepard. I yank out the still-cool dry Riesling and make fast work of the cork. "How about some wine?"

Rooney sits up on her elbows, eyeing the grocery haul on the counter. "How about wine *and* another cooking lesson?"

An uneasy hum settles in my throat. Cooking in my economically sized kitchen with Rooney. Wine in our systems. I feel like it's a disaster waiting to happen.

Rooney smiles like she's read my mind.

Maybe a little kitchen disaster wouldn't be the end of the world.

# EIGHTEEN

## Axel

Playlist: "Talk Too Much," Coin

"How's that?" Rooney points the knife toward the potato she's been chopping.

I pause stirring the pot that has sautéed leeks and celery, glancing her way. "That's . . . something."

She narrows her eyes at me. "I would appreciate *constructive* criticism."

Setting down the wooden spoon, I step closer. "May I?"

"By all means." She lays the knife on the cutting board but doesn't move. As I pick up the knife and rotate the half-chopped potato, our sides brush. Heat rushes through me.

"Cut it in half." I show her, slicing the potato, then laying each half on its flat side. "Next, cut it in lengthwise sections, then spin it and cut the other way."

When I peer up, her eyes are on my mouth and she's flushed, her throat and her cheeks. "Everything okay?"

"I'm just really hot," she says suddenly, stepping back and dragging my hoodie off her body, then tossing it on a chair at the dining table. It makes her shirt ride up, revealing a tantalizing flash of skin along her stomach.

My gaze wanders up as she gently tugs her shirt away from her body to fan herself. The woman doesn't wear a bra, and it's been slowly killing me—the slight, soft curve of her breasts inside her shirts, how her nipples bead beneath the fabric when she's cold. I don't blame her for not wearing a bra, because based on how Freya's whined about them since middle school, they sound like torture devices, but God, am I suffering for it.

She drops the shirt, and it settles, revealing Ms. Frizzle behind the wheel of the Magic School Bus. Rooney smiles as she sees me staring at it. "Are you a fan of the Friz?"

"I liked the show, but I hated how loud it was. I read the books, though."

"Wow. Now that you say it, Ms. Frizzle does basically yell everything."

I shrug. "She's enthusiastic. Did you like it?"

"Loved it." Rooney returns to the potatoes, tongue stuck out in concentration as she attempts to follow my example. It's unbearably sweet. "She was my first exposure to a woman in STEM, and she made it seem okay to be *excited* about it, you know? I felt like she loved science for the same reasons I did."

"And what were those?" I watch her chop another potato, this time with more confidence.

"Science made the world make sense, and that made the world feel so beautiful and vast and full of potential. With science, my curiosity could always be answered, every magnificent thing I saw or learned about could be explained, and that was incredible to me. It still is."

Her hair keeps slipping into her face as she chops. I step behind her, smoothing it back. "May I?"

She glances slightly over her shoulder. "What?"

"Pull your hair back."

She smiles at me tentatively. "Okay?"

Rooney's tall but I'm half a foot taller, enough that I have a good angle to section her hair, starting at the top. "You can keep chopping," I tell her. "I won't jar you. Your fingers are safe."

Slowly she picks up the knife, then starts back on the potato. I braid the top part of her hair, sliding my fingers into that silk-smooth blonde, adding pieces from one side, then the other.

"So, Ms. Frizzle," I ask her, eyes on my task, "any favorite lines?"

"Hm." She dabs her forehead, then resumes chopping. "Well, there's the classic that everyone knows, and it's probably my favorite: 'Take chances, make mistakes, and get messy!' And then another one that my parents definitely didn't always appreciate me taking to heart: 'If you keep asking questions, you'll keep getting answers.'"

Tugging another section of hair together, I tighten the braid. "You sound like Skyler."

"She reminds me a little of myself," Rooney says. "But she's smarter. I'm intelligent enough, but mostly I just worked my ass off. With Sky, you can tell everything's firing so fast in her brain. She's going places."

"She's brutal at board games, too."

Rooney laughs. "I can picture that. When we played with Harry that morning they showed up here, she was trying to make everything a competition. I went along with the game she made up using the stick we were throwing for him, and I happily lost."

"You're a better person than I am." A strand slips loose from the braid as I approach the ends of her hair. I tuck it back in.

"I think I'm getting the hang of this potato-chopping thing. Am I hired?"

I peer over her shoulder. "Definitely."

"So," she says, reaching for another potato. "Is there an artist who's inspired you? A quote of theirs you love?"

I finish braiding her hair, then reach for the hair tie that's on her wrist. As I slip it off, my fingers brush her skin, goose bumps trailing in their wake. I watch her, head bent, the profile I've already memorized, dragging my charcoal down the paper as I rendered the soft slope of her nose, the shadowed dimple in her cheek, that lush, full mouth. "Picasso said, 'Art is a lie that makes us realize truth.'"

Setting down the knife, she faces me. "That's very beautiful."

My eyes roam her face. "It is."

Silence stretches between us, and the ache inside me morphs into hunger. Hunger that makes me want to slide my hands up her shirt and feel her, to make her feel what I don't know how to say, to explain what it is to kiss her and talk to her and cook with her, how inexplicably right that feels when it's never felt right with anyone else.

But what's the use when my place is here, and hers is there, and our lives are worlds apart? So I push past the impulse and the comfortable quiet, reaching for the potatoes, telling her, "You did a good job. Now we'll just stir them around and give them a few minutes."

"Got it." Rooney brushes a flyaway off her face, then runs her hand over her hair, feeling it. "French braid?" she asks.

I stir the potatoes, then set down the spoon. "Mm-hmm."

"Who taught you to French braid?" she says, reaching for her wine and taking a long drink. "A girlfriend? Boyfriend? Sorry, I have to get out of the habit of making those gender assumptions. *Partner*, I should have said. Whoever they were, I'm sure they were supercool. Talented. Artsy. Incredible cooks. Definitely didn't need a lesson in chopping a potato." She gasps for air, then takes another long drink of wine. "I talk too much."

I bring my wine to my mouth and have a sip, too. "It was Freya. She made me do it for her soccer games. Mom was usually too busy with the other kids, and Freya could never get the hang of doing it on her own head."

Rooney blinks at me. "You braided your sister's hair?"

"Entirely for my own benefit. She'd sit in front of the mirror, trying to do it, and end up swearing and scream-crying so loud, my ears hurt. If I braided her hair, I didn't have to deal with that."

"Uh-huh." She smiles, then turns back to the food. "What's next?"

"First, stir the potatoes again, before we add the vegetable broth."

She leans over the pot, stirring them. I open up two cartons of vegetable broth, which she adds. "Now dial up the heat," I tell her. "Once it's boiling, we'll turn it down and let it simmer."

"Okay," she says, tapping the spoon. "I'm pretty far into making a meal, and nothing has caught on fire or blown up. This is big."

"Move aside, Julia Child. There's a new chef in town."

She tips her head back and laughs. "I don't know about that. I'm content with celebrating that I'm not burning your house down."

"You're doing great." I pick up my wine and take a sip.

Rooney's gaze goes to my mouth again before she glances away, tugging at her shirt. "God, it's hot," she mutters. "Can I open the window over the sink?"

"Sure."

She turns and leans over the sink, revealing the beautiful silhouette of her body. Long legs, a round, sweet ass, the soft slope of her hips. I grip the counter and start counting backward from one hundred in Swedish.

"Aren't you hot?" she asks.

Hot? I'm burning from the inside out. "Uh. A bit. Yes."

"Do you want to take that shirt off?" she asks. Her cheeks turn raspberry. "I mean, not *off* off, but, like, off-and-replace-the-flannel-with-a-T-shirt kind of *off*—you know what? I'm going to stop talking now."

"No, you're right. That's—" I clear my throat, pushing off the counter. "I'll do that."

While she turns back to the pot and stirs, I stroll into the main room, past the bed, and open my dresser for a shirt. I yank off the flannel and set it aside.

As I'm tugging down my T-shirt, the fabric just above my pecs, Rooney glances up from the potatoes.

"Do you—holy *shit*." Her mouth falls open. Her gaze rakes down my torso. Then she shuts her eyes. "Sorry. Just—yep. Sorry."

I tug my shirt down the rest of the way. Walk carefully back into the kitchen. "Why are you sorry?"

"Never mind." Her voice is unnaturally high. She clears her throat. She's flushed, eyes bright as she tugs her shirt away from her chest again. I tell my eyes not to rake down her body, but I can't stop. God, the things I want to do to her.

"Do you, um, want some help with the spinach salad until the soup's ready to puree?" she says, snapping me out of it.

Salad. Right.

"Sure." That comes out gravelly and rough. My turn to clear my throat. "You can peel hard-boiled eggs?"

"Great." We stand side by side, working on the salad, each brush of our bodies a torture I never knew I'd experience simply by cooking beside someone. Once the salad's assembled, she follows my instructions and pours the soup into the blender.

"So." She grips the base of the blender, eyes on the buttons. "Which one do I push?"

"Which one do you think seems best?"

"I'd think the lowest setting, to ease the motor and food into it, instead of whipping it at a high velocity, right away."

I nod. "Right, but first—"

Trigger-happy, Rooney jabs the button. Lumpy potato soup explodes like a geyser for the two seconds it takes for her to turn it off.

"Make . . . sure . . . the lid is on all the way," I mutter.

Rooney stands, open-mouthed, hands up, shocked. Slowly, she

turns and faces me, blinking rapidly. A mushy potato slides down her hair.

I pluck a potato chunk off my shoulder, then push off the counter, stepping close to her. There's a piece of potato nestled in her braid that I remove, setting it on the counter. "An understandable mistake."

She bites her bottom lip, and peers up at me, her eyes big and sad. Then she starts to sniffle. It makes me feel like my chest is being sawed open.

"Rooney, don't cry. It's okay. Remember? 'Take chances, make mistakes, and get messy!'"

The sniffling intensifies. "I'm such a kitchen disaster," she whispers, blinking away the wetness glistening in her eyes.

I wipe some soup off her temple, then her cheek. We're both a little messy, but thankfully, most of the food seems to have painted the cabinets and counter. "You're not a kitchen disaster."

"Yes I am," she says miserably, shoulders slumping. "I got potato soup on your cabinets and in your hair—"

"I . . . needed a shower anyway."

A burst of laughter leaves her. Then another. Then she's laughing so hard, her forehead thumps into my chest. Basking in the relief that tears have been avoided, I pick more potato out of her hair, tossing it in the sink, until she straightens again and wipes her eyes.

"Right," she says. "You're right. Trial and error. Mistakes are opportunities to learn. I'm fine. I'm okay. This is fixable." She strolls past me, wets the drying towel, and quickly wipes potato soup from the cabinets and counters. I pick up what's on the floor and toss it in the compost bucket.

Once we've cleaned up, I point to the blender again. "All right. Take two."

Rooney sets her hand on the lid this time. "Ready?" she asks, her smile nervous.

"Hold on." I backtrack to my coatrack, tug my rain jacket off the hook, and throw it on. "Go ahead."

Her eyes narrow. Then she laughs so hard, this time it echoes in the kitchen.

"Smart-ass," she mutters. Then she grabs me by the rain jacket and yanks me close.

I stare down at her, flushed, eyes sparkling. And then I cup her face and walk her back against the counter. She presses on tiptoe, and our mouths meet, then open. Her tongue flicks mine softly, and it's a flipped switch. We're kissing with the kind of frantic energy that just sent the soup flying in the air.

I tug off the rain jacket as she grips the front of my jeans, dragging my hips against hers. Her fingertips brush low on my stomach, while her mouth travels my throat—slow, hot kisses, her tongue tasting my skin on its way to a sensitive space below my ear that makes me moan like I'm dying.

"Okay?" she asks as her hands slide up my torso, rest over my chest, splayed wide. Hard pressure, smooth and even. Fucking perfect.

I nod, kissing her deeply. "Yes." My mouth travels her lips, her cheeks, her neck. My hands wrap around her ribs, down to her waist, then back up. "Can I touch you?" I ask.

"God, yes." Taking my hand, she slips it under her shirt. I'm so fucking hard, but now, somehow I'm harder, feeling her soft skin, warm beneath my fingers, the slight weight of her breast in my hand. "Shit," she says breathlessly.

I drop my hand, grab her by the waist, and lift her onto the counter, stepping in between her legs. My hands find her hips and yank her close, but not close enough. I slide my touch around her back, then lower, kneading her ass, rocking her against me.

Her hands wander up my neck, thread through my hair, scrape over my scalp. "Okay?" she asks.

"Mm-hmm." I nod against our kiss, my tongue doing to her mouth what I want my body doing to hers so badly, it's difficult to stand or think or function.

It's a thousand fucking degrees in here, the small space echoing with our panting breaths, the quiet friction of us moving against each other, but I can't stop, and I can't get enough.

My hands wrap around her thighs. I want to feel her, wet and warm. I want to taste her and breathe her in. Only *thinking* about it is about to do me in.

I've been celibate for too damn long.

# NINETEEN

# Rooney

Playlist: "Green Eyes," Joseph

Axel stills my hips and pulls his away. He presses a kiss behind my ear, his breath whispering over sensitive skin. "Can I touch you here?" he says quietly.

Air rushes out of me as his hands slide over my thighs, his thumbs circling higher. Higher. His mouth brushes mine. A faint kiss. Then harder.

I nod frantically. "Yes."

As soon as the word's out of my mouth, he's tugged off my leggings and tossed them aside. I'm sitting on the kitchen counter in fuzzy wool socks, a painfully boring pair of underwear, and a vintage *Magic School Bus* T-shirt. This is basically my uniform for life when other people aren't around, but I harbor no delusions that it's sexy.

Except the way Axel's breathing, how he cradles my face and kisses me, then runs his hands down my body and pulls me closer like he can't get enough, says otherwise.

"Jesus," he breathes, rubbing my nipples through my shirt. Then he dips his head and sucks one right over the fabric, chased by a soft scrape of teeth. I brace myself on the counter as he holds me, one hand low on my back, then my ass, the other cradling my neck as he tongues my nipples. "You don't wear bras," he mutters, switching to the other breast, kneading my ass, rubbing me against the thick, hard jut of his erection inside his jeans. "It kills me."

"They're small," I tell him faintly, gasping as he sucks that nipple harder and teases it more with his teeth. "And I hate bras. I hate clothes. I'd be a nudist if I could."

He groans, kisses up my throat, claims my mouth. "Torture," he mutters. "Fucking torture." And then his hand wanders my stomach—soft, tender touches. His knuckle brushes my clit through my panties, and I nearly bow off the counter.

"Please." I'm begging, rubbing myself against his hand, so desperate to orgasm, I can barely get enough oxygen in my lungs, can barely form a coherent thought.

Axel watches as he rubs one finger, then two over my underwear. Then, slowly, he slips them beneath the fabric, the first brush of his fingertips where I'm wet and exquisitely sensitive making me cling to him. Faint kisses brush my temple. His thumb circles softly right where I need it. And then he sinks a finger deep inside me, curling softly and stroking my G-spot.

My mouth falls open. And then I bite his neck like the animal I've turned into.

He grunts as I chase it with a kiss, as I lick his collarbone, his Adam's apple, and press long, hot kisses up his throat. "I'm sorry," I say against his skin.

"Don't be," he mutters. "God, you feel so perfect. So warm and wet and—*fuck*."

I'm rubbing him through his jeans, savoring the thick outline straining the fabric.

"Rooney, not now," he begs.

"Why?"

He groans as I rub him again, but then he gently removes my hand. He kisses me deeply, then adds a second finger and pumps faster. "Because I want to give you this, and I can't when you touch me. I'll fuck your hand and forget my name, and that's not what I'm doing right now."

"I . . ." Swallowing, I tip my head back as he kisses my throat. "I want you to feel good, too."

"I do," he says softly, earnestly, as his touch brings me closer and closer. "This makes me feel good. Tell me what feels good for *you*. I want to know."

I sigh against his kiss. "Rub up and down, too, not just circles. A little gentler."

His touch lightens, changes to rhythmic up-down strokes. It's so perfect, I can't ride his hand hard enough, chase release faster.

"I feel you," he whispers. "So close."

I nod furiously, eyes shut, lost to the weightlessness of being held in his arms, savored, and touched, and kissed. My thighs tighten around his hips. Our tongues stroke and suck as heat climbs up my chest and throat. My breasts brush against his chest, my clit throbs against his hand, and when I come, it's on a tight, breathless gasp.

It's only our breaths, heavy and fast, echoing in the kitchen as Axel kisses me deeply once more, then softly pulls away. He shuts his eyes as he sets each finger that was inside me against his tongue and sucks it clean. I touch him again through his jeans as he does it, earning a groan and long sigh as I pop the first button, then stroke over his boxer briefs.

His hand stills mine. He shakes his head. "It's all right."

"What?"

He presses a soft kiss to my temple, then my cheek. "Sometimes I get off on not getting off. Getting you off was pleasure enough."

My mouth falls open. He said *what*?

"MEOWWWW!" howls Skugga from the studio.

I sigh and shut my eyes as Axel eases even farther away, discreetly adjusting himself. "I'll go check on her."

I'm left sitting on the counter. Dazed. Stunned.

Maybe adopting a kitten wasn't such a good idea after all.

---

"You sure you don't want to try a bite?" I hold up a morsel of brownie.

Axel shakes his head. "No."

"Well, this is a disaster. You don't like sweets, and there's a whole tray of brownies to be eaten. Gluten-free, *dark chocolate* brownies." I pop the bite in my mouth and sigh happily. "My favorite."

His mouth lifts faintly in the corner, the closest thing yet to a smile. "I suppose you'll have to eat them all."

I sigh dramatically as I pick up the knife to cut another brownie square, a chewy delicious corner. "If I must. Though, maybe I'll save some for dinner tomorrow night with the crew, to share with Skyler."

"Those are done," he says.

I falter with the knife, stunned by how disappointed I am. I loved those rowdy dinners. "Oh. Why?"

"The time-sensitive projects are complete, so no need to pull long days anymore." Axel frowns, searching my expression. "What's wrong?"

"Nothing," I say automatically, out of long-ingrained habit. *Smile, smooth things over, everything's fine.*

Axel's foot gently nudges mine beneath the table. He peers down at his plate that was piled high with bacon and eggs and spinach salad, completely clean. The man eats like a teenager.

"Rooney," he says quietly. "I—" Clearing his throat, he looks up at the ceiling and says, "I don't read between the lines very well. You said nothing's wrong, but everything about your body says it is. I don't know what to do with that."

I slide my foot against his, socked feet against socked feet. "Sorry. Bad habit. I should have said I'm . . . disappointed. I'm going to miss everyone, mostly Parker and Bennett and Sky."

"I can ask Bennett to bring Skyler around after school one of these days before you go. Maybe we can have dinner with them, too."

I smile. "Really?"

Axel pushes away from the table, then reaches for a notebook and fine-tipped pen that sit on the edge of one of the floating shelves. "When it makes you smile like that, how could I say otherwise?"

My blush is spectacular. "I smile all the time. Doesn't take much."

"True." Flipping open to a fresh page, he sits back in his chair at an angle so I can't see what he's sketching. "But there are different smiles."

I tip my head. Is he flirting with me? "There are?"

He nods, hand moving quickly. "There's the small smile. Maybe that's . . . the polite one. For people I'd generally frown at."

I laugh.

"There's the bigger smile. Maybe that's the content smile. I see that a lot at my parents' house."

"That's because I like your family a lot. I'm content with them."

He narrows his eyes at the paper as his pen dances across its surface. "Then there's the smile you just pulled out. That one's harder to earn."

My heart's doing this wild jig in my chest, knocking against my ribs, making breathing difficult. "What smile is that?"

His mouth lifts at the corner again as he stares at his sketch. "It's not the biggest, but it's the most *you*. Your smile when no one's watching. When you think they aren't."

"Correct me if I'm wrong, but I can only conclude that since you've observed this smile, you *have* been watching."

He clears his throat. A faint blush warms his cheeks. "It's an artist's prerogative to observe humans."

I pop another bite of brownie in my mouth. "Says the artist who paints abstracts."

He tips his head, adjusts his pen in his grip. "Abstract art is deeply human."

"How so?"

"Good art—no matter how representational it does or doesn't appear—*is* representational of human emotion. It expresses and evokes our feelings, not just with color on the canvas, but with every space where color isn't. Absence has presence. Abstraction is representational."

"That's a whole lot of paradox."

"All art is a paradox," he says, eyes down, still sketching.

I smile, remembering what he told me in the kitchen. "'Art is a lie that makes us realize truth.'"

He nods. "Exactly."

"I've never known what to make of art. I just knew that your art spoke to me. Now I understand why—it makes me both feel *and* feel seen in my feelings."

Axel's pen pauses. He glances up, his gaze flicking to my mouth, then back down. "Really?"

I nudge his foot under the table again. He pins my foot under his. "You've only shown once in LA, but I was there as long as I could be. I thought it was pretty obvious I love your art, Axel."

The blush deepens. The pen tumbles from his hand. He shuts the notebook. "Hm."

"I would have said it." I set my other foot on top of his beneath the table. "But I was trying not to be a blatant fangirl. You certainly have enough of those, given the attention you got at that show."

Heat floods my cheeks. I just made it pretty damn clear that I've been watching *him*, too.

If Axel picks up on it, he doesn't let it show. He stares down at his notebook, a deep frown on his face. "Hm."

"What's all this *hmm*-ing?"

He drags his knuckles across his mouth, and there's something wrong with me, because every time he does that, it's like he's flipped the switch on my libido. I shift uncomfortably on my chair.

"Nothing," he mutters.

"Oh, no, I don't think so. If I can't get away with a 'nothing,' neither can you."

Axel drums his fingers on his sketchbook. Then he sits up, tosses it on the table, and rakes his hands through his hair. He shuts his eyes and takes a deep breath. "I honestly don't care what strangers think of my art. I like that it sells, but I don't care about their opinion beyond that. I was a little panicked when you all showed up at my LA show. If my parents had come, I'd have lost my shit."

"Why?"

Slowly, he opens his eyes, staring at the ceiling. "It's sort of like the painting-sunrises-and-sunsets thing. I want them to get it and connect to it, and I can't stand the thought that they might not. So I have yet to allow my parents to attend a show."

My mouth drops open. "Axel Bergman."

His eyes lower and land on my mouth. He swallows roughly. "Yes?"

"Your parents will love your art because they love you. Let them come to your show."

"Just because you love someone doesn't mean you understand them," he says. "You said yourself, when you told me about your family, sometimes the way people love you isn't enough."

I stare at him. "That's a very different context. You really think your parents won't understand your work and love it?"

He peers down at his hands. "I don't know. I just know I'm not sure I could handle it if they didn't. Maybe that sounds ridiculous, but that's how I've framed it in my head."

I stare at him and lean a little closer. "Think of what you're missing by not trusting them, though. The way you do it now, sure, you avoid the possibility that they might hurt you by not connecting with what you've done. But you're also missing out on the opportunity to experience their pride and love. What if they love it, Axel? What if they're glowing and thrilled and in love with your art?"

Slowly, he peers up. "I never thought of what I was missing. Just what I was avoiding."

"Give them a chance?"

He nods.

I smile, pleased. "Good."

Axel leans in, too, elbows on the table, eyes drifting to my shoulder. Reaching for my braid, he tucks a loose piece back in. The braid drops softly to my shoulder, but Axel's fingertips stay, sliding along my collarbone, his gaze following his touch. His expression is so serious, so focused.

"What are you thinking?" I ask.

He tips his head. His eyes darken as his finger slides lower, over the swell of my breast. "I'm thinking about what I told you earlier when you came back. About kissing you."

Heat rushes through me as it replays in my memory.

*I want to kiss you so badly, it's obliterated every other thought in my brain. There's nothing but wanting it. Wanting you.*

"Oh?" I ask a lot more breathlessly than I'd intended.

"Would you—" He clears his throat. "That is, would you want to . . . Fuck." Pulling back, he buries his face in his hands.

"Would I want to . . . fuck?"

"No," he groans. "Wait. I mean, yes, but that's not what I meant, not that I wouldn't—shit." He grasps my hand, tracing my palm with his fingertip, and exhales slowly, then says, "I'm so fucking terrible at this."

I should say something to put him at ease, but it's very hard to think when he's stroking my palm, one calloused fingertip swirling in a mesmerizing circle that I want happening where I'm feeling so achingly deprived again, it's almost unbearable.

I've been celibate for way too long.

"Ax—" My voice comes out Lollipop Guild high. Clearing my throat, I try again. "What do you want to ask me?"

"I . . ." Peering up at me, he says, "Do you feel this?"

I stare at him, my heart pounding. "Feel what?"

His thumb slides over the tender base of my hand. "This . . . *thing* between us. When we kiss. When we touch. What happened in the kitchen—"

"Yes," I blurt as his hands move down to my wrists. I have a pulse in my clit, and my entire body aches so badly for him, I can hardly breathe. "Yes, I feel that."

"Do you . . ." He's quiet for a moment but for his breathing, which is as unsteady as mine. "Want to *do* something about it?"

I arch as he hits a tender spot. "Sex?"

He nods. "We could . . . get it out of our systems. One time, work it all out."

"One time?" I squeak.

"One night," he amends. "One night is more reasonable."

"Definitely. That would be. Yes. I want that. If you do."

"I do," he says, stopping his massage, snapping us out of the erotic fog. "But this is . . . are you comfortable with this? Being married for, you know, obviously nonromantic reasons, and having sex for . . . also nonromantic reasons?"

*Yes* doesn't fly out of my mouth like it should, but why wouldn't I be comfortable? Sure, I care about him beyond the sexual attraction that's become obvious to both of us. I probably feel a bit more about him than I should, but it's hard not to, given the situation we're in—always with or near each other, sharing space . . . married.

I stare down at his hand. The one that was wearing the wedding ring and no longer is. "Where'd your ring go?"

He reaches inside his shirt and pulls out a chain that holds both our rings. Slipping it off over his head, he undoes the chain, then slides off the rings.

We stare at them stacked on the table, silent.

"I took it off when the man cubs came," he finally says.

I pick up mine, warm from his skin, and examine it. "I felt naked without it, at Willa's."

He runs his thumb along his ring finger. "We should keep them on. Don't want Vic getting ideas."

I laugh softly. "He's harmless."

"Hm." Axel slides my ring back on, then his. "There," he says. "Better."

I stare at our hands, his wedding ring beside mine. It hits me, as it tends to from time to time when I see it, that I'm in a loveless, lusty marriage.

And now I'm discussing having loveless, lusty sex with my husband.

Is there a part of me that wonders if there could be more, if Axel's as curious about what could be between us as I am? Yes. But . . . he offered only one night, and I think I should respect that. Haven't I insinuated myself enough into his life already, without asking for even more?

"One night," I tell him as much as myself. "Just sex."

He swallows thickly. "Just sex."

I rearrange our hands so that they're clasped tight, poised to shake on the one promise—unlike those many wedding vows—that we'll make and actually keep. Only one night of sex, no awkward lingering afterward, no temptation to prolong the inevitable. He'll go back to being busy, I'll keep to myself, then I'll head home for Thanksgiving—

Wait. Thanksgiving. Seeing his family. Socializing. Where will that leave us? Will we *both* be comfortable, after we've worked this out between us?

"I'm comfortable with it," I tell him. "But, afterward, will it be possible . . . will you be comfortable being around me? Like if I came to Thanksgiving at your parents', would you be okay with it?"

He tips his head. "Of course, Rooney. That's the point, right? We'll move on from *this* and then we can be around each other more easily. You have to come to Thanksgiving. My family, they'd miss you if you didn't."

I smile faintly as his thumb strokes my palm. "So can we be friends?"

"Yes." His gaze is serious, his hand warm and strong as it holds mine. "Friends."

———

Axel stands on the welcome mat outside his house, ready for his traipse up the hill to the A-frame where he's sleeping now. I lean in the doorway and smile up at him. "Thank you for dinner. And dessert. And the cooking lesson. Sorry about the potato soup explosion."

He runs his finger down my braid and curls the ponytail end around his finger, looking like he's very much lost in his thoughts. "Mm-hmm."

Harry the greyhound emerges from the shadows, his happy lope making an uneven rhythm against the ground. I scratch his ears and bend to give him a kiss on the head. "I missed you," I tell him.

The dog goes up on his back legs, and I give him a hug.

"Down, Harry," Axel says.

The dog drops and nuzzles my hand.

"So you've caved, have you?"

Axel shakes his head as the dog licks his knuckles. "He answers best to Harry. What could I do?"

"MEOWWW!" the kitten shrieks from the studio. Harry's ears perk up before he wanders away toward the studio end of the cabin to explore the sound of this new feline intruder.

"Well." I throw a thumb over my shoulder. "Motherhood calls."

Axel's mouth tips, deliciously close to a smile. And then suddenly the air feels different, something filling the space between us, quiet and unspoken and unsure.

This feels dangerously like . . . *feelings*. Which it can't be. No, it isn't. Not when we've just agreed all we need is to screw each other out of our systems, then part ways as friends. Maybe it isn't feelings, then. Maybe this is simply what it is to feel safe with someone. Safe and understood.

"Do you . . ." I swallow my nerves and blurt it. "Do you think we could hug?"

Axel's quiet for a moment, staring down at his boots, before he picks up his head and steps closer. His hands slide down my arms until our fingers tangle together. He rests his temple against mine.

"Hugs are a little weird to me," he admits. And now I know why he's telling me this way, when we're touching but not looking, close but not sharing revealing eye contact. He feels vulnerable when we do that. "But if you don't run your hands all over my back or tickle me, it should be all right."

His beard is surprisingly soft as it brushes my cheek. I breathe in the warmth of his skin, that comforting cedar-sage soapiness that I'm hooked on. Affection tugs at my heart. "Show me?"

Axel pulls me closer, making me list toward him and bump into his chest. With our interlaced hands, he brings my arms around his waist and says, "Hold me tight."

I do what he's asked, locking my hands together around the

breadth of his lean waist. My head rests just above his heart. I hear it pounding.

"Ax, if it's not—"

Before I can say another word, his arms wrap around me, one hand low on my back, curling around my waist, the other sliding up my spine, making me arch into him, until it settles on my neck. "Okay?" he asks.

I nod, speechless. A hug has never been so sexual. Finally, I find my voice. "Very okay," I tell him. "Okay for you, too?"

"Surprisingly pleasant."

I laugh, but my laugh fades as his fingers slip into my hair, scraping softly along my scalp. The hand wrapped around my waist holds me tight. I feel every part of our bodies, close. How well we fit. How good it'll be when he's touching me, moving with me, his hips pinned to mine like they are now, his arms around me. I breathe in against his sweater and drink him in as his grip on my hair tightens, his hand slides lower down the curve of my back and draws me closer.

"You're a good hugger," I whisper.

He's quiet and still, but I feel how that pleases him. The way his cheek nuzzles my hair and his nose sneaks into my braid and breathes me in, too. "So are you," he says.

The last of autumn's stubborn leaves *swoosh* in the wind. The air is cold, but Axel is hot, his hug so soothing, I dissolve into it. It's the strength of a tree rooted to the ground, the comfort of a fire on a frigid night. It's perfect.

And I'll only have it for a little while longer.

"Thank you," I whisper as I let go. As he lets go of me.

His fingertips brush mine before he steps back and turns toward the path.

I watch him and Harry until they've dissolved into the darkness. And then I slip back inside to hug the screeching kitten down the hall.

But as I pass the bed and nightstand, I notice a neatly torn piece of sketch paper glowing under the lamplight. I stop and pick up what must be the drawing he did while we sat at the table. Harry the greyhound lies on his stomach, face serene, a black-pen sky of stars, clouds, and crescent moon hanging above. Nestled into his side is a tiny kitten, shaded faintly to resemble the gray fluffball meowing down the hall, a wide, sleepy smile brightening her face.

I slip that one safe into my suitcase. Another treasure from here that I never want to forget.

# TWENTY

## *Axel*

Playlist: "Sunlight," Hozier

I have a headache, and it's not from the wine we drank last night. It's from the pinball machine that is my brain, ricocheting with conflicting thoughts. Relief that Rooney and I will get this inconveniently intense attraction out of our systems, part ways as friends, and life will go on. Worry that this twisting, aching *something* in my chest that doubled overnight is some kind of warning I should heed.

"You're extra quiet today." Parker wipes the sweat off his forehead as we sit slumped against the wall, taking a break from our work on the upstairs bedrooms' floors.

"Sarah foisted wine on me," I tell him. "Rooney and I drank it, and I may or may not have backed myself into a corner."

Parker lights up. "Sounds promising."

"It's not."

He stands up on a groan, rubbing his knees. "Well, I'm all ears. Get it off your chest. It's about Rooney, of course."

I scowl at him.

He snorts and starts in on the last of the flooring we need to rip up. "You know, I've done a very good job of minding my own business since you told me to stop trying to set you up with people. Which was . . ." He glances up at the ceiling. "What? Two years ago? And don't ya know, Rooney happened to have mentioned in passing that's about how long you've known each other."

My scowl becomes thunderous.

Parker shrugs. "Of course I'd like to pay it forward, do a little matchmaking with you two, since I owe you, but I won't."

"No you won't. Because being matchmade with my wife is *entirely* inappropriate."

He hoots. "The irony of this. It's too rich."

I'm not acknowledging that. "Besides," I tell him. "You don't owe me anything."

"Yeah I do! You're the reason Bennett and I met and ended up together."

"That was unintentional and entirely self-serving," I point out. "Bennett wouldn't stop talking my ear off at that show, so I introduced you two to get him off my ass. I had no idea that you would hit it off."

"Or that he was hitting on *you*."

"I never know when someone's hitting on me. How anyone knows such a thing is beyond me."

Parker laughs. "That was priceless. He was so pissed."

"Until he realized he was much better off with you."

The cadence of people's voices downstairs grows louder quickly, breaking the moment. Voices holler, laughter intermingled with shouts. I frown. "What's that about?"

Parker shrugs and rips out a strip of water-damaged wood flooring. "Who knows. Probably just one of the guys cracking dirty jokes. They're children. Excellent with tools, but children. Listen, can I just ask—why are you against exploring if there could be . . . more with Rooney?"

"Because I'm a borderline recluse with the emotional bandwidth of a grumpy badger when his food has run out, whereas she's the warmest, most pleasant social butterfly to ever exist, *and* soon she's heading back to exist in the actual world. 'More' hasn't even entered our minds. And it won't, thank you very much."

"How do you know?" he insists. "Have you talked to her about it? Axel, she fucking lights up when you walk into a room."

"I compared myself to a badger *constitutionally*. I didn't say I looked like one."

"Christ," he laughs. "You're a headache."

"What? I know she's attracted to me. I'm attracted to her, too. That's it."

"You're both clearly attracted to each other. I'm not denying that. What I'm trying to say is, on *top* of being attracted to each other, shouldn't you talk about whether you have feelings for each other?"

"We did talk about it! And the only thing we're going to have is sex."

"What?" His pry bar clatters to the ground.

Shit, I didn't mean to blurt that. Parker just rivals Viggo for pushiness. I can only take so much before I lose my cool.

"I told you, I backed myself into a corner." Picking up my pry bar, I start in on the floor.

"Axel, whoa. Hold on. Hold the fuck on. If this is what you want, no feelings, just sex, why are you wigging out? Shouldn't you be—dare I suggest this emotion for you—happy?"

"I'm going to sleep with the woman I married!" I snap. "You'll excuse me if I'm a little on edge."

He stifles a laugh. "Are you listening to yourself?"

"Drop it. Pretend I never said any of this."

I pull back the pry bar with a savage rip. I'm dealing with this internal chaos the good old-fashioned way. Smashing shit.

"Come on," Parker says. "What are you worked up about?"

I rip out more flooring and don't answer him.

Parker slams his pry bar over mine, halting my motion. "Axel."

"It doesn't feel like it has with other people. That's all I'm saying. Done. No more."

Parker's quiet for a moment. "And you really don't think you might be developing feelings for her?"

I think back to those aching, twisty, sharp pains in my chest. They aren't feelings, are they? I've never felt them before, not for anyone. And the people I care about—my family, my small social circle—well, I don't feel that way about them at all. What I feel for Rooney is lust. Desire. Plain, simple want. That and some weird-as-hell heartburn. That's the logical answer.

Parker shakes his head as if he knows what I'm thinking. "I think you should consider it."

He can say what he wants. There's nothing to consider, nothing to figure out. I'm doing what I do, which is get anxious when things change. Taking things further with Rooney, no matter how much I've wanted it, isn't straightforward for me. I get worked up when shit is different. I always have.

At least I'll have some distance from her, after we have our one night, which I plan on proposing be *tonight* because I think I'm about to keel over from sexual frustration. I'll spend the daytime hours up here. She'll do her thing at my house. We'll have fucked this right out of our systems—with that, plus our daily distance, I can fall out of lust with her and move on.

Laughter erupts downstairs again. I hear a voice that I didn't the first time things grew louder. *Hers.*

"Parker," I say, deathly quiet. "What did you do?"

He clears his throat, pointedly moving out of reach from me and my pry bar. "She said she's getting antsy, asked about chipping in around the place. I told her she could. There's sanding and painting. Plenty she can safely do."

The pry bar slips from my hand and lands sharply on my knee. "Mother*fucker*!"

"Jesus, Axel," he says. "Is it so terrible to include her? To let her help if she wants to?"

"Yes!"

"Fine. Then hide in your tortured-hero tower up here, if you must. The guys on the ground will keep her entertained."

I see red. "Excuse me?" I point to my left hand and the wide tungsten ring on my fourth finger. "Wife. Mine."

Parker snorts. "Wow, caveman mode activated. Relax. I didn't mean it like that."

I spring up and walk to the landing with its view of the great room below. Rooney's body is in perfect push-up form, flying as she goes through reps side by side with one of the crew, who's started flagging and then falls into a heap and waves in surrender.

She finishes one last rep, then drops to the ground, rolling onto her back, and her blonde hair fans out like a halo. Her cheeks are flushed pink, and her chest rises and falls quickly. Then her eyes meet mine. Her smile widens.

The worst ache yet hits me, a line drive straight to the heart.

––––––

Everyone's gone for the night. Except me. And Rooney.

I may or may not be hiding in my Parker-named "tortured-hero tower." Whatever, it's quiet and free of a beautiful wife who I'm suddenly feeling deeply nervous about screwing out of my system tonight. I'm desperate for her, and I'm also . . . a little overwhelmed at the thought of working everything into one night that I want with her, hoping it can be everything she needs it to be, too.

A knock sounds on the threshold, and I glance over my shoulder. Well. No longer free of said beautiful wife.

*Wife.*

When I hear *wife*, I think of when my brother-in-law, Aiden, gruffly says it to my sister Freya. When Dad calls Mom that and she magically appears, eyes narrowed, knowing he's about to give her playful hell for something.

It's an intimate word. The kind of word I never considered that I'd use, let alone think.

And yet here she is, my . . . wife, leaning on the doorway, sweaty and smiling. "Hi," she says.

I set down the roller. "Hi."

She glances around, pushing off the doorway. "Want some help?"

*No*, I plan to say, but my tongue does something terrible and says, "Sure."

Her smile widens as she bends and helps herself to the brush I was using to cut in. "I was going to offer to handle dinner, but Parker just said on his way out he'd see us soon for Mexican?"

I pause, the roller suspended in the air. Paint drips to the drop cloth. What the *hell* is Parker up to? "Oh?"

Eyes narrowed in concentration, tongue stuck out, she drags the brush along the baseboard. "I figured you'd made plans with him earlier, and that works for me. I just wasn't sure if tonight was our uh, night to, you know . . ."

I roll the paint onto the wall in Ws, working quickly, racking my brain for how to handle this. It's only five thirty in the evening, but once we get to Parker and Bennett's and have dinner, that'll be hours I've lost. Stopping, I face her. "Let's . . . let's wait a night. After dinner with them"—I really am going to throttle Parker for this cockblocking interference—"it'll be late."

She blushes and nods. "Yeah. Good plan."

"I'm sorry it's past dinner already. I didn't mean to work so late."

*Liar. You were hiding in your tortured-hero tower.*

Dammit. Parker needs to get out of my head.

"It's okay, Axel. I was planning on heading down to cook, but Parker intercepted me, which is probably for the best. I'm not sure what your fire insurance is, and I feel like you have enough home disasters on your hands."

I snort, unexpectedly tickled by that. "At least you'll be able to eat what they make. They know you're vegetarian and their kitchen's safe for you."

She makes a hum of approval. "Yes. I see lots of veggie tacos in my near future."

"Gotta carb up for whatever CrossFit challenge is next with the crew."

"Listen," she says, "Vic wouldn't let me help knock out that drywall that has to be replaced. Said I couldn't even hold a sledgehammer, let alone swing it. And thus the push-up challenge was instated. I told him if I could do more than him, I got to knock down that wall myself."

Vic. The one who calls her *sunflower*. My chest burns, like a hot poker is being pressed right between my ribs.

"I wasn't actually sure I'd beat him," she says, eyes on her task. "I've always been decent with push-ups, but I haven't exercised since I got sick. I think the adrenaline helped—that and the big lunch Vic ate, slowing him down. If it were chin-ups, I would have been toast."

I glance at her, concentrating on the brush. She's going really slow. "It doesn't have to be perfect, Rooney. Just drag it along."

"Ha. Doesn't have to be perfect. Do you know me?"

"Enough to know I need to remind you that this work, which you are under no obligation to do when you're supposed to be taking it easy, does not need to be perfectly done."

She falters with the brush, then peers up at me. "I know everything you're doing here at the house really matters to you. I just want to respect that."

Looking at her, I feel the sharp burning ache intensify right in my ribs. Shit. This is the world's worst heartburn.

"I . . . appreciate that," I manage. "But I don't want you doing all this work, stressing yourself out about it. Stress is bad for you, right? I mean, that's what makes you feel worse."

She smiles softly, then stands, wiping her forehead. "I'm not stressed. Promise."

"Do you . . ." I glance at the roller. "Do you want to do this instead? Rolling's a little physically harder, but seeing as you out-push-upped Vic, I imagine you can handle it."

Her smile brightens. "Yeah, let's do that. You're the artist, anyway. You could probably do these corners in your sleep."

We switch tools, brushing fingers, our wedding rings winking in the overhead lights. I have an odd, terrifying sense of déjà vu, and I back up hastily, tripping on the drop cloth.

"Wow, whoa!" Rooney grabs my elbow, but it ends up just doing what it did last time she tried that, when she first got here— taking her down with me. The paint roller falls with her, swiping my face. I move the cut-in brush fast, but not fast enough, painting a thin slice of pale blue across her cheek.

"Oof." I land hard on my back as Rooney moves her knee just in time to avoid crushing my nuts and ends up straddling me.

She grimaces. "One of these days my physics background is going to override my savior complex. I should know how grabbing a falling person who's six inches taller than me and many pounds heavier is going to go."

I slide my finger along a hair stuck to the paint on her cheek and tuck it back behind her ear.

"Sorry," she whispers. Her eyes dip to my mouth.

And suddenly I am deeply aware of her body on mine. The soft give between her thighs nestled over my groin. I exhale roughly and sit us up, making Rooney squeak as I lift her to stand in one smooth motion.

But then my hands are on her arms, and she's staring up at me, and I'm staring down at her, and *fuck* do I want to kiss her.

Rooney reaches up on tiptoe and slides her fingertips across my temple. "I got paint on you."

"I got it on you, too." I wipe the paint from her cheekbone.

Our eyes search each other's, a soft smile tipping her mouth as Rooney kisses me. It's gentle and warm, such a delicious tease, it makes me want to throw her over my shoulder and tell Parker just exactly where he can shove his meddling Mexican dinner.

Before I devolve into doing just that, I pull away. Rooney blushes as she peers up at me, her smile wider. "I can be done for the day," I tell her. "Want me to walk you down to the cabin so you can get cleaned up?"

She nods. "Yeah."

I stare at her mouth again and steal another kiss because I can't stop myself. "Okay."

"Okay." Her smile deepens, and the dimples come out. "It's a date." She gasps, backing up. "Not like—I mean, you know what I mean, not a *date* date, but like 'it's a plan' kind of 'it's a date'—*mmph!*"

I kiss her, to stop where I know she's going—apologizing for the sweet way words tumble out of that luscious mouth, for the excitement and joy that she radiates and that I soak up like rare sunlight on a gray day.

Pressing a soft kiss to the corner of her mouth, then that dimple that shows itself again, I tell her, "It's a date."

# TWENTY-ONE

# Rooney

Playlist: "In the Waiting," Kina Grannis

My stomach is in hell, and it's my fault. I ate an infernally spicy bean taco, because God bless Bennett, he knows I'm vegetarian, and he clearly put a lot of love into making a dish that I could eat that he was very proud to say "actually tasted like something," but what he doesn't know is that spice murders me.

Murders. Me.

It's only been a few hours since I bit into the bean taco Bennett carefully made—"from scratch!"—but it doesn't take long for me to start hurting when I've eaten something that's going to make me pay. At first, I told myself it would only be a little rough later but worth the slight discomfort to be polite and eat what my host had made me.

Then I tasted the spice.

And it just kept getting spicier, and that's when I knew I was fucked. High-fiber foods are my stomach's nemesis, but spice is its ruin. I decided I'd make it through one taco. Just one. Because Bennett was beaming, and he was so happy I was smiling and enjoying it (read: trying not to die from the heat).

When he offered me another, I told him this one was so filling, I couldn't possibly, but I'd happily take leftovers. So here I sit in Axel's car, holding a wrapped-up plate of stomach assassins.

And now I'm going to die.

I'm going to die in stomach agony alone in a bathroom, and it's just about enough to make me cry.

"Rooney?" Axel says from the driver's seat.

I force a smile his way. "Yep?"

"What's wrong?"

My smile fades. "Noth—"

"Please don't say 'nothing.'" His eyes are on the road as he shifts gears, but his words say he sees straight through me. "You're clutching your stomach. It hurts, doesn't it?"

"I'm fi—"

"Don't say that, either," he says. "Just be straight with me, Roo."

My nickname on his tongue melts a part of me that's stayed tensile strong this whole time. He called me *Roo*. And now I'm even more of a mushy, emotional mess.

I watch Axel's jaw clench as he shifts gears once more and passes the car meandering in front of us. Our speed goes up fifteen miles per hour almost instantly, and as the spasms worsen, I'm really grateful Axel's tired of my *I'm fine* bullshit because suddenly I am, too. I'm glad he knows I'm hurting and that he's driving like a speed demon.

"Talk to me," he says, eyes flicking my way for just a moment.

"I don't feel very well," I admit. And then I bite down a whimper as the pain worsens.

Now we're going faster, the Jeep flying down the road.

"How bad?" he asks quietly. "Do you need to go to the hospital?"

"No. Just home."

*Home.* Not *my* home. Or *our* home. *His* home. And yet, shutting my eyes, pressing my forehead to the cold window glass, I picture that little house in the woods, and it feels more like home than any place has in so long. Somewhere I've been safe. Somewhere I've been myself. Somewhere I've been welcomed and cared for and . . . loved.

No, I'm not saying I think Axel loves me. But he's *shown* me love. In quiet, caring ways. In giving me home and comfort these past few weeks. A home I'm about to go die in.

Smoothly, Axel pulls off the main road, cuts down the path to the house, and just a moment later sets the car in park.

"Can I do anything?" he asks, unlocking the door to the house.

"Check on the cat, then go for a walk," I tell him as I rush inside.

And come damn near close to dying.

---

My brush with death isn't *that* close, but the pain is not fucking around. When I'm finally not sick to my stomach anymore, I take a hot shower and let myself have a good cry.

Somewhat less miserable, I dress myself in pajama pants and a thermal long-sleeved shirt. I plug in the heating pad clutched to my stomach, cuddle into Axel's bed in the fetal position, and decide I have sixty seconds to wrap up the pity party. Then I'm going to breathe deeply, open my notepad, and make a to-do list. Because to-do lists make the world go round.

One minute gone, I open my phone and start a fresh note.

1.  Never eat beans again.
2.  Never EVER eat spice again.
3.  Schedule therapy to talk about everything, particularly professional future, childhood shit, and parents. (Blergh.)
4.  Spend time thinking about what makes me happiest and healthiest until therapy can be scheduled. (Double blergh.)

"That's enough of that," I tell myself, tossing my phone aside and trying to breathe around the unease tightening my ribs. My future is not something I've dwelled on since I got here. In fact, I've been pointedly ignoring it. But tonight was just one of those reminders that while my body's a badass, resilient miracle, it's also chronically ill and it isn't invincible. And that has implications for . . . everything, including the kind of education I undertake, the kind of work I do, and the amount of stress it entails.

Part of me wonders if I was just doing law school wrong, if I've been doing everything achievement-oriented wrong. Too hard, too intense. Maybe I can go back and just . . . be healthier. But another part of me wonders if I'm just dooming myself for a relapse, if going back is digging into that stubborn, overperforming part of myself that got me this sick in the first place.

Yeah, that's what the therapy's going to have to help me figure out.

My phone buzzes, drawing me from my thoughts, and as I read the screen, I feel my heart skip. It's from Axel.

Skugga's litter has been cleaned & while she enjoyed eating my shoelaces more than her dinner, dinner was served. Harry & I are out for a moonlit stroll, but he's worried about you. Updates appreciated.

There's a starlit photo of Harry, twig in mouth, head tipped sideways. I tear up, and I can't even blame it on the hormones. I'm not PMS-ing—I already dealt with that bodily fun the second week that I was here.

No, the truth is that I am feeling genuinely emotional about that adorable dog. And the fluffball cat. And this cozy house. And the man who's the heart of it all.

Dammit. I think I've caught feelings for my husband.

I swore to myself just last night, as we shook hands on our one-night-stand plans, that I wasn't going to let my feelings get away from me. It only goes to show how good I am at lying to myself, how stubbornly I can live in denial of what my body and my heart already know—that Axel's come to mean much more to me than he was ever supposed to.

Great. Now my heart hurts as much as my stomach. Sighing bleakly, I type, Please tell Harry I'm feeling a bit better and am snuggled up in bed.

Three dots appear, then Axel's response: Harry's wondering if visitors are welcome.

I smile. Visitors are not only welcome but wanted.

A few minutes later, there's a soft knock at the front door before the latch turns and Axel enters, Harry trotting behind him, tongue hanging out. He whines, rounds the bed, and sets his head right on my torso.

"Gentle, Harry," Axel says, easing onto the other side of the mattress. His hair's wet, his beard shaved to a tight stubble. He's in a midnight-black hoodie and jogger sweatpants. And he's wearing those glorious glasses.

What a fucking sight to behold.

I smile at him ridiculously, but it can't be helped. It can't.

"What?" he asks.

I hold my fingers to my face in the universal spectacles symbol, making a delicious pink blush rise on his cheekbones. "You wore them just to cheer me up, didn't you?"

He clears his throat and leans back on one elbow, reclining along the bottom of the bed. "Did it work?"

"Yes," I tell him, laughing.

Then it happens. His mouth twists into a wry smile. Two long-line dimples carve his cheeks. And then—Jesus Christ, save me—his nose crinkles.

That's when I die and go straight to heaven. I gasp and clutch my heart, flopping dramatically back on my pillow.

That's when Axel *laughs*. A deep, husky sound straight from his chest that makes delight dance down my spine.

"Gah," I say, writhing in bed.

"What are you doing?" He leans over me, looking at me like I'm a strange creature he's still inexplicably drawn to. I tug him by a fistful of ink-black sweatshirt and pull him in for a kiss. A slow, deep kiss that stops time and silences the world around us.

And then Axel gently pulls away, eyes searching mine. "Oh."

I smile and straighten out his glasses. "Sorry."

He drops to his elbow next to me and scratches Harry's head, which is still resolutely settled on my stomach. "Why?"

"Because I can't stop kissing you. And that's all I can manage right now."

"Rooney, I didn't come here—" He sits up, frowning. "You think I came here expecting that, after how terrible you were feeling? I wouldn't—"

"Axel, no!" I try to sit up, but Harry's head weighs a ton. I flop back on the pillow. "I only meant . . . I *regret* that it's all we can do tonight."

"Oh. Well." He rolls off the bed, then walks into the kitchen and futzes around. He puts the kettle on and opens the cabinets where he keeps the tea. "I can never tell when people are saying they're sorry as in they're blaming themselves, or when they're just 'regretting' something," he mutters. "Literal mind. Sorry about that."

"You don't need to be sorry," I tell him. "In fact, I propose a no-sorry pact. Unless we're being jerks to each other, obviously."

"Signed," he says. "Want tea?"

"No, thanks."

He watches the kettle. Spins his mug. Drops a sachet of Sleepytime tea in the mug. Then meanders back into the main room. "Can I get you anything?" he says.

I smile up at him. I've seen him on a construction site, muscles flexing in filthy old jeans and a sweat-soaked shirt. I've seen him sell his art, polished and smooth in a charcoal suit stitched from sin itself. But here he stands in those delicious glasses and head-to-toe black, sweatshirt hanging off his broad shoulders, long legs in joggers that hug the muscles of his thighs and kiss his anklebones—he's the most beautiful I've ever seen him.

Judging by the way I feel myself looking at him, by the way he looks at me, Axel knows it. A fresh blush hits his cheeks. He turns and faces the bookshelf. His ass. In those joggers.

I bite my fist and sink deeper into the bed.

"Want me to read to you?" he says.

I whimper, but the universe does me a solid and covers my tracks, because it happens right as Skugga says, "MEOW."

Axel sighs, book in hand, then tosses it onto the bed. "I'll check on her."

"Actually . . ." I sit up as much as Harry will allow me. He's so intense about his position over my stomach, he doesn't seem to care that he just heard the cat. "Do you think she could come for a visit, too?"

Axel glances from me to the dog. "Seriously?"

"He seems okay?" I shrug. "He didn't even blink when she meowed."

"If Harry attacks me when I bring her in, and I die, it's on your conscience."

"Fair. I attend confession once a year so my nana won't haunt me. I'll deal with it then."

Groaning, Axel disappears through the studio door and returns a moment later, the tiny fluffball cradled in his arms.

Oh dear. That wasn't well-thought-out. He's somehow even

sexier with the tiny cat in his arms. It's pretty similar to how I felt watching him hold Skyler at dinner earlier, when she crushed his nuts when she sat on his lap and then directed his entire artistic process on the drawing she'd commissioned from him. He bore it all like a saint. Very much like Harry is bearing the curious inquisition of Skugga as she trots across the bed and playfully bats his nose. His eyes flick from me to her, back to me.

I pet his head. "Good boy."

Skugga glances up at me and says in the dainty voice that everyone now knows is a total act, "Meow."

"Meow yourself," I tell her as she curls up onto my chest. She purrs and kneads the blankets, then licks my chin.

Axel watches with interest as she settles in. Then he turns to Harry and gives him a good rub of his head, behind his ears, down his back. "Good boy."

Harry shuts his eyes, sighing contentedly. That's what I do, too. I listen to Axel pour his tea. Then I feel the bed gently dip as he eases onto the mattress.

"How are you feeling?" he says.

I take the book that he set between us, fanning through it. Wanting something to do. "Not awesome. But not like I'm about to die anymore, so, progress."

"I'm sorry," he says quietly. "I should have told Bennett no beans—"

"Gah." I thump my forehead with the book. "We don't have to talk about this. It's embarrassing."

Axel shifts slightly on the bed, toward me. "Why?"

"Because it's . . ." I wave a hand. "I don't know, bathroom stuff, and that's no fun to talk about with someone you're going to have acrobatic sex with—"

"Acrobatic sex?"

"You heard me. Not sexy. At all."

Axel sets his tea on the nightstand, which requires reaching across me. When he sits back against the pillows, he's closer, his hard shoulder brushing mine.

"Rooney." He picks up my hand and gently massages it. "First of all, I don't know where you got the acrobatic sex idea, but just because I run a lot does not mean I am flexible. And second, what happened tonight, that doesn't make you less attractive to me." He's quiet for a moment, staring at my hand. "*Nothing* could do that."

My heart free-falls, then finds its wings, soaring higher and higher. "Eh. You haven't heard me sing."

His mouth quirks. "It doesn't embarrass me, and it's not sexy or unsexy. It's just . . . life. It's your body. I hate that it makes you hurt and that you get sick. But it's not a turnoff."

I swallow a lump in my throat. Why did I have to marry someone so perfect? And why am I leaving him so soon? "Okay."

He tugs gently on each finger of my hand, releasing tension I didn't even know I was holding. I melt into the mattress, and Skugga climbs down from my chest. She helps herself to Axel's stomach, curling up in the folds of his hoodie. Her purr doubles in volume.

"This little fluffball's growing on me," he mutters. Her purr intensifies. She stretches out a tiny paw and touches his arm. "You said where you found her was a secret. Why?"

Of course he asks now, of all nights. And of course, for some inexplicable reason, I'm going to tell him.

Because Axel has made me feel like that most vulnerable part of my life, the most embarrassing aspects of my illness, won't change how he sees me. Not like my parents who *need* me to be better than I am, or the friends who I've projected that onto. He's made that tired, worn-out part of me sit down and put her feet up and *feel* that it's okay not to be okay.

So I'm going to tell him, and it'll be mortifying, and hopefully it'll keep this growing tenderness that's crept up on me over the past few weeks in check.

"I found her because I had to pull over," I tell him. "Because I wasn't going to make it home before I got sick. So I got off the highway and . . . *availed* myself of a field."

Oh God. Why did I do this again? I feel like I just leaped out of a plane and realized I forgot my parachute. "That's where I found her."

Axel tips his head, looks back down at Skugga. "Talk about silver linings. That had to feel terrible. But at least you got her out of it."

That's it. That's all. He's moved on.

I blink at him, stunned.

Axel reaches past me for his tea, sips it, then sets it down. When he leans back against the pillow, he says, "One time, Ryder and I went hiking. This was years ago. We used to come up here for Christmas fairly often, and he and I would go on this big Christmas Day hike. And I swear to God, he put something in my oatmeal that morning. We got up early, just the two of us, ate breakfast, and about halfway through our trek—" Axel shakes his head. "I was so bundled up, and suddenly I knew I had, like, ten seconds, maybe. I have never stripped so fast in my life."

I bite my lip. "Did you make it?"

"Barely. And Ryder was laughing so hard. Fucker."

"Oh, God, Axel. That's a nightmare. Being bundled up when you're at the crisis moment."

He nods grimly, his hand gliding along Skugga's back. "I break out in a cold sweat just thinking about it sometimes. Ryder denies it to this day, but I beat his ass so bad at *Mario Kart* the night before, and he'd been riding the high of a pretty sick victory streak until I crushed him. He did what he's good at—played cool, acted unaffected, lulled me into lowering my guard. He acted so chill about it, I figured things were fine between us. Which was naive. I know what kind of revenge Ryder prefers. Stealthy and swift. I think he stuck a laxative in my oatmeal when I got up to get milk, because when I came back, I could have sworn it tasted different."

I've been trying not to laugh, but I can't stop myself. "Your family doesn't do anything by half measures, do they?"

He sighs and peers down at me. "No, they really don't."

After a moment's silence, I tell him, "You're the only person I have ever openly admitted that to."

He tucks a loose hair behind my ear and says, "Why?"

"Because all our lives we're taught it's shameful and undesirable to discuss that aspect of our bodies, let alone when it malfunctions. It's not a part of myself that I can trust other people to handle compassionately. So I guard it very carefully."

Axel frowns at the cat, hand running rhythmically along her back. "I don't get it—why it's seen as shameful, when it's just our bodies working the way they were made to, or for you, a medical condition that affects that." He's quiet for a minute, hesitates, then says, "But I do understand guarding a part of yourself."

I peer up at him. "You do?"

He nods. And then, after a long stretch of silence, he says, "A couple years ago, I figured out that I'm . . ." He clears his throat. "That I'm autistic."

My heart flips. Words rush to the surface of my thoughts, but I don't say anything. I stay quiet. Because Axel told me, when he's trying to find the right words, he needs time. So instead, I set my hand on his and squeeze. He flips it so our palms connect, then he laces our fingers together.

"I don't talk about it," he finally says. "Not because I'm trying to hide it. I'm not ashamed. But it's . . ." He swallows thickly and squeezes my hand. "I think even though *I'm* at peace with it and it makes sense to me, I know that's not the case for everyone else. So, each time I consider telling someone, I have to brace myself, decide if they're worth that risk."

He's quiet long enough that I venture to say, "But your family?"

"They know now. For a while, I . . . I didn't know how to tell them. Like I just didn't know the words, and every time I tried in person, I just . . . couldn't. So I put it off way too long. When my sister Ziggy had her breakdown, then was diagnosed, I felt so guilty. We're very different people, and neurodivergence is unique from person to person, but there were enough signs that I should have seen before she was in such a rough place. I should have been there for her, but I was up here, wrapped up in *my* shit, and . . ." He sighs. "That's when I decided I had to figure out a way. Because Ziggy deserved to know, and my family did, too.

"I know they love me, my family. Rationally, I knew they'd be entirely supportive, and they were. I just . . . had to find a way to tell them that I could handle it. It took me forever, but I wrote them each an email because I do better that way. I'm sure that seems weird."

"I don't think that's weird." I squeeze his hand. "I think that's wonderful. You found a way to tell them that felt safe and allowed you to do it."

He nods. "But even then, it took time and courage, with people who love me unconditionally." He glances up at me, and when his eyes meet mine, something devastatingly sharp pricks my heart. "Because it's that part of myself that you just talked about. The part that I protect most deeply."

I smile at him. My vision's a little watery, and my chin trembles.

His expression tightens. "Why are you crying?"

"Because you told *me*," I whisper. "You just shared that part of yourself."

He lifts his hand, softly runs his knuckles along my jaw. His thumb whispers over my lip. "You shared yours, too." His throat works with a swallow. "I still don't know why that made you cry, though."

I laugh and wipe my eyes. "Happy tears. It means a lot to be trusted. Thank you."

Axel stares at me behind those glasses, so serious, like he's trying to puzzle me out.

"Still want me to read?" he says.

"Yes, please."

I pop my nighttime meds and turn off the electric heating pad. Harry curls up on the floor as Skugga makes a tiny mewling kitten noise in her sleep. Axel opens the small paperback and holds it in one hand, flipping nimbly to the dog-eared page. His free hand finds mine again, and our fingers lock tight.

I shut my eyes, telling myself I'll stay awake, because I don't want to miss one minute of this. But then I rest my head on the comforting solidity of his shoulder, and I know it's a lost battle. Safe, peaceful. That deep, soft voice, lulling me to sleep.

# TWENTY-TWO

# Rooney

Playlist: "Hotel Song," Regina Spektor

The next day, I'm up at the A-frame with Axel after everyone's left. I'm telling myself it's because I want to compensate for sleeping in (thank you, stomach, for the numerous previous-night wakings) and not showing up to help as early as I did yesterday. Not because I can't stop wanting to be around the guy I married for completely nonromantic reasons and haven't caught remotely romantic feelings for.

And it's definitely not because I woke up to another Harry and Skugga doodle that's so fucking adorable, it made my heart pirouette. The sketch sits safe in my suitcase beside the others, this one featuring Harry serenely flopped onto his side, Skugga leaping off him, reaching for a butterfly. It's the happiest sketch yet, and I'm disturbingly attached to it.

I've been a bit wiped out and probably less than extremely helpful today because my stomach is still not pleased with life, meaning I haven't eaten much and coffee was out of the question, and because I had another sex dream about Axel. I woke up so uncomfortably aroused, it took no time at all to finish what my dream had started, and yet it didn't even take the edge off.

So today has passed in a series of tiny tasks being done with a vague sense of dissatisfaction. I'm tired and hungry and horny. I need caffeine, but I can't drink it. I want food, but I won't eat it.

I want sex, but I haven't had it. In short, I am dangerously close to being grumpy.

Traipsing up the steps to the second floor of the A-frame, I feel my butt buzz. I stroll down the hall to the room Axel's painting and check my phone. I have a text from my dad.

> Hey, sweetie. Hope you're enjoying your
> downtime. Coming for Thanksgiving? No
> pressure. I've got a set I can be on if not.

I take another step on the grumpy-o-meter. He's basically asking my permission to go do his fancy producer thing on set rather than celebrate the holiday.

The old me would have already texted him back and told him to do what he needs, that I'd be fine. But the new Rooney who's found her footing here at the A-frame isn't so eager to preemptively smooth things over. I'm taking my sweet time. Because I don't actually know how I feel about that. My dad can wait for my honest answer.

When I walk into the bedroom, Axel glances up from cutting in along the door's trim molding. "Okay?" he asks.

I pocket my phone. "I'm avoiding my dad."

He frowns. "Is he bothering you?"

"Nah. Just being Dad."

Axel returns to painting. "I'm almost done, so we can go home. . . ."

*And finally have sex* is the unspoken rest of that sentence.

Heat floods my body, in every place I can't wait for his hands and tongue and body to touch. Axel's cheeks pink as he dips his head, and a lock of chocolate hair falls rakishly forward. I am going to do deliciously filthy things to this man tonight.

"I have to clean up first," he says, "but then we can get out of here and I'll make us something to eat."

"I'll clean up these brushes and rollers," I tell him. The sooner I clean up, the sooner we leave, the sooner we're having *alllll* the sex.

"Thanks, Roo."

I tap the paint cans shut, then pick up the rolling pans and rollers to rinse them out. When I'm halfway down the stairs, my phone buzzes again.

I've already heard from Dad. Maybe this one's Mom's typical vague but well-meaning, Love you. We should talk sometime soon. I decide I'm not really in the mood to read or respond to one of those texts, so I ignore the buzzing until it stops.

Once I'm in the basement, I dump the paint stuff into the work sink and wash everything. My phone buzzes again, right as I invert the last pan to dry. Willa's been out of town and pretty quiet, but maybe she's back and texting.

Curious, I check it. Then I gasp. And I yell, "Axel!"

"What?" he yells back.

Panicking and breathless, I sprint up the steps, round the hallway, and crash right into him.

He's breathless, too. His hands are running up and down my body. "You okay?" he says frantically. He spins me around, then back, then he grips my shoulders hard. "Don't do that! You scared me."

I blink up at him, stunned. He looks so upset. "I did?"

"Yes!" he says, dropping his hands. "You screamed. I thought you were hurt."

"I'm sorry. I didn't mean to scare you. I—"

My gaze clocks his hands . . . they're shaking. I watch them turn into fists at his sides, then fold across his chest.

*He cares*, the little voice of hope whispers. *So much that he sprints through a house and pats you down for injury. So much that he's shaking, he's so unsettled. He cares.*

"I'm sorry," I say again, peering up at him.

Axel narrows his eyes at me. "It's fine. Was there something you'd like me to know, seeing as you screamed from the basement?"

"Right. Yes." I hold up my phone. "We have a problem."

He grabs my phone and reads Willa's texts:

Hey! Ry and I are in the area picking up some fancy doodads I can't spell that he needs for his place's climbing wall. We thought we'd stop by the A-frame to say hi before you head home!

And the one from ten minutes later.

Haven't heard from you, but figured we'll at least try. I'm in Rooney-hug withdrawal! Be there in fifteen.

"Shit," he hisses, glancing around. "Turn off all the lights. Fast."

We bump chests before peeling out in opposite directions, frantically flicking off lights, grabbing keys and phones, then hustling out the front door. Axel locks the old bottom lock, then the new bolt he had installed on both the front and back sliding doors, which requires a new key.

"Tell Willa to come to my place instead," he says. "Come on."

I text Willa back, a quick, Hey! I'm actually just having dinner with Axel at his place. Meet us there?

"Done," I tell him.

He nods, then he takes off down the path. I mean *takes. Off.* I pocket my phone, staring at him, before, on a delay, breaking into a run myself.

Except that run doesn't last very long. Which is a bit frustrating, seeing as I used to run. A lot. And be very fit. But then I remember I've been a pretty sick human up until recently, and today I managed only a few gluten-free rice cakes and a banana. I have no coffee in my system and not nearly enough calories. My legs are noodles. I think I'm running in place.

"Go on without me!" I yell, waving him away, bent over. "I'll catch up."

But then footsteps are coming back toward me. Axel crouches down and sweeps up my legs. By sheer reflex, I grab his neck and hold tight. I'm riding piggyback on Axel Bergman. And he's fucking flying.

Wow, it's like my own personal *Twilight* reenactment, when Edward zooms around with Bella on his back. My speed demon hottie is hurtling me at the speed of light toward the cabin.

"This is not natural!" I yell into the wind. "This is freakish fitness, Axel."

His grip on my thighs tightens. I think I see the tiniest grin sneak out. "I run every morning for an hour, Rooney."

I glare at him. "Show-off."

"Imparting information," he says. He's on a full run with me on his back, talking like we're strolling down the sidewalk. Asshole.

But he's a fast asshole, so now we're at the house, Axel shoving me inside, then toward the showers. "Hurry up," he says.

"Okay! I'm going!" I'm peeling off my shirt and shucking my leggings as I step into the bathroom.

"Shit!" he yells. "I forgot clothes to change into at the A-frame. Be right back."

"Okay, Flash!"

"This isn't funny, this is fucking stressful!" he yells.

While he's gone, I wash as fast as possible while taking care to scrub all evidence of paint off my body. I hear the front door slam just as I drop the towel and pull on my robe.

"Come on," I call. "Your turn."

I open the bathroom door and hold it. Axel stands there, clothes under his arms, staring at me. He blinks away. "Sorry." It comes out gravelly and quiet.

"No worries." I slip by him, my front inadvertently brushing his arm. I hear him suck in a breath, and right before the bathroom door slams, I could swear I feel his eyes on me.

It's absurd, how ridiculously clumsy I'm being, tugging on jeans and a hoodie over half-wet skin. I trip, fall on the bed, get my elbow stuck in the sleeve. But eventually I get everything where it should be.

Finally dressed, I rush into the kitchen and pull out the last of the potato soup. I dump it equally into two bowls, place the bowls in the microwave to warm up, and quickly set the table.

I'm winded like my nana used to be after taking the stairs. This is the worst.

The microwave beeps. I place the soup bowls on the table, add a sprinkle of cheese and chopped parsley we still had in the fridge, and fall into my chair just as Axel sprints across the room and dives for his seat, too.

We both take bites. They fall right out of our mouths back into the bowls. Axel does a convulsive whole-body shudder. "*Christ*, woman. At least microwave it."

"I did!" I hiss, starting to laugh.

Axel buries his face in his hands, making his voice come out muffled. "For how long? Thirty seconds?"

"A minute!" I say, kicking him under the table. "I was in a rush, okay? I panicked!"

His shoulders start to shake. He's *laughing*. "A minute," he says hoarsely. "And you said you could microwave a mean bowl of soup."

"I'm used to soup for one, you jerk. Microwaving for two is a whole other ball game."

The sound of a car pulling into the clearing brings our laughter to a screeching halt. Axel's hands fall from his face. Our eyes meet.

"They're here! We have to eat it," I tell him, frantically spooning cold soup into my mouth and trying not to gag.

"Why?" he says bleakly, staring at his bowl.

"Because," I say around another bite of horribly cold soup, "I said we were eating dinner fifteen minutes ago, and it's going to look really weird if we don't show signs of having eaten dinner?"

Axel groans, lifts his bowl, and downs it in one long gulp. "Oh fuck," he says, shuddering again as a grimace racks his face. "Oh, God, that is horrible."

Axel sets down his bowl, and that's when I notice his wedding ring.

There's a knock on the door.

"Your ring!" I whisper.

Axel's eyes widen. He grabs at his ring. I grab mine. And both of us freeze. "Mine's stuck," I whimper.

"Mine too," he says, yanking at it.

"Stop. That'll make it worse. It's because we've been—"

He bursts out in hoarse laughter again as I start losing it, too. "Running around like panicking fools?" he whispers.

If I weren't freaking the fuck out that his brother and my best friend are about to see us wearing wedding rings, with no explanation that won't defeat the whole damn point of this marriage of convenience, I'd be a gooey, happy blob, devouring Axel Bergman, who is laughing so hard, he's tearing up.

"Ah, Christ. What a nightmare," he says, still laughing and wiping his eyes. "Okay, just keep your hand under the table or your hoodie sleeve over it until you can work it off."

"What are you going to do?" I whisper.

He turns and demonstrates as he says, "I'm going to casually slide my left hand into my pocket."

It doesn't look casual at all.

"That's not going to fly," I tell him.

"Hello!" Willa says. "We're here!"

"Well, I'm literally out of options, Rooney, so it's going to have to."

I slump back in my seat, waiting for disaster. The door opens, and Willa walks in, high-fiving Axel. I spring up, sleeves tucked down over my hands, as I hug her. She gives me a warm hug back, then inspects me, hands inside my sleeves. "Cold?" she asks.

I nod. "Yeah! Just a little. Axel's going to build a fire."

Ah, shit. With his hand in his pocket?

"Um, later," I say. "I'm just a smidge cold. But I bet I'll be colder later."

Willa gives me a funny look. "Did you drink too much coffee again?"

"Uh, yes. Yep. Way too much caffeine. Come on in! We were just finishing our soup."

Axel stares up at the ceiling in a plea for divine help as he shuts the door. Ryder gives him some kind of dude handshake—thank God Axel is right-handed.

"Hey, Rooney," Ryder says. Then he glances over at Axel, who's leaning—casually—against the doorframe, hand still in his pocket. "Everything okay?" he asks.

"Yeah!" we say in tandem.

Willa glances between us, then tips her head, staring at me. "Sorry to spring a visit on you. I just got back, and we were running errands. It was a last-minute run and . . ." She shrugs. "I'm just freakishly happy I can do that right now, pop in on you."

Axel shakes his head silently. *All your fault*, he mouths.

I bite my lip. I will not laugh. "Me too!" I tell her. And I mean it. I've loved being closer to Willa, even if, with her busy schedule, we haven't seen tons of each other. "I'm glad you came."

"So." Ryder eases onto the sofa and stretches out his legs. "What's been going on?"

Willa plops down next to him. "Yeah, what have you been up to?"

"Oh." I sink back down into a dining chair and work on my ring beneath the table. "Well, I've been doing a lot of nothing. It's been great."

"Really?" Willa smiles. "Still? Are you feeling okay?"

"Yeah, I am. Turns out slowing down from Energizer Bunny mode is actually really nice."

She nods. "Good. You've been overdue for a rest, and I'm glad you got it here."

"How's our host treated you?" Ryder says, glancing over at Axel, who's still standing, looking moody in the corner.

"I've been nothing but welcoming," Axel says coolly.

Ryder grins. "Sure you have."

"He has," I tell him. "We've decided we're friends."

Axel's mouth twitches, followed by an eyebrow arch.

*Friends who make out*, that expression says. *Friends who are going to bang the life out of each other if we can finally get an uninterrupted night around here.*

My thighs squeeze under the table.

"Tell me about your game, Willa." While she answers me and we chat with Ryder, Axel does the least casual swipe ever of his hand through his damp hair. I imagine he's trying to get the ring wet enough to twist off. After a few unsuccessful tries, he tugs harder and bangs his elbow into the door, making Willa and Ryder glance his way.

"I'm fostering a kitten!" I say too loudly, trying to draw their attention back to me. "Axel's letting her stay in his studio."

Ryder balks. Glances back at Axel. "You? A kitten? In your *studio*."

Axel tries to cover up what he's been doing by lacing his hands over his head and leaning back. It's the most un-Axel thing I've ever seen him do. "Just until Rooney leaves. Then Parker and Bennett are taking her."

"Do you want to meet her?" I ask.

"Sure!" Willa says.

I lead the way and open the studio door, then flick on the lights, gesturing them in. When their backs are to me, I do one last thing I can think of, which is stick my finger in my mouth and give it a good suck, wetting the band and twisting it with my teeth. Finally, the ring pops off, and in the world's most perfect timing, I manage to spit it out and slip it into my pocket just as they turn around.

Willa makes a big-eyed *Oh my Godddd* face. "She's so precious. Ry, we should get one."

Skugga hams it up, stretching exaggeratedly from her drop cloth nest and prancing out.

Ryder frowns at her. "She looks like a dust ball."

"Hey," I tell him. "That's my dust ball baby you're talking about."

Willa lets out a high-pitched squeal as Skugga pulls the move she did with Axel, stretching her tiny paws on Willa's shins. "Ryder, pleeeeaase."

"Uh-uh, sunshine, nope." He shakes his head. "I'll be the one who's home all the time, shoveling her shit and making sure she doesn't scratch everything. And they're scary little fuckers." Skugga pounces on his bootlaces. "See! She's attacking me."

"She's honing her hunting skills," Willa argues. "Besides, she could be an outdoor cat. Eat the barn mice."

"We don't have a barn," he says. "Or mice. We have a bungalow."

"So? You said it yourself, I'm gone a lot. You'd have company. Cats are good companions."

Ryder gives her a face. "Good companions? Says who?"

Axel's now on the threshold, just behind me, hand still in his pocket. I glance back at him and quickly try to mouth, *Suck on it.*

He frowns at me. Willa and Ryder are still doing their usual innocuous bickering, so I mime it. Axel's eyes widen. "What the fuck was that?" he mutters.

"Oh!" I say loud enough for Willa and Ryder to hear. They give us only a distracted glance. Willa has picked up Skugga and is making big, sad eyes at Ryder as she pleads for a cat. "I just remembered, Axel, I need you to come look at the toilet. It was making this weird sound right before they got here."

I yank him with me to the bathroom, stick his finger right in my mouth, and suck it.

Air rushes out of Axel as he slams a hand on the wall, steadying himself. My tongue swirls around the ring, before I grip it gently with my teeth, rotate his hand just a little, and twist it right off.

Axel stares at me, open-mouthed, eyes dark as I spit out the ring and then rinse it in the sink. "You could have just *said* it."

"Sorry." I peer past him, where Willa and Ryder stand talking, and then meet his eyes. "I tried to tell you, but time was of the essence."

I slide the ring into his pocket and can't help but notice the significantly larger bulge at his groin.

"Get out of here, trouble," he says, nudging me out of the bathroom, then pointedly shutting the door behind him.

I rush back to our guests, my face on fire.

There are not enough cold bowls of potato soup in the universe to cool my burning cheeks.

# TWENTY-THREE

## *Axel*

Playlist: "Movement," Hozier

"Whew." Rooney slumps against the door, eyes shut, face slack with relief at the sound of Willa and Ryder's Subaru rolling down the path.

I stare at her lips, pink and softly parted. I still can't unsee my finger disappearing into her mouth, then pulling out with a long, wet *pop*.

Christ, I'm hard again.

I turn back to the table, gathering up the cards. "Fun time to find out my wife's a card shark," I grumble.

She evil-cackles, then pushes off the door. "Fun time to find out my husband's a sore loser."

"Competitive," I mutter, shuffling the cards, then stacking them neatly.

"Euchre isn't supposed to be ruthless, Axel. It's a chill, hang-out-and-visit card game."

"You had two Bergmans playing with you. All games are ruthless."

She smiles, and God, it aches, hot and bright in my chest. "Well, ruthless or not, you Bergman boys got your asses handed to you. Willa and I cleaned the table with you fools."

I slide the cards into their box, then set them on the floating shelf. The fire snaps and pops below me, painting the floors and my bed with glowing orange light. It's so easy to picture what I've been waiting for, wanting with a hunger that gnaws at my bones: laying Rooney out on my bed, stripping her slowly until she's only soft skin bathed in firelight.

I have never wanted someone so badly, so totally, it makes my hands shake, makes breathing around her and speaking to her and looking at her all feel like some form of torturous foreplay.

"Everything okay?" Rooney asks.

I glance at her, suddenly stunned by the depth of my denial. I really thought I could give myself one night with her and that would be enough. But when I picture her beneath me, on top of me, beside me, my body and hers moving, her moans and sighs . . . that vision keeps reeling through time, and it's dangerously detailed. It's Rooney bent over the table, surrounded by papers and a laptop, reading whatever it is lawyers read for their jobs, Skugga in her lap, Harry at her feet, the door open in my studio so I can watch her work while I work, too. It's holding her hand as we hike and watch the sunrise, as I clasp her against me, her back to my front, and breathe her in and know this is all I need—the sun breaking the horizon, another day that's a gift, because it has her in it.

And those are absurd things to picture with my strictly platonic wife who's got one foot out the door.

"Hey." Her hand slips inside mine, pulling me from my thoughts. She stands, glowing in the firelight that casts her blonde hair bronze.

"Sorry." I squeeze her hand, then release it. "What did you say?"

She smiles gently. "I asked if you were okay. That was kind of stressful."

"Yeah. It was. But I'm okay."

"Once I wasn't petrified we were going to give away *everything* that's going on, I actually had fun. Did you?"

Fun? Did I have fun?

There were certainly good parts. Watching Rooney smile and laugh as they won, the way she got extra playful and relaxed with her best friend. Seeing her so at home in my home, making tea and popcorn for Willa and Ryder, settled at the table across from me.

But I can't say I had fun, feeling my wedding ring burn a hole in my pocket, battling an erection because Rooney's every move turned me on, all while praying to God Ryder didn't have some random thing he wanted to grab from the A-frame that I'd have to take him to get and then the jig would be up.

"It was . . . fine."

Her smile dims. She glances away, a gesture I've recognized means the last thing I'd want to make her feel: crestfallen, disappointed. Knowing I caused that feels like a body blow.

"I didn't mean . . ." I step closer, wrapping my hand around her elbow. My throat is tight, my chest tighter. I hate when I do this. When I'm honest and honesty proves *not* to be the best policy, when what I say doesn't say everything I meant.

This is why my social circle is so small. Because with strangers and casual acquaintances, there's no benefit of the doubt for me, no way for them to know that while I try my best, translating what I've experienced into how I feel about it then articulating that to others is harder than the most grueling morning run. With people who don't know me well, there's no patience when I need time to straighten it out in my head and find the guts to try again. There's just misunderstanding and frustration.

But Rooney shows me what I already knew. That she's safe. That she's listening.

She turns and faces me, head tipped.

"I didn't mean it wasn't fun *at all*," I manage. "I was just . . . distracted with what could go wrong. I felt . . . anxious."

She turns more fully, her expression softening. "Hard to enjoy yourself when you're anxious. Isn't anxiety such a jerk? Just plays everything that could go wrong on a loop. I'm sorry."

Relief floods me. She understands. "Exactly."

"Well, want to sit in front of the fire and mellow out for a bit?" she asks. "I can make us more tea. Throw a little whiskey in it. We can get some therapeutic animal cuddles in and zone out."

Warmth spills through my chest. I nod.

Her smile returns. "Okay. Good. Where's Harry?"

"He'll come around." I stroll toward the door and open it, whistling softly into the air that's taken a sudden turn for the cooler. "He tends to wander in the evenings, but he'll come home to warm up for the night."

Rooney fills the kettle, then turns on the burner, smiling as Harry bounds in and runs straight past me toward her.

"Nice to see you, too," I mutter.

He jumps up and she hugs him, letting him lick her chin, laughing as he sneaks a lick of her ear, too. "Harry Styles!" she yelps. "Behave yourself."

Skugga scampers out of the studio and pounces on my shoe-laces with a tiny, feral "Meow!"

I pick her up, then hold her right in front of my eyes. "Quit it with the shoelaces."

The tiny fluffball tips her head, just like Rooney did a moment ago. "Meow," she says.

I sigh and set her on the bed. She runs across it, then topples off, chasing one of her feather-tipped jingle balls and disappearing back into the studio. It's weirdly familiar and . . . homey.

I never thought sharing space with someone could be like this. Not since growing up with a family that I love but whose noise levels and chaos had me in a perennial state of sensory aggravation. Living alone, it's the first time I've felt sustained calm and peace in my home. I never imagined it would be that way with another person, too.

With her.

Rooney pours us tea as the kettle starts to whistle. "Sleepytime, right?" she asks.

I nod. "Thanks."

She smiles, eyes on her task. I'm back in physical hell again, looking at her, the way she bites her lip idly, how she tucks a strand of hair behind her ear, revealing the long line of her throat. That I want to kiss and suck and taste—

*Shit.*

I turn away and add another log to the fire. That's when the first *boom* of thunder echoes around us. Rooney glances up. "Whoa. That was out of nowhere. Is it calling for storms?"

"I didn't check the forecast. Now that the roof's done, I've stopped worrying about it."

She pulls out her phone and swipes open to the Weather Channel app, dunking the tea bag rhythmically as she does.

Then she turns her phone, revealing a screen flashing the same colors as the fire—a vast stretch of deep red, circled by burnt orange, fringed in yellow. "We're about to get our asses handed to us," she says.

There's another flash of white light chased by a formidable boom.

That's when the power cuts out.

---

"Oookay," Rooney's voice says from the kitchen. It's dark, our only light spilling faintly from the fire. I move quickly, finding the candles where I keep them in the closet and the flashlight. "So, has this happened before?" she asks.

"Yes."

She sets down the kettle, by the sounds of it. "This does not happen to me. And . . . listen, don't laugh."

"I don't generally laugh, do I?"

"Fair point," she says. "So . . . I might be a *smidge* afraid of the dark. I know that's ridiculous, but I am."

"I have experience with this." Walking toward her with the flashlight, I offer my hand. "Viggo is, too. Don't tell him I told you."

I can hear her smile. "His secret is safe with me."

"Come here." I guide her out of the kitchen with the flashlight, Harry whimpering behind her. "Harry's in your boat, too," I tell her as we lower onto the floor in front of the fire.

Rooney opens her arms as Harry crawls toward her and lies across her thighs. She strokes his head in a long, slow rhythm. Her hands are shaking.

"Are you afraid of storms, too?" I ask her.

She stares down at Harry. "I don't like how dark they make everything. My mom always used to let me come into her bed during a storm. She had twinkle lights she'd plug in and drape across the headboard, which, if you knew my mom, you'd understand is really funny, because everything about her and her clothes and her home decor is the height of fashion, but she kept this junky string of twinkly lights that she'd turn on just for me when it was dark and I was scared."

Skugga darts across the room, tumbling awkwardly over our legs and sprinting into the kitchen, clearly enjoying having free rein of the place and entirely unaffected by the raging storm outside. Rooney stares after her and smiles, and that's when I see the wetness in her eyes.

"You get sad when you talk about your mom."

Rooney sighs heavily, rubbing Harry's ears. I set a hand on his back, too, where he's trembling, hoping the weight of my touch soothes him. He sighs just like Rooney.

"It's tricky with my mom. There's distance, especially now that she lives in Positano with her husband, Paolo."

"When does she visit?"

"Oh, she doesn't. I'm invited to visit her, but seeing as I've barely come up for air since freshman year of college, finding time to hang out in Italy has been kind of difficult."

I stare at her and try to imagine a world where my mother wasn't chasing me down, phoning me to get on a plane and come see her. I don't know what to say.

"It's okay," Rooney says, reading my concerned expression. *It's okay.* That's the refrain that I'm learning accompanies her *I'm fine but not really* smile. "I get why she doesn't visit. She wasn't happy here. In a loveless marriage, usually solo parenting an opinionated, high-energy kid with nonstop questions about vegetarianism and planetary science and animal rights. I'd want an early retirement and an Italian lover, too."

"But you miss her?" I ask. "And you'd like it if she visited, wouldn't you?"

Rooney peers up at me, her smile watery. "Yeah. I miss her. And I'd love it if she visited."

"Have you told her that?"

"No. I . . . I don't tell my mom things that I think will upset her. She doesn't visit, and if I told her I wish she would, I'm worried it would make her feel guilty and upset."

"That sounds like you're responsible for her feelings. Aren't each of us responsible for our own feelings?"

Her expression turns reflective. "That's a good point. I never really thought of it that way. I suppose it's just our dynamic. I learned to hide my problems from my mom because she was miserable enough as it was, and I was supposed to be her happiness. But . . . I don't think that's very healthy." She glances at the fire. "Willa says I should go to therapy, and she's right."

"Therapy isn't easy, but it's exactly what we need sometimes."

Rooney's hand finds mine. She picks it up and holds it in her grip, her finger tracing my empty ring finger. "Have you gone?" she asks.

"Not very often," I admit. "But yes. The therapist was the one who suggested emailing to tell my family about my diagnosis. Therapy is difficult for me. Figuring out what I'm feeling and finding the words for it, that's an involved and sometimes delayed process for me. It's also very hard for me to talk about my feelings with a stranger. So I've found it's best if I don't go too often. I schedule when I'm feeling the need to process, when I'm feeling ready to articulate those feelings."

She peers up at me. "What do you mean, about figuring out your feelings?"

I stare at her, my heart pounding. It takes me a minute to find my courage, to find the words to explain it. "I just don't . . . know sometimes, how I feel. It's like my emotions are deep inside me, and I don't surface them as fast as other people. Other times, my emotions are there, right below the surface, and I'm so overwhelmed with them, words swarm my brain, and I can't quiet them enough to concentrate and find the right one. I know it might seem like it sometimes, but I'm not emotionless. I *have* feelings."

"Of course you do, Axel." Her hand's grip tightens on mine. "You just feel them differently."

A knot forms in my throat, hot and thick. I have never felt so seen by the very last person I ever expected to understand what it's like to be the way I am. "Yes."

That knot in my throat dissolves as she stares up at me and her hands cup my face. Rooney presses the softest kiss to my forehead, then my temple, then my mouth, and I melt into her. I nudge the dog right off her lap, then drag her into my arms. I feel raw and relieved, shaky with adrenaline singing in my blood.

Rooney sighs, threading her fingers through my hair as our kiss deepens. "I want you," she says breathlessly as my mouth trails down her throat.

A grunt of agreement leaves me, because it's the only sound I can form when her hands are sliding under my shirt, whispering along the front of my jeans.

I stand with her as our kisses grow hungrier, our touch wilder. My shirt comes off. Her sweatshirt does, too. We fall onto the mattress with twin groans and a much louder groan from the bed.

I pick up my head. "Did you hear that?"

Rooney shakes her head. "No. Why are you stopping? Don't stop."

I lean into her, kissing her deeply, my palm sliding down her stomach, touching her gently where she's warm and wet. I'm lost in the feel of touching her and being touched, grinding against the sweet give of her body, the warmth between her thighs, so much so that I tell myself to ignore the next groan from the bed that comes when I slide my arm beneath her back, drag her higher up the bed, then settle us heavily against the mattress.

She's urging me on, and we're dry-humping frantically, too impatient to take off clothes or do anything except chase release. But on a particularly rough thrust of my hips, the bed groans its loudest yet, creaks ominously . . .

And breaks right down the middle.

# TWENTY-FOUR

## Axel

Playlist: "Happy Accidents," Saint Motel

The mattress starts sinking slowly beneath us. Rooney stares up at me, wide-eyed as we continue our descent into the valley of the busted bed.

"Did we just break your bed?" she whispers.

"Uh. Yes."

A laugh jumps out of her. "Sorry. It's not funny. It really sucks. But . . . it's kind of funny."

Thunder cracks in the sky, and her arms tighten around me.

I yank her up from the bed as I push off, making her yelp.

"Yeesh, muscles." She blinks up at me. "I think we know who broke the bed. Is that thing made for someone your size?"

I narrow my eyes at her. "The bed handled my weight just fine until *you* got here."

She gasps. "Excuse me!"

A log rolls off the flames in the fireplace, dimming the light. Rooney might be aggravated with me, but she clings even closer.

"Let me build up the fire again." I pull away from her, add another log, and blow on the coals until it burns brighter again. Then I turn back and face the damage. My house is intentionally compact. I don't need a lot of space. Enough height not to feel claustrophobic, and a layout that feels streamlined. But it means that when my bed breaks, I have to do something about it. We're not going to be able to do anything we wanted to tonight.

"Right." I sigh. "Time to do some rearranging."

---

It's a sweaty job, dealing with the broken bed, because the platform I built is made of solid wood. Apparently not solid enough.

With the broken bedframe hauled into the studio, the mattress now sits on the floor. Rooney and I are both sweating, and my lower back is tight and hurts like a bitch, like it has off and on for days. I can't believe how sweaty we are, except I guess it took Ryder and Parker and Bennett to set the thing up with me, and Rooney and I just did it with half the manpower.

My sweat has now become damp and chilly on my skin. Which I *hate*. I tug my shirt away from my chest, thoroughly miserable.

Rooney flops onto the mattress on the floor. "There should be enough hot water for another shower or two, right?" she asks.

I drop my shirt. "Probably. Want one?"

She glances my way and smiles. "*You* want one. I can tell you're feeling gross. Go shower. I'll be okay. The fire's bright, and I can be a big girl."

"You're sure?"

"Of course, Ax. Go on."

"I'll be quick. You can shower after me."

"Sounds good." Halfway up from the mattress, she freezes. "Shit." Rooney springs up the rest of the way and digs through her suitcase, which is tucked along the wall. "I forgot my clothes were in the wash. I have . . . a pair of jeans, and a *Reading Rainbow* T-shirt."

"Here." I cross the room to my dresser and raid my drawers. After I broke down the tent and sorted through what I wanted up at the A-frame, I left a few worn-out stragglers behind. There's an old hoodie of mine and sweatpants that have seen better days. I toss both of them onto the mattress for her. "Sorry. They're pretty beat up, but it's what I have. Most of my stuff's not here."

"No, that's perfect. Just as long as they're not hard pants."

"My sentiments exactly." I find myself another pair of old sweatpants, a threadbare, faded T-shirt, and an old crew-neck sweatshirt. "Be right back."

My shower's fast as possible so that I leave hot water for Rooney. We trade places, and while she's in the shower, I realize I need to do something about this sleeping situation.

Or . . . maybe I *want* to?

I suppose I could just throw a blanket on the floor and call it a day, but something in me wants to make it special for her. Special and . . . cozy?

What is going on with me?

I don't have an answer to that, but I can't seem to stop myself. I just keep going. I dig in the closet and find an older tent, more compact than the one I used while I was sleeping outside those first few weeks. Harry follows at my heels, whining softly.

"It's okay, bud." I pat his side. "Just some rain. It'll pass."

He whines again, then drops right in front of the fire as I pull the tent to rest on top of the mattress, which is close to the fire but a safe distance from its flames. It looks weird from the outside, but inside, it's promising. Just not quite cozy, though. It's too dark, even with the fire nearby.

I traipse back to the closet, find the LED battery-operated twinkly lights that Freya gave me as a housewarming gift *for wherever you want a little extra sparkle*, a turn of phrase I vividly remember making Ryder snort and resulting in Freya punching his arm. I unravel them, then thread them through the tent's opening and use clothespins to anchor them to the dome of the tent. It's . . . definitely a hack job. But it's lit and cozy.

I hope it will make her feel safe. The way Rooney makes me feel safe.

Parker's voice echoes in my head. *You really don't think you might be developing feelings for her?*

Oh, God. I'm not. I can't.

But then what were those scenes I was picturing in my head just a few minutes ago, imagining her here, part of my life, at home in my home? Why couldn't I stop myself from admitting one night was never going to be enough?

The floorboard creaks, breaking me from my thoughts, and I turn. Rooney stands by the fire, hands laced in front of her, hair wet but combed, my clothes swallowing her up. Her eyes meet mine, and that moment feels like a new color, brushed across my heart's canvas. One that I never even dreamed could grace my life, because I didn't know it existed.

Now I can't imagine what my life would look like without it.

That's when I know. When every question I had is answered, and I know this twisting, aching, terrible, beautiful *something* that's grown and deepened inside me for weeks is a feeling, and that feeling is all for her, and it's nothing like I've ever felt for anyone.

And that feeling . . . is love.

I love her.

Holy *fuck*. I love her.

Blithely unaware, Rooney smiles at me, holding out the sweatshirt. "Bob Ross, huh?"

I stare at her, transfixed. Besides the famous TV painter's face on it, the sweatshirt is the same ivory color of the sweater dress she wore on our wedding day. For some reason, it feels purposeful—a wink from the universe.

"I loved his show," she says. "I'd sit there and mellow out, listening to him, watching him paint those scenes that . . . well, they kind of remind me of the landscape here."

"M-me too," I finally manage.

"He had such great sayings. 'We don't laugh because we feel good, we feel good because we laugh.' Obviously, I love that one." Rooney glances down at the sweatshirt, frowning. "There was another one, though, that I can't fully remember. It started with 'No mistakes . . .'" She peers up at me. "Do you remember how it went? 'No mistakes . . .'"

"'Just happy accidents,'" I tell her quietly, moved by the truth in those words. That's what they are, the circumstances that led her here, that made us collide and our paths converge . . . not mistakes, even though they felt like it, but the happiest accidents.

The ones that gave me her.

Her smile widens. "That's it."

I'm still staring at her, stunned, reeling. I'm . . . in love. And it's a little frightening. Like staring in front of a blank canvas when I'm aching to paint, colors ready, brush in hand. I just have to prepare to become completely absorbed.

Will loving her be like painting? Like building this home? Like running? Immersive, consuming, so intensely possessive of my thoughts and energy and time?

Do I like that? Or am I back to being frightened? Who knew love would be so complicated.

Her hand slips inside mine, and every thought dissolves. Maybe love isn't complicated, then. Maybe love is simple. Maybe it's people who make it complicated. Maybe I can just be—here, now, touching her, lost to this moment and every moment I get with her.

Maybe that can be enough.

"Where'd you go?" she asks quietly.

I squeeze her hand. "Just . . . thinking."

Peering at the tent, she seems to register it for the first time. "What is this?" She smiles, then crouches down, lifting the flap. "You put lights in it."

"You don't like the dark."

She stands again, then steps closer, wrapping her arms around me. Her head rests on my chest. "Axel," she sighs, and presses a slow kiss right over my pounding heart. "What am I going to do with you?"

# TWENTY-FIVE

# Rooney

Playlist: "New Song," Maggie Rogers, Del Water Gap

I stare at the tent sparkling with twinkly lights. A comforting, cozy setup that Axel put together to make the storm feel less stormy and the dark not quite so dark, and my heart bursts, like a kaleidoscope of butterflies taking wing.

And that's when I know that all this rationalizing I've been doing, telling myself it's only a crush with a few surmountable feelings tacked on for this tough nut who finally cracked just for me is nothing but lies.

I love him. I think I've been falling in love for quite a while. Like a domino effect, it's been moment after moment, one tipped onto the other, building speed and beauty as they connected. Before the last inevitable *click* as that final piece fell and revealed itself.

*Love.*

Oh, I would do this. I would fall for the guy who has every plan to fuck the lust right out of us and send me on my way. My heart's soaring, and it's breaking, and even while it hurts, I have never felt so safe. Because that's what this has been—not passionate, though it's had its moments, or romantic, which we've tried very hard to avoid. It's been safe.

What an irony, that a loveless marriage became the safest place to build love after all.

I hug Axel hard, my ear resting over his heart. It's racing. Why?

His arms wrap around me, slowly, cautiously, like he's worried I might shape-shift while he's holding me. I stay still, hugging him like he showed me—hard, with my hands locked low on his back. I hope that whatever is making his heart pound inside his chest isn't me. Or if it is, it's the good kind of pounding.

*Does* he feel the way I feel? Is his heart soaring and snapping and crashing to earth? I won't know, will I? Not unless I tell him. Not unless he tells me.

I want to be brave. I want to ask and profess and bare my heart.

But it's dark, and it's storming, and I'm so terrified to be alone. Even though I want to know, even though I'd be euphoric if I asked and I learned that I have his heart the way he has mine, I'd rather have just some of him tonight than risk losing him entirely.

Tomorrow I'll be brave. Tonight I need to be safe.

"Axel," I whisper against his sweatshirt. It's worn and soft, and it smells just like him. I breathe in deep and sigh. "Thank you for my twinkly light tent."

"You like it?" he asks.

I nod, squeezing him just a smidge harder. "I love it."

*I love you.*

Swallowing the lump in my throat, I pull away, enough to peer up and drink him in—that stubborn lock of chocolate hair kissing his temple, the fire glowing in his deep green eyes. The artful loveliness of his cheekbones and jaw, the softness of his lips.

He peers down at me, too, looking at me in a way I don't think he has before. With an openness, an unguarded curiosity as his gaze travels my face. He smooths back my hair behind my shoulders, then softly cups my face.

Thunder booms outside again, and a flash of lightning illuminates the room. I clutch Axel tighter. "Sorry I'm so jumpy. I shouldn't still be afraid of storms, but I just . . . am."

He holds me close, one hand slipping rhythmically through my hair, and says, "One of the first things we learned from my dad when we started hiking and camping was that it's important to have a healthy fear of nature, to know our place in the grand scheme of things. Because then we can make wise choices. Fear can teach us. But it can also lie to us." He leans his cheek against my head. "Try something?"

I nod.

"Shut your eyes."

I tense. "But . . ."

"I know, it makes it dark. Just try it, though."

Exhaling slowly, I close my eyes. The world feels twice as strange and much more disorienting. But I hold tight to Axel, and I keep my eyes closed. "They're shut."

"Now . . . listen."

"To what?"

His hands slip steadily through my hair. His heart pounds against my ear. "What's around you. Feel what you can't see. Let it orient you."

I try another slow breath to calm myself and listen. To the crackling fire, the quiet breathing of Harry at our feet. Skugga's ball jingling around as she chases it in the studio. I hear rain pelting the windows and the faint creak of tall trees swaying in the wind. Another boom of thunder shakes the earth, but this time it doesn't frighten me. It just . . . is. It's there, the same way the fire is, and the animals, and Axel holding me. I hear its pounding like I hear my heart. I hear the storm like I hear my own breathing, like I hear Axel's.

"It's like one of your paintings," I whisper. "Big and complex and abstract and . . . I just *feel* it."

And then I feel his smile against the top of my head, the way his arms clutch me a little tighter.

"That's it."

Slowly, I open my eyes, blinking as they adjust from darkness to the dim glow of the fire and the twinkly lights. Axel stares down at me, a new light in his eyes as he searches my face. "How do you feel?"

I smile. "Safe."

He dips his head and kisses me once, soft as the lightest rain whispering over my skin. Then he pulls away. "Want s'mores again? With those gluten-free chocolate chip cookies?"

My smile becomes a ridiculous grin. "Yes! You're a genius, you know that, right? Gluten-free chocolate chip cookies are a brilliant substitute for gluten-free graham crackers."

Turning toward the kitchen, he says, "I didn't even know gluten-free graham crackers existed."

"You haven't been missing anything. They are *rough*."

When he rounds the counter into the kitchen, I notice him jolt, like he's been stung, then roll his shoulders.

"Okay?" I ask.

"Fine," he says. "My lower back's been a little tight."

"Well, considering you work twelve-hour days of construction, then sleep on an air mattress, despite a perfectly serviceable bed and sofa being available to you, I'm not entirely surprised. Aren't any of the beds good to use at the house?"

He opens a cabinet, then starts pulling out the s'mores fixings. "We wrapped them up in protective plastic bags. They're still sealed while we work, and I can't stand sleeping on that plastic material."

"So you're sleeping on a plastic air mattress?"

"Vinyl." He throws me a look over his shoulder. "And it's a fabric top, thank you very much."

I open my mouth, ready to put up a real stink about this sleeping-arrangement nonsense, but I'm interrupted before I can.

Because as Axel bends to pick up the bag of marshmallows he just dropped, he lets out such a low, sharply pained sound, I forget everything I was going to say.

And then he crumples to the floor.

I run around the island and slide into the kitchen in my socks, dropping to my knees.

He's sprawled on his back, legs jerking up until they're bent. I see a fine tremor ripple through his torso. "It's okay," he says hoarsely. "I'm fine."

I'm the queen of *I'm fine*. And I see right through it. "You don't have to be fine."

He doesn't say anything. Just shuts his eyes. "Please don't touch me," he says.

"I won't," I say quietly, hands on my thighs. And then I simply sit next to him while he breathes, palms pressing into his eyes. I wait. And I wait. And I wait. Until I can't stand it a second longer. "So, when are you going to admit that you actually aren't fine?"

His mouth tightens as he drops his hands. "My back . . . might be slightly aggravated."

"What happened?"

"My lower back. Ever since I fucked it up in the spring, it's not hard to piss it off."

"How?"

He lowers one leg and winces. "My soccer league got a little physical."

"I feel like you're not telling me the whole story. Was it serious?"

"It wasn't a big deal. Bennett acts like it was, because I had to call him to come get me from the hospital—"

"The *hospital*? Axel, that's serious—"

"No. It was because they had me on muscle relaxers, so I couldn't drive. It was just a really bad spasm. That's what this is, too. Actually, speaking of muscle relaxers." He points stiffly to the small cabinet right over the fridge. "Mind grabbing the bottle for me? Right next to the whiskey."

"Oh sure. Real healthy."

He groans, shutting his eyes. "I didn't ask for them *together*."

"I'm teasing you." I stand and grab the muscle relaxers, having to reach on tiptoe. "You made everything giant in this place. I'm five eleven, and I can't even touch your top shelves."

"I actually fit in my own house," he deadpans. "The cruelty."

I fill a glass with water and bring the pill bottle with me. "How many?"

"One."

I shake out the pill, then screw on the cap. "Those cabinets might be perfect for you, but what if someone who isn't six five wants to live with you one day?"

He peers up at me, gaze searching my face. "I never thought they would."

"Shortsighted of you." I set the pill in his hand, then watch him throw it back, his Adam's apple working while he leans up just enough to chug the entire glass of water. "Does massage feel good when it locks up?"

He coughs a bit on the last swig of water, then lowers the glass. "You don't have to do that."

"That doesn't answer the question I asked."

"It . . ." He lowers back onto the ground. "I don't know. It's only happened when I'm alone. At the hospital, they didn't do massage— just gave me muscle relaxers and an electrostimulation unit. I do *not* like e-stim, by the way." He shudders, then winces.

I feel impossibly protective of him right now. I know Axel's no sob story. He likes living alone and his solitary life, but it still just makes me wish someone were there to take care of him when he needs it. Thankfully I'm here now, and I can.

I *want* to.

"Well . . . if you're comfortable with it," I say, "we can try."

"I guess," he mutters. "Once I can get myself out of here."

"I'd offer my heating pad, too, but that's off the table until the power's back on. When you feel ready to move, you can lie down on the bed, and I'll rub you for a while."

His mouth twitches.

I snort. "Okay, pervert. *Massage* you. *Rub* you. Whatever. There is no way to say that without it being innuendo."

"You're right. I apologize."

"You're forgiven. Your penance is to lie down on that bed."

"If I must," he groans. Slowly, he rolls onto his side, then gets on all fours. He cautiously tries to stand. "That's not happening," he says. "Crawling it is."

"Oh, Axel. This is terrible."

Harry barges into the kitchen, whimpering and sniffing Axel, who crawls toward the living room. I move the chair, and next I'm aiming to move the tent when Axel says, "No, leave it."

So I do. I just pin the flap open and let him crawl in. Slowly, he stretches onto the mattress like a slow-motion slide into home plate on a low, pained groan.

Trying to give him some privacy to get comfortable, I get to work, doing what always makes me feel better when things are upsetting, which is to make things tidy. I stoke the fire and add another log. I light the candles that he set on the floating shelves above the fireplace.

And when I turn back, Axel's lying on his stomach, only in sweatpants. My heart stalls. He's so beautiful. I stare shamelessly at the muscles in his back, the dip of his spine and two soft dimples right above the waistband of his sweats.

When I glance up, our eyes meet. "Sorry for the show," he says.

"I just can't stand that feeling of fabric on my skin when my back's like this. It's aggravating."

"You're fine." I crawl into the tent, too, which is surprisingly spacious, but then again, for it to fit a six-five guy, it sort of has to be. "Okay for me to touch you?"

"Yes," he says, face muffled in the sleeping bag he's laid out. "Can you sit on my butt? It'll give you better leverage, and pressure on my tailbone feels good."

I straddle him and mentally slap myself as I feel the hard muscles of his ass. This is not sexual time. This is take-care-of-Axel time.

Gently, I set my hands on his lower back, his skin taut and smooth. I'm no massage therapist, but I've been an athlete long enough to know what hurts and what generally makes it feel better, so I do what I know feels good. I slide my thumbs gently along the large muscles on either side of his spine and earn his groan.

Right. Nope. Not sexual at all.

Just tell that to the ache between my thighs and my nipples tightening beneath the Bob Ross hoodie. *No mistakes. Just happy accidents.*

I repeat the motion a few times, spreading my hands and kneading with my palms next. Air rushes out of Axel. His ass tightens beneath me.

"Is that okay?" That comes out a little breathy. Oops.

Axel's hands fist the sleeping bag he laid inside the tent. "Yes."

I can feel the lockup low in his back, and I work my palms down right to the two small dimples on either side of his tailbone.

"There," he groans.

Pausing, I sit back as I remember a shiatsu massage I had earlier this year. The therapist stood at my head, then slid their hands down my spine, toward my butt. I remember vividly how it opened up my lower back.

"I'm going to try something else, okay?"

Axel opens his eyes only halfway. I can see the muscle relaxer has started to kick in. "Sure."

I ease off his butt, then crawl toward his head. He glances up and frowns. "What are you doing?"

"I'm not going to go wild here, because I'm not a professional, but I just wanted to try something a massage therapist did for me. It'll come at that low part of your back really well."

His eyes are pinned on me as I kneel closer, then lean over him, my knees straddling his head. I slide my hands down his back. "Don't you dare say anything remotely innuendo-related."

Sighing heavily, he presses his forehead to my knee. Then he brings his hand gently to my thigh and slides it up to my hip, then back down. "This is cruel."

"Does it hurt?" I ask.

"Yes," he groans. "So bad."

I pause. "I can stop."

"Not the massage," he mutters. "This." He squeezes my thigh. "It's so close to being exactly what I want."

My cheeks heat as I laugh quietly. "I think the muscle relaxer has relaxed your tongue, too."

"Mm-hmm," he says, nuzzling the inside of my thigh. "It has. And my tongue doesn't want to be relaxed. It wants to be busy."

I snort a laugh. "Wow. Are you this fun drunk?"

"Nope. I just get really quiet."

"As if you aren't already really quiet."

"Even quieter," he says seriously. "Like a mouse."

I peer down at him and bite back a laugh. "I don't know. I bet if I got you in front of a dartboard with a few beers in you, you'd get a little rowdy. You seem like a darts guy."

He smiles, a devastating trifecta: bright teeth, long-line dimples, and the grand finale—that crinkled nose. My heart stutters like an engine that just might quit.

"When you come for Thanksgiving, you'll find out," he says. "We have darts in the basement. Oh *fuck*, yes." He grips my thigh as I slide the heels of my palms into the muscles of his ass. "Do it again. That felt so good."

It's taking everything in me not to collapse and just give up, because I'm so turned-on, it's unreal, and I'm also about to bust a gut laughing, massaging Axel's ass while straddling his face as he moans beneath me. None of it is sex and we both wish it was. If this isn't us in a nutshell, I don't know what is.

"Yeah," he says breathily, gripping my thigh harder. "Fuck, that hurts. Good hurts. Don't stop."

"If you'd told me the day I drove up here that just a few weeks later I'd be married to you, straddling your face, and rubbing your butt while you told me it hurts so good, I'd have laughed so hard, I would've cried."

Axel groans. "Just wait until I'm not doped up on muscle relaxers. You'll be in my face, all right. And you won't be laughing."

"I'm holding you to that." I keep up my massage, kneading deeply into those tight muscles. I hear his breathing grow even, his groans space out.

"A little better?" I ask.

He mumbles something. His eyes are shut, firelight dancing on his skin and the long muscles of his shoulders and back. I ease away so that I'm sitting next to him and brush back his hair, indulging in one soft caress of his beard. I have to use the bathroom, and then I'm planning to park it on the sofa, where I'm close and I can at least see the twinkly lights in the tent. I'm not sleeping next to him, not when he's out of it and we didn't talk about sleeping arrangements. But before I can even leave the tent, his hand flies out, wrapping around my wrist.

"Come here," he says quietly.

I hesitate. "Axel, you just need to sleep—"

"That's why I want you to come here." His eyes open and hold mine.

"Just for a few minutes," I tell him.

He narrows his eyes, but he doesn't say anything.

Carefully, I ease onto the sleeping bag beside him. Axel lifts his arm just far enough to wrap it around my waist. He tucks me closer, then buries his nose in my hair and breathes in.

And that's how he falls asleep, holding me close, my name on his lips, a soft, breathless sigh.

# TWENTY-SIX

# *Axel*

Playlist: "Make Out in My Car," Moses Sumney and
Sufjan Stevens

I wake up when it's only the faintest light. The tent's still open,
Harry right in my line of vision, out cold in front of the dying fire.

Slowly, I push onto all fours, wincing at my back. It's still pretty
bad. Not as bad as last night, but definitely not good. Leaning, I
peek out just far enough to see Rooney curled up on the sofa, a
blanket tucked tight to her chin. She looks small and cold, and it
makes protectiveness roar in my chest.

"Rooney," I call. My voice comes out hoarse and low like it always does in the mornings.

Her eyes slowly open, and Christ, it's stunning, like the first
peek of blue sky after days of clouds. They lock on me as a slow-
dawning smile warms her face.

"Hey," she says quietly.

"Come here?" If I had any pride left, it would be in jeopardy,
but I don't. She saw me drop to the floor, then crawl across it because of my jacked-up back. Then I probably said God knows what
on the muscle relaxer—those things make me *completely* unfiltered. She's seen me pretty much at my lowest.

Sitting up, Rooney stretches, a tiny squeak leaving her that
makes the world glow rose-petal pink, the vivid smudge of color in
a sunrise, the shade of a blush on her cheek. I ease back inside the
tent and wait for her. I hear her rustling around, talking to Skugga,

whose jingle ball heralds her arrival. I watch a new log land on the fire, the hand bellows creating enough air to coax the dying coals to make a small flame again. Then Rooney appears, smiling and framed in the tent's opening, like the perfect painting.

My heart twists.

"Hi," she says, crawling in. She extends something small and white to me.

"I take muscle relaxers for pain only, Rooney. I'm not into the hard stuff."

She laughs. "It's a mint, you goof."

"Ah." I open my mouth, and she sets it softly on my tongue as she pops one in her mouth, too. "Holy shit, that's strong."

"I burn through these things all day at school." Her expression dims a little as she stares up at me, curled on her side, her hands beneath her cheek. "Speaking of school . . . can I ask you something?"

"Of course."

"How did you know you wanted to paint, like for that to be your work?"

Gingerly, I ease onto my side, too, and face her. "It was the only thing I was pretty good at and enjoyed deeply enough that I could envision doing it for work. Once I knew my art could sell, I went for it. I figured if it crapped out, I could always do construction for Park and Bennett, but I haven't had to so far. What does that have to do with Stanford?"

She sighs, her gaze drifting past my shoulder to where the first bit of sunlight makes the tent glow. "I don't know what to do about law school."

I stare at her, her blonde hair frizzy and gnarled in a little bird's nest, a pillow wrinkle on her cheek. I trace that line down to her jaw. "What feels right?"

"I don't know," she says. "That's what's so hard. I don't know . . .

and normally, I always know. Sometimes I tell myself going back, I could try to do things more healthily, more balanced. Other times, I tell myself I should just move on and pick something that's more compatible with my health issues, something remote or flexible for when I'm home and stuck in the bathroom."

"You'll figure it out," I tell her quietly. "I know it's hard, because you want to feel sure in your choice, but maybe this is one of those things you just have to figure out like science—trial and error." Viggo's words come back to me, and I repeat them to Rooney. "You won't know until you try."

The words hang between us. Or maybe they just linger in my thoughts. Because I have never done this before. Loved someone the way I love her. Loved so much, I want to give her everything and protect her from everything and love her with every possible part of myself that I can. I don't know how, or if I can, but I won't know until I try.

Rooney smiles faintly. "You're right. I'm sorry for spiraling. Here I am, having an existential crisis before we've even had coffee. I should make coffee, shouldn't I?" She starts to sit up, but I set a hand on her waist and hold tight.

"Rooney." I tug her close. "I don't want coffee. I like listening to you think and talk."

Her smile returns and she curls in closer. "Thanks."

I tuck a strand of hair behind her ear and kiss her forehead. "You can get coffee, if you really want."

"No." She shakes her head, then leans in and kisses my neck. "No, I'm okay. But I don't want to talk about school anymore. I don't want worrying to take away from my happiness right now."

I slide my fingers through her hair, savoring the softness, gently rubbing her scalp. She shuts her eyes and sighs. I watch her as I touch her, the lulling crackle of the fire wrapping around us. The tent is warm, and my home feels like it's flooded with sunlight, not just because there's a fire and the sun's breaking the horizon, but because Rooney's here, right beside me.

Because I love her.

And that's the last thing I can tell her. Because that isn't what this was supposed to be. It's not what she married me for, and it's not why she came. Even so, knowing I won't tell her, knowing she doesn't see me the same way, it feels so right to know. So freeing, to have a name for this. To understand what's inside me and alive for her in a way it's never been for anyone else.

Harry pokes his head in the tent, resting his snout on Rooney's waist. Rolling onto her back, Rooney runs her hand down his head and his back, in long, steady strokes. His mouth twitches almost like a smile, and he lets out a heavy sigh.

"How am I supposed to say goodbye to you?" she asks quietly.

The ache is back, twisting sharply beneath my ribs. Love. I have a name for it now. Love only for her.

"Goodbyes are hard. He's going to miss you."

"Until he forgets me," she mutters.

"No." I swallow roughly. "He won't forget you. And he'll always be glad to see you whenever you want to visit."

Rooney's hand falters, before she runs her fingers gently over his ears. "I can visit?"

The pain in my chest grows sharper. I take a deep breath that doesn't help. "Yes. Visit anytime. He'd love that. Maybe not once you've found your own . . . companion. I think if you brought them, it would be hard for him. You know how dogs are."

Rooney glances at me, her expression tight and unreadable. "What if I told him I don't want someone else? What if I wanted him?"

I stare at her, torn. I'm terrible at subtext, but I'm trying to speak in a subtext of my own. One that tells her how I feel without risking it fully. Because I'm not sure what's right in this situation.

I've never loved someone like this, let alone when they had one foot out the door.

If I tell her how I feel, how would that make *her* feel? Would she want to stay? Would she feel guilty for leaving? And if so, is that loving someone, to tell them something that could make them torn about their future?

Searching her eyes, I tell her, "I think he'd say he wishes he could come with you and make his life fit with yours, but he's not made for the places you are. He needs this little world he's built for himself and a small, safe space, and he would never *ever* want you to alter your plans for him."

I tuck a ribbon of golden hair gently behind her ear, my fingertips tracing her throat. "He'd say he wants you to be happy more than anything, and he could never live with himself if you ended up losing your happiness while trying to share it with him."

"What if I told him I'm not so sure about those plans? What if I said I've felt happiness I didn't know existed until I shared it with him?"

I search her eyes. Is she saying what I think she's saying?

But what if she's not?

And if she's not, and I get it wrong, what if I ruin everything? This sliver of time with her before she goes. The tenuous friendship I've found with her. The possibility that I could simply see her again whenever she wanted to be here, even if she wasn't mine.

"He would tell you something the wise Bob Ross once said. 'It's hard to see things when you're too close. Take a step back and look.'"

Rooney frowns. "Very enigmatic for a dog."

"Dogs are philosophical creatures." I steal another ribbon of hair and spool it around my finger. "And he'd give you that advice because, whatever you chose, whatever plans you made, he would only want them to be truly what *you* wanted and the instruments of your happiness. Not his happiness or anyone else's. Yours. And he knows that takes time to figure out. Time and perspective. Just like a good painting."

"And he'd wait?" she says, her hand leaving Harry and finding mine, twining our fingers together. "While I figured that out? While I took a step back and looked?"

I let the ribbon of hair unspool into a soft firelit coil and bring it to my lips. "Yes, he would wait."

Then, in the safety of another language, I whisper against her hair, *He'd wait forever.*

"What's that?" she asks. "Swedish?"

I nod, letting her hair fall from my fingertips. She frowns. She's adorable when she frowns because she so rarely does it. Maybe it's how she feels when I smile. "What's it *mean*?" she says.

"If I told you, that ruins the fun."

The frown becomes a glare. "What fun?"

"Come here." I grab her arm and pull her close. She tumbles into me, and it's not entirely pleasant, my back being jostled, but I have so little time. I wasted so much *fucking* time, and I'm not going to waste any more.

Rooney peers up at me, searching my eyes. "What is it?"

I ease back onto my side, facing her as I slip my arm around her waist, my hand running gently along her back. "I want you."

"I want you, too," she says quietly, pulling herself closer to my body.

"It'll have to be a little different, because my back, but—"

"I don't mind," she whispers. Then she leans in and kisses me softly.

Rooney peels off her sweatshirt, then her T-shirt, revealing slight breasts and rose-pink nipples. I groan when I see them, and I pull her close, until they're pressed against my chest and we're kissing deeply.

"They're not normally this small," she says. "I mean, they're small. But it's because when I'm sick, I lose weight, and it's always first from my boobs—"

"Rooney," I whisper, kissing her nipple, then nuzzling it. "They're beautiful. I love them."

"I'm just a little self-conscious. There's my boobs, then my stomach is sensitive to the touch and . . . bloated, for lack of a better word. I just don't feel super sexy when I don't feel like myself, with these itty-bitty titties and a tender belly."

"Small breasts and a belly is a work of art," I mutter against her skin. "Just ask Botticelli. You know his most famous painting, I bet. *Birth of Venus*."

"Ohhh." She smiles. "You're right. She does have a little belly and bitty boobs."

I kiss her other breast, thumbing her nipple. Heat spills through my body, and I'm so achingly hard, the brush of my cock against her thighs, even through my sweatpants, makes my eyes fall shut. "I was the thirteen-year-old kid who stood in front of that painting in the Uffizi for an inappropriately long time. Mom had to drag me away. Totally embarrassed her."

Rooney laughs. "I didn't know you made a family trip to Italy."

"We didn't. It was a birthday present to me from my parents. Each of us was given a big birthday gift when we turned thirteen, a way to honor becoming a teenager and taking another step toward adulthood. I wanted to see art in Italy, so Mom took me for a whole week." I press another kiss between her breasts, my hands roaming her appreciatively. "And now I'm going to stop talking about my mother while I kiss you."

"Good idea."

I slide my hand down her stomach, careful and light in my touch. "What do you like? How do you like to come?"

"Well, um . . ." She clears her throat. "I don't often get off on the whole p-in-v setup, and when I do, it takes a lot of time and touching."

"So what *do* you get off on?" I mutter, kissing her neck.

"H-hands and tongues and . . . other things."

"Like what?" I ask.

She exhales shakily, her touch traveling my thighs, then stroking me over my sweatpants. "Is this okay?"

"Yes," I breathe. "But I might actually come if you do it much more."

She pauses. "Want me to stop?"

"Probably, just for a moment." I kiss her gently, then with tongue. I taste her mint and mine and the sweetness that's only her. "Why aren't you answering me? When I asked about 'other things'?"

"Can I ask something? As a way of answering you?"

I pull away, listening. "Yes."

"That night in the kitchen. When you said sometimes you get off on not getting off. Did you mean . . . like orgasm denial? And other things . . . in that vein?"

Lust slams into me. I take her hand and set it over my pecs, guiding her, until her thumbs are rubbing my nipples because it feels so good, and I need her to touch me, but I don't want to shoot my load yet. "Yes. I like denying myself, but not when I'm with someone else. I tried, and it didn't feel right for me. I like my partner to delay it, though. I like edging, having my control tested."

Air rushes out of her. Her thighs rub together.

"Do *you* like . . ." My voice comes out low and gravelly. "Delaying? And edging? Are those your . . . 'other things'?"

She nods. "Yes, they're my 'other things.' I don't so much like it being done to me because it takes me forever to get there, and when I'm ready to come, I just want to come. But I do like doing it, when it makes my partner feel good, when it makes it more pleasurably intense for them. But I haven't . . ." She swallows thickly. "I had a bad experience in college. A guy told me I was a freak for it, and I didn't force it or demand it, I'd just . . . brought it up."

Anger rolls through me. "You're not a freak, Rooney. Everyone likes different things."

"I know. I just . . . it just put me off trying to share that with someone for a while. A few times it happened organically with a partner, but it's not the same as having an understanding."

I guide her hand up to my ear, showing her how I like it touched, then down my neck and shoulders. "You told me."

Her smile's wickedly sexy, just like the flush in her cheeks, the heat in her eyes. "I did."

"I'm probably not a great candidate for delay today, but I want to try."

She licks her lips. "Not a great candidate? What do you mean?"

"Because . . . it's been a while."

"Hm." She tips her head, her touch trailing back down to my pecs. "Me too."

I shift, wanting to touch her more, but my back burns, and I stiffen. "Sorry," I hiss.

She leans closer, kissing me. "No sorries. Let's just keep it simple. Just face each other like this? Is that good?"

I nod, wrapping my arm around her waist, pulling her closer. And then carefully, both our hands slide down each other, until they're sinking beneath our clothes, breaching waistbands and underwear. I feel her, and she feels me, and we gasp.

Rooney moans as I dip my finger inside her and find her slippery wet, so warm and soft, I have to kiss her. Hard. She sighs against my mouth as I circle her clit and then rub up and down how she showed me that night in the kitchen. Her touch slides along my length, a firm grip that makes me see stars.

"Tighter," I tell her. "Just a little. And my balls. Touch me there, too."

She nods, her hands pumping, then softly cupping me, rubbing that spot behind them that makes a fresh wave of lust crest inside me.

"Like that?" she asks.

I nod and steal another deep kiss, our tongues working rhythmically like our hands. And it's not long after that that I whisper, "Close." I'm too far gone to be self-conscious that it's so soon. Everything is reduced to the feeling of her hands touching me, her mouth moving with mine. Her sighs and moans and her body beneath my fingertips.

When I'm about to come, I guide her hand to the tip of my cock and close her grip around it, making the impending need fade just enough to be a heady, sweet torture. I still touch her, keeping one finger, then two inside, stroking that soft-smooth part of her that makes her hips move, makes her ride my hand.

"Okay," I breathe. She releases her grip, then slides it down my length, trying different moves and touches, learning the ones that make me thrust harder into her grip.

Once more I get close, and this time she recognizes it, gripping me, and making me groan with the teasing pleasure of it. Once more she holds me, kissing me harder, her breathing erratic. I know she's almost there before she tells me, because I watch a beautiful pink flush climb up her chest, to her neck. I watch her chest arch higher and higher, her body starting to shake.

"I'm gonna come," she whispers.

That's when I guide her hand to release me, to work me in firm, fast pumps that make my head fall back, my own breathing turn frantic.

I spill into her hand, onto my stomach, over and over. And then I guide her touch away, and let it fall limply at her side as she comes, too.

I watch Rooney lose herself to her release, her hoarse, near-silent cry, the sharp spasm of her legs around my touch. I watch her, and I love her in this new way, in another facet of something I still barely know how to explain but know is as real as the heart pounding in my chest.

Rooney curls toward me, wrapping her arm around my waist. "Okay?" she asks breathlessly. "To touch you?"

I nod, holding her close, slowly easing myself onto my back.

We clutch each other, half-naked, messy, panting. Rooney clasps my jaw and gives me a slow, gentle kiss. Lying quietly, we stare at each other, hands wandering, stealing kisses. I trace her breasts with the tip of my finger like it's a piece of charcoal, shading where there are shadows, swirling around her nipple as I would drawing it.

She smiles and tangles her legs tighter with mine.

"Axel," she says quietly, her hand gently kneading my muscles. "With your back like this, should you fly down for Thanksgiving?"

I frown. "I have all of tomorrow to get it in good enough shape before I fly down. It won't be terribly comfortable, but I can probably manage."

She blushes as she bites her lip. "But theoretically, if it was going to be too uncomfortable . . . *would* you want to stay? And if *I* theoretically wanted to stay back, too . . ." Her eyes search mine. "Would you want me to?"

I pull her in for a deep, long kiss, and the world colors itself sunburst gold. More time with her, more precious, fleeting time. "Yes," I whisper against her lips, holding her close, savoring this dizzying, euphoric—is it *joy*?—coursing through me. "I want that. I want . . . you." Tucking a ribbon of hair behind her ear, I kiss her again. "So much."

# TWENTY-SEVEN

# Axel

Playlist: "Looking for Love (Acoustic)," Birdtalker

"Happy Thanksgiving, Harry!" Rooney plants a kiss on his snout, then stands as the dog runs inside to stay warm before I lock the door to the house. "You promise you're up for this?" she asks. "A hike isn't too much?"

The smidge of guilt I felt for both of us making our excuses to family and friends, instead of joining them for Thanksgiving, evaporates as I pocket my keys and drink her in. Dark leggings and her hiking boots. A chunky sky-blue sweater that makes her eyes sparkle. That heinously yellow hat with its fuzzy pom-pom that I'm unnaturally attached to.

"I'm up for it," I tell her. "Walking feels good."

*And I'm trying. I'm trying to show you that I love you.*

I think I'm trying to be romantic, too. I'm not sure, because I'm honestly clueless about what's involved, and the only romance novels Viggo gave me as possible points of reference aren't exactly relevant, considering they involve waltzes, corsets, and trysts in libraries.

Thanks for nothing, Viggo.

Rooney smiles and tugs the fuzzy yellow hat tight on her head. "Okay, as long as you're really feeling up for it."

"I am. I better be, considering I literally slept and did nothing all day yesterday."

"For the first time since I've been here!" she says, falling into step beside me. "It's good to rest."

I give her a pointed glance. "Says the woman who insinuated herself into a home renovation when she's had a flare-up and is supposed to be *resting*."

She blushes. "Well, we're all works in progress."

"That we are." I use my walking stick more than I normally would, and we're not going very fast, but it feels good to stretch my legs and warm up my body. I haven't missed a morning run since the first time I threw out my back, and a few days without has made me desperate for movement.

Our steps are quiet, the light faint, and when we make it to the same spot I brought her to on our wedding-day hike, Rooney gasps softly, because I timed it just right.

The sun peeks over the horizon, painting the world a watercolor peach pink, long plum shadows stretching across the ground. The lake below sparkles like a mirror, and everything is hushed, nothing but a faint wind and a few hardy songbirds who'll stay for winter.

"Axel," she breathes.

I watch her watching the sunrise, knowing I could do this the rest of my life: witness sunlight painting Rooney better than I ever could, the day wrapping its arms around her, illuminating what's inside her heart—warmth, hope, a depth of joy I never thought I'd know, let alone love, yet here I am.

So fucking gone for it. Gone for *her*.

I've been afraid to tell her. I'm terrible at risking changes like this. What if she doesn't feel the same way? What if it chases her off? What if? I've spun my tires for days, wondering, but what finally stopped me is this: reminding myself who she is. Rooney. Rooney who stayed. Rooney who wanted me, just as I am. Rooney, the safest person I've ever met. If I can be brave for anyone, it's her.

She glances my way and catches me staring at her. "You're not watching the sunrise," she says.

"No."

A blush stains her cheeks as she smiles faintly, her expression perplexed. "You love sunrises."

"I love you more."

Her mouth parts. Her eyes widen. And then a smile I've never seen, never earned before, lights up her face. She drops her walking stick, takes the one step between us, and gently wraps her arms around me, careful of my back.

"Say it again," she whispers.

"I love you," I tell her. "And I don't . . . I've never done this before, Rooney, so I might do a really rough job of it at first. I'm telling you because, while I want you to love me back, I'll understand if you don't. I just needed you to know—"

"Axel." She brings both hands to my face, her thumbs sliding along my cheekbones, eyes searching mine. "This feels like one of my daydreams," she whispers. "It's not a dream, is it?"

I slide my hands up her arms, until I'm cupping her cheeks, too, my thumbs circling those deep dimples. I meet her eyes, a breathtaking stained glass striation of grass green and sky blue.

Then, pressing my forehead to hers, feeling her, drinking in the soft, soothing scent of blossoms at twilight that clings to her hair, her clothes, her skin, I tell her, "You're not dreaming."

"Then I'll tell you what I've known and tried so hard to hide," she says quietly, pressing onto tiptoe, whispering against my lips, "I love you, too."

The world inverts, hearing those words—words I never thought I would—and I pull her closer, hold her tight, anchoring myself to the truth of what I'm holding, the woman I love, the woman who loves me. Clinging to Rooney, I kiss the words I can't say. I tell her with soft nips of my teeth and a firm, deep press of my lips, everything my heart feels but doesn't know how to articulate. Not yet. But it will learn.

Her mouth parts for mine on a soft sigh, as I hold us together, her body and mine, as our lips brush and retreat, then seek and devour, as our tongues do what our bodies have—touched and danced and learned the steps that make us wild.

But I don't want to be wild right now, and if her tender touches, her languid sighs say anything, Rooney doesn't, either. So I pull back, just enough to press a final kiss to her forehead, to breathe her in and imprint this moment in my memory.

Rooney tips her head, peering up at me, and adjusts my glasses. "I might have bent them. I got a little worked up."

She fiddles further with the frames as I peer down at her. "I don't care."

"I do. I am *deeply* attached to these," she mutters before she finally drops her hands. "There. I fixed them."

I steal one last kiss. "Hungry?"

She smiles. "But of course."

I unpack our haul, handing her a thermos of tea before extracting my coffee, then unearthing the container of cinnamon rolls I commissioned from Bennett and Parker with no small amount of eyebrow wiggling and knowing grins. I unfold the blanket and spread it out. Then I sit and gesture between my legs. "Come here."

Rooney settles in, her back to my front, our knees bent as we watch the sunrise. Her smile is content, her eyes on the horizon, narrowed against its building brightness.

"This is perfect," she whispers.

I press a kiss to her temple. "It is."

"You said you've never done this before." She rests her head against my shoulder. "What does that mean?"

"It means I'm thirty years old, and I've never been in love or remotely interested in being in love, and I've never been romantic with anyone. I've had consensually casual partnerships but nothing serious. Nothing like this."

She's quiet for a moment, staring at the sunrise, before she glances up and meets my eyes. "How did you know this was different?"

"It just . . . was. I . . ." Clearing my throat, I sip my coffee, then set it down. "Don't laugh."

"I won't," she says.

"Whenever I saw you, whenever you were around, and especially once you got here, my chest would . . . ache." I rest my hand over her heart, showing her. "Right here. I thought I had a cardiovascular problem. I was googling shit, worrying I had some kind of corrosive disease, or the most severe case of heartburn ever known in medical history."

She bites her lip and fights a smile. To her credit, she doesn't laugh.

"Turns out," I say to her, "that's how it feels to fall in love with someone you're telling yourself you shouldn't, no, *can't*, fall in love with. I mean, that's how foreign all of this is to me."

Rooney slides her hand up my thigh, a soothing, affectionate touch. "Now it can be familiar. Just you and me."

I kiss her softly, brushing back a strand of hair the wind's sent streaking across her face. "What about you?"

She reaches for the cinnamon rolls, pops off the lid, and extracts one. "I'd say I've been cautious about love and skeptical of marriage. Seeing what I have, from my parents, from other friends of theirs in the entertainment industry, I was really put off. The last decade, since I was aware of desire and attraction, I haven't looked at people, wondering if they could be my true love. I've wondered if they'd be fun to dance with and a good time in bed. I didn't want anything more. I had a career path. Financial stability. Parents who loved me in their way, who would be there in a heartbeat if I had a crisis. A few good friends, all the time in the world. Why did I need to fall in love? Why would I ever need to marry?"

She peels off a bite of the cinnamon roll where no icing has touched it and brings it to my lips. I take it, and softly nip her finger, making her yelp and then turn and give me a kiss.

"But?" I prompt her.

"But," she says. "Then I married you, because I needed somewhere to . . . belong for a while, and I told myself I was the perfect person for a loveless marriage. I was pretty sure you barely even registered my existence, so I told myself there was no danger of the intense attraction I felt for you becoming love."

"Barely even registered your existence?"

"Yeah!" she says with a laugh. "Considering you used to walk out of a room when I walked in."

"You gave me heart palpitations. I was supposed to think that was a good thing? You scrambled my brain to the point that I downgraded from stilted conversationalist to grunting."

She laughs again and softly strokes my cheek. "Well. We figured each other out, eventually, didn't we?"

Moved, I rest a hand over hers. Rooney knows because I've told her, but she doesn't *understand* how hard it is for me to figure out people. She doesn't realize how much it means that she feels figured out. Known. Connected to me. I pull her close and kiss her hair. "Yes."

"And in figuring each other out," she says around another bite of cinnamon roll, "I've learned marriage is what you make it. Some days it's felt like there was nothing between us, and others, like there was everything. Some moments I'd stare at that ring and think how odd it was to be legally bound to you, to have pledged my life to you, to have vowed to cherish and believe and honor you, and yet how easily I could break those vows.

"And that . . . that *ease* with which vows can be broken—what I grew up seeing unfold in my parents' marriage, as my friends began having committed relationships and torching them with a few bad fights and poor choices—it made me think that kind of commitment, marriage, would never mean anything to me, because how strong is something that can break so easily?

"But now, I think I understand. It's not that marriage is this fortifying element in and of itself. It's not the teary wedding-day promises or the legal license or the indestructible rings that make a marriage strong. It's the people. It's their choices. It's how strong *they* make it."

"No pressure," I mutter.

Rooney nods. "Right? It is. It's a lot of responsibility." She turns and plants a kiss on my jaw, then settles in against me. "But I want that with you," she whispers. "I want to learn how to have it."

"We'll learn," I tell her as I hold her close. "Together."

———

Back inside the house, we're greeted by Harry, who bounds happily toward Rooney. I don't even exist to him anymore, and that honestly hurts a bit more than I'd like.

"Hey, handsome," she says to him, letting him jump up and lick her. "Down, Harry."

He drops and follows us, until we stop at the foot of what is now only a mattress on the floor, the tent put away yesterday evening when I felt good enough to move and break down our setup.

"At some point," I tell her, "I'm going to have to get a real bed again."

Carefully, she removes the bag from my shoulders. "Your back would probably appreciate an actual support system beneath the mattress you're sleeping on."

Skugga darts into the room from the studio, meowing and twining between my legs. She's been all over me since I threw out my back.

Zipping back into the studio, she meows loudly and stares at me from just inside the doorway. I feel a tug toward the place like I haven't in months. Everything inside me that's been building since Rooney got here feels like it's spilling over. I want to paint her, and I want to paint more. I want to paint what's inside and what I can't quite name, what feels different now that we've said it. Now that I know what this is.

*Love.*

When I glance away, I catch Rooney watching me. Smiling. "You want to paint," she asks, "don't you?"

I shift on my feet. "I mean . . . I could paint, yeah."

Her smile deepens. "Then paint."

*But how long will you be here*, I worry, *and how can I spend a single moment away from you before you're gone?*

"You could . . ." Clearing my throat, I take her hand, lacing our fingers together. "You could come with me. Hang out while I do. I can make up a little nest with the couch cushions and blankets. I could get a chair actually, so you can be in there—*mmph!*"

Her mouth is on mine, her hands tight around my waist. "Yes, please," she whispers.

# TWENTY-EIGHT

# Rooney

Dreams really do come true. I am tucked into a nest of pillows and blankets in Axel's studio, with a cup of hot chocolate, the romance novel he's been reading to me, and the best damn view in all of Washington State:

Axel Bergman painting.

He's got noise-canceling headphones on and his hair's going every direction. His paint-splattered jeans hang low on his hips, and the white T-shirt he's wearing is so threadbare, I can see his back muscles shift as he moves his paintbrush across the canvas and then grabs more paint. When he sets down his brush and swings his arms, his rounded shoulder muscles flex. Head tipped, he examines his canvas.

And *I* examine *him*.

"How much of that book have you read?" he asks, tugging off his headphones and giving me a wry glance over his shoulder. "And how much of the time have you spent staring at my ass?"

I arch an eyebrow, snapping my book shut. "I got a few pages in."

"I've been painting for two hours."

"Don't I know it."

He smiles as he glances away, eyes on the task of wiping his hands clean.

Abruptly ending the quiet, the kitten drags a paper from one of the thin shelves of a tall cabinet near Axel's paints. "Skugga," I chide. "Get out of there!"

Axel glances up, panic tightening his expression as he watches her. If his back weren't still on the mend, I bet he'd have beaten her to it, but Skugga's darted off with the paper that's so big compared to her, she trips on it running my way.

I scoop her up and gently extract the paper from her tiny teeth. "Bad Skugga." I set her down. "That was very bad."

"Meow," she says in the tone of a disingenuous *oops*, before running off and pouncing on a fabric mouse.

I smooth the corner that's dented from Skugga's mouth and tell myself I shouldn't look at something of Axel's without his permission, but then my eyes catch on the outline of a breast, the curve of a hip.

"Holy shit," I mutter. "That's *me*."

Axel reaches for the drawing. I yank it away. "Rooney," he pleads.

"What is this?" I ask him.

Pink blooms on his cheeks. He's quiet for a long, drawn-out moment. "You said it yourself. It's you."

Peering back at the drawing, I'm reduced to my suddenly tender breasts, the pounding ache between my thighs, as my entire body turns hot. He drew me *naked*.

"When?" I ask.

Axel's quiet.

"When, Axel."

"For months," he says.

My head snaps up. "*What?*"

"I . . . I use art to process," he says, lowering to the ground across from my blanket nest, sitting with a groan. He runs a hand through his hair and sighs. "I didn't know why, after each time I saw you, it was harder to pick up a brush and paint what I used to. Why every night I'd dream about you, laughing, smiling, sighing, coming, with *me*."

I stare at him, stunned, then glance back down at the drawing. I can barely breathe, I'm so turned-on. "You thought of me like this? You've been thinking of me like this the whole time?"

"I couldn't get you the fuck out of my head. I couldn't think or sleep or function, so I started drawing what was in my head. I'm sorry, Rooney. I promise it was never meant for or seen by anyone except me. I never . . . did anything inappropriate with them. I drew them, then put them away, and never looked at them again. It was just to get you out of my head, and my dreams, and my art." He sighs bleakly. "Obviously it did not work."

I stare down at the drawing again, clutched in my hand. "So you . . . you've been wanting me. This whole time."

"Rooney, I have wanted you since the moment I met you. Since you were screaming in the stands at Willa's first game and she scored and you smiled while you cried. Your hair was half out of its braid, and your eyes were red-rimmed, and you were *screaming* with joy. You were so fucking beautiful and alive, and I felt like I'd been clubbed over the head. You scared the hell out of me, how much you . . . *felt*, how much you said and expressed, so freely. I had no idea what to do with you, except want you. Helplessly. And for a good long while, I thought, hopelessly. So I tried to do everything I could to stop it."

I close the distance between us, straddling his lap. He's warm and solid, and he smells like paint and sweat and his woodsy soap, and I shut my eyes to memorize this moment as I bury my face against his neck. Because I never want to forget it.

"I would love to know what's going on in your head right now," he says, his voice tight. "You're being unnervingly quiet, for you."

I laugh. "I feel very, very flattered. And very, very turned-on."

His head jerks up sharply. He looks at me, frowning. "Y-you like it? That I drew you?"

"Yes," I whisper. My hand slides down his stomach and lifts his shirt. "Actually, no. I don't like it. I love it."

Air rushes out of him as my palm touches his warm skin, the trail of soft, dark hair arrowing beneath his jeans. "Just wait until you see what I've been painting."

"You painted me?" Realization dawns. "That's why you couldn't sell it. You didn't have a creative block, you liar."

He grins. "I had a creative block of sorts. I couldn't paint what I could sell. All I could paint was a woman I couldn't have, in a way I'd never share with anyone."

I crawl off of Axel's lap before he stands slowly. He pulls drop cloths off bulky canvases stacked against the wall, his back to me as he spins one around and faces it my way.

It's incredibly moving, not because it's me but because it's a chance to experience how Axel sees me. It's also shockingly accurate, given he painted this before he saw me naked. My small breasts, a curve at my stomach, the length of my thigh and calf.

I'm . . . flooded with longing, with how loved I feel. I wrap my arms around him, my chest to his back, and rest my head gently between his shoulder blades. "I love it."

He sets his hands on mine, clutched tight to his front. "Really?"

"So much." I sigh as my hands wander down his stomach. "Can I?" When he nods, I slip my fingers beneath the waistband of his jeans, waiting to encounter his boxer briefs—

I gasp. "Axel Bergman. Are you going commando?"

I hear the smile in his voice. "These jeans feel weird with underwear."

A happy hum leaves my throat, and I slip my hand lower. A

rough breath leaves him as I unbutton the first button, then the next, until I have him, velvet-hot, hard and thick, in my grip.

"You were giving me hell for being distracted by you," I whisper, "but I'm wondering how much painting versus paying attention to *me* you're guilty of, based on this erection in my hands, Mr. Bergman."

A groan leaves Axel as I stroke his cock—a firm, slow tug, my thumb rubbing gently over the head. "This is a fantasy," he says roughly. "You, here, while I paint and try not to think about all the things I want to do to you. I've been hard since I picked up a brush."

I work him, tight and fast, my other hand sliding up his chest, tracing his nipples. His breath grows ragged and he arches back, hips moving. I feel that moment he starts to lose himself, fucking my hand, and that's when I stop and grip him how he showed me, tight pressure right at the head of his cock.

"Oh," he groans. "Oh fuck." I do it once more, touch him how he likes, feel him grow harder, soaking up his groans and sighs, before he stops me. Wrapping his hand around mine, Axel loosens my grip on his cock, then tucks every hard inch haphazardly into his opened jeans. He turns and kisses me, walking me straight back until I'm pinned against the glass wall of his studio. "Now," he says between deep kisses. "On the bed. Mattress. Whatever."

We both laugh as Axel drags me with him, shutting the studio door behind us, where Skugga's sleeping on her drop cloth bed. Harry's outside wandering around, maybe napping in his little A-frame doghouse. We're alone, and it's quiet, only faint light and the sound of our rough breathing filling the room.

And suddenly all the rush and fervor die away. Axel's hands don't wander me anymore. They simply rest on my waist as he stares down at me.

We didn't have sex yesterday, on my insistence. I didn't want to make his back any worse, which it seemed to be after our first time in the tent. Longing has felt like a third person in the room with us, and now it's finally here, time and ability for more of what we shared the other day.

I think we're both a little breathless from it.

Our hands link, fingers dancing. I feel the absence of our rings that neither of us wear since the night we yanked them off. Instead Axel wears both of our rings around his neck on a chain. I look at him as his thumb rubs my ring finger, realizing I miss mine. I miss that little piece of metal that reminds me of our awkward, sweet day, of pancakes and a sunset hike and a skunk vigil and the way he slid me down on the bed and pressed his weight against me and kissed me like I was *his*. Like he was *mine*.

When did it happen? When exactly did I fall in love with him? I always thought realizing you loved someone would be this epic moment, an emotional firework grand finale. But this wasn't. It was quiet and steady, tender and unexpected. Just like the man I married.

The man that I love.

The man who looks at me and says, "I love you."

"I know," I tell him, smiling, bursting with the joy of it. "I love you, too. How's your back?"

"No acrobatic sex," he says on a faint smile, "but I'm better than I was the first time. Or I will be, with you, very soon."

I run my hands through his hair and watch his eyes slip shut. "I did not come up here expecting to have sex. Ergo, I did not bring lube. And we're going to need it if you find yourself inside me."

"Rooney," he says quietly, opening his eyes. He walks us backward until he hits the dining table, and then he slowly lowers himself onto it, so we're almost eye to eye. Leaning in, he presses a kiss right between my breasts. "I have what we need."

"Oh. Great. Because Rooney on a p-in-v dry spell and Axel with his hammer dick—"

He laughs. Actually laughs, husky and deep. "I don't have a hammer dick."

"Says you."

"I think I'd know."

"I've touched that thing. I know what dimensions I'm dealing with, and I'm not going to lie, you're going to have to warm me up for a while."

He smiles now, the biggest one yet. It makes his eyes sparkle, makes my heart overflow with love. God, it just swallows me up, how much I love him, how quietly, perfectly he wrapped me into his life and made me never want to leave.

"It will be my pleasure," he says, softly running his fingertips along the hem of my sweater. He drags it off, leaving me in only a camisole and no bra. "Anything else you want to tell me before I start that warm-up?"

"Yes. Absolutely no backdoor business. It hurts too much."

He nods. "I understand."

"Do you mind?" I ask hesitantly.

His mouth brushes my hip, his tongue tasting my skin. "Not in the least. What else?"

My eyes fall shut as he lifts the camisole just enough to kiss higher, up my stomach. Soft, slow kisses that make my knees weak. "J-just what we talked about the other day, that my body is a little tricky for me right now."

He stares up at me, hands drifting over my stomach, feather-light, then gently cupping my breasts. My vision blurs with tears that spring up from his tenderness. "I love your body. I love *you*."

My head falls back as he kisses his way across my breasts, then nuzzles my nipple. He sucks it softly through the fabric, rhythmic, wet tugs that make me gasp as he rubs the other with his thumb. Peering up at me again, he slides his hands beneath my camisole.

Slowly, he stands, towering over me, and lifts it away, letting it fall to the ground. His eyes travel me in absolute quiet. And finally I know what kind of quiet this is. The adoring quiet. The reverent quiet. The one that drinks in beauty and savors it. And under his intense gaze, his hands roaming my waist, savoring my breasts, I know right down to my bones that I am cherished. I am the woman he finds light in the darkness for and holds close when the storm is raging. The woman he loves.

Like so many vital moments with Axel, his love is loudest when he's quiet. It's here, in how he looks at me and touches me, in his short, ragged breaths and the tremor in his hands as he steps closer to kiss me. A kiss that says:

*I love you.*

*I want you.*

*You are beautiful, just as you are.*

Slipping his fingers inside the waistband of my leggings, he slowly drags them down. I take over, to save his back, and step out of them, then peel off my socks.

Axel reaches behind his head, dragging off his shirt as I set my hands on his jeans and push them off his hips. He shoves them down, then steps out of them quickly.

And here we stand, naked, fingers brushing, then tangling, before hands wander carefully, learning slopes and curves, smooth planes and hard ridges. His palms slide along my waist and down to my backside. Mine drift up his chest, threading softly through the fine, dark hairs on his chest, then resting on his shoulders.

Gently, he bends his head, and our mouths meet in a slow, deep kiss. I melt into him, the warmth of his body, the satisfaction of his arousal, hard and hot between us. And then he backs away and lowers himself onto the mattress that's no longer covered in a tent, but simply pushed against the wall, the twinkly lights strung above the window overhead. He lies down slowly, props his arms behind his head, and meets my gaze on a wry grin.

"Well?" he says. "I made a promise when you gave me that massage."

I bite back a smile, dragging my lip between my teeth. "Seriously? You just want me to sit on your face."

His cock jumps, and his tongue darts out, wetting his lip. "That's exactly what I want, yes. If it's what *you* want."

"I mean . . ." My cheeks heat. I'm wet between my thighs, my breasts throbbing from his kisses and touch. There's a soft, beating pulse in my clit. "Yes. I want."

Smiling, he eases away the pillow behind his head as I crawl up the mattress, over his long body. I stop and rub myself along his hard length, teasing us.

Axel slips his hands between us and rubs me gently, kisses my throat, my collarbones, my breasts. I steal a messy, hungry kiss that's tongue and teeth, a kiss that makes him groan and wrap his arms tight around my body and then softly push me away and drag me up by the waist.

"So beautiful," he says, hands sliding along my ribs, teeth nipping my thigh. "So, so beautiful." And then he pulls me closer, making me gasp and grip the windowsill for leverage.

His beard is soft on my thighs, his mouth warm, and his tongue a fucking master—slow, flat glides where I'm aching and wet that make me shiver with pleasure. I move against him in a lazy rhythm, moaning as his hands drift higher and cup my breasts and then gently tug my nipples. A gasp leaves me as his tongue does what I've taught him to do with his hands, teasing circles, then fast up-down flicks that make my hands white-knuckle the window ledge, my back arch as I press closer, wanting *more*.

It's quiet and peaceful and hot and raw, nothing but his body and mine, the warmth of the fire, the faint creak of the windowsill when I tug on it to steady myself against such intense pleasure, I have to shut my eyes because all I can do is feel.

I'm climbing higher and higher, as my hand slips into his hair, threading through the cool, silky strands. Touching him, I hear his satisfied groans, feel the rhythmic dip of the mattress. My eyes open as I glance over my shoulder to see his hips moving, his cock tall and thick, long legs bent and flexing as he moves like he can't help himself.

My fingers sink harder into his hair as I watch him, as molten pleasure melts my limbs, then floods right between my thighs. "Ax," I whisper. "Oh God."

Crying out, I arch into him and come, wave after wave that rack my body. His tongue moves gently, his hands caressing and soothing as I call his name and anchor myself against him, riding my release until it ebbs to a peaceful lull.

Gasping for air, I flop clumsily onto the mattress. It's not at all sexy, but I'm too deceased to care.

"Okay?" he asks.

"Dead," I mumble.

Axel pushes up slowly onto his elbows. "Better not be. I'm not done with you."

I laugh breathlessly and roll toward him, tangling our legs, wrapping my arm around his waist. Then I clasp his jaw and kiss him, tasting him and me, and somehow I'm already aching again, which turns out to be convenient, because what Axel says next is "Rooney. I need you."

Stroking his cheek, I run my hand along his beard and kiss him once more. I slide my leg over his hip before Axel tugs me across his waist so that I straddle him.

"I want to be inside you," he says breathlessly. "But we don't have to if—"

"I want that, too," I whisper against his lips.

He moans against our kiss, slips one finger, then two inside me and works me steadily. As he touches me, his mouth travels my skin, his groans rumbling against my jaw, then my neck. Then he drags himself away and gingerly reaches into the nightstand drawer, pulling out condoms and lube.

I roll the condom over his length as Axel uses the lube and his fingers, tenderly, lovingly, making sure I'm plenty ready. Air rushes out of us both as I guide him to my entrance and start to sink down. I don't make it very far before I have to stop and say a very bad word, very loudly.

He looks up at me, his face pained. "Are you all right?"

"Just need some time." I gasp as I ease down a little more.

His hands slide up my thighs, around my backside, gentling, soothing touches. "I'm sorry."

"Don't be," I tell him, bending toward him to steal a slow kiss. His hand slips between us and rubs me again, as I ease myself down a little more. "Though, maybe you should be. It's your fault I'm like this."

He frowns. "Why?"

"Because many months ago, I stopped wanting anything except to touch myself to the thought of you, wishing it were the real thing. That's how it's been since."

He moans, either because of my words or because of the fact that I finally managed to lower myself almost all the way. His hands drift up my back, pulling me down over him, until our fronts touch and his mouth brushes my ear. "Me too," he whispers.

Primal, possessive joy surges through me, knowing he's wanted me the way I've wanted him. I turn my head and meet his lips, rocking gently with him as his hips move. Listening, watching, I whisper, "Tell me what you want."

"Harder," he says tightly. "When you can. Hard and slow."

Moving against him in languid, deliberate strokes, until I can sink all the way down, I feel him filling me, my body exquisitely tight around every throbbing inch of him.

Axel stills my hips, holding me close, my chest to his, our hearts thundering against each other's. "Stay?" he says quietly.

And the word breaks my heart a little. Because I want him to mean it not just for now but for days and weeks and months and years. Because even though there's a life I have to face down in California, I want to be with Axel, no matter where I am. No matter where I go, my heart will be with him—I understand that now—with this man in his quiet home in the woods, with his paints and his books and his home-cooked meals. I hope Axel understands that, too.

"Just like this," he whispers.

I nod, blinking back tears, kissing him as we move together, in a desperate embrace and an undulating rhythm. Time dissolves into a daydream world of endless minutes, of deep, slow thrusts and warm skin and salty sweat and breathless sighs.

Axel feels my thighs trembling, my body's fatigue, so he pulls away, gently pressing me back onto the mattress, turning me so I'm tucked against him, my back to his front. He presses slow, hot kisses down my neck. "Is this all right?" he asks, hand gliding over my hip, affectionately rubbing my ass.

"As long as you're using the entrance I think you're using."

That deep, husky laugh dances over my skin. "I know that's off the table. You told me, and I told you I didn't mind."

I glance over my shoulder, uneasy. "You really don't mind? You won't miss the butt stuff?"

"Hey." He clasps my jaw, a familiar scowl tightening his features. "I told you I don't. I meant it. Believe me. Please?"

I search his eyes as his hand slips forward, gentling my stomach that's not flat or taut or anything I used to tell myself it had to be to be desirable. His hand dips lower, stealing wetness, then touching me so gently, tears spring to my eyes again. "I believe you," I whisper.

Then Axel smiles. A new smile. A soft, secret smile that I know no one else has ever earned. He kisses me as his hand leaves me for only a moment, as he guides himself only just inside my body. Touching me again—every achingly sensitive place—he rocks into me. Slow, patient, gentle.

I rest on one of his arms like a pillow, and his fingers toy with my hair, soothing and sweet. His other hand is a dedicated lover of my body, teasing my nipples and then my clit, working me into a frenzy as I move against the incredible fullness of him. As beautiful as it is, Axel's body inside mine, so is every other sensual touch we share—my back against his chest, his kisses to my throat, my hand weaving through his hair, the soft, sweet words he whispers in my ear.

I feel him get close, the building pace of his thrusts, how his breath catches, and that's when Axel stills his body inside mine, controlling himself for me, even as he's pulsing, aching to come. His fingers caress where we meet, then higher, circling my clit patiently as his mouth grazes my neck. He stays with me, denying himself, as I climb higher and higher to a stunning precipice.

I clutch him tight, breathing Axel's name when my release begins deep within me. White-hot, aching waves crest through my breasts, low in my belly, every inch of me wrapped around him.

"Please," I whisper, begging him. "Move inside me. Please, Ax."

"Rooney." He breathes my name like a plea and a prayer with every torturously slow roll of his hips, before his desperation takes over, and he pumps into me, fast and deep. Just as my orgasm fades to a sated echo, Axel clasps my jaw so that our lips meet in a frantic kiss, and spills in long, jagged thrusts, his mouth open against mine.

I touch and kiss him through each exquisite drive of his hips, every helpless gasp of my name. And when he falls onto his back, easing gently away, relieved and breathless, I follow and curl around him, a sleepy smile on my face as Axel wraps me in his arms.

Our eyes meet as he kisses me, then says, "Happy Thanksgiving."

"Same to you," I whisper. "I am feeling very, *very* thankful."

# TWENTY-NINE

# Axel

Playlist: "San Luis," Gregory Alan Isakov

Three weeks. Three weeks of finishing work on the A-frame, then putting it back together, yet still traipsing through the dark to the little house in the woods because it's home. Three weeks of every kind of sex on every surface at every time. Three weeks of sunrise and sunset hikes. Three weeks of days off in the studio, while I paint and Rooney reads, the dog and cat draped over her, napping in the sun. Three weeks of card game nights with Willa and Ryder, dinners with Parker and Bennett and Skyler. Three weeks of watching her fall asleep in my arms, bathed in firelight, feeling time dwindle like the dying flames at my feet.

Because time's been closing in. Christmas is coming, which is when Rooney will go home and resume her old life. We haven't talked about what's next, because Rooney hasn't known what she's doing about school, what's coming beyond spending Christmas with her father, and I refuse to ask her for an answer before she has it. The last thing I will ever do is repeat the hurt her parents have caused, what Rooney's told me in the dark after making love. That her father asks for too much of her heart and gives too little of his own, that her mother loves her from a distance, but it's not the kind of love she needs.

I'm not great at reading between the lines, but I've spent weeks listening, learning the woman I love, and this is what I know:

Rooney has hidden and hurt herself trying to love people who didn't love her how she deserved. I know what Rooney knows all too well, thanks to them, because she told me once: sometimes love isn't enough.

This is one of those times. I know it, even though she might not yet. Rooney is going to go back for Christmas, feeling better, having energy to socialize and meet people and be out in the world. She's going to see friends and rub shoulders with someone and realize that twenty-four is really fucking young to set her heart on me, to decide that I'm it. She's going to see what she'd forgo if she stayed with me, a man whose sole time in the outside world extends to his art shows and the rare important athletic match for one of his siblings. She'll realize she loved me, but that doesn't mean I fit in her life.

So I'm going to see her off with all the restraint required not to kiss her breathless and beg her to come back. Because I've learned that's what my love for her is—wanting her happiness, even if it means it's happiness without me.

And I won't love her any less.

"Axel?" Rooney pops her head in the studio, and thank God my canvas is facing away.

It's dripping with such bitter, bleak shades of blue, it puts Picasso's Blue Period to shame. I tried not to do it at first, because I knew she might see, but it was the only way to cope, as each day crept by and my happiness dimmed and my sadness grew. I had to paint it, to ease a sliver of the building pain inside my chest that's going to crack with the pressure of loss when she leaves tomorrow morning.

"Hey." I set down my brush, wipe off my hands, and cross the room. I can't force a smile, but I try to hide the sadness, to set my jaw and meet her eyes and touch her in a way that puts her at ease.

Rooney's smile is a little unsteady as she clasps my face, her thumbs sliding along my jaw. "The beard is getting formidable."

"It is." I scrub it with one hand. "But my wi—"

I stop myself. It's become a thing the past few weeks, to lob the words affectionately, teasingly at each other—*wife, husband*. I just can't seem to force it past my throat right now.

"You've seemed to enjoy it," I manage.

Rooney's gaze searches mine. "I do." She drops her hands from my face, threading her fingers with mine. "Are you at an okay stopping point?"

*Painting my bleeding heart onto a canvas?*

I don't say that. I don't tell her painting like this won't be stopping anytime soon.

"Yeah, I can take a break."

Gently, she takes me by the hand into the main room. My jacket and hat are there. A small bag she packed. Our walking sticks.

A goodbye hike.

I swallow roughly. "A walk?"

She nods and tries to smile. "Yes, if that's all right."

"Okay." It comes out hoarse. I clear my throat. "Just . . . need the bathroom real quick."

She nods again. "Sure. I'll get bundled up. Takes me long enough."

Since the temps have dropped, Rooney has to wear a comical number of layers to stay warm, unaccustomed to December weather in the Northwest. I know her referring to it now is supposed to amuse me and make me smile. But it doesn't. "Be right back."

"Okay," she whispers.

In the bathroom, I grip the sink and try to breathe. It's hard. It's so fucking hard.

I turn on the water, splashing my face over and over, hoping it helps. It doesn't. My hands shake as I shut off the faucet and avoid my reflection in the mirror. I know what I look like, and I know it's pathetic.

Out of the bathroom, I focus on tugging on my knit hat and jacket. I scratch Harry's head as he whines up at me. "Stay, Harry."

He *harrumph*s, dropping to the ground. As if trying to lighten his mood, Skugga pounces on his torso, crawls up his side, and bats his ear. He only *harrumph*s again.

Rooney stands, bundled up in an old coat of my mom's that I found when it got cold and Rooney was without a winter jacket, seeing as she never expected to stay this long. It's puffy, the color of pale blue winter skies, and when Rooney wears it with that damn yellow hat, she looks like a ray of sunshine popping out from behind a cloud.

I zip up my jacket, then step closer, zipping hers the rest of the way out of muscle memory. Rooney stares up at me. Her hands rest on my wrists, squeezing gently. "Thanks," she says.

I nod. Grabbing our walking sticks, I slip the bag onto my back, not knowing what's in it, only that Rooney wants it to come with us.

After I step outside, she follows me, locking up. I watch her, head bent, blonde hair swishing past her shoulder, the same order of operations as so many mornings before we walked across the field, hand in hand, and up the hill to the A-frame.

She turns and meets my eyes, offering another tentative smile. "Ready?"

*No*, I think. *I was never going to be ready for this.*

"Yes," I lie.

Rooney takes the first step, and I fall into place beside her. Our sticks hit the ground, none of her usual chatter accompanying us. No questions about what species this is or what genus that is. No *Look, Ax!* as she points out something that lights up her face and makes her smile. Just quiet, boots and walking sticks striking the hard earth. Nothing but soft puffs of warm breath materializing in the cold air as we walk. And when we get to the spot, I almost turn around.

She had to bring us here.

I've shown her other places now that she's felt up for it. Rooney's built stamina and strength in just a few weeks of increasingly difficult hikes. She's started learning her way around. She could have taken us to a half dozen places.

But no. We're here. Where I brought her when we married. Where I brought her to be brave and say I loved her.

And now I have to be brave again and let her go.

"It's not quite a sunset view," she says, staring out at the landscape. "But I wanted it to be here."

I swallow around the lump in my throat. "Okay."

She blinks my way, her expression unreadable. "I wanted to talk about what's next."

Oh, God, it hurts, this new ache. It's not the love-ache, or at least, it's not just that. It's the ache of a sword glowing from the forge, dragging through my heart. White-hot. Brutally sharp. The ache of loss.

Rooney walks my way and gently eases the bag off my back. Crouching with it, she opens the flap, unfolding a blanket. "Sit," she says. "Please?"

I don't want to sit. I want to run. I want so badly to run from this pain.

But that's not what I do anymore, not with Rooney. I don't leave when she draws close. I don't hide when things are hard. At least, I try not to. So I sit slowly on the blanket, watching her reach inside the bag again. She pulls out a water bottle, just one, for us to share. A bag of jerky for me, and a gluten-free chocolate chip cookie for herself.

"Hungry?" she asks.

I shake my head. "No."

Sitting, she pulls the cookie from its container and spins it in her grip. She breaks it in half, then breaks it in half again. Then she drops it in the container. "I'm not going back to school," she blurts. "At least, not yet. I'm going back to LA for Christmas, and then up to Stanford to talk with my advisor." She meets my eyes. "I'm going to take a full-year leave, then reevaluate as I get closer about whether to finish or leave for good."

I blink at her. "A . . . full year."

She nods. "I'm so sorry it's taken me this long to talk about it. I've been weighing the decision heavily, and I only just figured it out."

I nod, breathing as the ache burns deeper. "You don't need to be sorry. It's your future to figure out, not mine."

Her brow furrows. "I was hoping . . . maybe while I was figuring things out, you'd have figured some things out, too?"

"Like what?" I ask.

She glances down at her hands and bites her lip. "I thought maybe you'd have something to tell me, too. Or ask me?"

Confusion makes anxious bands tighten around my ribs. What does she think I'd have to say to her, when she's leaving and I'm staying?

"I'm not sure what you're expecting me to say," I tell her slowly. "Except that I'm happy for you, Rooney, for whatever brilliant things await. And . . . I'm honored to have been even just a temporary part of your life, before you were back on your way to chasing that bright future."

"Axel . . ." She shakes her head, blinking like I've shocked her. "I've never been happier than I have been here. I love what we've built in every meaning of that word, even though I never expected it to happen. Where did you get the idea that we were temporary? We've shared such . . . safety and trust and love. Haven't we?"

"Of course," I tell her, swallowing the lump in my throat. "But you told me yourself, sometimes love isn't enough."

Tears fill her eyes. "W-what are you saying?"

I so badly want to tell her that I take it back, that I'm confident our love *is* enough. That when Rooney returns to her real life, what we've shared will still feel real then, too. That whenever she visits, when I can work myself up to being with her, it'll be frantic and loving and condensing weeks into hours and making the most of it until she's here for good.

But what about my bleak social ability? Terrible on the phone, terse in texts. What about my need to stay home, in my space? Hermit, recluse, loner. What about the fact that I can barely sustain a long-distance relationship with my understanding family, let alone with a woman who thrives on touch and talking and intimate connection?

What about her needs that have gone unmet from the people who were supposed to love her best? What about how she's hurt herself trying to love them back, with that deceptive *I'm fine* smile and her brutal determination to make everything work if she just *pushes* herself hard enough? What if that's how we become— distorted and damaging, the last thing I'd ever want—our love turning into something that hurts her?

What if we try, and she leaves and comes back, and she doesn't want me anymore?

I stare down at my hands. "I'm saying it's best for us to let this end. If you want me after you've had time in the real world again, seen what's out there, I'll be here."

She reels, like I've struck her. "'Seen what's out there'? Axel, I'm not shopping around. I love you."

Hearing those words, I want to wrap my hands around them and hold tight. I want them to tether us unbreakably. I want to trust they're stronger than any outside force that could come at us.

But I know better. I know my limitations, and I know her harmful patterns. And I'm so scared loving each other won't be enough to overcome that. "I love you, too, Rooney. That's why I'm saying this. Because I love you and I want you to be happy."

"I *am* happy. Or I was, until five minutes ago. I mean, I was really fucking nervous because long-distance relationships aren't easy and you haven't said a single thing in the past few weeks like, 'Hey, Roo, I want to make this work. Come here as much as you can. Or, hell, I'll fly down to you.' But now," she says, wiping away tears, "I realize you haven't said anything because you don't *want* to make this work. You only wanted me while I wasn't work, while I was convenient, and now that I'm not, you're ending it."

Hearing that hurts, sour and sharp, like my heart's one big paper cut and her words are pure acid. "That's not true. I'm not ending it. It's ending on its own. You're going back. I'm staying here. It's a natural end."

"But it doesn't have to be!" she says. "It's ending just because I'm leaving for a while? Because I have an apartment in California? Bullshit, Axel. You *say* it's because I'm leaving. But it's time you own your part in this. You're being distant. You're pushing me away."

*Because I have to, to cope. Because if I feel all of this, I'll drown in it, and I'll drag you down with me.*

"I'm here, Rooney."

She shakes her head. "No you're not. You're acting like the guy I met, not the man I know. Not the man I married."

"Please don't say that," I snap, because it cuts too deep. "We didn't marry for love. It's not real."

She stares at me, eyes wet, chin trembling. "Not real? If this isn't real to you, what *has* it been? You showed me that you loved me even when my life was such a fucking mess. You made me feel brave to own that truth and ask for love when it's about to get messier, and then the moment I take a chance on it, you rip that love away from me."

Words slip through my mind like a sieve. I stare at her, terrified. Terrified that I've hurt her when all I wanted was to love her like she deserves. Terrified of what I always have been: that my love isn't her kind of love, that my best isn't best for her.

"Talk to me," she pleads, grabbing my coat. "Please!"

I jerk away instinctively and stumble back until I'm upright, standing out of her reach. Panicking, I'm so confused and overwhelmed, I feel like I'm going to crawl out of my skin if I'm touched.

Rooney looks up at me, wounded. Her face crumples. Then she picks up the bag as she stands, throws it on her shoulder, and runs out of the clearing.

For once, I'm not worried about Rooney finding her way home. This time, it's me who's lost.

———

Hours later, after a walk home that I don't remember, I step inside the house, knowing she's gone. I slump into a chair and scrub my face—sharp, bitter pain twisting inside me as my thoughts turn bleak and despairing.

My phone dings, which is deeply irritating, seeing as I hate that sound and always try to have it on vibrate. I pull it from my pocket, ready to silence it, when I see new email notifications lighting up my screen. Notifications I've ignored because I've been too busy to acknowledge them, too busy soaking up every moment with Rooney.

I'm so desperate for a distraction from the gnawing ache building inside me that I swipe open my phone, prepared to lose myself in oppressive administrative details and too-long-ignored correspondence. Bills. More bills. My agent poking me—as they rightfully should—about how my art is coming along.

"A lot of depressing-as-shit blue is coming, Emory," I mutter, scrolling through the emails. "Blue and black and gray and . . ."

My thoughts come to an abrupt halt as I see the subject line, and the sender. I have a new email from Uncle Jakob's executor. I open the email and start to read.

Dear Mr. Bergman, it begins. Attached is a confidential file that I was directed by your uncle to forward to you on the first December 13 after your marriage. I regret that originally I did not realize the file failed to send, so I am resending. Please accept my deepest apologies for this delay.

Frowning, I click open the attachment and start to read, then freeze. "What the *fuck*?"

Axel—

If you're reading this, it is because you are now married, either for love or for money. I can imagine if it is the latter, then you aren't terribly pleased with me, and that is your right. Who am I to have asked you to be married? Quiet, solitary Uncle Jakob—what do I know about love?

I know more than anyone knows I did. Not your grandparents, not your mother, not my friends. I married Klara after your mother had left for the States, and your grandparents had decided to sell the business. I'd moved to Östersund and that's where I met Klara, and befriended her, much as I tried to avoid her because I was hopelessly taken by her and I was the last sort of man someone like her would want.

I won't bore you with details, but I will tell you our marriage did not begin as one of love but for money, and that's the only reason I consented to it. Klara needed someone, and she made me a shrewd offer, a not-insignificant cut of the funds she received upon our marriage, which I needed, as a starving artist in a new city. We were married on Saint Lucia's Day—yes, this is my romanticism showing, sending you this letter on December 13, having written it on our anniversary date as well. We shared a flat because it was necessary for appearances, and at first I hated it. I was used to doing things on my own, in my own way, and Klara was incapable of not pulling me into her energetic thoughts and questions, her small dinners with friends and her quiet walks at night. Yet somehow, along the way, I let myself fall in love with her.

And then I lost her too soon. So soon, I never got to introduce her to my parents, to my sister, to my feisty niece and her new baby brother—you. She was my secret and then she was my secret loss. Klara had broken open my heart and loved me, and then she'd broken my heart by leaving me. I was . . . beyond consolation. I became reclusive. I shut myself away from the family for many years.

Until your mother demanded I come to the house in Washington, to meet my nieces and nephews and see her. So I came. And I struggled. I was still angry and bitter and lonely, and being surrounded by a chaotic gathering of people I knew I loved but still struggled with was harder than I'd anticipated. Until the third morning I was there, outside, sketching and drinking coffee, and you came outside, quiet, serious, your own pencils and sketchbook tucked under your lanky arm. You caught me drawing her—Klara. Your eyes traveled from the paper to me, and I begged you in my thoughts not to ask, because it was too difficult to talk about how deeply I still hurt.

You said nothing. Only nodded, then quietly sat beside me, opened your sketchbook, and drew studiously. And you did it with me every morning after that, while I was there.

That's when I knew what I would do with the money Klara, in her infuriating sweetness, had left to her husband in the event of her death, the money it made me sick to contemplate using, but made me just as sick to contemplate letting go to waste: I decided I would leave it to you, and in some distorted gesture of hope or cosmic justice or delusion— call it whatever you want—I placed a condition that I suppose I hoped might give you what I had for far too little time: love.

I saw so much of myself in you, Axel, and I could so easily picture you growing up believing all the things I'd believed of myself, things that made me only agree to marry someone for reasons entirely divorced from love. I hoped I was wrong, and perhaps I have been. Perhaps you fell wildly in love and married and have lavished Klara's legacy on the person who captured your heart.

Or perhaps I was right.

And if I was, I hope your story has ended happier than ours. I hope you at least gained a friend, and the understanding that every one of us is worthy of loving and being loved in whatever way is true to us. I hope, if I have hurt you in my machinations, you will forgive me, that you will understand this was my final chance to honor Klara. The woman who changed my world. The only woman I ever loved.

I hope, if you have found love such as I did, that you have cherished it. That you will do everything in your power to protect it, for as long as you both shall live.

—Uncle Jakob

I shut my eyes, breathing unsteadily against the ache that spills through my chest, climbs up my throat, and burns past my eyelids. Tears wet my face. Then tears become heaving, gasping breaths. But they aren't tears of despair. They aren't sobs of hopelessness. They're relief. Relief and love tinged with a glimmer of hope. Because it's so profoundly simple: I love Rooney, and my fears don't get to stand in the way of that.

My uncle's words are here before me, and they're exactly what I needed—true and convicting and undeniable: *I hope, if you have found love such as I did, that you have cherished it. That you will do everything in your power to protect it . . .*

I didn't cherish our love or protect it. I feared our love and protected myself, and I hurt Rooney when I pushed her away. I clearly have some personal shit to work on as I figure out how to tell her how sorry I am—I know that. And my fears won't disappear overnight, they'll be a battle—I know that, too. But most importantly, I know our story doesn't end here, that my mistake has shaped us, but it doesn't get the final say.

I made a promise to the woman I love—*to love and to cherish, now and forever.*

I'm going to show her just how much I mean it.

# THIRTY

# *Axel*

Playlist: "Blue Christmas," The Lumineers

"HO! HO! HO! Merry—" Viggo freezes on the threshold of the A-frame. "Christ. You look terrible." He glances over his shoulder at Ryder and says, "You said he looked good. That he was doing good. What the hell happened?"

Ryder blinks between us, frowning. "I did. He was. I don't know."

Viggo rolls his eyes. "Come on, let me in. Move. Merry Christmas and all that."

I hold the door as Viggo walks in, then Willa in front of Ryder. She gives me a faint smile and her usual high five. "Hey," she says.

"Hey."

Willa's quiet around Christmas, not her usual feisty self. Her mom passed away shortly after the holiday just a few years ago, and the family knows it's still a tough time of year for her. I always expect her to be subdued, but I'm not sure what else I should expect from her since Rooney left, if she'll be angry with me for how badly I fucked up.

I haven't told Ryder what happened with Rooney, and it doesn't seem like Rooney told Willa, either, because she doesn't seem upset. She just hikes her bag higher on her shoulder and says, "Thanks for this idea. Not gonna lie, I don't miss flying with everyone and their grandmother for Christmas."

"True that," Ryder says.

"Must be nice!" Viggo calls from the kitchen, where he's already poking around the snacks Mom set up. "Some of us had to sit on a plane next to a guy who was eating salmon jerky."

Oliver traipses in last, carrying so much shit, I can't even see him. I just know by process of elimination that it's his long legs poking out from a mountain of Christmas presents my parents mailed here, rather than pack for their flight, which must have just been delivered.

My brother Ren and his girlfriend, Frankie, are upstairs getting unpacked, as are Mom and Dad, who caught an earlier flight and are down the hall in the first-floor bedroom. Ziggy, who flew up with my parents, is stretched out on her stomach in front of the fire, reading. Aiden and Freya, my brother-in-law and sister, are out on a walk.

At least, it'd better be a walk. Aiden's hands were all over Freya as they put on jackets and boots. I told him if he defiled the property with an outdoor tryst, I was coming for him. To which he responded with a middle finger and a door slam.

"Here." Oliver dumps Christmas gifts into my arms. "Make yourself useful."

If I felt capable of it, I'd laugh at the irony. Since Rooney left, I've been nonstop. First, I painted around the clock, only pausing long enough to feed the animals, let out the dog, and mindlessly eat a granola bar so I could stay upright. Then I exhausted myself cleaning the A-frame and decorating it, anything that could distract me from constantly thinking about her.

Following Oliver in, I set the boxes of presents under the Christmas tree, which I cathartically chopped down and is covered in every single ornament I could find. There's also fresh garland on the banister and throughout the house, strung over doorways. I even put up fucking mistletoe, which—*gross*—my parents are currently taking advantage of.

The mistletoe was a bad call.

"It feels different around here," Frankie says as she gets to the bottom of the steps. She's in head-to-toe black, except for a reindeer-antler headband with jingle bells.

Ren's wearing his truly ugly Christmas sweater from the stash that we keep here, complete with Rudolph's blinking nose. Landing at the last step in Frankie's wake, he sets a hand on her back. "Besides being decorated for Christmas?" he asks. "What do you mean?"

Frankie does a double take at his sweater. "Wow. You weren't lying. That sweater is heinous."

Ren smiles and boops Rudolph's nose. "Isn't it?"

"Mine's worse!" Oliver says. "I gotta go put it on. Where are they again?"

"Upstairs hallway closet," I tell him. He's already taking the steps two at a time.

"Hm." Viggo crunches thoughtfully on his cheese-and-cracker sandwich. "Maybe I'll break out the *Christmas Story* bunny suit. Is it still here?"

"No!" Ziggy yells. "You look demented in that thing."

Viggo wiggles his eyebrows. "That's the point. Also, it's toasty as hell, and I need all the layers when I'm here. Though, it's actually pretty warm right now. Has it always been this warm with just the woodburning stove?"

"Yes," I lie. "It's a pretty efficient heating system."

Frankie glances around the foyer, eyes narrowed. "It feels different, doesn't it? Good different. Did you deep clean?" she asks me. "Burn a new candle? I swear it's different."

I latch on to that explanation for what she's picked up on. "Uh. Well. Yeah. I cleaned a bit. Touched up paint here and there. Took care of odds and ends. You know, the usual."

Poking the floor with her cane, she says, "That floorboard definitely used to squeak."

"Yep. Fixed that, too."

Ren smiles at me. "You've been working hard around here, huh?"

I swallow nervously. "Nah. Nothing big."

"It's definitely less drafty," Ziggy says, rolling onto her back, eyes on her e-reader. "Did you seal the windows or something?"

More of the family's glancing around now, inspecting the place, and I feel my grip on the situation slipping. If Rooney were here, she'd know just what to do, how to change the subject and make it seem effortless. But she's not. I sent her the email two days ago, set up everything, and I haven't heard a word.

I rub my chest. That ache hasn't left once.

"Glogg is warming," Mom says, unknowingly saving me. "And I've set up Scrabble."

"Ooh." Ziggy shoots up from the floor. "Yes! Come on, Ollie. You and me, to the death."

Oliver groans as he hits the bottom step and tugs on his sweater. Peering down, he changes the Grinch's grin from mischievous to menacing with a glide of his hand over the sequins, flipping their direction. "Must I?"

"Yes," Ziggy says, dragging him with her.

"You're just going to annihilate me with your absurdly large reader's vocabulary."

"Of course I am." She settles at the long dining table, dumping out tiles. "But you need *someone* to keep your ego in check."

Oliver glances my way, a moment of understanding passing between us. "I've had my ego checked plenty lately," he mumbles.

Ziggy gives him a confused look. "Fine. I'll take it easy on you."

Having avoided a full-on inquisition about the house, I stand in the foyer, relieved and surveying the space as people disperse and settle in. Ren and Frankie cozy up on the sofa in front of the fire, sharing some kind of private exchange that involves Ren blushing bright red as Frankie cackles. Ryder hands Willa a glass of glogg and slips his arm around her waist, pressing a kiss to her hair. She stares out at the patio where the hot tub sits, a secret smile on her face. My mom laughs as Dad whispers in her ear, leaning in behind her as she cuts more salami at the kitchen counter.

And suddenly I am keenly aware that most of the people here use this house for one primary reason:

A shit ton of sex.

I groan and scrub my face. Right. I'm going to keep telling myself my childhood home away from home is an innocent place that brings us together for wholesome, familial love reasons. *Not* that I just spent months and the majority of an inheritance I only got access to by marrying the woman I was in lust with, then fell in love with, then had to part on terrible terms with, all so these horndogs could have updated plumbing and environmentally conscious insulation for their sexual escapades.

God. Fuck my life.

"Axel," Mom calls from the kitchen.

I close the distance between us and force myself to eat a piece of cheese. "Hey, Mom."

She clasps my hand, holding tight. "Everything looks beautiful. Thank you."

It's bittersweet, hearing that. I'm grateful for all I was able to do to make the place ready for my family. And I'm gutted that I'm not sharing it with Rooney. "Thank you for coming up."

"Oh, goodness," she says, smiling and adding grapes to the massive charcuterie board she's built. "I'm delighted to have a break from hosting. I love having everyone home, but to show up and only have to cook, it's a treat. All the gift I need."

My stomach knots as Rooney's words echo in my head. *Your parents will love your art because they love you.*

"Speaking of gifts," I say a little hoarsely. I clear my throat.

Mom tips her head. "Yes?"

"I, uh . . ." I scratch the back of my neck. "I have something for you. And Dad. For your Christmas gift."

Mom smiles. "You want us to have it now?"

"Probably for the best." Before I lose my courage.

"Alexander," Mom calls over her shoulder. "Come here."

Dad leaves his conversation with Viggo and joins us, setting an arm around her waist. "What is it?"

Mom smiles up at him. "Axel has a gift for us."

Dad grins. "That so?"

A cold sweat breaks out on my skin. Oh fuck. Why did I do this?

Mom's smile deepens. Dad plants a kiss on her temple and meets my eyes. "Well?" he says. "Let's see it!"

———

"Why's Mom crying?" Viggo asks, handing me a beer. I take it and drain half in one gulp.

"I gave her and Dad a painting."

His eyebrows fly up. "Correct me if I'm wrong, but that would require you allowing them to *see* the painting?"

"Yes," I say tightly.

He grins. "You finally did it. Good for you."

I take another gulp of beer. "I feel like a jerk, taking so long to get comfortable with showing them."

"You're not a jerk. We each do things in our own time," Viggo says. "What matters is you did it when you could."

"I guess." I stare into my beer, such a fucking mess of emotions. Touched and elated that my parents loved the painting. Sick to my stomach that Rooney's not here. That I haven't heard anything.

When I glance up, Viggo's staring at me very closely. "So when are you going to tell me what's got you all torn up?"

"What?"

"Axel," he says patiently. "You asked us to come here for Christmas. You *asked* us."

"Via email."

"You never ask for anything. I mean, don't get me wrong, despite the salmon-jerky-on-the-plane trauma, I'm glad I'm here. I love having everyone together, and it's a nice return to the tradition of Christmas at the A-frame. But you have a reason, and I don't think it's an entirely happy one." His voice softens. "I'm your brother, dude. I love you. I want to know."

I glance around. And in a moment of weakness, I mutter, "I fell in love with Rooney, and then I really fucked it up."

Viggo gapes at me. And then he pulls out his phone and attacks his text messages.

"Did you just send a Bat Signal GIF to the guys?" I ask.

"Hush up. I hear you judging me." Viggo pockets his phone. "Report to the basement in five."

"What? No—"

He's gone, sauntering out of the room nonchalantly. Ren's next, planting a kiss on Frankie before he stands and stretches, then wanders the way of the basement. Oliver whines from the pantry, followed by a slapping sound, then an "*Ouch!*"

Ryder kisses Willa's temple, then strolls through the kitchen, swiping a beer from the fridge before he turns the corner.

And then Aiden walks in the front door, dark hair dappled with snow, bright blue eyes shining from behind his thick-framed black glasses, looking like a pissed-off, nerdy Lucifer. "This better be good," he growls, before he stomps down the hall.

Resigned to my fate, I clutch my beer and head for the basement, too.

---

"So you told her you love her," Viggo recaps, perched on a box in the basement that's way less dusty than it used to be. I really hope they don't notice that. Or the fresh lines of concrete indicating where the sewage pipes were ripped up and replaced. "Romanced the hell out of her for a month. Then, when you knew she was leaving for home, you broke up with her, preemptively losing her on *your* terms, rather than risking a long-distance relationship and the possibility of losing her down the road."

They all stare at me.

"Uh." I clear my throat. "I would say that's accurate. Yes."

A collective hiss of disapproval echoes in the basement.

"Axel." Ryder scrubs his face. "Why? She told you she loves you. You don't trust her to make it work with a little planning ahead and a three-hour plane ride between you?"

Ren chimes in and says, "Have you tried to call her? Oh, well. You don't do calls. Texts are inadequate. So are emails."

I open my mouth, but Viggo jumps in.

"Definitely no emails," he says. "It's one thing to handle your pain-in-the-ass family via email, but this is grand-gesture-in-the-freezing-rain material. She deserves his words, face-to-face. He needs to go to her."

My stomach drops. "What if—hypothetically—I *had* sent an email?"

They all suck in a breath.

Viggo grimaces. "You didn't. Tell me you didn't."

"I did."

The room erupts in various sounds of despair.

"But . . . it wasn't my apology," I explain. "It was directions."

Viggo blinks at me. "*Directions?*"

Taking a deep breath, I stare down at my hands and tell them what I did. When I finish, it's very, very quiet.

"Damn." Viggo sets down his beer and opens his arms. I think he wants a hug. He's not getting one. "That is glorious. That is— God, I'm proud of you."

"Well done," Ryder says.

Ren dabs his eyes. "That's beautiful, Ax."

"Can I ask something?" Oliver says, hand raised. We turn toward him. "Is Rooney Peach Panties?"

Viggo sighs. "Yes, sweet, innocent child, she is."

"I'm with them," Aiden says, pushing off the wall. "I think she'll love that. I know I've been quiet, but it wasn't long ago I was in the same spot you are—well, metaphorically—and I'm honestly just feeling deeply bad for you because it sucks—the emotional aspect, and being subjected to the brotherly gathering."

"Hey." Viggo throws an old stuffed animal from the neighboring box at Aiden's head. "A Bergman Brothers Summit is a place of loving care. It's not a punishment."

Aiden catches the black cat stuffed animal that's seen better days and tucks it under his arm. "Says you. You have yet to sit in the hot seat. I'll keep my speech brief: Communication is hard. Even when you love someone, it's hard. When you fall short, yes, you say sorry and forgive, you learn and get better, but it's not just a walk in the park after that. Sometimes, you still mess up."

"Still?" Viggo says disbelievingly.

Aiden turns slowly, pinning him with an arctic glare. "Yes, Viggo. Still. It's called being a work in progress. A mere mortal. One day, when you fall from your idyllic cloud in the sky and hit earth, you're going to learn that loving someone is a lot more than reading romance novels and being emotionally intelligent. And frankly, I'm going to bring my beer and soak up every goddamn minute."

Ren whistles. "Wow. I think Aiden's had that on his chest for a while."

Oliver stares at Aiden like he hung the moon. "I wish I could hit replay on that moment."

"Back to the matter at hand," Ryder says pointedly.

"Right." Aiden clears his throat, then lobs the stuffed animal cat Oliver's way. "What I'm getting at is, what happened with you and Rooney is normal. It happens. You were a couple, having your first fight, which was really just a misunderstanding. Now you're going to work through it."

I glance around at them. "You think it'll work?"

Viggo grins. "Uh, yeah, Axel. Pretty sure it's going to work."

"I agree," Aiden says, before clapping his hands. "Well, my part's done, then. If you'll excuse me, my wife's now waiting in our room for her Christmas gift, which is hopefully a—"

"Ay!" we all yell.

"In short," he says with a grin. "I'm leaving. You got this, Ax."

Oliver pets the stuffed animal cat thoughtfully and says, "I know you're worried that you haven't heard from her, and yes, you messed up, but Rooney did, too. She didn't stay and try to talk it out. She left. Maybe she's figuring out how she wants to say sorry, too."

"That's a good point," Ryder says.

Viggo plucks the stuffed animal cat from Oliver's arms and fixes the bow around its neck. "Here's a thought. You really want to knock this out of the park?"

"Here we go," Oliver sighs. "An elaborate baseball metaphor is coming."

"Not today," Viggo says, facing me. "I say you get on the plane. Chase her down. To hell with us. We'll be here. Go win the girl—woman, I mean—then bring her back."

"But I didn't want to have you all here just to leave you."

Ryder makes a face. "Axel. We're going to sit around, drink too much glogg, fight about board games, and be exactly where you left us. Go. If you want to, that is."

"I second that," Oliver says.

I stand, determined energy thrumming through me. "All right. I'll do it. Well, at least I'm going to try. First, I have to find an open flight to LA the day before Christmas Eve."

Viggo sighs dreamily, clutching the cat to his chest. "This is going to be epically romantic. I can feel it."

# THIRTY-ONE

# Rooney

Playlist: "Home," Edith Whiskers

Twenty-four hours into my return to LA, I knew what I needed to do. My body ached with sadness. I couldn't stop crying. I felt sick to my stomach, and for once, my illness wasn't to blame.

I hated how I'd left, with so much hurt, so many unspoken words between Axel and me, sobbing as I hugged Harry and Skugga, not knowing if it would be the last time I saw them. Because Axel didn't want me, at least not the way I wanted him. I was the woman he married for convenience and inconveniently fell in love with.

Once again, I was a fucking mistake.

And that's when I had a not-so-small epiphany: I've been trying to prove I'm not a mistake for a very long time, meaning my childhood, my relationship with my parents, my sense of self, and Axel are all tangled into a really fucked-up knot.

So I pulled out my laptop and opened the browser, found the website I'd visited, then x-ed out of, a dozen times while staying in Washington. This time, I found the number. I entered it into my phone. And I scheduled my first therapy appointment.

Now I have three sessions under my belt. Yes, God bless Sue, she has made time for me three times in six days, because I've needed it. I've needed to talk about things I told myself were in the past and best left there, to cry about hurts I'd never let myself feel.

I've never spent this much time submerged in sadness, and yet, shockingly, I'm all right.

Well, no, I'm not. But I'm starting to learn that I can survive being not all right, that accepting my not-all-rightness is a necessary part of life.

So, here I am, the day before Christmas Eve, just all right enough to clutch this printed-out email from Axel in my shaking hands. An email that I just saw this morning, when I finally felt mentally capable of facing my inbox.

I've followed its directions, unsure. Maybe the tiniest bit hopeful.

Because I'm standing outside a boutique art gallery in Santa Monica, the same neighborhood as my childhood home, where Ax knew I planned to spend Christmas.

Step one, the email reads. Arrive at the gallery at 10 a.m.

I peer at my phone. Ten on the dot.

Step two. Knock.

Lifting my hand, I knock. I hear clicking heels, the sound of a lock turning. The door swings open, revealing a smartly dressed woman who steps back and smiles. "You're Mr. Bergman's guest?"

My heart races. "Um. Yes, I think so. That is, his email—" Taking a deep breath, I steady myself. "Yes. I'm his guest. Rooney Sullivan."

"Ms. Sullivan," she says. "Right this way."

She locks the door behind us, which makes sense, given the gallery's hours say noon to six. I decline her offer to take my coat, and then follow her through a modern, open space of cool white walls and floors that gleam beneath soft recessed lighting.

"Take your time," she says at the threshold, before she turns and disappears down the hall, leaving me alone.

I glance over my shoulder, surprised by her abrupt departure. But then my curiosity wins out, and when I turn the corner—

Air rushes out of me. The email flutters from my hand to the floor, landing with a soft *swish*.

I only get a moment before tears blur my vision, and I'm furious with myself, because now I can't see the two canvases in front of me, massive and bold, the only art on this entire gallery wall.

I wipe my eyes quickly, and once again, I can see.

Night's darkness fades in one canvas, deepens in the other, and on both, it's borne out in a painstakingly fine gradation of cerulean, sapphire, and indigo. Sweeping strokes of dreamy lavender seep into ripe plum. Rich apricot blossoms into buttery marigold. Like a lover's embrace, the edges glow with a delicate, whispering brush of palest pink, shades of soft skin and kitten noses and lush peonies.

He painted them. Axel painted sunrise and sunset.

That's when I see it, an envelope poking out from the corner of sunset. On unsteady legs, I bend and pick up the email that I dropped, to read my next direction.

Step three: read the letter.

I walk up to the canvas, tug out the envelope, and see my name. Shakily, I tear it open and pull out the paper.

*Rooney,*

*If you're reading this, you got my email, and you're here at the gallery, seeing what took more courage than I ever thought it would to paint. After you left, I knew I had to do this: to face my fears and show you what you mean to me, to tell you how sorry I am.*

*There's a reason I painted sunrise and sunset, and it's not just because you challenged me to paint what I love, but because dawn and dusk have always made me think of you. The crew called you "sunflower," which you know drove me up the wall, but they weren't wrong, and they weren't the first to have thought it. I've looked at you before as the Swedish word blossomed in my thoughts—"solros"—sun-rose, that's what it translates to. It's so perfectly you. The sun-gold warmth of your hair, the rose pink of your lips when you smile and your cheeks when you blush. The feelings they evoke, too: the joyful hope of a sunrise, the comforting gratitude of a sunset, the sense of wonder they both herald, for another day of life that I once considered a gift but learned to call a miracle because you were there, sharing life with me.*

*So here they are, dawn and dusk, bursting with your colors, reminding me of you and what we've shared. They're memories of kisses and healing touch, of early mornings and late nights, of laughter and peaceful silence. They capture the life we built that I was so afraid to lose.*

*I was so afraid, Rooney. Afraid you'd realize that our relationship and the outside world you'd come to me from were incompatible, and then you'd have to break my heart or break yourself for me. I told myself that in releasing you from our relationship, I was placing your happiness above mine, and that is what I want, your happiness, above all else. But then I clung to my fear when you tried to tell me I'd gotten it wrong— that _we_ were your happiness, and I was taking that away.*

*I didn't listen. I didn't believe you. I'm so sorry.*

*While painting these, I found my words and spoke with my therapist. We talked about the judgment I've internalized for myself and how I live. I thought I was at peace with who and how I am. Turns out it's a bit more complicated than that. I will keep working on it. For myself, and if you can forgive me, for you, too. For us.*

*I want to be there with you, but I'm here, hosting my family for Christmas, because it was what I needed, so I asked them,*

*and they came. I wish I was there to hold you, because I know
you're crying, hopefully not because the hurt I caused is
irreparable, but because you see how much I love you
and how sorry I am and you're proud of me for being
brave the way I know you're being brave, too. I know you
went home and reached out for help the way you told me you
wanted to.*

*If you can forgive me, I want to be brave with you, Rooney.
I want to stretch and grow side by side. I want to wait for
you, and trust you, and show you that we can do this.
Together.*

*There's a first-class plane ticket in this envelope, and it has
your name on it. If you're ready, if you can forgive me, please
come.*

*Because I want us. I want you here, with me. Yesterday. A
week ago. Forever.*

*Love,*
*Axel*

I close his letter, and I cry.

Because I'm learning how much it takes to be brave the way
Axel has been, and I'm in awe. I'm learning that being brave isn't
being fearless but rather facing our fears and not letting them dic-
tate our lives. It's living honestly in the imperfection of existence.
It's finding love in those messy places and fighting for it. And that
is deeply vulnerable.

I've spent too long hiding from that vulnerability, behind the
lies and smiles and *I'm all right*s. But I'm not doing that anymore.
I love myself enough to face my fears and grow, and I love Axel
enough to share that journey with him.

Now I know, clutching his heart poured out on paper, my

eyes locked on his bravery brushed across canvas—Axel loves me enough, too.

―――――

Twinkly lights sparkle in the darkness, draped along the outline of the A-frame. It looks so much like the tent Axel put up during the storm, my heart skips a beat.

I stand on the porch, hand hovering over the doorbell. If I step even a foot to the right, the windows will show anyone who wants to see that I'm here, and I don't want them to know. Not yet. I'm hiding and saving up my bravery for one person. And thank God, he's the one who opens the door.

"Axel." I breathe his name, drinking in cold winter air and the sight of the man I love after a week that feels like a lifetime.

He stares at me, wide-eyed, gripping the threshold. "Rooney?" he croaks.

Viggo appears behind him and waves, then with a hearty shove, sends Axel stumbling onto the porch and slams the door behind him. We face each other, our places identical to the day this all began. My hands are trembling, and my knees feel weak as I take him in.

The beard's thick and a bit neglected, dark circles beneath those beautiful eyes. His hair's tousled, and he's wearing a black winter coat over a cream cable-knit sweater that renders him both rugged and handsome. A rucksack drops from his shoulder and lands between us with a *thud*.

"You're here?" he says as I ask, "You're leaving?"

"I was coming for you," he says quietly, his hands approaching me shakily, hesitantly, like he thinks I'm a dream. "You're here," he whispers.

I smile, tears slipping down my cheeks. "I'm here."

"You came." His hands drift up my arms, past my shoulders,

then my neck, until they cup my face and thumb away my tears. "I'm so sorry, Rooney. I'm so, so sorry. I was scared to hurt you and scared to lose you and scared I'd mess it up when you went back, and I didn't tell you any of that, and I should have."

I shake my head. "I should have stayed and talked it out, tried to understand where you were coming from. I heard you say it wasn't real and—"

"It was real," he says urgently. "It was and is the realest thing I've known."

"Me too," I tell him tearily. "I just didn't stay long enough to hear you figure that out. Instead, I touched you when you needed space, and I pushed you to talk when you needed time to articulate yourself. I'm so sorry, Axel. Forgive me?"

"Forgiven," he says quietly, searching my eyes. "Forgive me, too?"

"Of course," I whisper.

"You got my note?"

"Note?" Tears slip down my cheeks. "Axel, that was the most beautiful *letter* I've ever read."

His mouth tips faintly, but there's no smile. Only serious, ever-green eyes traveling my face. "You read it. You saw them."

"I read it. I loved it as much as I loved the paintings and what they meant. I loved your bravery and your words, and I want everything you said. Is that . . . is that still what you want?"

Stepping closer, he cradles my face, and our eyes meet. "It's exactly what I want. *You're* everything I want, and I'll do whatever it takes to make life together possible. I love you more than I'll ever be able to say, Rooney, but it's no less true."

"I love you, too," I tell him. "So, so much. I want it all with you. Messes and mistakes and forgiveness. I want to love you and never stop."

The words have barely left my mouth when his lips meet mine, his kiss deep and tender and loving, so perfectly him.

"Ask me what I want again," he whispers.

I smile up at him. "Axel, what do you want?"

"I want to date my wife."

I laugh happily. "I would love to date my husband."

He presses his forehead to mine. "But most of all . . . I want to be with you forever. Not just for a whirlwind month. Not even until death do us part. I want every day, cramming as many lifetimes as possible into the one we've been given because finding you thirty years into my existence and only getting one chance to love you isn't nearly enough."

"Axel." I pull him close for a kiss that's a little wild and a little reverent, as achingly familiar as it is wondrously new. Clutching him tight, I sigh happily as he walks me back and pins me to the wall. Our kisses deepen, hot and slow, savoring, remembering, our touches desperate to rediscover each other.

"Sorry," he says breathlessly, pressing his forehead to mine. "As soon as I've kissed you, I want to kiss you again. It's a vicious cycle."

A smile I haven't felt in too long warms my face. I peer up at Axel, searching his gaze, drifting my hands through that silky, tousled hair, smoothing it away so I can see all of his striking, serious face. "You aren't alone," I tell him. "I've been waiting a week to kiss you, and now I don't want to stop."

He runs his hands along my back, over my waist. "I've been waiting, too."

"While I'm still in California, there'll be more waits like this," I tell him quietly.

He nods. "I know. But we won't have to wait long. My work is flexible, and I can do that flight in my sleep. I'll come to your place, cook for you. Leave you with lots of soup to microwave."

"You will? I mean, you know I love it here, and I'll be up here tons, but when I'm not—"

"Yes, I will. And yes, I know." He nuzzles my temple, then presses a kiss to my forehead. "I told you, I'm going to date you. You'll come to me. I'll come to you. I'll have to pass on the social mixers, and I won't be taking you to any clubs, but we can go to museums and have picnics and—"

"It's perfect," I tell him through a teary, incandescent smile. My hands settle on his chest, where our rings rest safe and warm beneath his sweater, our secret lovingly guarded. "And when I'm sick, you'll make me blanket nests and tea, and when you're burned out, I'll hold your hand and take you for long, quiet hikes."

His face grows even more serious as he tucks a loose hair behind my ear. "The hard parts and the easy parts," he says. "We'll figure them out together."

I peer up at Axel, the man I married, a stranger I barely knew, now the person I know best and love most. I steal a kiss, up on tiptoe, before I sink into his arms and hold him tight as I tell him, "I can't wait to live life with you."

His smile is dazzling—bright and rare. "I can't wait to live life with you, my wonderful"—*kiss*—"darling"—*kiss*—"Rooney."

I laugh, delighted and swept off my feet, quite literally, as he scoops me up and I throw my arms around his neck. "Someone hit the historical romance hard this past week."

"So hard." He kisses me tenderly, first my temple, then my cheek, then my lips. "Come inside?"

"I'd love to. But, tonight, afterward, can we go home?"

"Of course." He tips his head, and the smile deepens. "You called it home."

I beam at him, my heart glowing and full. "I did."

Axel gently lowers me to the ground, takes me by the hand, and opens the door, where mistletoe hangs above us. Stopping me, he wraps me in his arms and loves me with a kiss as soft and quiet as the rare snow that's begun falling from the sky.

"I love you, Rooney," he whispers.

"I love you, Axel."

He smiles and takes my hand again to lead me inside, but I stay stubbornly in my spot, pulling him back. Peering down at me, he searches my eyes, a soft smile warming his face. "What is it?" he asks.

"I want you to know . . . home, yes, it's that cabin in the woods that I love, with a bed we broke and pets we adore, and a place we made ours. But, more than anything, no matter where I am or where you are, *this* is home." Placing my hand over his heart, his hand over mine, I tell him with each kiss:

*Here.*

*With you.*

*Forever.*

# *Axel*

Playlist: "Do You Realize??," Vitamin String Quartet

*Five months later*

My first spring with Rooney. That's how I think now, how I see my life's seasons, milestones, whatever unfolds, *with her*. Ever since she was standing there on the A-frame porch at Christmas, snow drifting down, silver-white flakes weaving a veil on her spun-honey hair, Rooney is the frame around the canvas of my world, the color that transforms its palette to the loveliest, most vibrant hues. For so long, I never thought I needed more, wanted more than I had. But here she is, reminding me daily how wrong I was, how glad I am that I was wrong, that I opened my heart to the "more" that I so stubbornly believed wasn't mine to have.

Seated at the table in our little house in the woods, I watch the tree's blossoms sway in the wind, sunset glinting through the branches. It's a beautiful view. But it's got nothing on the view in my kitchen.

Rooney, my wife, standing in the kitchen, hair braided down her back, wearing nothing but my T-shirt, a mug of tea cupped in her hands.

I smile at her. Because I do that now. I smile. Not a lot, not for many. But I do for her.

Rooney beams at me, her simple gold wedding ring clinking

quietly against the mug as she taps her finger to its side. "That went well, I think."

I peer down at my own mug of tea, a knot twisting my stomach. "Seemed to."

She's talking about my family being here, about seeing them for the first time since I wrote them each letters last month explaining that Rooney and I had been together quietly since the fall, that we'd gotten married and I was sorry we weren't able to share that with them, but that we wanted to celebrate our marriage with them now.

I wrestled with how to tell them about Rooney and me, about our marriage. I don't communicate the way the rest of my family does. I don't text often. I never call. And that's for everyday life things. So telling them about this? The prospect of how it might go, if we told my family when we were all together, their collective curiosity, the inundating questions, being pressed for details, timelines, all sorts of things that would require our origin story, and with it, the details of what I did to the house, let alone the personal details of Rooney's and my beginning that felt so private, so tender—too precious to try to put into words—made my throat constrict, my chest pinch sharply, until I realized letter writing was the best I could do.

"Hey." Rooney crosses the space from the kitchen toward the table. I open my arm, wrapping it around her waist as she eases onto my lap. She sets her mug on the table and faces me. Her hand, warm from cradling her tea, cups my cheek. "What is it?"

I sigh.

She's quiet, waiting. Her fingers scratch along my scalp, the way I like. I shut my eyes and tell her the truth: "I just . . . hope I didn't disappoint them."

Her hand stops in my hair. My eyes drift open, meeting hers. "Axel."

"Rooney."

She tips her head, her eyes searching mine. "You didn't disappoint them. At *all*."

I swallow roughly. My throat feels thick. "How do you know?"

"Because there's a houseful of Bergmans right up the hill at the A-frame, delighted for us, happy and well-fed, who are here because you asked them to come and they want to be here. Every single member of your family is here because they love you—"

"*Us*," I tell her. "And loving someone is not the same as not being disappointed by them."

Sighing, she eases off my lap, then drags a dining table chair toward the fireplace with its floating shelves and tidy baskets on them. I'm out of my seat in a flash.

"Rooney, you are not climbing a chair only to fall and break a bone the night before I marry you."

"We're married already," she tells me.

"You know what I mean." I drag the chair out of her reach. We're renewing our vows in front of everyone tomorrow afternoon. It *feels* like I'm marrying her in a whole new way tomorrow. I want everything to be perfect for her, for them. Rooney banged up and bruised from tumbling off a rickety chair is not part of that perfect plan. "Tell me which basket you want. I'll get it."

Rooney rolls her eyes, then points. I reach for the basket, then hand it to her. She roots around until she finds what she was looking for.

My stomach drops. It's a manila envelope. I know what's in that manila envelope.

"Sit your bossy butt down, Axel Jakob." Rooney makes a shooing motion with the envelope.

I do as she says, sitting back at the table. Rooney returns to my lap and empties the envelope. Letters scatter across the table's surface. She spreads them out, then turns toward me.

"This," she says, tapping the letters, "is not the response of a family who is disappointed in you."

I stare at the letters spread across the table. A lump forms in my throat.

"They wrote you back," she says, her eyes shining, searching mine. "Every single one of them wrote you back because they love you, because you showed them how you needed them to know about us, and they showed you right back that all they want to do is connect with and love you the way you need to connect and be loved, Axel."

"I could have flown down, told them in person, like you told Willa."

"You weren't going to do that. Not when I was sick."

My grip on her waist tightens. Rooney had a flare-up right after Christmas. It was terrifying, heartbreaking; I felt so helpless, witnessing her wrestling with pain, how often she got sick. She said it wasn't as bad as the flare-up last year, which was both hard to wrap my head around and deeply upsetting to know she'd gone through alone. Thankfully, her doctor's quick work to get her on steroids and increase her infusion dosage helped significantly. Rooney's felt much better, and her symptoms have quieted. But it's only been about a month of her feeling okay. Which was when she asked if I was ready to tell everyone about us, when I came up with the idea of renewing our vows, inviting her parents and my family to celebrate.

"I got to tell Willa in person," she says, "because, unlike nearly all your family, she lives close and could easily visit me, which I asked her to, so I could finally tell her. *I* was the one who slowed us down. My health has thrown a wrench in life before this, and it will again. If anyone should worry about disappointing people, it's me."

"Rooney—"

"I'm the reason you did what you did. I'm the one who was sick.

You stayed here for me. You took care of me, even when I told you that you didn't have to."

"There wasn't a chance in hell I was leaving you."

She smiles down at me from her perch on my lap. "Of course there wasn't. And did I disappoint you? My body doing what it did? My sickness keeping you from going down to see them, to try to tell them in person?"

I scowl at her. "Of course not."

She arches her eyebrows, a pleased smile lighting up her face. "And why is that, Axel?"

"Because I love you. And I could never . . . I would never be disappointed by you being you."

"I rest my case, Your Honor." She taps my nose softly and grins. "I really would have made a great lawyer."

I clutch her waist tightly. She says that so offhandedly, but I know there's a tinge of sadness beneath that phrase, *would have*. She's still only officially on leave from law school, not formally withdrawn from her program, but every time she talks about it, the surer she sounds that she's not going back. And though I can tell there's peace for her, in having decided on the next step in her life, that doesn't mean she's not grieving the path she's no longer going to take.

Rooney taps those letters again on the table, her eyes holding mine. "You and I are not disappointments. We are certainly imperfect. We have our limitations and our struggles. But nothing about how we live and operate makes the people who matter to us see us as anything less than the people they adore.

"Your wonderful family showed us that. In their letters. In their care packages to me. In being here, ready to celebrate us."

At first I thought she might find it romantic, if I surprised her with this plan, to renew our vows in front of the most important people in our lives, but the more I thought about it, the more I worried it would make her anxious to be caught off guard. In the end, I told her what I had in mind.

I still remember how her eyes lit up, the way she threw her arms around me. "A surprise like that *is* romantic," she whispered, before pressing a kiss to my cheek. "But I like knowing, so we can plan it together. Let's surprise everybody else, though. I think they'll be delighted by the unexpected gift of getting to see what they missed."

And now they're all here, and I know tomorrow they *will* be delighted, just like she said. Because they love us, and they're happy for us. I search her beautiful eyes, then finally nod. "You're right."

"Of course I am," she says primly.

A deep laugh rumbles out of me. Rooney gifts me with one of those soft, sweet smiles that makes my heart race.

I stare at her, my hand sliding up her back. She bends her head, kissing me, slow and savoring, her fingers scraping through my hair.

When she pulls back, Rooney pauses. Her eyes search mine. "Is that all this is really about? Your family?"

I hesitate, my grip tightening at her waist. "No, it's not just about my family."

"I didn't think so." Slowly, she stands, holding out her hands. I take them and stand, too. In our silent, understood way, she steps into my arms, hands tight around my waist. I wrap her in my arms, too. We stand in a hug, my chin on her head, her cheek resting against my chest.

This is how we talk sometimes. When all that eye contact feels so intense, the words jam in my throat and my mind blanks. This way, Rooney still feels close to me and I can find my words to stay open with her.

"What's got you thinking like this again?" she whispers.

I rub her back. "Before today . . . being married to you, it still felt . . . safe, contained in our little world here. My family knew, and they were undeniably wonderful in their letters, but just surrounded by all of them with you today . . ." I sigh. "I felt it again, how hard all the peopling is, how drained I get. And I saw how happy you were, surrounded by all that. . . ."

Rooney lifts her head. She presses a gentle kiss right to the hollow of my throat. "You worry that one day I won't be happy about how differently we socialize. That I'll resent you needing breaks from busy environments, that you don't talk much in group settings, and you'd prefer having me all to yourself rather than sharing me."

I swallow, then nod.

Rooney smiles. I feel it as she turns her head and rests her cheek on my chest again. "I can't make you believe me, Axel, that I'll never resent or grow tired of how your lovely brain and body work. Same way you can't make me believe the same about you and how you feel about me."

My grip on her tightens. "But you do believe me?"

She nods. "And I doubt it sometimes, too. Because I'm human and I'm scared of trusting someone to love and want all of me, in sickness and in health, for better or worse, forever."

I swallow thickly. "I do love you that way. And I always will."

"I know. That's what tomorrow's about. Standing in front of everyone we love, promising that to each other. Promising we'll believe in each other's love, even when doubt and fear creep in."

She lifts her head again, cupping my neck, drawing my forehead to hers. "What we're doing, Axel, every day we wake up and live and love together; what we're doing tomorrow—none of it is suddenly going to be free of fears like this, just because we put rings on our fingers and made promises to each other. But that doesn't mean we're wrong or messing up. It just means we're seeing that fear, and choosing not to believe it. 'Courage is not the absence of fear, but rather the assessment that something else is more important.' That's what we're doing. Being courageous, together."

The beginning of a laugh catches in my throat. I peer down at her, the woman I love beyond words, and brush her hair back from her face. "Did you just quote a US president to me, you big nerd?"

She smiles. "Damn right, I did."

I kiss her, and she laughs. I laugh, too, shaking my head. "You're perfect," I whisper.

"Hardly."

"You are," I tell her, kissing her again. "Thank you. For listening. For what you said, reassuring me."

Rooney searches my eyes. "Thank *you*. For telling me. For hearing me."

Gently, she brings my head toward hers. Another soft, slow kiss. Until her tongue strokes mine and heat pounds through me. I wrap her tight in my arms, scooping her up, her legs around my waist, my hand cupping her ass, pulling her close.

"Take me to bed," she whispers as her mouth dances with mine. Her smile blooms across our kiss. "This time, just try not to break it."

"That was one time and months ago. Am I ever going to live that down?"

She laughs, a bright, sparkling laugh that makes me dizzy with pleasure. I love when I make her laugh. "Not in a million years."

## *Rooney*

I stare down at my husband sleeping in our bed. The man I'm going to marry today. Again. I smile, filled with love, with gratitude. I'm the luckiest woman in the world.

Sunlight dances in his hair, caramel and bronze sparkling in the depths of his bed-head waves. It slips the way my finger loves to, along the thoughtful frown creasing his brow, down his nose, to his mouth, pursed in sleep.

Slowly, I bend and kiss his forehead. "Axel."

"Hmm," he mumbles, turning in his sleep, wrapping his arm around my waist. He nuzzles into my boobs and sighs peacefully.

"Ax, we slept in. You have to get up so we're not late for lunch up at the A-frame."

"Uh-uh."

I smile wider. He's adorably grumpy in the morning. "Come on," I whisper into his hair.

He grumbles something indecipherable into my scant cleavage, squeezing me tighter. But only a few seconds later, his grip goes lax. A snore leaves him. He's fast asleep again.

Gently, I ease out of his arms. I'll make coffee, then take another stab at coaxing him to consciousness.

The floors are cool as I step out of bed and tug on Axel's T-shirt. I steal a pair of his woolly socks and pull them on, too.

Standing at our dresser beside the studio door, I'm reminded Skugga's in there. Axel put her there last night, when she kept pouncing on his feet in bed while we were trying to have sex. A tiny laugh leaves me as I remember the image of Axel, completely naked, scowling as he gripped her by the scruff, muttering about cantankerous cats as he wrenched open the door to the studio and firmly but gently plopped her in her cat bed before shutting the door resolutely behind him.

I felt a little twinge of guilt as he exiled her, but as soon as he crawled back into bed, that little mischief-making kitten was the last thing on my mind.

Opening the studio door, I peer inside and call Skugga with the little *pst pst* she always answers to.

But Skugga doesn't come running my way. The cat bed is empty.

Frowning, I step into the studio, scouring the space. "Skugga?"

My gaze snags on the open window in the back of the studio. Axel has screens in all of the windows because he often needs them open for ventilation for paint and turpentine fumes, and he understandably doesn't want critters and bugs coming in.

One of the screens now has a gaping hole in it.

My stomach drops. Skugga escaped. That's the only explanation. I run through the studio, toward the window, searching for some clue to help me figure out where she went next.

"Skugga?" I call, whipping open the back door of the studio that leads into the yard behind. My heart's pounding as my gaze darts across the clearing, to the edge of where the grass grows tall, thick with wildflowers.

"Skugga!" I yell.

There's commotion behind me. Banging and swearing. I glance over my shoulder to the sight of Axel with bed-head hair, in his sexy glasses, shirt only halfway down his chest, hopping into a pair of sweatpants. "What is it?" he asks. "Did something happen to her?"

"She's gone," I croak. Tears spill down my face. "Skugga's gone."

His gaze flies around the room. "She has to be here."

I watch him tearing around the studio, looking for her, as I wipe the tears from my cheeks. "There's a hole in the screen," I tell him. "She must have scratched the screen apart and made a break for it."

Axel swears under his breath, then stands from where he was crouched, searching the drop cloths. He rakes his hand through his hair. "We'll find her."

"She's so s-small," I whisper, my chin trembling. "She's never been outside."

Axel gets one look at me, and his entire expression falls. Before I know it, I'm wrapped in his arms, held tight. "We'll find her," he says, pressing a kiss to my hair. "I promise."

"H-how?"

Harry barks on the other side of the glass windows at the front of the studio, loping unevenly along the length of the room.

Big eyes, unsteady gait. Panting happily. Seeing him makes my heart ache. Harry and Skugga are pals. I can't look at him and not think about her. An idea dawns on me. "Harry can find her," I tell Axel.

He peers down at me, brow furrowed. "Roo, he's not trained to do that. There's no way—"

"He loves Skugga. He knows her scent. He'll find her."

Axel's right. I know, rationally, Axel's right, but I can't just stand here, crying. I have to do something.

"Come on." I rush past him, yanking the small blanket draped across Skugga's cat bed with me, back into the main room of the house, whipping open drawers to find clothes, tugging on shorts, then a sweatshirt. I pull back my hair as I step into my boots by the front door.

Axel's quiet behind me but moving quickly, too, stomping into his boots, then following me outside.

Harry runs our way, barking again.

"Harry, come on." I crouch, letting him give me a big good-morning lick up my cheek. "We have to find Skugga."

He cocks his head, curious.

"Skugga?" I say again, lifting the blanket to his nose.

Harry sniffs it, then barks.

Axel sighs behind me, scrubbing his face beneath his glasses. "Rooney, sweetheart—"

"Come on, Harry." I urge Harry forward, tucking Skugga's blanket into my waistband like it's capture the flag. "Let's go find Skugga."

Harry lopes ahead of us, sniffing the ground, barking, then starting toward the woods behind the house. I follow him, Axel quiet behind me.

I know it's a stretch, but doing something helps, makes me feel better. I hate the thought of our kitten lost and alone.

Harry trudges through the brush and sniffs around. Suddenly he picks up his head, barks, then breaks into a run.

I start to jog so I can keep up, and Axel's right behind me. "Rooney, wait a second."

"He's onto something. I can't wait a second!"

Harry's running now, as fast as his weak leg lets him. I'm running, too. Harry leaps over something up ahead. I tell myself to keep my eyes open for whatever it is, so I can leap, too.

"Rooney," Axel yells. "Watch out. There's a—"

I screech as I realize I'm about to fall into what looks like a giant puddle, thick with mud, swollen from the heavy rain we've been getting. I leap and teeter on its edge, pinwheeling my arms. I start to slip toward the puddle.

"Rooney!" Axel yells again, shoving me forward as I start to fall. I tumble onto my stomach in the grass. There's a splash behind me.

No, not a splash. It's not the sound of a body slapping against shallow water. It's the *thwump* of a body falling *into* water. Deep water.

Scrambling to my feet, I turn and scream when I see the top of Axel's head poking through the surface. Instinct kicks in. I jump into the water after him.

The water swallows me up as I sink, but my toes touch the bottom quickly, and I push up, wrapping my arms around Axel's torso as soon as I feel him. I'm tugging him, at least I try to, until I realize he's tugging me, that we're launching up onto the ground, gasping for air.

"What the hell was that?" he yells.

"What was what?" I wipe my eyes, spitting muddy water off my lips.

He looks furious. "You came in after me."

"Of course I did."

Axel wrenches me close, until I'm splayed across his lap. His eyes hold mine. "That's not your job. I was fine. I didn't need you to come save me. You could have gotten hurt, you could have—"

"Everything you were afraid of just now, I was afraid of, too," I tell him sharply. "Don't you dare tell me I get to matter this much to you but you aren't allowed to matter that much to me, too."

"Dammit, Rooney." He wrenches me into his arms. "You scared me."

"I'm okay," I whisper. He holds me so tight, it almost hurts. "I'm okay. And you're okay?"

"I'm fine," he says roughly, his hand sliding up and down my wet shirt, my waist, my ribs, my back, like he's reassuring himself I'm still here in one piece.

Pulling back, I search his face for signs he's not just telling me what I want to hear. My stomach plummets as I realize what's different now. His glasses. They're not on his face.

"Your glasses," I say brokenly. His sexy bookish woodsman glasses are gone.

He shrugs, wiping water from his eyes. "I'll get a new pair."

"I can go back in and look—"

"Don't. You. Dare." Axel hauls me upright with him. "You even look at that filthy water, woman, and I'll throw you over my shoulder and carry you home."

I smile faintly, brushing away the hair stuck to his forehead and temples. "Not exactly a disincentive."

He sighs, shaking his head, but a tiny smile lifts his mouth, too. "Life is never dull with you, Rooney, I'll give you that."

A laugh jumps out of me. But it's broken off abruptly when I hear Harry's bark, and then the tiniest kitten meow.

My eyes widen. Axel's do, too.

"Skugga!" I yell, darting past Axel toward Harry, where he stands at the base of a tree, peering up, then turning and barking at us.

This time Axel runs ahead of me, his long strides smooth and effortless, in his long-distance runner way. I watch him fly past me to the base of the tree. He glances up and then curses so loudly, it echoes through the woods.

I follow his line of sight, coming to a winded halt at the base of the tree. There, up much higher than should be possible, is our little kitten.

"I'll get on your shoulders," I tell him.

Axel gives me a scathing look that speaks volumes. I remember how he rushed to stop me from even stepping on a chair last night, which, with my track record with those chairs, was probably a fair intervention. If climbing a chair was off-limits, this is definitely not going to fly with him.

"Stand back," he says. "Please," he adds, a grumpy afterthought.

I do as he's asked. Axel takes a few steps back, breaks into a run, then leaps up, reaching the lowest branch and gripping it tight. He swings, like a gymnast on the uneven bars, then wrenches himself up onto the branch.

My mouth drops open. I knew he was athletic, but good grief.

I watch my husband climb branch after branch, fluidly, calmly, until he's reaching out, that impressive arm span allowing him to hold tight to the trunk as he grasps Skugga by her scruff. She mewls, swinging her paws. Axel pins her to his chest with one hand, then uses the other to leverage himself down again, branch by branch.

I stare in awe as he climbs to the final bough, maneuvers himself to its edge, and then eases down, holding on by one hand, before he drops the safe few feet to the ground.

"She's okay," he says. He's winded now. But I know it isn't fatigue. It's adrenaline.

I rush toward them both, wrapping my arms around Skugga and Axel. Harry bounds toward us, barking happily.

"Here." Axel hands her to me. I take Skugga, curling her in my arms like a baby, hugging her close. I peer up at Axel, muddy and wet, squinting without his glasses, breathing heavily, hands on his hips. Tears crest in my eyes.

"Thank you," I whisper.

Gently, he cups my head, kissing my forehead. "Couldn't leave Skugga stuck up in a tree, could we?"

Harry barks, leaping at Axel. Axel bends and scratches behind his ears. "Good boy. You found her. I never should have doubted you."

Harry barks again, then lopes ahead of us, back the way we came.

I feel a swell of love. Of gratitude. For my little family. For our pets who've burrowed so deeply into my heart. For the man who'd do anything for us. Searching his eyes, I tell him, "I love you so much."

He steps close, so close, our noses nearly touch. Then he presses the softest kiss to my lips. "I know. I love you, too."

Gently, Axel wraps his arm around me, pulling me against him. "Come on." He smiles down at me, then scratches Skugga's cheek. "Let's go home."

———

"Windows all latched," Axel says, peeling off his sopping, muddy shirt. "Triple-checked the doors are locked, too." Next, his muddy sweats and boxer briefs. He rakes his hair back from his face, then tips his head sideways, like he's got water in his ear he's trying to work out. "That cat doesn't have a chance in hell of escaping again."

From my place under the shower water's spray, I stare at Axel, naked and glorious, mud stuck to his skin, his hair going every which way. He washes his hands, then bends over his contacts case so close, his nose nearly touches the sink. It's the only way he can see to put them on.

I bite my lip, so full of love, of desire. My husband. Who climbs trees to save a kitten, who shoves me out of harm's way even when it means harm finds him instead. The man who loves me in all my chaos and emotionality. My Axel.

I watch him in the mirror, blinking as he gets his contacts comfortable in his eyes. He turns, then catches me staring at him. "What is it?"

I smile, fighting tears. "Come here."

He steps inside the shower, right under the water, wrapping me in his embrace. I sigh as I feel his hard, warm chest, its springy hairs tickling my skin. My hands rest on his shoulders as I stare up at him. I reach past him for the bar of soap, with its little exfoliating beads he loves, and rub it down his arm. "I love you," I tell him again.

He smiles at me, soft and tender. "I love you, too."

My hand drifts lower with the bar over his stomach. The muscles jump beneath my touch. He tugs in a deep breath as I scrub down his thigh, over his hip. "Thank you," I whisper, "for all the ways you take care of me and our pets I made you keep."

He huffs a soft laugh. "I'm grumpy with them half the time, but you know I love them as much as you do. Well . . . at least, almost as much."

I laugh.

"You don't need to thank me," he says, his voice catching as I scrub gently between his legs, dragging the soap up his thigh, my other hand finding sudsy soap bubbles and working it along his cock, which is thickening rapidly in my hand. "I always want to take care of you, Rooney."

"I know you do. But I like to take care of you, too."

He swallows roughly as I stroke him in my hand. His eyes fall half-shut. He cups my neck and stares down at me. "You do."

A happy hum leaves my throat as I press up on tiptoe, reaching for a kiss. Axel tries to deepen our kiss, his hand slipping between my legs, too, but I pull away, then drop to my knees.

"Rooney," he protests. "You don't have to—*fuck*."

I take him deep into my mouth. His head falls back. His hand slaps against the tile wall. He gasps as I pump him, lick the tip with my tongue in that way he loves, before I take him deep again. For a few minutes, it's just this, me pleasing him, loving him, taking care of him in one of the many ways I love to.

His hips rock forward as I take him deep into my mouth again. His hand slips into my hair. "God, Rooney. I can't . . . Roo, stop, I'm gonna come."

I murmur enthusiastically around him, but he pulls away, drags me to my feet, then presses me against the tiles. His mouth finds mine, hot and slick, his tongue stroking mine in the same rhythm of his finger as it slips inside me. He swirls his thumb over my clit. I arch up, moaning as he rubs me so perfectly, light and quick, his finger inside me curling deeper.

Pleasure winds tight inside me, makes my toes curl. I grip his shoulder, riding his hand, and cry his name as release breaks through me, hot and sweet, wave after wave.

He kisses me deeply, then spins me, until my body, warm from the shower, hits the cool tiles. Fresh pleasure spikes inside me, in my nipples, pebbled against the tile, right between my thighs, where he rubs me again as Axel eases himself inside, just the tip, the faintest tease.

His hand finds my throat, guiding my head back, until our mouths meet for a kiss, deep, hot, desperate. His thumb strokes my jaw. His tongue serenades mine. He rocks into me, gentle, steady, while his other hand builds my pleasure, making me climb higher, higher.

I reach behind me, and find his hard, firm ass, squeezing it, pulling him closer, showing him I want him deep. Axel drops his forehead to my shoulder and fills me, making air rush out of my lungs, sparks burst behind my eyelids. He strokes that space inside me that makes my knees weak, my legs tremble. But he's holding me steady. He always is.

Axel's hips move hard, losing their rhythm. He rubs me faster, sinks his teeth into my earlobe, and drags gently. I wrench my head back as my orgasm tears through me, and Axel clutches me in his arms, rubbing me through it, stroking into me. And then he seats himself inside me, shouting my name as his hips falter while he holds himself deep inside me, as if he wants not an iota of space between us.

Panting, breathless, we pull apart slowly, only to turn around and find each other again, under the water. We smile at each other, brushing hair from each other's faces, me on tiptoe, his head bent, finding each other for a slow, sweet kiss.

"I love this," I whisper.

Axel smiles against our kiss. "What? Shower sex?"

I laugh, pulling back enough to search his eyes. "Well, not just shower sex. I mean . . . this, you and me, just the two of us, our quiet, occasionally chaotic life."

His expression turns more serious, his gaze darting over my face. "Just . . . the two of us? That's enough?"

I nod. "It is." Gently, I stroke his jaw, along his beard. "I mean, I will be occasionally persuaded to share you with others—family, friends—but only if I'm heavily compensated with shower sex afterward."

An almost smile lifts his mouth.

"I mean it," I tell him, my hand resting over his heart. "I want this. I want our cozy, secluded home, sunlight and birdsong waking us up, nothing else. I want to live here all the time and figure out what comes next. I want years to soak up life with you and take care of you and let you take care of me."

Axel strokes my cheek with his knuckles, his eyes holding mine. "I want that, too."

I press up on tiptoe again and kiss him, sweet, soft, slow. "Good. Because I think it's about time we got dressed and walked up that hill, so I can tell you this all over again, in front of the people we love. What do you say?"

My husband, my love, bends and kisses me, tender, reverent. "I say, I can't wait. For today. Tomorrow. Every minute we have. So long as it's with you."

"Well, then," I whisper. My hand rests sure and steady over his heart. "You have lots to look forward to. Because you've got me with you. Forever."

## ACKNOWLEDGMENTS

Writing *With You Forever* was, like Rooney and Axel's love itself, a gently paced and unexpectedly emotional journey. I fell hard for these two as they fell for each other, as layers of their backstories and wounds and motivations deepened and then turned even more soft and complex than I'd originally planned.

What came from this process was a book that—to me, at least—feels reflective and vulnerable, equal parts playful and painfully self-conscious. It's a book that speaks from my heart as I continue to learn who I am as an autistic and how I work. While Axel's experience of being autistic draws somewhat from my own, I also owe thanks to the many neurodivergents who've openly shared about their lives and lent nuance to his characterization, particularly in their experiences as they self-diagnosed and decided how and when to be open about that.

As for Rooney's IBD, ulcerative colitis, I have my dear friend Jennie to thank for walking me through her history, for lending it to Rooney and answering my countless, often bizarre writer questions. I am honored to bring my friend's lived experience of this disease to the page in a fictional character, and so deeply thankful for her time and trust.

My own experience of celiac disease, which went much too long undiagnosed and has left me with permanent intestinal damage, shaped my knowledge of gluten-free eating and life. To all my GF and celiac folks out there, hard hugs. I'm not sure there's a heaven, but if there is, that's where we'll get to eat whatever pizza and doughnuts we want.

I'm also profoundly thankful to my sensitivity and beta readers, Mae, Ellie, Sarah, and Katie, who offered me thoughtful, thorough feedback that made this book so much stronger.

This story is truly one from my heart. I hope its message has both resonated with and encouraged you, even if you aren't chronically ill like Rooney or neurodivergent like Axel: that self-acceptance and self-love are multilayered and delicate, that the bridge we cross to entrusting that tender place within ourselves to worthy others is frightening, but it is also a gift. I hope you feel affirmed by this story as a human who lives daily with your own fears and vulnerabilities, and that you remember this: You deserve to be safe, accepted, loved, and cherished for exactly who you are. Nothing less.

The Bergman Brothers series, continuing with this book, portrays a big, messy family, found family, and friends—imperfect people trying exceptionally hard to love each other well. There are rough patches and plenty of struggles along the way, but ultimately, their love is accepting, affirming, and profoundly safe. Some might say this isn't very realistic. To which I say, I'd like it to be, and this is why I write. As Oscar Wilde said, "Life imitates Art far more than Art imitates Life." I believe stories affirming everyone's worthiness of love and belonging have life-changing power—to touch us, heal us, and deepen our empathy for ourselves and others. Stories have the power to reshape our hearts and minds, our relationships, and ultimately the world we live in.

I hope by now that, as it has been for me, this Bergman world is a haven for you, reader, where these intimate relationships with oneself and others, platonic, familial, romantic, and beyond, affirm the hope for all of us—that we can be curious, not judgmental, open-minded and openhearted; that we can welcome and embrace one another, just as we are, and become better, wiser, kinder, for having experienced all that is possible when we do.

Keep reading for an excerpt from
the next Bergman Brothers novel

*EVERYTHING FOR YOU*

# Oliver

Playlist: "Capsized," Andrew Bird

I will be the first to admit that I am not my best self when intoxicated. A generally upbeat, sociable guy, I don't seek alcohol for its loose-limbed, easygoing buzz, and after throwing back a few, I don't get it. I simply turn, for lack of better words, into a highly unfiltered, emotional mess.

Which is why I will not be drinking this weekend. Nope, not a drop. Not when I've just started to feel like myself again, months after getting my heart crushed. Not when I'm about to spend spring break celebrating my brother's marriage alongside my still-very-much-in-love parents and six siblings, four of whom are also happily partnered.

Drinking would be a bad choice. Not only because, as I've said, I'm no peach when drunk, but because it won't take much to send me spiraling into the bleak thoughts that have plagued me since my breakup.

"Oliver."

My brother Viggo, so close to me in age and looks that we operate like twins, turns off the rental car's stereo, bathing us in silence.

I glance his way from where I've been staring out the window. "What?"

"I'm *talking* to you."

"So keep talking."

Viggo sighs and rakes a hand through his unkempt brown hair, our only discernible difference, compared to my dark blond. Same angular jaw and faint cleft chin as our dad, same high cheekbones and pale blue-gray eyes that we inherited from Mom. Same tall, lean bodies, except I've started putting on more muscle, thanks to weight training so I can hold my own on a D-1 soccer field.

"I could keep talking." Viggo throws a concerned glance my way, eyes on me much longer than they should be for how fast he's driving. "But I don't think you've been listening."

"I'm listening," I tell him so he'll keep his eyes on the road and not get us killed before we even make it to the party.

"Uh-huh." Thankfully, he trains his gaze ahead even as he leans my way, wrinkling his nose.

"What are you doing?" A smile I can't help tugs at my mouth. Viggo drives me up the wall, but he's just about the only person who both indulges my rare foul moods and can pull me out of them.

"I'm sniffing you," he says, throwing on his turn signal and passing a slowpoke in front of us.

"Sniffing me."

"Mhmm. I smell the angst wafting off of you."

"Shut up." I punch his thigh. He twists my nipple. I yelp in pain. "Dammit, Viggo! That hurt!"

"Serves you right," he says. "That's my gas leg you hit. I could have caused an accident."

I slouch down moodily in my seat and stare out the window. Sharp lemon-yellow sunlight slices through the slate-blue sky marbled with clouds. It's early spring and—unlike our family's current home base of Los Angeles—Washington State, where Mom and Dad first lived and started their brood of seven Bergman kids, feels like it fights for every fragile blossom and green shoot that muscles its way through the cold, hard earth. In the Pacific Northwest, there are edges and effort. Here, hope feels hard-won.

That's how hope feels inside me, too.

Lowering the window, I suck in a gulp of mid-fifties wet air—petrichor and the promise of full-blown spring just around the corner. God, I love this place.

"So . . ." Viggo clears his throat, yanking me from my thoughts. "I know you're dreading seeing everyone in their coupled bliss."

"Coupled bliss?" I snort a laugh, trying to deflect how on the mark Viggo is. Annoyingly, this is typical, his confident and freakishly accurate emotional intuition. After reading hundreds of historical romance novels, my brother considers himself an expert on the human heart.

"I'll be fine, Viggo. I'm over it."

*Mostly.*

For once, my brother lets it go and stays quiet, though his skeptical arched eyebrow speaks volumes as he takes the hairpin turn preceding the entrance to our family's getaway home, a lakeside A-frame nestled in the woods.

Well, we call it "the A-frame," but it's actually been expanded extensively. As Viggo pulls into the drive, the view hits me like a direct kick to the chest. Dark wood and steep roof, tall glass windows across the front, the sprawling addition that made it spacious enough for all of us looming to the left, smoke curling from the chimney. Tiny green leaves and pink buds kiss wet black branches forming a canopy over us.

It's a view so bittersweet-beautiful, it hurts. A lump forms in my throat.

"I have a plan to cope, okay?" Viggo slows as we roll over a pothole.

"A plan."

He nods. "So, Axel and Rooney are already married—"

"I do remember being informed of that last month. Sort of hard to forget, along with the sight of your face when you found out."

Viggo scowls. He hasn't recovered from the devastation that

his romance-reading radar didn't pick up on our brother Axel and Rooney's covert marriage.

He mutters darkly, "I'm still salty about that. A secret marriage! An elopement! How did I miss it?"

"Because they weren't speeding off in a horse-drawn carriage to Gretna Green?"

"Shut up."

I pat his back to console him as Viggo mutters under his breath about emotionally constipated siblings. "Even if you did read romances postdating the nineteenth century," I tell him, "you weren't going to have a clue what was going on until Ax was ready to tell us. That's just how he is."

My oldest brother's a man of few words. Deeply loving but intensely private and quiet, Axel lives on the family property, here, in his own cabin, so we see and hear from him less often, and when we do hear from him, it's frequently via the written word.

Axel's on the autism spectrum and finds writing the easiest way to tell us personal things. Which is why, when he told us how twisted up he was over Rooney this past Christmas—when I saw how long they spent alone on the porch after she showed up, how close they seemed while she spent the next few days with us—I wasn't *terribly* surprised to receive a beautiful handwritten note from Axel last month, explaining that since the fall, he and Rooney had been together and that they were now married. The letter also said that he was sorry he hadn't been able to make us a part of their wedding, but he still very much wanted to celebrate their marriage with us.

The only thing that made getting that heartfelt letter written in Axel's tall, sloping scrawl even better was watching Viggo's dawning horror as he read his letter, too. Not because he disapproved of Axel's methods but because he'd been clueless about what was going on.

"As I was saying." Viggo sniffs, maneuvering around the other vehicles parked in the clearing. "My plan to cope. It's a low-key party.

It's not like you'll have to see them get married. Knowing Axel, it'll be chill. Practical. Relaxed. We'll pound some delicious food. I'll get you good and liquored up, tuck you in, and you'll sleep it off. Tomorrow it'll be back to the same old family shenanigans, and you can blast me in the face with a soccer ball when we play pickup."

"For the hundredth time, it was an *accident*."

He rubs the bridge of his now slightly-less-than-perfectly-straight nose. "Uh-huh. And it had nothing to do with the fake snake I put in your bed the night before."

"If it *did*," I say testily, throwing my phone, water canteen, and snacks into my carry-on bag between my legs, "it was subliminal. And you deserved it."

Wrenching the car into park, Viggo turns and looks at me. "Listen, something I tell myself regularly, as I wait for my one true love—"

"Here we go." I slump back in my seat and scrub my face.

"—is that someone's romantic gain does not equate to my loss. Most of our siblings are happily paired off, and while I wish I was, too, I can be happy for them while I wait. Our time *will* come." He sets a hand on my shoulder and gives it a squeeze. "Until then— well, more like for the next seventy-two hours—let's be the untethered man cubs and have some fun. Got it?"

I sigh and throw open my car door. "Fine."

---

Well. I'm intoxicated. Thankfully I haven't veered into shitshow territory.

Though I think I might be on my way.

Stashed in a shadowy corner of the A-frame's wide back deck, I'm outside the golden reach of countless twinkly lights strung overhead. A cool late-March breeze weaves through the small gathering, and as I nurse my who-knows-what-number beer, my gaze travels my family.

Mom and Dad sway to the music, eyes only for each other. Mom slips her hands through his copper hair, which is threaded with white, and smiles softly up at him. Dad's eyes crinkle as he grins at her, wrapping his hands tighter around her waist.

They look so in love, and I love that my parents are still gone for each other, but I don't need to see them kiss, which they're about to. So I look away just in time and catch the oldest of us, my sister Freya, with her arms around her husband Aiden's neck—*ack!*—kissing him.

I shut my eyes briefly, and when I open them again, there's Axel, next in birth order, swaying his wife, Rooney, to the music's rhythm. He's the tallest of us, which makes him gigantic, seeing as no one in the family is under six feet. His hair, chocolate brown like Viggo's, falls over his forehead as he stares at Rooney, her spun-gold waves adorned by a crown of flowers. He kisses her forehead, eyes shut, his world nothing but her.

Then there's Ren, so much like Dad, with his broad build and ginger hair, and just a little like Mom with her pale blue-gray eyes and sharp cheekbones. I try not to watch him make his girlfriend, Frankie, flash a rare wide smile and laugh as he whispers in her ear.

I was hoping I could count on my grumpy lumberjack-looking brother Ryder—with Dad's feisty green eyes and penchant for provoking the woman he loves—to cut me a break, but even *he's* being romantic. A heated grin plays on his mouth as his girlfriend, Willa, smiles up at him and sinks her hands into his dirty-blond man bun, tugging him down for a deep, hard kiss.

My sister Ziggy, the only one younger than me, sits happily curled up on a deck chair, a lock of long, red hair twirled around her finger, smiling to herself as she reads one of her thick fantasy romances. I know that look, her green eyes darting down the page, a fiery blush heating her pale skin—she's being swept away by another dark-haired, sardonic villain who'll somehow be redeemed and turn into a love interest by the end, if the past few stories she's gushed about are anything to go by.

Among a few other close friends are Rooney's parents, too. And though they're divorced, they share what seems like an amicable dance between friends now, their loving gazes directed at their daughter.

In short, I'm surrounded by all kinds of happy endings, which is lovely . . . but also terrible.

"Okay." Viggo plops beside me and swaps out my beer for a glass of water. "I didn't know Axel was going to surprise Rooney with renewing their vows in front of their families and closest friends."

I rub my chest, where it still aches with the knot of joy and sadness that's been there since I watched them promise themselves to each other again just a few hours ago. "You told me it was only gonna be a party."

Oh boy. My words are sloppy. I sound very drunk.

Focusing on my diction, I try to sound more sober as I tell my brother, "They already got married. It was just supposed to be a *party*."

"I know, bud," Viggo mutters, cupping my neck, an affectionate, steadying gesture that's common in our family. Tipping back his beer, he takes a long pull. "But it seems our surly, silent oldest brother turned into a full-fledged romantic somewhere in the past three months and had the swoony idea to invite the most important people in their lives for an intimate gathering so they could share a wedding with us after all."

I glance back at Axel, who's holding Rooney. He kisses her so long, they stop dancing, until their rescue dog, Harry, bounds up and breaks them apart with a cheerful bark.

I shut my eyes again. "I'm happy for them," I whisper.

"I know you are," Viggo says. "It's still hard to see though, and that's okay. You and me, Ollie, we do nothing by halves. You fell in love, and you fell hard. Healing from heartache takes longer for big hearts like ours."

As I open my eyes again, they land on Axel's close friends, Parker and Bennett, who dance with their daughter, Skyler, nestled between them. That's what I used to think I'd have with Bryce. What I dreamed about.

I know I'm young, and I know not everyone finds their forever-person when they're a sophomore in college. But I was so sure I had. We had everything I thought you were supposed to—we talked easily and got along right away. Bryce was all play and fun, which balanced my brutally disciplined work ethic both on the field and in the classroom. It was easy with him, straightforward. Wasn't it supposed to be easy? When did I miss the signs that my boyfriend was losing interest? That his eyes had started to wander?

My chest tightens as those unanswered questions, those obsessive worries, shout over each other in my brain until the familiar, anxious noise inside my skull threatens to make me scream.

I suck in a breath and exhale steadily, coaxing myself to focus on sensations around me—the cool air on my skin, the sound of soft music nearby. A trick my therapist taught me since I realized those "anxious days" I'd been having were every day, that anxiety wasn't just a byproduct of my busy, high-pressure schedule, but a reality of my brain, my body, my life.

While I was learning to cope, while I started trying anti-anxiety meds, Bryce was my fun, lighthearted person. My happy place. I thought I knew that so fully, so completely. And then with one sweep of remorseless infidelity, down came the house of cards.

"I never wanna feel like this," I mutter. "*Never* again."

Viggo's quiet for a moment. "I know. I don't want you to either."

I shut my eyes. The world's starting to spin as I say to Viggo, "Why's he have to play on the team and be in half my classes? I'd be fine if I could just . . . get away from him."

"And to address that, my offer still stands."

I snort a drunken laugh, blinking open my eyes. "While I 'preciate your offer to prank Bryce so bad he'd leave UCLA, I'm pretty sure two-thirds of what you have planned is felonious, and I don't want you to go to jail."

Viggo scoffs. "I'm a stealthy guy. I could get away with it."

"Or I could say yes to the Galaxy's offer and get away from it all."

His head whips my way. "What?"

I tuck my lips between my teeth. "*Shooot.* I said that out loud."

Viggo turns to face me fully. "I'm not surprised they want you. I'm surprised you're considering it. You've always said you wanted to complete your degree, no matter what."

"I did." I feel unsteady, so I lean back against the house. The world's spinning even faster now. I hiccup drunkenly. "I wanted—I *want*—my pre-med degree."

At least, I think I do.

Do I?

My brother's quiet for a minute. "Why do you do it, Ollie? Work *so* hard? You know how good you are at soccer, how much you love it. When was becoming a doctor ever a real plan for you, when going pro was inevitable?"

"It wasn't inevitable." I try to sip the water Viggo gave me and mostly miss my mouth.

Viggo rolls his eyes. "Yes it was. And I've never understood why you've been busting your ass since freshman year of *high school* to prepare for something you never really intended to pursue."

I laugh emptily. I can tell Viggo almost everything, but not this. How hard it is to be the fifth son, to live in the shadow of a decorated military veteran and physician father and four older brothers who, each in their own way, are profoundly capable and talented and confident. How difficult it's been to find myself amid all of that, to feel seen and . . . maybe just a little admired?

Axel's a brilliant, successful artist. Ren's a professional hockey player, an NHL darling. Ryder's quickly building an accessible wilderness-experience-and-outfitter-store empire. And Viggo's so damn good at everything he tries, even if he doesn't seem to stick with his interests very long, he could literally do *anything* he wanted.

Then there are my sisters. Freya, the eldest, a physical therapist who's already managing her practice, for God's sake. She's just barely in her thirties! And Ziggy, who's always known what she wanted and singularly pursued it: soccer. She's the beloved baby, the adored and wanted second daughter, the perfect bookend to our family.

Then there's me. A hard worker. A diligent student athlete. Someone who got swept up in medicine because it was fascinating but most importantly because it was something Dad and I could always talk about. Someone who aced every test because that was the one thing I did that made Mom smile and hug me hard with relief that I wasn't getting into trouble again or making mischief with Viggo.

Being on a pre-med track, getting good grades, I've derived pride and satisfaction from it. I've always liked doing well, knowing I've exceeded expectations, pleased the people who matter to me in doing so. If soccer weren't the one place I felt freest, most joyful, most myself, I would like to be a compassionate, competent doctor. But soccer is my heart, and the opportunity I've wanted for so long is finally here, begging me to be brave, to give up these familiar, safe places of validation and straightforward reassurance, to take a risk and grab this opportunity with both hands.

"I think . . ." I lick my lips, which feel tingly, almost numb. "Med school was my backup plan."

Viggo snorts. "Only you would have medical school as a backup plan."

"Will they be proud of me?" I mumble.

His amusement dies away. He leans in, his hand slipping down the middle of my back. "Who?"

"Mom and Dad. All of you."

"Ollie, of course. We're already proud of you. If you did nothing but exist the rest of your life, we'd be proud of you. Because you're ours and we love you."

I hiccup a laugh. "Sure."

Viggo frowns. "What's ever made you doubt that?"

I shrug off his arm. "You wouldn't understand."

"Then tell me so I will."

Drunkenly, I lean my elbows on my knees, hiding my face. One elbow slips off. "I'm gonna do it. I'm gonna tell the Los Angeleeees Galaxy yes."

There's a thick pause. "Maybe," Viggo hazards, "this decision should wait for daylight. And sobriety."

"Pff." I wave a hand and lose my balance so badly, I nearly fall on my face. Viggo wrenches me back up. "Who needs sobriety?"

"You do, my brother. Now, c'mon, let's get you to bed—"

"No way, José." I stagger as I stand. Viggo wraps an arm around my waist, and I use his steadying influence to reach into my pocket for my phone. "Gonna get on my gmaaaaails and tell them my answer *right* now. 'Yes, please, Galaxy! Signed, sincerely, yours truly, Oliver Abram Bergman.'"

"I'll just take that." Viggo plucks the phone from my hand. "You're not emailing anyone right now."

"Good*byeeee*, Bryce," I sing as Viggo starts us toward the deck stairs, away from the party. He's going to sneak me around the side of the house, in through the front door, so I don't embarrass myself around the family, and in some dim, not-as-drunk part of my mind, I'm grateful for it. "Good*byeeee*, collegiate soccer," I croon. "I was better than you anyway."

A quiet laugh rumbles in his chest. "This is my favorite part of your drunkenness. You finally find your ego."

"I am fast as a panther," I sing to the sky. "And excellent at organic chemistry! And I have a great ass! Hear that, incorporeal celestial being up there? Ooh, I think I see the Little Dipper. He's my favorite." I hiccup. "Oh dear. I think I'm very drunk. How did that happen?"

Viggo laughs again. "You had a lot of beer, Ollie. What did you expect?"

*What did you expect?* That sentence. It sends me hurtling back to earth from my stargazing as the world's spinning worsens, memories blurring across time and space. That's what Bryce said to me when I walked into his place and caught him with someone on their knees, his dick down their throat, and asked what the hell was going on.

*What did you expect?*

As if we hadn't been exclusively together for months. As if expecting my boyfriend to be faithful was an absurdity. As if I wasn't *worth* his faithfulness. Or his remorse.

My stomach heaves. I groan, "Gonna puke."

Viggo seems to have anticipated that, because he's ushering me across the lawn, where the light doesn't reach and there's a row of hardy rhododendron bushes. Just as we round them, we both stop. My sister Freya's bent over, doing exactly what I'm about to.

I open my mouth to ask if she's okay, but vomit comes out instead.

Freya takes one look at me, then turns and pukes again.

"Okay." Viggo lifts his hands, backing away. "I love you both. Deeply. But I—" He gags. "I do not have your medical-people iron stomachs. Be well. Call for help if you need it, but I'm sending in reinforcements if you do."

Then he bolts back up the steps of the deck.

After another wave of hurling, Freya moans and sinks to the grass, flopping onto her back. I feel one last surge of alcohol churning up my throat, wretch it out, then turn and face my older sister. She looks like hell, starfished on the grass, eyes shut.

I, however, feel eight thousand times better already after having puked up my liquid bad decisions. I have a hankie in my pocket that I use to dab my mouth. Then I crouch and offer Freya my backup from my other pocket. She takes it listlessly, wiping her sweat-beaded brow, then her mouth, before she shoves it in between her cleavage and winces.

"Hit the wine too hard?" I ask.

She sets a hand over her mouth. "Please don't talk about alcohol. The thought of it makes me nauseous."

"What's wrong?" I flop down beside her and lie on my back. Side by side, we glance at each other, same pale eyes and Mom's blonde hair, though Freya's is still white blonde, while mine's darkened, like Ryder's.

Sighing, Freya glances up at the dusky sky, glittering with silver stars. "My boobs hurt," she whispers, wiping a tear from the corner of her eye. "And my period's late."

Discussing this topic isn't taboo in the Bergman household. When each of the boys got the puberty talk, that included my dad sitting us down and saying, "You don't turn into a juvenile jerk about your sisters' periods. You ask them if they need anything, and if they do, you go to the store and get them pads, tampons, pain meds, comfort foods, whatever they need to survive, then thank God your body doesn't do that to you every twenty-eight days."

"Last month's was light, too," Freya says, her voice soft. "Almost like . . . not a real one."

I push up on one elbow. "Wait. Are you—"

"Pregnant," she whispers, smiling so wide up at the sky, tears streaming down her face. "I've been so scared. It was too good to be true, after waiting and hoping . . . I couldn't take a test yet."

I clutch her hand because I know her. I know when Freya's emotional, she doesn't need you to fix anything for her, she just needs a hand to hold. So I hold it tight.

"Does Aiden know?"

She bites her lip. "He knows I'm a few days late and feeling wiped out. I promised him I'd take a test tomorrow morning if I still felt this way when I woke up, but . . ." She shakes her head, wiping away more tears. "I didn't have high hopes. I didn't think it could finally—" A half sob, half laugh jumps out of her. "I *never* puke. And my boobs never feel like this. It has to be a baby, doesn't it?"

I laugh softly, but my throat's tight with emotion. "Yeah, Frey. I think so."

My sister's smile widens. She starts to laugh through happy tears, and then I'm laughing with her, like I haven't in months. My heart feels full, its cracks and bruises bandaged by hope.

The clarity of this moment feels surreal. How sure I am, how free I feel having made this decision—albeit under the influence of alcohol, but in vino veritas, as the saying goes—to move on, to be brave, to step into this new season, believing in myself and the possibilities awaiting me.

No more brushing shoulders with Bryce. No more relationships complicating my happiness or risking my joy in soccer. My friends and family, playing the beautiful game, that'll be enough for me. And soon, there'll be a tiny Bergman baby to adore and pour my love into.

I'll protect my heart, keep my head down, work my ass off. Those will be my worlds, two distinct ones—the people I love and the game I love. As I glance up, hope burning as bright and hot within me as those stars lighting up the sky, I make a promise to myself: I will never let them be one and the same again.

**Chloe Liese** writes romances reflecting her belief that everyone deserves a love story. Her stories pack a punch of heat, heart, and humor, and often feature characters who are neurodivergent, like herself. When not dreaming up her next book, Chloe spends her time wandering in nature, playing soccer, and most happily at home with her family and mischievous cats.

To sign up for Chloe's latest news, new releases, and special offers, please visit her website and subscribe.

---

VISIT CHLOE LIESE ONLINE

---

ChloeLiese.com

Chloe_Liese

Chloe_Liese

Chloe_Liese

ChloeLiese

Ready to find
your next great read?

Let us help.

**Visit prh.com/nextread**